The Little Moment Of Happiness

by

Clarence Budington Kelland

Double 9
BOOKS

The little moment of happiness
by Clarence Budington Kelland

ISBN: 978-93-63053-58-8

Published by

DOUBLE 9 BOOKS

2/13-B, Ansari Road
Daryaganj, New Delhi – 110002
info@double9books.com
www.double9books.com
Tel. 011-40042856

ABOUT THE AUTHOR

Clarence Budington "Bud" Kelland was an American writer. He was a notable literary personality in his heyday, describing himself as "the best second-rate writer in America" and being prolific and versatile. Kelland's career as a fiction writer from 1913 to 1960. He was featured in numerous publications, including The Saturday Evening Post and The American Magazine. A prolific writer, he wrote 60 novels and almost 200 short tales. His most well-known juvenile works were the Mark Tidd and Catty Atkins series, while his best-known adult work was the Scattergood Baines series. Kelland's other famous adult books include: Conflict (1920), Rhoda Fair (1925), Hard Money (1930), Arizona (1939), and Dangerous Angel (1953). Kelland's name lives on in hundreds of films based on his works, notably Speak Easily (1932), starring Buster Keaton. The film Mr. Deeds Goes to Town (1936), starring Gary Cooper, was based on the Kelland serial Opera Hat from The American Magazine. Opera Hat was eventually adapted into the short-lived television series Mr. Deeds Goes to Town (1969–70) and the film Mr. Deeds (2002). One of Kelland's most well-known characters, Scattergood Baines, appeared in six Hollywood pictures from 1941 to 1943, starring Guy Kibbee as Baines. The Baines character was a benevolent but often misunderstood guy who tried to aid the residents of his little village.

CONTENTS

CHAPTER I 7

CHAPTER II 20

CHAPTER III 30

CHAPTER IV 43

CHAPTER V 55

CHAPTER VI 63

CHAPTER VII 79

CHAPTER VIII 91

CHAPTER IX 106

CHAPTER X 117

CHAPTER XI 132

CHAPTER XII 145

CHAPTER XIII 159

CHAPTER XIV 166

CHAPTER XV 171

CHAPTER XVI 183

CHAPTER XVII 194

CHAPTER XVIII 208

CHAPTER XIX 223

CHAPTER XX 232

CHAPTER XXI 241

CHAPTER XXII.. 251

CHAPTER XXIII 259

CHAPTER XXIV 270

CHAPTER XXV 278

CHAPTER XXVI.. 289

CHAPTER XXVII... 302

CHAPTER I

Those low-lying hills were France!

They had not lifted into view suddenly, but had rather emerged from the east, solidifying slowly out of a slate-colored blur which to the eyes of unaccustomed voyagers might or might not have been land. There was no ebullition of spirits. The two thousand men and women aboard the vessel crowded to the rail and strained their eyes toward that land in which great events awaited them, for the most part in utter silence. Conversation failed. There was an impressiveness about the moment akin to the impressiveness of entering some great cathedral—there was awe!... There, rising out of the east was France!... *France!*

The sentiment that stirred them was more profound than a thrill. The day had held its thrill for them—a thrill that for many of them had followed a sleepless night. Those who had slept had done so fully clothed, with life-jackets within instant touch of the hand. For the kindly ocean had been made dangerous, not by the elements, which throughout the voyage had held themselves in restraint, but by men. It had been a morning of mists which lay upon the placid waters and glowed in response to the touch of the rising sun. Then, as the luminous grayness dissipated, there came into view far off to the northward, a spot which grew and approached until it became a grim and business-like French destroyer to be greeted with cheers of relief. It was the convoy. There was a thrill. It spelled safety—that little boat with ready guns—but it spoke of danger as well. The early passengers who watched the approach of the little vessel of war warmed with affection toward it. It was their guardian, come out of nothingness to protect them through the remaining perilous miles of ocean.

In the cabin a little party of women had remained through the night, fearful of the unseen, impressed by the perils which might hide beneath the dark waters which the bow of the vessel turned up into wonderful patterns of phosphorescence. They had grouped together to draw what comfort they could from companionship. Now they emerged on deck relieved, almost jubilant, until one of their number said, suddenly, "I am told it is the last ten miles which is most dangerous."

The destroyer ran alongside, and a sailor with two little flags waved a long message to the bridge; then she dropped back astern, and with her passed that thrill which had stirred the ship's company.

No, it was no thrill that moved the passengers on the vessel as the hills of France arose before them; the emotion was more profound, more impressive. To many of them it was the first sight of a foreign shore, but, more than that, it was their first sight of France—of that France which by the greatness of her spirit during three years of peril, of suffering, of horrors, had become not a country, but a *symbol*.

For the most part the passengers were in uniform. In these days there were no tourists, none who traveled abroad for amusement or recreation or to accomplish that object so dear to Americans—to improve the mind. These voyagers went as servants, to take their part, great or small, in that war which America had come to see at last was *her* war.

There were many young officers among the first-class passengers, boyish lieutenants proud of unaccustomed uniforms, a little set up because they were not as other men; but all eager to be at their grim work. In a month their swanking would be a thing of the past, for they would have encountered reality, and out of the reality they would emerge as men. There was a captain or so, themselves boyish; there were Red Cross men who, before assuming their uniforms, had been lawyers, merchants, brokers. Older men there were, wearing well-tailored uniforms and carrying themselves with assurance. There was a considerable company of Y. M. C. A. workers, on their way to do what came to hand. They were not certain yet what it was to be, but they would learn. Their uniforms were not so well tailored, their puttees were not of expensive leather like those of the officers and Red Cross men. As one reviewed them he saw that all but a few were not members of the *executive* class, but workers. They were coming to drive trucks, to sell meager supplies over the makeshift counters of huts and canteens, to serve the soldier in such ways as offered.

And there were women—Red Cross women, Y. M. C. A. women, a few musicians and entertainers come to lighten the tedium of the boys in khaki. There were a few civilians, French people, returning from America for purposes important only to them. And there was a sprinkling of French officers, among them a boyish hero much followed by women's eyes because he was a handsome boy made more handsome by the splendor of his uniform—trousers of red, long coat of black, and most of all, perhaps, by the cluster of medals upon his breast. He was only a youth, but he was France's most famous aviator.

There were third-class passengers. Forward were six hundred Poles in vivid red coats, recruited in the United States and Canada for the Polish Legion, going to fight for their country, which could only be a member of the family of nations if the Allies succeeded in crushing the enemy. Aft there were six hundred American boys—machine-gun men and a signal-corps unit.

All of them—officers, men, women—knew that those hills concealed something, something tremendous. Resident in each individual was a consciousness that beyond there lay a new world, but how new and how different none was capable of realizing. The old life, the old ways, the accustomed rules of the game of life, had been left behind and few had the vision to perceive that they were left behind forever, that nothing could again be as it had been, and that they were standing poised for a step through a doorway which led into a new era.

They were about to find contact with another civilization, with another philosophy, another method of life. It was not alone that they were to be set down in an alien land, amid a people speaking a tongue which was meaningless to them, and living their lives according to a manner which seemed good to them—and which *was* good to them and to all who saw it with clear eyes and open mind—but because they were about to become a part of events through which no soul can pass without being so modified and molded as to emerge a different soul, detached, unrelated, cut off by experience and knowledge from the soul that had been.

Behind those low-lying hills lay France.... What was France? It was, for every man and woman aboard that vessel, the great adventure of the soul. Just that. Each one of them was to be born again. With the touch of the soil of France beneath their feet would come a new birth, the entrance into a new life in which each would find much to wonder at, much to admire, much to puzzle over.... But they would find *themselves*. Moreover they would find a world which had resolved itself into genuineness, a world which was true, because war had stripped it of pretense.

The American soul is a peculiar affair. It is circumscribed by environment, by inherited prejudices. It is, for the most part, incapable of comprehending itself, much less the soul of another people of another temperament and genius, ripened by plenitude of years and by a hundred generations of genius which has studied the art of living. The American soul is a living thing imprisoned in a cage of concealments. It was to come into intimate contact with a people who do not believe in imprisoning the soul, who have sought for and discovered the essentials, and have cut away—perhaps have never found the necessity for cutting away—the shame, the self-deceptions, the glossings-over, the self-imposed blind spots, which make us what we are. The American soul recognizes food and admits it to thought's decent society, but it declines to recognize the existence of processes of digestion. The French soul knows that food must be digested as well as eaten. To the French soul digestion is respectable.

So the American soul was to meet the French soul—a meeting of the poles. From such a meeting must result something worth while to the world....

From that day, the 18th of May, A.D. 1918, those men and women would calculate the events of their lives. It was the beginning of a new dispensation. As the world dates events as A.D. or B.C., so these Americans would date their events as, "Before I landed in France," or, "After I landed in France."

It was from the port side of the vessel that the best view of the now distinct land was to be obtained, and the rail was crowded from end to end of the long deck with men and women who looked and looked as if land were a new and tremendous curiosity, a something which they had never seen before and might miss altogether if their attention wavered for an instant. Tea and wafers had just been served by the deck stewards. Well forward stood a young man with the bars of a captain on his shoulders; he stood back from the rail, alone, looking over the heads of the other passengers, as his height made it practicable for him to do. He held in his right hand a cup of tea and was eating one of a handful of square wafers. Not as a man eats who is dallying with the quaint foreign custom of afternoon tea did he bear himself, but as a young man who is honestly hungry. He addressed himself to those biscuits and washed them down with tea because it had been long hours since the midday meal and because his big young body was demanding food.

In his uniform he presented a figure to admire, as did most of the young officers aboard. His back was broad, his legs straight, and, though not bulky, gave one the impression that he was graciously and strongly made. One may read much from a man's legs. More especially is this so in uniform and leather puttees. Indications of character are resident in a calf, but more especially in knees and ankles. These things are concealed by the trousers of civilian life. Some day an astute judge of character will write a monograph on masculine legs and revolutionize the appraisal of men. The captain's legs were a credit to the United States, the army, and himself.

He was not handsome, nor was his face delicate with overmuch intellectual labor. If you had met him in a crowd you would have said immediately that here was a young man who could play a bully game of football. That was the impression his features gave—of ability to play a rough game splendidly. It was not the face of a pugilist nor of a society man. It was the face of an average young American of the class which goes to college, acquires enough education to make him easy in the presence of gentlemen, and upon which to base a greater success in life than had been possible to his father who came before him. When you looked at him you thought in physical terms before you considered his possible mentality. There was nothing dull about him; there were indications of a reasonable amount of good nature, and some intolerance, and much of boyishness. His attention was equally divided between France and biscuits.

A young woman just in front of him turned and looked up at him. "Here comes something," she said, pointing.

"Dirigible," he replied, following the direction of her finger.

The dirigible buzzed out to the vessel, looked it over, and evidently with satisfied mind turned and hurried away toward shore again....

"There's a convoy or something," said the young woman.

The captain was interested. "Probably coastwise ships coming down from England. Six of them, aren't there?... And see all those other little boats in there. Must be close to the harbor."

"We're slowing down.... See, there's that little boat like a tug with a cannon up in front. It's signaling us."

"Pilot, probably."

The vessel lost headway and everybody watched the pilot come aboard as if it were some strange phenomenon—as it was to all but a few.

"I wonder if we'll be allowed to cable home that we have arrived?... What do you think, Captain Ware?"

"Haven't the least idea in the world. Don't see why not, though, Miss Knox.... War Department 'tends to it for us."

"My people will be terribly worried until they hear I am safe, and then they'll keep on being worried until I'm back in New York again.... I'm going to sit down. Come on."

Maude Knox's tone approached the proprietary, not that she had asserted any permanent claim to Captain Ware, but only those property rights *in transitu* which arise even in war-time aboard a transatlantic liner. She had promenaded with him, had played bridge with him, and had sat out on deck—the lightless decks—with him as other young men and women aboard ship had embarked on friendly alliances for the voyage. These two had talked, or rather Miss Knox had talked and Captain Ware had listened, and rather liked each other—that was all. There had been nothing sentimental in their relations, even under the moon and in the not unromantic precautionary darkness enforced by the peril of the submarine. They were recognized by the passengers as having paired off, just as a dozen other young couples were similarly indulgently recognized. It was youth making the best of its every moment. That was all.

"I simply can't imagine what it is going to be like—living over here," she said. "It must have been terribly interesting for an American to live in France before the war—but now, with all the effects of war to see, it will be like living in a thrilling book, don't you think?"

Ware had thought of France mostly in terms of war, of ruined villages, lines of trenches, strategic positions. The romance of going to war in France had not missed him; he felt it, but he felt it with a vagueness, an ignorance of what he was to find, and a chaotic conception of the French people that, perhaps, but made the adventure the more romantic to him. He was aware that something great, something that was going to interest him as he had never been interested before, was about to happen to him. But what it would be like he could not picture, did not try to picture. He knew he wanted to see Paris, because he had heard tales of Paris. Most of them he was inclined to discount, but enough remained to make him feel that the city was well worth his investigation. That is as far as he had thought of civilian France.... What his thoughts and sensations were, now that he was nearing those shores, he was unable to put into words, and if he had been able the natural reticence of the young man afraid of appearing sentimental would have caused him to remain silent. Not so Maude Knox.

Maude was the daughter of a professor of philosophy in a Mid-Western university. From her babyhood she was accustomed to the dissection of souls. She had seen her own soul on her father's mental operating-table, and, somehow, the reserves which are inherent in the common run of girls seemed to be what she called *piffle*. She had grown up with her father and a housekeeper, and theories and philosophies and iconoclasms had been the commonplace staple of her mental diet. A great many of them, too, she catalogued in her small head as piffle. On the whole, she was a bit *queer*, or so her girl friends said, but by no means unwomanly or otherwise than girlish. She had a way of liking to look facts in the face, and of discussing them critically. That made her queer. She liked to talk about things, and inquire into things, and was fairly capable of analysis. She fancied she knew a great deal about life and the complexities of human conduct—because she had heard them discussed and had discussed them herself. Actually she was an exceedingly unworldly young person, with more than the usual amount of tolerance for the peculiarities of other folks.... She was rather small, with hair that crinkled close to her head and which no amount of breeze seemed ever to disarrange; her eyes, when she laughed, closed to twinkling slits, and tiny wrinkles ran out from their corners in a droll sort of way; her cheek-bones were high, and her cheeks not at all rounded. She was pretty, but she was also undoubtedly *chic* and agreeable-looking.... She wore a leather coat, and when she walked she thrust her hands into the side pockets and strode with a swing of the shoulders from side to side that was almost a boyish swagger. One might have been excused for concluding that she had only recently emerged from tomboyhood. She had a certain confidence of bearing that was at once attractive and a safeguard. There was something about her which seemed to say to young men who looked at her with interest, "No nonsense here."

There are girls who are advertised by their appearance as amenable to shaded porches, moonlit nights, and sentimental interludes. Maude Knox was not one of these. Yet she did not impress one as being exempt from emotions and sensations; she gave no warning that one must expect no warmth. It was rather that emotions, sensations, warmth were there, but surely controlled, not to be manifested lightly or frivolously. Somehow it was easier to think of her as a wife than as a sweetheart....

Ware was thinking how his father would enjoy all this, the arrival in a strange land, the sights, the anticipation of events to come. His mother would not have enjoyed it. There was too much bustle and confusion for her, too much to upset the nerves. In all likelihood she would be confined to her cabin with one of those nervous headaches.... But his father—his father was one of those men who never grow beyond their enthusiasms nor beyond naïve manifestations of their enthusiasms.

"Yes," he said, in answer to Miss Knox, "the folks will worry, of course.... Dad won't worry so much, but mother'll be in a stew. She's usually in a stew."

"I had a *time* to get father to let me come. He said a war was no place for a young lady.... But this seems to be a different kind of a war, doesn't it. Women are going to it."

"I can understand nurses...." he said, hesitatingly.

"But not the rest of us. That's because you're old-fashioned and Middle-Western.... The army wouldn't let us come if we weren't useful."

"What, exactly, are you going to do?"

"Why, ... *something*—something *useful*."

"There's that girl that plays the harp, and a choir-singer, and a couple of actresses. I can understand them more or less, but you ... I really don't. You're not a stenographer, nor anything like that, nor an entertainer, nor a nurse, nor an ambulance-driver."

"Maybe I'll be a chaperon," she said, taking refuge in lightness, for she really did not know what she *was* going to do. She was classified as a canteen worker. Her uniform was that of the Y. M. C. A., and she had remarked with feeling that the hat was already beginning to fade....

"I presume you know as much about it as any of us do.... I wish you could hear dad on the war and on Germany. He reads the papers to the last punctuation mark, but, somehow, he never seems to grasp it. Possibly most folks are that way, but father always says what he thinks, and goes ahead pronouncing the names of French towns, and has opinions about everything. He gets excited and pounds on the table.... Dad's all right. We've always done things together since I was a kid. He's that kind."

She was able to see that a very real affection for his father was stated in those phrases. She wondered about the father—if he resembled his son in appearance or character.... He did not. The father was a middle-sized man of no education except what an undirected reading of many books had given him. He was a great reader of novels, especially of historical romances, and his knowledge of the past of the nations came from these.

His idea of France was Athos, Porthos Aramis, and d'Artagnan, with Miladi and a few cardinals and intriguing duchesses thrown in.... He owned a grocery in Detroit which did moderately well. His soul was filled with admiration and love for his son. He had a temper given to sudden, brief flashes ... and he had no bad habits except that he chewed tobacco surreptitiously.

People liked him, especially children. He was good personally, but had no vindictive attitude toward evil. Every Sunday he went to church without complaint and without thought of it; though he would have enjoyed himself much more in a boat with a fish-line. When Captain Ware was younger and got into difficulties which his mother magnified into crimes and wept and foresaw disgrace, Mr. Ware would say, "Now don't you worry, mother; that boy's coming out all right...."

"Mother's more worried about my coming to wicked France than about my being shot up," he said, presently, and smiled.

His mother was the dominant member of the family. She was the last word in orthodoxy and was stubbornly dogmatic. She was religious after the manner of a zealot, but in her life economy took place just before religion. One had to save money and be economical to enter the kingdom of heaven; she could even overlook a few moral lapses in an individual who was frugal and laid by systematically for a rainy day.... All his life Captain Ware had been afraid of pulling down on his head what he privately called his mother's "tantrums." These were hysterical outbursts following some escapade of his, or possibly following a mere argument in which economy or religion was mentioned. She could cast stinging darts with her tongue, and when she was opposed, it did not much matter where, she was reckless in dispensing them. Anybody who stood near was likely to be wounded.

But she loved her son savagely and jealously, and lived her life and practised her economies for him. Anything which appertained to the perpetuation of the species was somehow abhorrent to her. Here, as everywhere, she was an extremist. Before her son was ten years old she was already in a state of mind, and embarrassed him so that he exerted himself to avoid being alone with her, by questioning him and by very frank warnings.... At ten she gave him a book to read entitled *Plain Facts*. She worked as she thought, frantically, without sparing herself or anybody else ... and the result was that she was burning herself out.... She was a remarkable woman, sometimes a lovable and companionable woman, but so intense, so intolerant of any belief which did not agree perfectly with hers, that people always felt the necessity of being on their guard with her so as not to "set her off."

It was from these parents that Captain Ware inherited, and he was like neither of them.... But traces of both were easy to find in him. When one looks for explanations of his acts, one would do well to study his parents and to see if his acts did not spring from inherited characteristics and tendencies, or were not the result of a revulsion against parental characteristics which had irked him as a boy.

Now, for the first time in his life—and he was twenty-six years old—he was cutting loose from family contacts, and cutting loose in this total and revolutionary manner. His first adventure in freedom was into a new world which would not understand him and which he was not equipped to understand himself.... He had always lived at home, except for his four years in college, and his mother's figure had been always present, for she had made it her business to keep it ever present.... In a few hours he would set his foot on the soil of France.... With one sudden wrench, war had snatched him from an environment dominated by his mother—and set him down in France.

"I wonder if we'll get ashore to-night," said Miss Knox.

That question presently answered itself. After a short progress up the river, the vessel dropped her anchor, there to remain until morning.... That night Captain Ware sat late on deck with Maude Knox, watching the strange river thick with anchored craft which busied themselves by sending flashing signals to each other—mysterious signals that seemed to say: "You have arrived at the war. We are busy about the war...."

The Polish volunteers forward sang the weird songs of their land; the Americans aft manifested their relief at a safe arrival by wildly cheered boxing-bouts followed by enthusiastic, if somewhat ragged, singing of many popular songs.... There was a preference for that sentimental type of song which had to do with weeping sweethearts left standing on the pier, and with mothers dedicating their boys to death for the flag....

In the morning came the distress of customs examination and the woes of finding and identifying baggage. Ware assisted Miss Knox as other young officers were assisting their partners of the voyage.... The vessel tied up to the dock. Miss Knox shook hands and said good-by, marching down the steep incline of the gangplank with the members of her party.

"I wonder if I'll ever see him again?" she thought.

As for Captain Ware, the girl passed completely from his mind. He had other things to think about and a great curiosity to satisfy.... So far as he was concerned, she had passed out of his life.

He stood at the rail, looking down upon the wharf. Below him an American soldier thrust his head out of a port-hole, looked about him sternly, and then demanded of a Frenchman below, "Say, mister, where's all this trouble, anyhow?"

His attitude was typical of those boys. There was trouble some place and they wanted to get to it and settle it with promptness. It was the attitude of a policeman a little late at the scene of a fight....

Kendall Ware arrived in Paris early on the evening of May 19th and alighted from the crowded train in the Gare d'Orléans. He was excited. It was impossible that he should actually be in Paris, but he was unmistakably there. It rather astounded him and he wanted to rush out of the gray old station to see it at once.... To arrive in Paris was a fitting climax for such a day as he was completing, a day that had given him his first glimpses of beautiful France, glimpses from a rapidly moving train that had caused him to say to himself, "It's no wonder the French will fight for such a country." Already he was impressed by France; already admiration for it was beginning to grow within him.... That beautiful, smiling, rich, clean expanse of hills and fields and vineyards, punctuated by little red-tiled villages and by ancient sprawling stone farm buildings, had touched the sentimental in him. He thought he understood why Frenchmen love their land ... but he had not scratched the outer husk of that reason yet. It would require weeks for him to discover that it was not the material, not land nor soil nor the structures reared by men, that caused the Frenchman's passionate love; it was, he would discover, the imponderables, the immaterial—it was the soul that resided in the material....

He climbed the stairs from the train-shed into the station proper, and paused a moment to regard with boyish interest the crowd composed of women and soldiers, of *poilus* carrying full equipment—sturdy little men whose age seemed greater than it was by reason of four years given to such affairs as Verdun, the Marne, the battles in the Champagne. These men had been in it. They had heard cannon roar with deadly intent; they had taken part in charges and in retreats; the trench and the dugout were more their homes to-day, through years of custom, than their own farms or cottages.... They were *soldiers,* and they looked to be soldiers.

There were uniforms of other nationalities, too: of the British, the brown and tasseled caps of the Belgians, the gray and peaked caps of the Italians— and the khaki of Americans. There was a boy with an arm-band bearing the letters M P, with which he was to become very familiar—the everywhere present and remarkably efficient military police of the American Army....

Presently he was in the dark street. The darkness came as a surprise to him until he recalled that Paris nights slept under the constant threat of German *Gothas*. The street lights—casting a dim-blue glow—were shaded above so that no light might rise to tell hostile raiders that a great city lay here.... Strain his eyes as he would, he could not see Paris, only a vague hint of buildings that might be palaces or warehouses, for all that he could see.... He looked for a taxicab.

Then it occurred to him that when he found a conveyance he had scant language with which to direct the chauffeur. He was going to the University Union, once the Palais Royal Hôtel, now taken over by American universities and colleges as both club and hotel for American university men in the army.... A tiny taxicab rattled up to the curb—all Paris taxicabs rattle in this way—and he approached it with some embarrassment.

"University Union," he said to the chauffeur.

"*Comment?*"

"U-ni-versity Union," said Kendall, speaking very slowly and distinctly.

"*Comment?*" repeated the chauffeur, waggling his head.

Out of the crowd stepped a Frenchman, smiling. "What is it monsieur desires? May I be of assistance to monsieur?"

"I want to go to the University Union, and I don't know how to tell this man."

"The University Union? I do not know it. Is it that it is an hotel, monsieur? Do you know its location?"

Kendall searched for a note-book and read the address. "Number eight rue Richelieu," he said.

"*Huit rue Richelieu,*" the Frenchman said to the chauffeur.

"Thank you," Kendall said, and took the hand which the Frenchman extended cordially.

"It makes nothing, monsieur. I am delighted to serve *Monsieur l'Officier Américain.... Bon soir, monsieur! Bonne chance!*"

Kendall's heart was warmed by the little courtesy. It was a sort of welcome to him. It surprised him, rather, for in America one does not expect assistance to leap to one from a crowd of strangers. He was soon to learn that it was different in France; that all Paris seemed to be on the lookout to be of service to American soldiers, on the lookout almost to the point of embarrassment. He was to discover that the heart of France had a very special niche set aside for Americans. Even though it had already a saying, "*Tous les Américaines sont fous*," it loved them for their very madness....

The little taxi rattled and strained at breath-taking speed around the corner, across the Pont Royale, under the arches which allow a street to pass through the Louvre (though he did not know it was the Louvre), past the Comédie Française, and finally brought up with a lurch before the building that had been the Palais Royal Hôtel before the coming of the Americans.

Here he registered, passed through a lobby filled with American officers and sergeants and corporals and privates—for in this one spot in all France military rank ceases to exist and men are not soldiers, but university men—and up-stairs to the Bureau of the University of Michigan.... In half an hour he was in a comfortable room with windows which opened upon a balcony facing toward the east.... He stepped out upon it and gazed into the darkness. Scarcely a hundred feet away, across a narrow street, was the dark bulk of a mammoth building, and the black silhouettes of a multitude of quaint chimney-pots.... It was the ancient Royal Palace. Kendall did not realize this, nor that his eyes were gazing at a spot rich in history, in intrigue, in romance—and not unbaptized with blood.... But one thing he knew—at last he was in the heart of Paris....

CHAPTER II

Captain Ware felt singularly young, boyishly exhilarated, as he walked out early next morning for his first view of Paris. It was not yet eight o'clock, but the day was beautiful, promising warmth; the skies were clear; the whole appearance of things one of perfect peace and quiet. The city did not seem one threatened by war. The streets, as he walked up the rue de Rivoli, were almost deserted. It was early for Parisians to be abroad.

The city astounded him, captivated him, gave him a feeling of humility. He was familiar with Detroit, had seen Chicago and New York, but Paris— Paris was different. His experience gave him nothing with which to compare it. Chicago and New York were unsightly upheavals; the fantastic work of tremendous industrial forces in irresistible motion. They reared. Paris did not rear; it reposed; it had not been upheaved tumultuously—it had been dreamed and dreamed by genius which comprehended beauty.

The city affected him almost to breathlessness as it opened before him when he passed the ancient grayness of the Louvre. He turned to the left and stood between the wide jaws of the Louvre, the mouth of the Place du Carrousel, and, standing there, looked westward through the reaches of the Tuileries and beyond to where, silhouetted with massive grandeur, uprose Napoleon's Arc de Triomphe.... It was impossible—incredibly magnificent. At that instant began the first great change in his life. He might not consciously have dated it from that instant, and possibly he never dated it at all, but Paris had set the hand of her beauty upon him; her spell had touched him with its magic.

"Why," he said to himself, "anything could happen here!" And presently, "The Germans drop bombs on this ... they try to destroy this."

For the first time came an appreciation, not yet a full appreciation, but far more than an inkling, that a great event had overtaken him: he had left the Middle West behind him; he felt that he was not only about to see, but to be a part of, a new and wonderful mode of life and of thought. There came to him a hint that there might be something to life besides merely living it. Though he did not know the phrase, he felt something of the meaning it bears—*Joie de vivre*. Later he would, perhaps, appreciate a remark made to him by a French officer. "It is not *savoir faire* that is the great knowledge, it is *savoir vivre*." It is not so important to know how to conduct oneself as it is to know how to make the most of life....

He retraced his steps to the rue de Rivoli, stopped to regard the golden Jeanne d'Arc about which he said to himself that he would have liked it better if it had been bronze or marble, and that the sculptor had made Jeanne "huskier" than he had pictured her to himself. That was the word he used—"huskier." Somehow he had always conceived Jeanne d'Arc—what slight conception he had of her—as rather anemic and thin and fragile.... His conception of Jeanne was like the conception many good Americans have made for themselves of France. Two millions of them would soon be on French soil to see for themselves that it was not an anemic, fragile country, but robust, healthy, capable not only of visions, but of battles....

He walked on to pause again in the Place de la Concorde and to marvel at such prodigality of open space in the very heart of a great city. He even tried to calculate to himself the money worth of so many acres in the retail section of New York, say along Fifth Avenue from Thirty-fourth Street north and west.... It was a typical American calculation. Beyond him the Champs Élysées reached on, climbing its little gradient to the Arc de Triomphe. It was splendid and beautiful. It "got under his skin," as he phrased it.

He stood there looking off across the river toward the Chamber of Deputies, over the roof of which could be seen the dome of Napoleon's Tomb. Then he turned and surveyed the path he had just traversed, that reach of low, symmetrical buildings facing the Jardin des Tuileries. He was not exactly inarticulate, but he was not eloquent. "I'll be damned," he said under his breath. "Well, I'll be damned."

Now he was hungry, and, walking more rapidly, he returned to the University Union to find the dining-room open and a few American officers at *petit déjeuner*. For the most part they were eating bread and confiture and washing it down with chocolate. A few were taking the American breakfast, actually eating *two eggs* and other food—a thing to convince the Parisian that these visitors were indeed mad, or at least barbarians.

"Yea, *boy!*" said a loud voice, just as Captain Ware was endeavoring to give his order to one of the two pretty French girls who were the waitresses. It was his first sight of the Parisienne, and it had rather surprised him. They did not wear short skirts and high-heeled slippers, with more than enough black-stockinged ankle to regard. They had not saucy eyes and *rétroussé* noses, nor did they whisk about flirtatiously. They were pretty, indeed they were charming, but they were quiet, even subdued, and they looked *nice*. That was a good American word he could apply to them. He liked their looks, even if they failed to come up to his ideas of what a French waitress should be.

He looked up from the pad on which he had been checking off the *petit déjeuner*, to see facing him across the table, in a captain's uniform and Sam Brown belt which made him almost unrecognizable, a man with whom he had been more than friendly through four years in Ann Arbor.

"Bert Stanley!" he exclaimed, jumping to his feet and extending his hand.

"They all come here," said Stanley to himself, "all of them—if you just wait long enough.... When did you land?"

"Day before yesterday."

"And got to Paris so soon? How did you work that?"

"Ordered.... What are you doing here?"

"Making marks on pieces of paper. That's what I got for knowing anything about architectural engineering. I'm in the Signal Corps and I'm drawing plans for aeroplane-sheds.... What are you?" He looked down at Kendall's collar markings.

"Intelligence! I'm one of the fellows who find out everything about everything in the world and tell it to the army for its good."

"Stationed here?"

"Don't know. Report this morning."

"Fix it, son, fix it.... It's a great *guerre*, and this battle of Paris—"

"*Beurre, monsieur?*" asked the waitress.

"Eh? What's that?"

"She wants to know," explained Stanley, with exaggerated patience, "if you want butter. It's extra."

Kendall signified his desire for butter. "I've just been out looking at the town," he said. "The fellows that built it knew what they were doing, didn't they?"

"They knew how to do a lot of things. Staying here, of course."

"Didn't know where else to go. You, too?"

"Have been a month, but if I'm going to live here for the duration, and it looks as if I were, I'd like to get somebody and take a little apartment somewhere.... Over in the Quartier Latin or up on one of the streets off the Étoile. Have some comfort. Live cheaper, too. Get a cook for sixty or seventy francs, and be regular people.... Say, if you're set down in Paris, come on in with me."

"Sounds reasonable," said Kendall, tentatively. "Haven't the least idea what they'll do with me, though."

"Well, you run up and see, and, whatever happens, meet me here at half past six and I'll take you to a regular place to eat, and then we'll go out and look at the sights."

"You're on," said Kendall, "bigger than a house."

Captain Ware had hoped to be assigned to active duty with a combat unit. He had studied and trained himself for the duties of an intelligence officer at the front, and for months had looked forward with enthusiasm to those interesting and invaluable duties which such an officer performs. He was not a young man to welcome a desk job or to be contented with a position in the Safety of the Service of Supplies region. In that he resembled thousands of other young officers whose fortune it would never be to hear a cannon fired in battle, to take part in a charge, or to be nearer to the front than some small town in the interior of France. None of them had chosen their places. They had been sent where they were most needed and where their work was essential to the victories to be won against the enemy.... Captain Ware, like these others, must perform the task set for him, wherever it might lie—hoping always for a new assignment that should carry him to the dugout and to the trench. It was, therefore, with grievous disappointment that he learned he was to be stationed in Paris, apparently in permanence. He could still hope, for in the army in France no man can tell what to-morrow will bring him. Orders come and men go.... Somehow it did not seem possible to him that he would thus go to war without going to war; that he should journey across the ocean to this mightiest of all conflicts without the experience of battle....

At half after six he was again at the Union, where he found Bert Stanley waiting for him in the lounge, whiling away the time very pleasantly in conversation with charming Annette of the pert face, white teeth, and busy chatter—a chatter made up in very large part of excellent American idiom learned from the patrons of the cigar-and-candy case of which she was custodian. Hundreds of American officers will return to their country after the war with pleasant memories of wise little Annette, the little French girl who sold cigarettes and candy and wrist watches and post-cards at the stand in the Union.

Kendall ascended to his room in the queer little elevator whose conductor was a tiny Belgian boy, proud of a few words of American, and presently walked down the five flights—for in France it is not considered good manners in war-time to use an elevator for descent—and rejoined Stanley.

"Well," said Stanley, "what luck?"

"It looks like Paris for mine," said Kendall, still depressed by his disappointment.

"Might be worse.... Might have been Chaumont."

They walked north on the rue de Richelieu, past the Molière fountain, and by the door of Marty's which Kendall was to know very well later on. At the rue St.-Marc they turned to the left until the Opéra Comique uprose before them, and then made their way into the up-stairs dining-room of the Café Poccardi on rue Favart.

"It's early. The crowd doesn't show up before seven-thirty, so we can get a table up front where we can see the show," said Stanley. "Besides, there's a waiter there who speaks English."

They found seats with their backs toward the windows, a point of vantage from which they could view the large, mirrored room with its rows of small, closely set tables. Only a few were occupied, but gradually the patrons straggled in—a truly Parisian gathering. There were handsome men in officers' uniforms with many gold service stripes on the sleeve, and some with two, three, or even four wound chevrons on the opposite sleeve. They were accompanied by well-dressed women, mostly young, always very neat.... It was their shoes that demanded Kendall's attention. This was a matter that had been impressing itself upon him through the day— that the Parisienne knew how to dress her feet. There were *poilus* on leave, each with his girl, or even with two girls. There were one or two old but immaculate men with women young enough to be their granddaughters.

A few women entered alone and seated themselves quietly at tables to await their partners—perhaps the café was their place of rendezvous.... Two women, beautifully dressed in black, with widows' veils, occupied a table just across from Kendall and his companion. They were very young, and one was remarkably lovely.... The sight rather depressed Kendall. This was one of the meanings of war—this youthful widowhood! Here was the cruelty of it, the bitterness of it!

"France must be filled with widows," he said to Stanley.

Bert grinned. "Camouflage," he said.

"What do you mean?"

"If you're thinking about our friends opposite, don't get too sympathetic. They're no more widows than I am. Camouflage. It's the style. But they're overdoing it. Everybody's next, now, even us Americans. Bait, sonny, bait, that's what it is."

Bert looked over at the widows and smiled, and the lovelier one smiled in reply, not brazenly, not with the red-lipped, painted-cheeked smile of the Anglo-Saxon siren, but demurely, pleasantly, as if she were merely returning his smile out of courtesy and from an abundance of gentle good nature.

"See?" said Bert.

"But they look *nice*." Again Kendall used that word.

"They are nice.... This isn't Terre Haute, son."

Everybody was drinking wine, Kendall noticed. It was universal, and as the meal progressed he spoke about it.

"Everybody is going to the wine," he said, "but nobody gets noisy."

"Nobody does," said Bert. "Do we get noisy at home when we drink coffee?"

Kendall watched. He saw a man half fill his companion's glass with red wine, then pour in as much water as there was wine. This, he saw, was almost universally done.... Conversation was animated. There was gay laughter and lightness, but it was not the gaiety of wine.

At a table well within view sat two *poilus* with their wives or sweethearts. Kendall watched them, for it was by far the jolliest, least restrained party in the room.... And then he saw the larger soldier throw his arm around the neck of his buxom companion and kiss her soundly.... It rather shocked him. The idea of demonstrative affection in, for instance, the dining-room of the McAlpin, or in one of the better-class cafés of Detroit, was impossible to entertain. He watched for a waiter to protest, perhaps to eject the couple from the place.... But there were only tolerant smiles when any notice whatever was taken of the event.... And it was an event which was repeated—the sound of hearty smacks coming even to Kendall's ear.... He saw other men come in, and before they sat down beside waiting companions they would stoop to salute with a kiss.... The thing was not universal, not even general, but there was enough of it for him to become aware that it was not exceptional.... But for all that, it made him feel embarrassed and uncomfortable. Apparently, if people had kissing to do they simply did it.... He was to recognize this later as one manifestation of the frank, unaffected genuineness of the people. Now it seemed rather gross to him, gross and exotic. The idea did not occur to him then that it was he with his American notions and antecedents, with his inheritances from Plymouth Rock, that was exotic.

He wondered who all these people were; he wondered if they were *married*. Were these men and women husbands and wives, or were the women those mysterious, very French, somewhat exciting persons whom he had read about in novels and who were called *mistresses*?

He did not put the question to Stanley because he was afraid of appearing provincial. He might as well have done so, for in all probability Stanley, with all of his month's experience in Paris, was pondering the same matter.... Anyhow, he felt that he was seeing life; that he was beholding things which he could tell about later to interested audiences.... It is a peculiarity of the Anglo-Saxon mind that everything which is strange to it appears to it as necessarily tinged with naughtiness.

At another table, over to Kendall's left, two girls were eating alone, and he watched them with interest and considerable curiosity, wondering who and what they were. One of them attracted him particularly. She was young, in the neighborhood of twenty, he judged. She was dressed in white, a suit of some knit material that reminded him of a light jersey, and on her very black and wavy hair was a shapeless white cap of the tam-o-'shanter variety. Her skin was a delightful olive, and her eyes black, with shadows under them. She was not beautiful, unless her eyes made her so. She was small and almost thin. She addressed herself to her food in a very business-like manner, not often looking up from her plate, but once in a while she smiled as she replied to some comment of her companion, and her teeth were very white and regular. There was no appearance of wealth about her, but every feature spoke of intelligence—indeed, of a certain keenness.... She was very attractive.

"Look," he said to Bert. "I wonder who she is. She looks as if she had 'class.'"

"Pretty kid," said Bert, who, just then, was more interested in *poule au riz* than in Parisiennes.

He continued to stare, unconscious of his rudeness, until she lifted her eyes to his. For a moment she regarded him, with no especial interest, certainly with no sign which could be interpreted as provocative, and dropped her eyes again to her plate.... Kendall was conscious at once of disappointment and satisfaction. Here was another girl that he had estimated as "nice," and this time, apparently, he was right.

In a moment he heard her name, for her companion uttered it. "Andree." Somehow it suited her, Kendall thought, and he thought, too, that it was a decidedly pretty name ... "Andree."

From time to time, as he was finishing his dinner, Kendall glanced at Andree. But he did not meet her eyes again. She was not interested in him, apparently, and even when he walked past her table on his way out she did not look up or manifest by a sign that she was conscious of his existence.

"Where now?" he said as they debouched onto the broad Boulevard des Italiens.

"Might as well take in the 'Folies Bergère.' It's one of the sights."

They walked along in silence, crossing the boulevard and turning up a narrow street toward the theater. Kendall continued to think about the little girl with the black eyes. Somehow she had made an impression of some sort upon him. He could not have described it nor estimated it. All he knew was that he liked her looks immensely and was curious about her. Probably he would never see her again, but he found himself hoping that he might.

They bought tickets for the "Folies" and entered, traversing the large hall filled with tables at which the audience was expected to refresh itself between the acts, or even during the performance, and, after buying programs, were conducted to their seats by a girl usher who stood sternly by until she received her tip—a tip that she would have suggested if it had not been tendered.

Then the performance began—a very disappointing performance to a Middle-Western young man who had heard tales of the naughtiness of the French stage. It turned out to be a rather clumsy musical comedy which was more vaudeville than either music or comedy. It was not naughty at all, he said to himself—but perhaps that was because he failed to understand the dialogue. Anyhow, he had seen much franker costumes and much more suggestive incident in Mr. Ziegfeld's "Follies" or at the Winter Garden.

The audience was more than half American; the music was adapted from American shows, and between the acts a jazz orchestra, "straight from Broadway," made the ears ring. Everybody got up between the acts and promenaded or sat at the little tables.... Girls wandered about and spoke to one, and made Kendall feel uncomfortable and embarrassed again. He was glad when they returned to their seats.

The performance rather bored him, and he suggested leaving. Bert was ready, too, so they sauntered out onto the dark streets, making their way to the Avenue de l'Opéra and past the huge bulk of that wonderful building which France had erected even while she was paying to Germany the billion-franc indemnity exacted after 1870. Once or twice soft voices accosted them out of the darkness, but they walked on toward the Union, and presently were ordering ice-cream and listening to a lieutenant play ragtime on the piano.

Then, suddenly, the air was rent by a startling, metallic shriek, a long-sustained, nerve-twanging, raucous blast.

"Raid!" said Stanley, getting to his feet.

"Bomb raid?" asked Kendall, instantly excited.

"Yes. Let's go out and take a look."

So, with characteristic foolhardiness, they sallied out and hurried up the rue de Rivoli to the Place de la Concorde, where they sat on a stone balustrade and waited. They were not alone. About that open space were scattered a dozen Americans impelled by absurd curiosity—a curiosity they would discard very shortly and become more circumspect in their behavior as well as more respectful toward the *Gothas*.

Still the *alerte* sounded, more terrifying than the sound of the barrage which was presently to begin. Sirens mounted on fire-engines were giving the alarm, tearing madly through the black streets, and with horrid voice commanding Paris to seek sanctuary in *abri* or in the tunnels of the Metropolitan.

Kendall was not frightened; he was hardly apprehensive. Even when the guns opened toward the north and he could see bright star-flashes as shrapnel burst high above, he was only exhilarated and very interested. The thing did not seem serious to him. But it *was* serious, he knew. It was war, and such barbarous war as held the world in a spell of horror. Presently the air was filled with the crashes of cannon, and one could trace the course of the enemy by the spreading of the ring of fire about the city.... Once in a while would come a deep, dull, thunderous *boom*, as a bomb, released by a *Gotha*, would fall in the distant suburbs, perhaps upon the home of some laborer, burying himself with his wife and babies in the ruins, or destroying them utterly so that no trace of their human shell would ever be discovered.... The firing moved westward, and then swung around to the south as the hostile aeroplanes strove vainly to penetrate the city.... This continued for half an hour. Then there was a time of quietness, after which came the pleasant voices of bugles notifying a cowering population that all was clear.... The raid had been abortive—it had succeeded in killing only half a dozen defenseless civilians!

Kendall and Stanley walked back to the Union—to have another dish of ice-cream. As they walked up-stairs in the darkness Kendall said to his friend: "I wonder who that girl was ... the one in the restaurant. Her name was Andree."

CHAPTER III

Kendall Ware had been two weeks in Paris; he had learned many things, absorbed many things, but as his observations grew he discovered depths to his ignorance that were not apparent to him on the day of his arrival. The greatest advance he made in those first weeks was in arriving at a knowledge of how little he understood or was equipped to understand of France—and when he said *France* he did not mean a country, but the people who inhabited the country. Continually he was amused by superficialities; daily he was impressed by profundities. Gradually he came to perceive that one cannot know France by looking at the surface any more than one can gather a knowledge of what is transpiring in the ocean by sailing a little boat over its waves.

A people which can produce Joan of Arc and Robespierre, a St. Louis and a Louis the Eleventh, a Madame Roland and a Madame du Barry, a Clemenceau and a Calliaux; which is capable of an 1870 and of a 1914, of the Terror and of Verdun—is not one whose complexities can be solved by a twenty-six-year-old American in fourteen days.... The American will make no impression on France, but France will make a profound impression on the American.

From being interested in a city, in its buildings and its beauties, Kendall became interested in its people.

His first reaction to the people was rather romantic. He saw romance in every one. Hotel porters with one arm, wearing the Croix de Guerre and the Légion d'Honneur, and perhaps the Médaille Militaire excited him. Each one was, in truth, a hero. These men had seen and done. Now they worked at menial tasks, still wearing uniforms, and with those medals on the breast which raised them into the aristocracy of manhood. It was strange to him that a man could be at once an honored hero and a porter.... *Liberté, Égalité, Fraternité* were inscribed on every public building. This was one of the manifestations of Liberty, Equality, Brotherhood. These things really existed, and so a porter could be a decorated hero.

If one addressed a taxi-driver one called him *Monsieur*, just as if one were addressing the President of the Republic itself. One addressed the *gendarmes* as *Monsieur*. One addressed even the turbaned and besashed and betrousered Moroccan street-sweepers as *Monsieur* if one addressed them at all. Monsieur Poincaré or Monsieur Clemenceau would have given them the same salutation. It was not an affectation; it was not what strangers have called French politeness. It was but a manifestation of Liberty, Equality, Brotherhood. At first it had seemed rather absurd to Kendall, American and republican though he was, but he grew to like it, and somewhat to understand it.

Everywhere he saw heroes wearing medals. It made him feel insignificant and somehow lacking. One could not walk a block without passing officer or *poilu* with the red ribbon of the Legion of Honor, or the rarer, even more precious, broad yellow stripe of the Military Medal. The narrow green stripe of the ribbon of the War Cross was everywhere. Sometimes the ribbons were elongated to give space to two or three, or, as was the case with one boyish officer, to eight palms.... And every palm the token that its bearer had fought back out of the clutch of Death, performing some act of valor which raised him above the level of an army of heroes....

These soldiers were the first to command Kendall's interest, but it expanded to cover every one. Ancient drivers of *voitures* whose horses were always too tired to take him where he wanted to go; the chauffeurs of taxi-cabs who could never understand his French, and who, when he had made them understand, told him they could not take him to his destination because they happened to be heading the other way; the crowds who occupied the tables under the awnings on the sidewalks of the rue de la Paix or the rue Royale; the old women who came to collect two sous if one took a seat along the Champs Élysées or the Avenue du Bois de Boulogne; the soldiers, French, Belgian, Italian, Austrian, Canadian, English, Moroccan, American, who promenaded of evenings and Sundays from the Place de la Concorde to Rond-Point, and the girls with whom they promenaded—all these interested him, and each, as he studied them with boyish *naïveté*, added something to his education.

He worked hard by day, and often far into the night, but for the most part his evenings were free to investigate life with Bert Stanley, whose investigations were merely of the surface and were rather questings for an hour of amusement.... Sometimes he played bridge with three other Americans at the Union, but he liked best to stroll about the darkened streets, without object or destination.

Little by little he added to his meager store of the language. When he spoke to friends about securing an instructor they laughed at him. "Pick it up.... Talk to people," they told him. "Sit down on a bench along the Champs Élysées and talk to a girl. They're as eager to learn English as you are French.... It's better than a teacher—and a darned sight more pleasant."

He voiced his distaste for this suggestion. He had been but two weeks in Paris, and very mistakenly had classified all the girls who promenade the Champs Élysées in the evening as women of the streets. His natural decency revolted at any contact, no matter how slight, with these.

"Nine out of ten of those little girls work in shops or offices," Bert told him. "You haven't got 'em right, son."

But Kendall was suspicious. He continued in that attitude until one evening a little girl—she appeared not more than seventeen—sat rather diffidently on the other end of his bench.

"Good night, monsieur," she said, with quaint pronunciation.

He did not answer, but turned his back with a gesture of repulse.

"Oh, monsieur, please," she said, timidly. "I am not a bad girl.... See." She turned her face so that the dim light shone upon it and pointed to her cheeks. "There is not paint. You see. No.... I am a good girl, but monsieur, I am—how do you say *solitaire*? I learn English.... It will not harm monsieur if I talk with him a little and learn English."

Kendall regarded her. She was a little thing with clear eyes and a rather pretty face, whose cheeks, as she pointed out, were guiltless of paint. She was not well dressed, though she was neat, *chic*. And she was so young.... It was apparent to him that she told the truth, and his manner changed toward her.

They talked. It was a conversation which would have aroused the mirth of a listener ... but it was remarkable how well each made the other understand; she with slowly pronounced French and a few words of quaint English—he with his small stock of atrociously articulated French.... She worked in a chocolate-shop. She was a refugee from Soissons and an orphan. Her two brothers had been killed at Verdun and her mother and father had died of the war.

"Now I must make to work," she said, simply. "But I am very *solitaire, monsieur.... Oui, je suis trés-solitaire—trés-solitaire.*"

"Poor kid!" said Kendall.

She shrugged her shoulders and said, with that calm resignation which is so much to be met with, "*C'est la guerre....* It is the war." That is a phrase which explains everything, excuses anything in France to-day. "*C'est la guerre.*" One offers it to explain the lateness of trains, the price of cheese, poverty, the lack of sugar, morale, everything great or small. "*C'est la guerre*" is the countersign of the epoch. It embraces everything.

After an hour she arose, offered her hand charmingly, and said good night and "*Merci.*" Kendall sat looking after her, feeling the first life movements of a comprehension of the womankind of France. From that moment they assumed a higher place in his thoughts, not yet so high as they deserved, but one rung nearer to the truth. He did not even begin to understand them—not their philosophy of life nor their conception of the relations between the sexes; but he began to ask himself questions to which his education and prejudices and narrownesses could provide no answer. He began to wonder if all he had heard were true; he began to consider, if it were true, was it then necessarily evil. He had been brought up to regard the drinking of any beverage containing alcohol as inherently wicked and as something to be done surreptitiously and with a sort of "devilish" feeling. Here everybody drank wine, and wine contained alcohol, and they did it with no concealment and with no thought that it could be other than normal and perfectly respectable. He considered that, and from it attempted to form a judgment of other things which to him seemed not as they should be. Apparently drinking in France was not a thing of moral turpitude, done as it was done by the French.... Perhaps, then, other matters were the same: evil in Detroit because custom and inherited moral conceptions had made them so; right in Paris because custom and inherited moral conceptions had made them so.... Dimly he was feeling for the conception that an act in itself is not a sin, but the manner of the performance of that act.... This may have been sophistry; it may have been alarmingly faulty moral philosophy, but it marked a step ahead for a young man come of such parentage as Kendall came of. It marked a willingness to listen to argument and to maintain an open mind. His mother, he considered, had never maintained an open mind. She had been dogmatic. To inquire into things was a sin to her. Nothing had been so quick to arouse her anger as an impulse on his part to look for the reasons of things, particularly religious things.... His father had not been like this. True, he had not been of an inquiring turn of mind, but he had seen no especial reason why somebody who wanted to inquire should not be allowed to do so. There was a certain sweetness about his father, a tolerant attitude toward life in general and toward transgressions in particular, that came nearer to the attitude of Jesus Christ than did the hard, unbending, dogmatic almost cruel religion of his mother.... He had inherited from both parents; each had given him something distinctly traceable to each, and both had joined to give him other qualities which were a strange composite of both of them. He was inclined to judge at first sight like his mother, harshly and dogmatically; he was inclined, on second thought, to look for excuses and to forgive what must be judged as evil, like his father. It was a quality composite of the characters of his parents that he placed the abstraction of *goodness* on a lofty throne, but was inclined to apply its laws with gentleness and mercy rather than with narrowness and hardness.... There were days when he was inclined to narrowness and dogmatism; there were days when he bent quite in the other direction and became over-indulgent.

Following his first experience in conversation with a casually encountered girl, and finding himself to have come off none the worse for it, he repeated the experience several times, and enjoyed it, and came to look forward to the evenings because of the possibility of a pleasant and instructive talk with some girl he would never see again, but from whom he would learn some French and considerable of France.... It was rarely that his sense of propriety was offended or that the attitude of one of his chance companions was other than "nice." He made no effort to follow up any of these casual meetings, or to centralize his attention upon a single girl. He preferred matters as they were. But he was learning that the ordinary French girl did not resent being accosted by an American, and that when he was lonely he might find charming company without fear of being rebuffed.

On his third Sunday in Paris he was sitting among the trees that border the Champs Élysées. He was lonesome, for Bert Stanley had been absent on a mission for several days. He and Bert were sharing a room at the Union now, a room with two beds, which cost them jointly ten francs a day—and he missed Bert. He had lunched alone that noon and now did not know what to do with himself. It was the first time he had been really homesick, but now he was homesick and uneasy and rather at loose ends. He wished something would happen; that some friend would appear with an entertaining suggestion. So he sat and smoked and watched the passage of the colorful crowd.

Presently he stiffened to interest. In the distance he saw approaching a girl dressed in white. It was the white tam-o'-shanter that had caught his eye. It was familiar. For a moment he could not remember where he had seen it, or why it stirred him to interest, and then he recalled the little girl of the Café Poccardi. He even remembered her name—"Andree." She came abreast of him and he identified her certainly. It was she, and really more attractive than he had remembered her to be. She walked along with little steps, her body very straight, her bearing very staid. As she walked her eyes remained straight in front of her, as though her mind were on some interest at her destination.... Her profile was prettier than his first picture of her full face had been; there was a daintiness about her lips and her straight little nose, and about the whole of her. If one had been compelled to limit himself to a single word in describing her, he would have been forced to use that word "dainty."

She passed, and his eyes followed her. Suddenly he stood up with a resolution half formed, a resolution to speak to her. Then he hesitated. She did not look like a person one speaks to without permission or presentation. But it was a chance.... He was lonely and this was rather an adventure, and, besides, he had learned that one is not often rebuffed when making a casual advance. Still Kendall was a bit apprehensive. He walked along behind her irresolute, wondering if he dared, and keying up his courage to dare. At any rate, he would wait until they were out of the crowd; he did not wish the embarrassment of being rebuffed too publicly.

The girl tripped along, almost birdlike in the carriage of her head and in the *ensemble* of her daintiness. At the Place de la Concorde she turned to her left up the rue Boissy d'Anglas, on one corner of which is the Hôtel Crillon and on the other a high, blank wall of brick. The street was deserted.

Kendall summoned his resolution and overtook her as she entered the shadow of the brick wall. He was rather excited and apprehensive, and stammered a bit as he lifted his hat and said in his best French, *"Bon jour, mademoiselle."*

She stopped suddenly and slowly raised her eyes to his face. She was not startled, not frightened, not thrown from her poise in the least.

"Bon jour, monsieur," she said, with a rising inflection, as one who expresses surprise and inquiry.

Kendall was at a loss. He did not know how to proceed or how to make plausible his action. What little French he knew departed from him, and he stood awkwardly by her side, feeling very idiotic indeed. She waited gravely, with no twinkle in her eye at the rather absurd figure he must have presented.

The Little Moment Of Happiness | 35

"*Voulez-vous promenade avec moi?*" he managed to articulate, at last.

"*Pourquoi?*" she asked.

Why? Why should she promenade with him? He felt his face reddening, and it was his impulse to clap on his cap and beat a hasty retreat. What answer was there to that *why?* He could think of nothing whatever to say, and the pause became awkward.

"*Parlez-vous anglais?*" he asked, desperately.

"*Non.*"

In sheer desperation he touched her arm and began walking. She walked with him, the merest hint of an amused smile at the corners of her mouth.... At any rate, she was walking with him. That much was accomplished, but, now that he had progressed to this point, what was he to do with her? She was difficult, and not inclined to help him in the least.

"Mademoiselle," he said, desperately, "I speak very little French. I am very lonesome." Then, of necessity, he lapsed into his own tongue. "Why in thunder don't you speak English!" he said, testily.

"Where are you going?" she asked.

"With you—if you permit," he replied.

Again that appalling why. He was to come to know that she used it often; that she shot it at one like an unexpected little arrow when one least looked for it, and rather upset one with it. There came a time when he called her Mademoiselle Pourquoi because of this. "Because—" he answered. "Because— Oh, confound it! I don't know why. I haven't any idea. No reason at all. I just want to.... Now if you could only understand that we might get somewhere."

She was amused—a little. She regarded him gravely, and it was apparent that she was appraising him, satisfying herself as to what sort of a barbarian he was, and possibly as to what he had in mind.

"Will you dine with me?" he asked. That was a phrase he had by heart.

"Why?"

"Same reason," he said, ruefully, in English. "I've got to dine, you've got to dine, we've got to dine.... *Pourquoi, pourquoi, pourquoi—toujours vous dit pourquoi.*" This was not remarkably excellent French, but she comprehended, and for the first time she uttered a little laugh. He amused her. From that moment they got along better, for, apparently, she had appraised him as not dangerous.

She began to ask questions, not idly, he judged, but the better to satisfy herself about him.

"Where do you live?"

He told her.

"You are an American?"

"Yes."

"From what city?"

"Detroit."

"I do not know it.... What is your grade?" She meant his military rank.

"Captain."

"Are you married?"

He had rather been expecting that question, for it had been put to him by almost every girl he had talked to. Apparently it was an important question.... In a land where so many, many young men have been sacrificed to war an unmarried man is an important personage. He offers possibilities. Suppose that one million, two millions of men of marriageable age have been slaughtered, there remain at home one or two millions of young women who have no one to marry. This, in France, is not a theory, but a condition, a very real and very terrible condition. A million girls of an age for marriage and no men!...

"No," he said.

She was silent while they walked the greater part of a block. He repeated again his well-learned phrase, "Will you dine with me?"

"Yes," she said, in the tone of one making a decision of some moment. "Where?"

"Anywhere you wish."

They were just passing a little café not distant from the Madeleine, and she stopped hesitatingly, rather speculatively, and there was a subdued twinkle in her eye.

"Here?" she asked.

She was looking for information about this young American, and this was an experiment. The cafe was one of the most expensive in Paris, and doubtless Andree wanted to see how he would act at her suggestion, for reckless spending of money is a thing which your Parisian does not indulge in. Possibly she wanted to find out just how much she attracted him, and one way to do it was to discover if he was willing to spend money on her. It is not impossible that she wondered a bit if he had lots of money, as all Americans are said to do. Your Frenchwoman is not mercenary, but she is practical—and lots of money is an excellent thing to have.

"All right," he said, in perfect innocence, for he had never seen the place before. It looked rather dingy and not especially attractive. It was very small. So they went in. There was a passage down the middle of the room, with tables on either side, set in solid rows. The waiter moved a table out to admit Andree to the leather bench which ran along the wall. Kendall waited for the table to be replaced so that he could sit across from her, American fashion, but she motioned for him to sit by her side. Young women and men in France sit side by side, not *vis-a-vis*—and it is a custom not without its advantages.

Ordering was a difficult matter, first because of lack of the language, and second because he was beginning to be very anxious to please this girl and to make a favorable impression on her. With characteristic American generosity or love of displaying his willingness to spend, he would have ordered more than four could have eaten, but she interfered and took the ordering into her own hands—a thing for which he was grateful when the check was presented.... Even when she was making an experiment she could not bear to see money actually wasted.

Kendall studied her covertly. She impressed him as being a grave, very self-possessed young person. The word demure conceals in its meaning something of the provocative. If it were possible to remove that shade of meaning from it, then it would have described Andree exactly. She was demure without being provocative.... And how pretty she was. She grew on one. Those heavily shadowed eyes were really beautiful, and her lips delicately sweet. He made up his mind that she was what he had been accustomed to designate as a lady, which was but another way of saying "nice."

Out of the corner of his eye he watched her eat. She was very dainty about it, but also very interested. Indeed, she ate in a thoroughly business-like manner, giving her attention fully to her plate. He thought of a bird.

Indeed, there was something birdlike about her, but what bird she resembled Kendall could not determine. Possibly it was a composite resemblance.... He liked her very much, but was puzzled by her. She was something quite outside his experience. Her manner puzzled him. She was not what he would have called "offish." She did not seem wholly at her ease, yet she was much more so than he. She was gravely expectant; concealing herself, perhaps, while she waited for self-disclosure on the part of Kendall.

She would drink but a fraction of a glass of wine and declined a cigarette at the end of the meal.... Then he called for the check and discovered that the rather light repast was to cost him seventy francs. He wondered if Andree were accustomed to eating seventy-franc meals, not knowing that this was the first experience of the kind she had ever had. Seventy francs would have sufficed nearly for her food for a month.... On the whole, she was a mystery to him, and as long as he knew her she continued to remain something of a mystery. He was incapable of solving her.

"Now what shall we do?" he asked.

"We shall walk," she replied, in quaintly stilted and accented English. The effect was charming.

"Eh?" said Kendall. "You—why, you said you didn't speak English!"

"Yes," she said, and smiled, but offered no explanation. But the explanation was clear, even to Kendall. It was because she was making no admission whatever about herself in those first few minutes. It was because she was on the brink of a new experience, was meeting her first American, and because she wanted to find out as much as she could about him without permitting him to learn anything whatever of her—until she was ready to permit it.... He was pleased. Evidently her judgment was favoring him.

"That's fine," he said. "Now you can teach me French and I can teach you English."

"Maybe," she said, with her reserved smile. "We shall see."

"Let's take a taxi out to the Bois de Boulogne," he suggested.

"It is very expensive.... It is not *nécessaire*. No, we shall walk."

They retraced their steps to the Place de la Concorde and walked slowly up the Champs Élysées to the Étoile, and then diagonally to the left and so along the Avenue du Bois de Boulogne, that wonderful promenade so dear to Parisians. There they found chairs beside the broad graveled walk and seated themselves. They had progressed very well conversationally, for, though Andree's English was but little more extensive than Kendall's French, the two supplemented each other splendidly. A little pocket dictionary which Kendall always carried worked wonders. The little dictionary was a splendid thing, anyway. It grew to be a little joke between them and they laughed over it gaily; Andree became less restrained.

Kendall would start a sentence in French and arrive at a point impassable. Neither English nor French could supply his meaning. "*Attendez,*" he would say, with mock solemnity, and then would produce the little book, and with heads close together in the dusk they would search it for the word. When they found it Andree would laugh at Kendall's pronunciation of it.... The dictionary was a great promoter of acquaintance.

He was more and more curious about her. He wanted to know who she was, and what she did, and if she worked for her living, and where she lived, but he could not screw up his courage to direct questions, and she volunteered nothing.

Finally she said, "I must be at my home, for every day I have very much work."

"What do you work at?" he asked, brashly.

"I must study. Many, many hours every day I must study."

"What are you studying?"

"Many things.... I must study much, much, for the time is not long.... So I must be at my home *now.*" She pointed down at the ground with a pretty gesture, a childish gesture, the first manifestation of the sort she had shown him. "I must be at my home *now*—at this minute. Make me to be there—instantly." Then she laughed gleefully.

What a charming little thing she was, he thought, and was enchanted by her.

"*Nous cherchons un taxi,*" he said, trying out his French. Apparently he did reasonably well, for she shook her head.

"It is not *nécessaire.* No, I shall go on the Metro.... Good-by."

"But—oh, now listen. I'm to go home with you, of course. And we must see each other often—to learn French and English, you know.... You're not going to send me away now."

She considered a moment.

"You may come with me—*some*…. When I say, then you shall tell me good night. Do you promise?"

"Yes," he said, "but—"

She arose and he accompanied her to the nearest station of the Metropolitan, into which they descended, he very curious to know where they were proceeding, and entered a passageway labeled "*Direction Châtelet.*" The train was crowded and there was little opportunity for speech until they changed to take another subterranean train which discharged them at Place St.-Michel—the heart of the Quartier Latin.

So, Kendall thought, she is a student and she lives in the Latin Quarter! There was magic in that thought, romance in it; the very fact of her residence in that fascinating quarter of the city gave her a higher valuation.

They entered the big lift which should have carried them to the street, but the lift declined to rise. They waited amid bursts of laughter from the crowd, and then everybody marched off again in perfect good nature—indeed, rather delighted at a little adventure, for the old soldier who operated the elevator had dined too well that Sunday evening, and in his abounding good spirits had forgotten how to operate his machine. The crowd trudged up-stairs, laughing, not at all peevish as an American crowd in like circumstances would have been; indeed, they were rather in sympathy with the old fellow. Just as they arrived at the top of the stairs the elevator came slowly into view, the conductor stepped off with the air of one who had done a noteworthy thing. He removed his hat and bowed low to the company.

"*Regardez!*" he said, magnificently. "*Voilà…. Voilà!*"

Andree laughed prettily and Kendall laughed, and they were advanced another step in their acquaintance by the little incident.

The streets were black as they emerged, and Andree took his arm, leading him diagonally across the Place, past the fountain, and up the Boulevard St.-Michel—the "Boul' Miche" of fable and story. She permitted him to accompany her for a few blocks, then she halted.

"It is here you must go," she said. "You must go now."

"But—"

"Your promise!"

He acquiesced. "I shall see you again?" He essayed the thing in French, "*Voulez-vous donnez moi un rendez-vous, mademoiselle?*"

"No, no, no, no. It is not so. *Écoutez.* The right way to say is this, *Voulez-vous me donnerai un rendez-vous?* It is the future time, do you onderstan'?... You wish to see me again?"

"Yes."

"*Pourquoi?*"

"Mademoiselle Pourquoi." It was the first time he called her so.

It was a liberty, perhaps, but it pleased her, for she gave a little laugh. "You really wish to see me again?"

"Yes, really.... I want to see you—to beat the band."

"To beat the band?... What is that, monsieur? I do not onderstan', oh, I do not onderstan'." She had a way of failing to understand with despair in her voice and her gestures that was very charming.

"*L'argot américain,*" he explained. "American slang. It means I want to see you very much."

"It is well."

"When?... To-morrow? *Demain?*"

"I cannot to see you to-morrow, for I must work, as I said. *Mais* in the evening, yes. *Sept heure et demi.* Do you onderstan'? In the Place St.-Michel, *près de la fontaine.*"

"At half past seven near the St.-Michel fountain.... And you will be there—*certainement?*"

"*Oui—et vous?*"

"*Certainement*—surely—you bet," he said, with increasing emphasis.

She held out her hand. "*Bonne nuit, monsieur.*"

"Good night, mademoiselle.... To-morrow evening at half past seven."

"Yes," she said, and disappeared into the darkness.

CHAPTER IV

Kendall stood a moment looking after Andree until the blackness of the boulevard swallowed her up. He was exhilarated. The girl had had a tonic effect upon him; the incident was not an incident, but an adventure, and he tingled with it.... He wondered why. He wondered why he wanted to see her again when he had not cared whether or not he saw again any of the other girls he had talked to. He hoped she would appear next evening as she had promised ... and then he felt a twinge of apprehension. The twinge was not an inheritance from his father.

If he did see her again—then what? Would he see her again and still again, and what were the meetings to lead to? What sort of affair was he getting mixed into?... He felt a sense of naughtiness, and, when he tried to discover why he should feel naughty, he was unable to say. Certainly there had been nothing in the least to warrant it in any word or action of the evening. But Andree was French—and she lived in the Latin Quarter.... What *was* he getting himself into, anyhow?

The part of his being inherited from his mother was in the ascendant. She suspected anything she did not understand. Because she did not understand it she believed something wicked must lurk in it somewhere.... He remembered how he had once dug a cave in a vacant lot next his home and how his mother had almost gone into one of her "tantrums" over it. She could not understand why a boy should want to burrow into the earth. It must be some squalid desire for wicked concealment on her son's part. She almost convinced him that it was a sin for a boy to dig a cave, just as she had almost succeeded in making him believe that so many of his other perfectly natural desires and impulses and doings were wicked.... She had a way of connecting everything with *sex*, and she suspected *sex* above everything else in the world. It was her nightmare. It was a squalid, wicked sort of a thing, to be thought of only in terms of aversion. Always she had hammered this into him, and though he could not quite believe her, he never quite outgrew her point of view. In this moment he knew exactly how she would regard his meeting with Andree.

Then his father came to his rescue—his father, whose dominant note was tolerance and a sweet inability to see evil, or, if he saw it, to see palliation of it, or even a vein of goodness running through it. His father never suspected anything or anybody. His father had never suspected *him*. Somehow that had always been very wonderful to him, because his mother had impressed it upon him that he was a person always under suspicion. He knew exactly how his father would regard Andree and what he would say and do. He could hear his father saying it and see him doing it. His father would have patted Andree on the shoulder and smiled. He would have said, "She's a pretty little thing, isn't she?" Then he would have proposed taking Andree and his son for an ice-cream soda. His father always did that—for ice-cream soda or candy. And then he would have whispered in Kendall's ear: "Got enough money, son? 'Cause if you hain't—"

Kendall wondered if it were better to see wickedness in everything and sometimes to be justified by finding it, or to see wickedness in nothing at all, and sometimes to be disappointed by having it suddenly thrust upon one.

He walked slowly toward the Place St.-Michel and there descended into the Metro. His antagonistic inheritances struggled within him, and his youth and his youthful desire for the joys of life took sides with his father. In one moment he determined he would never see Andree again, and then he would call himself an idiot and ask what harm could possibly come from it.... If ever he had seen a "nice" girl, Andree was nice. Well, then?... But he was disturbed, and had not been able to conquer his disturbance when he entered the Union. There he found Bert Stanley waiting for him.

"Here comes the wicked old man," Bert saluted him. "What you been up to, with me away? Have I got to keep my eye on you every minute?"

"Just walking around," said Kendall. Some young men would have wanted to tell about Andree and to discuss her, but not he.

"Let's split a bottle of beer.... Say, I heard about an apartment to let—up near the Étoile. What say to having a look at it to-morrow?"

"How much?"

"I heard it was three hundred francs—and we're paying that much here for one room with two beds."

"Sounds good, but I don't know. Anyhow, we can look it over."

"'Tisn't far from the office. We can walk over at noon."

Kendall yawned. "Let's go to bed," he suggested.

"What's the use? There'll be an air raid to-night. Better to sit up than just to get nicely asleep and have to roll out. I never get to sleep again."

Kendall persisted and walked up to his room, where he was soon in bed, but not to sleep. He was excited and restless. He wanted to sleep, not to think, but his mind persisted in its activity, and his thoughts became incisive, whitely clear as one's thoughts do of sleepless nights. It was rather the sensation of being subjected to a blinding light which hurt the brain.... It was not alone of Andree that he thought. He could concentrate on nothing, but kept running down *cul-de-sacs* of memories and speculations and plans which overlapped and confused one another maddeningly. He would shut his eyes and try to curtain off his mind so that no thought could penetrate, but it was not to be done, so he tossed and rolled and submitted.... Just around the corner of every avenue his thoughts followed Andree, lay in wait. Before he knew it he was building air-castles about her....

It was really a relief to him when the *alerte* sounded. He said to himself that he would not get up, and composed himself to wait. In a quarter of an hour the barrage started, sporadically at first, then worked itself up to a fury of sound such as he had never heard before. It sounded nearer, more menacing. Really, cannon might have been going off in the street below his window. So imminent did the sound become that Kendall got out of bed, not frightened, exactly, but impressed. He considered that there was nothing above his head but the roof. Half determined to dress and go down, he fumbled for the light-button and turned it before he remembered that there would be no light, that all light was turned off at its source with the sounding of the *alerte*.... In his pajamas he went to the windows which opened out on the little balcony which overlooked the Palais Royal, and stood there looking off toward the east, where the firing was most furious.... Over his head he could hear the angry humming of aeroplanes, and wondered uneasily if they were defenders or hostile bombers. Tremendous detonations rattled the windows and rocked the buildings, and these, he fancied, were falling bombs. The sky was alight with up-leaping flares from the mouths of the cannon and from shells bursting high above the city, searching the heavens for flitting *Gothas*.... Then came a series of tremendous upheavals which seemed to his tingling nerves to be almost at hand.... And then the sky was red with flames which uprose and spread and glanced and billowed over the tops of the buildings. Metallic fragments rattled on the roof of the Palais Royal, fifty feet away, and on the roof of his hotel and in the streets below. Kendall ducked inside, for he knew this was falling shrapnel from the defensive barrage.... For the first time he was seeing a real air raid, a serious raid, and one that was meeting with success. Already a tremendous fire had been started, and what might not follow?... It was enough to shake one's nerves, for the individual is so helpless! All one can do at such a time is to hope and to argue that Paris is large and a bomb small; that the chances of a bomb falling where one happens to be are almost infinitesimal.

The sound came very near indeed. Kendall could not see what caused this, but it was an anti-aircraft gun mounted on a truck which had come to a stop at an open space at the mouth of the Avenue de l'Opéra and was industriously blazing away at the moon.... Kendall wished he were dressed and down-stairs with company at hand; he would even have consented to descend into an *abri*, an experience which had not so far been his. He wondered what an *abri* looked like. At any rate, there were plenty of them, for nearly every building in Paris was defaced by a poster announcing, *"Abri, 30 places.... Abri, 60 places."*

The sound, the terrific crashings and retchings and tearing bursts of tremendous potentiality, gradually ebbed, then surged up with renewed vigor for a time, then subsided again, and, after a series of fitful outbursts, ceased.... But the light which glowed and danced over the roofs from the distant Faubourg St.-Antoine silhouetting the tangle of chimney-pots on the Palais Royal did not subside. The fire burned on....

Kendall returned to bed—and slept.

If that raid had made Kendall Ware fearful, what had it done to the teeming populations of the Faubourg St.-Antoine, to the closely packed poor who massed about the Bastille, and to the eastward of this monument to an event that owed its being to their own ancestors, to those who used to dwell in St.-Antoine, mother of revolutions!

Next noon Bert Stanley and Kendall lunched at a table on the sidewalk of a little café on the Place de Ternes and then walked down the Boulevard de Courcelles a few hundred feet or so to the number that had been given Bert as a place where a desirable furnished apartment was to let.

They entered through an archway and rang the bell of the *concierge's* apartment. A pleasant, motherly, smiling old woman came to the door and bowed them in. It was not difficult to make her understand that they were in search of an *appartement meublé*, whereupon she jangled a huge bunch of keys and invited them to follow her up four flights of stairs, and ushered them into the rooms that were for hire.... The apartment of five rooms was to be had for three hundred francs a month, with twenty francs extra for the *concierge*. Yes, a cook could be obtained, and madame would undertake to have her on hand when needed. Her wages would be seventy francs a month. Everything was very easy.

"Where is the bath?" asked Kendall.

"Oh, monsieur, we have a bath. Of a surety. It is but three blocks away...."

So it was arranged. They were to move in when they desired, and they left the building feeling quite like family men and proprietors. They discussed the apartment from all angles and were exceedingly pleased with themselves for accomplishing it....

"All France needs," said Bert, quoting some epigrammatic American friend, "is open plumbing to make it the greatest country in the world."

On the broad stairs of that huge hotel which the United States Expeditionary Force has taken over for its headquarters in Paris Bert stopped suddenly.

"I can't help you move in to-night," he said. "But there isn't much to do. Get a taxi to take up our boxes and bedding-rolls. I'm going to be busy."

"So am I," said Kendall, Andree recalled to his mind after she had been absent from it since morning.

"Huh!" grunted Bert. "Same one you were with last night?"

"Go chase yourself," said Kendall.

"If it is," Bert continued, "we might make a mixed quartet of it. Dinner and then *promenade avec.* Eh?"

Kendall hesitated. It sounded pleasant, but he was not sure Andree would like it—and he was not sure about the sort of girl Bert might have chosen for a companion. Andree, he had made up his mind, was not the sort of girl who would take up with anybody.

"Nothing doing," he said.

"Why?"

"Who's your girl?" Kendall countered.

"Girl I've known quite awhile. Cashier in a shop.... Say, what you getting at, anyhow? Madeleine's a darn nice girl, I'm here to tell the world. Looks it, too. I'd just as soon take her over to the Y. M. C. A. and introduce her to the head guy—and she'd get past, too."

"I don't know.... I don't know Andree very well. She might not like it."

"Rats!" Bert said, scornfully. "They might as well get acquainted one time as another."

Kendall wasn't so sure of that. He saw no reason why the girls should ever get acquainted. In short, he didn't follow Bert's reasoning nor comprehend the point he made.

"We can move in to-morrow," Kendall said, and there was an end of it.

It was a long afternoon for Capt. Kendall Ware, but at last he found his day's work at an end and himself in the street. He went into a café for a hurried meal and then took the Metro to the Place St.-Michel, arriving there a good half-hour ahead of the appointed time. He took a seat at a sidewalk table in a café from which he could watch the fountain, and ordered a glass of coffee into which he squirted *saccharin* from a bottle with a nozzle like those used by American barbers to put bay rum on one's hair. At ten minutes past seven he was fearful Andree did not mean to keep her appointment. At a quarter past he was sure of it.... And she was not due until half past. He was to learn that she was one of those persons who are never ahead of time, who never hurry, but who may always be depended upon to arrive eventually.

It was almost exactly seven-thirty when he saw her coming across the Place. At first he did not recognize her, for he had been expecting that white suit topped by its cunning tam-o-'shanter; but she was not in white this evening. Her dress was of some light summer material and she wore a dark tam. He never saw her wear anything but a tam.... She looked more slender, younger, than before. Why, she seemed to be nothing but a child! He knew she saw him, but she did not seem to see him, for she came forward sedately, with those staid little steps of hers until she was almost at arm's-length. Then she looked up and smiled.

Again he found that difficulty in opening the conversation, in organizing his French for action, and she—she seemed to have forgotten her English. But each was glad to see the other. He tried to tell her he was glad to see her, but made frightful work of his attempt to pronounce the word *joyeux*. It necessitated resort to the dictionary—and immediately awkwardness was dispelled.

"I have worked so—*so*—hard. All the day."

"At what?"

She held out her book. It was a volume of Racine. "I have been studying." She opened it to show him. "Regard this so long part. It is necessary for me to learn it. You do not know Racine.... You do not know this play. Oh, it is very sad, very *tragique*. But it is very beautiful...."

"What are you learning all that for?"

"I must.... I must learn many things. It is for the examination. I must to enter into the *Académie*. First I must pass the examination. If I can succeed to enter into the *Académie*, then I shall some day go onto the stage of the Comédie Française and be a great actress and make much money, and you shall sit and clap your hands. I shall then come to New York like Madame Bernhardt, for there is much money, and you shall be proud I am your friend. *N'est-ce pas?* But it is very *difficile* to enter the *Académie*. One must know a famous actor or musician to recommend one.... Do you know actors and musicians in Paris?"

"No."

"You must to meet these actor, then, and know him well, so you will say to him, 'Recommend my friend to the *Académie*.' It is very necessary." She looked up at him and smiled gaily at her little joke, which was uttered half in seriousness.

"So you're an actress, are you?" An actress! It rather startled him. He had ideas about actresses—American actresses! But a French actress!...

"*Non.... Non.... Non....* I am nothing. I am a young girl only, me. But I must do something. I have to live, is it not? Yes.... Then to be the actress in the Comédie Française is to be well."

He was rather relieved. There is a difference between being an actress and desiring to be one. He had an inspiration. "Maybe you would like to go to the Comédie Française to-night," he said.

She clapped her hands. "But yes—yes. Let us hurry. It is already late and we shall miss something."

They went to an adjacent bus-stand, where Andree tore two numbers from a packet fastened to a post. The bus appeared, passengers alighted, and the conductress began calling off numbers. Only those were allowed to mount whose numbers were called, for overcrowding is not permitted. The bus rolled away without them, but presently another appeared, their numbers were called, and in ten minutes they were walking down the Avenue de l'Opéra toward the theater.

Kendall bought seats, the most expensive in the house, and they entered, mounting the broad stairway to the gallery, where they permitted themselves to be shown into a species of box by an attendant. The play was just commencing.

"Do you onderstan' it?" Andree asked.

"Not enough to do any good."

"Then I shall explain it to you." And as the action progressed she pattered on with explanations and observations very cunningly and charmingly. "You see thees ol' man? He is in love with thees yo'ng girl. But she—she does not love him. It is ver' sad. Thees yo'ng man who is ver' handsome, she loves him." Suddenly she turned to him and asked: "Are men in America—oh, how do you say—what is the word? *Fidèle*. Do you know *fidèle*?"

"Faithful—constant—is that it?"

"Yes. Are American men so?"

"Why—generally, I guess."

She shook her head somberly. "Frenchmen are not. They are most *infidèle*. It is ver' sad."

"How about French girls?"

"Oh, some are *fidèle* and some not. Some Frenchmen are *fidèle*. The poor. *Oui*. It is the rich men and women who are not *fidèle*."

"Are you rich?"

She laughed. "No, I am ver' *fidèle*."

"So the poor folks always marry and are faithful?" he asked, with real curiosity.

"Oh, they are faithful. Not always do they marry. No. Sometimes they are too poor, sometimes they do not want to, but they are *fidèle*. But yes. Do young men and young girls in America always marry?"

"Yes."

"It is very strange. Not so in France. No."

"What then?"

"A young man love a young girl, and a young girl love a young man.... They marry, maybe. That is well. But maybe they do not marry. It is expensive to marry. Then they see each other very often and he gives her money so she can live.... That is well, because they are *fidèle*."

Kendall gasped mentally. What would Detroit, what would his mother think of such a theory of life as this? How would they regard a mode of living which places fidelity over the solemn forms of marriage? Here was a people who apparently valued love and fidelity more than marriage licenses and wedding-rings!... It sounded very naughty to Kendall. Also it made him think. His mother and his father tried to function in him simultaneously and made a chaos of his thoughts....

The play continued. "Oh, you should onderstan' French better. You must speak it well, *well!*" she exclaimed. "Then I can read poems to you. Do you know French poetry?"

He laughed. "I know one poem," he said.

"Tell it to me."

He recited:

> "*Je vous aime,*
>
> *Je vous adore,*
>
> *Que voulez-vous encore?*"

She turned to look full in his face, her lovely, childish eyes alight with mischief. "It is not a poem," she said; "it is a declaration."

"Exactly," he said, half seriously.

"Oh no, no, no! You do not love me.... It ees not *possible*. No. You do not know me enough yet."

Without thought he made the leap. "Of course I do. How could I help it?... Don't you love me?" He talked to her as he would talk to a child.

"I do not know—yet. I have not known you. We shall see."

She was perfectly serene and perfectly serious. It startled him. "By Jove!" he said to himself, "things move rapidly in this country." He was right. France has a way of omitting unessentials and of disregarding shams and subterfuges. If there is a destination to arrive at, France does not walk around the block to reach it, but cuts straight across.

"You are sure you are not married?" she said. "You tell the truth?"

"I'm not, and I'm not going to be," he said, decidedly. At least he would put an end to any such speculations.

"*Pourquoi?*" There it was again, that direct, troublesome *why*.

"Because I don't like it. I don't want to be married."

She nodded. Apparently the reason was perfectly good and sufficient to her. She directed her attention to the play.

"Now," she said, "thees ol' man he has make love to thees yo'ng girl. Also he has promise her much money, and she will love him."

"I don't like that," he said. "I can see, maybe, why people should love each other and all that, but the money part of it! I don't like that at all. That isn't—good."

"*Pourquoi?* It is that a girl must live. She must eat. Because she loves must she starve?"

There was practical France speaking, and France, in spite of temperament, in spite of surface excitability and eccentricity, is eminently practical—especially your France of the poorer sort. France may jump, but she jumps with her eyes open, and with a pretty sure knowledge of where she will fall.... The play moved on to its climax, Andree translating, but little translation was necessary, for the pantomime carried the story.

"It will be better for you to see a tragedy," said Andree. "This is *comédie*. The actors speak fast in *comédie*; in tragedy they speak more slow." She showed him how tragic actors speak, and it was deliciously funny.

Then came the climax in which "thees ol' man" took "thees yo'ng girl" to the railway station and delivered her into the hands of her youthful lover. Andree was in tears. The magnificent acting affected Kendall himself, touched his emotions. He felt Andree's hand move spontaneously to touch his arm as though in sympathy with the bereaved and forsaken old man, and Kendall took her little fingers in his palm and patted them very much as he would have stroked the hand of a weeping child.... She was so fragile, so childlike, so *nice*. He regarded her covertly, wondering what was going on under that curly black hair ... assuring himself that it was impossible for any one to think of anything but sweetness in connection with her. Yet she was a mystery. He was incapable of understanding her, and never came to understand her. A mystery she always remained to him—but a sweet mystery, a dainty mystery, a mystery never touched by unworthy things or thoughts.... And that was another mystery which he might one day understand dimly. He might come to a height from which his vision would be so clear that he could understand that she was good with that natural goodness which comes from God ... not with that conventional, rule-of-thumb goodness which is a product of narrow beliefs and set dogmas. Kendall was good himself, but he was not capable of attaining to a goodness such as Andree's, for he could never approach her naturalness, the instinct which was in her for following always a path upon which God could smile, even if men should frown.... Doubtless the frowns of men weigh but little in the judgments of God....

They left the theater silently, the emotions evoked by the drama still moving them and drawing them together. He felt a great tenderness for her and almost fancied he was in love. It was a fair imitation. Whatever it was, it was not bad, but good. He would not be the worse, but the better, for having experienced it.

"My friend and I have rented an apartment," he said, suddenly.

"Your friend? What is his name?"

"Bert Stanley."

"You will live together?"

"Yes."

"I will know him then.... You shall show him to me."

"If you like."

"Where is thees apartment?"

He told her.

"Is it very *grand*?" She used the word in the French, not the English signification.

"Two bedrooms, dining-room, *salon*. It is very comfortable. We shall move in to-morrow—and we're going to have a cook."

"Cook? What is cook?"

Again recourse must be had to the dictionary, and there followed a lesson in pronouncing the rather difficult word *cuisinière*.

"Has thees friend, this Monsieur Stanley, a friend—like me?"

"I think so."

"You do not know? You have not seen her?"

"No."

"That is droll.... And thees cook?"

"I haven't seen her."

"I must come to see thees apartment and thees cook. I must know how much you pay, and if it is too much.... Ah, you shall have a dinner and she shall cook, and I shall be there, and your friend, thees Monsieur Stanley, and *his* friend. We shall know each other."

"I don't know," he said, doubtfully, thinking of the proprieties and wondering what the *concierge* would say if he were to give a dinner such as she suggested. His acquaintance with *concierges* was limited.

Again they were walking up the dark Boulevard St.-Michel, and again she would not permit him to accompany her to her door. "Good night.... It was ver' nice, and I think you are ver' nice—perhaps."

"But you don't love me?" he asked, trifling with destiny without intention, as young men will trifle.

"I do not know—yet.... I do not know you. And you do not love me. Oh no, no! It is not possible. You make fun of me. I can see you make *grimace* even in the dark."

"When do we play together again?"

"Soon.... I cannot see you to-morrow, but the day after—yes.... It is not a good place to meet, the Place St.-Michel. It is far. No, it shall be the Metro, Place de la Concorde, at *sept heures*."

"Seven o'clock."

"Yes.... And you will not fail?"

"No."

"Good night."

He was of a mind to kiss her good night as he had kissed American girls whom he had taken home from parties and with whom he had played about, but he hesitated. He didn't want to spoil things, to make her take fright and disappear. She was becoming too much a delightful element in his life for him to take a chance of losing her now.... And while he hesitated she was gone.

As mysteriously as she appeared out of the mazes of the enormous city she disappeared into them again, and Bert was apprehensive lest she fail to reappear. He need not have been apprehensive. There is in life a thread of fate, of destiny, which attaches one person to another, so that, even though they separate to the ends of the earth, they will be drawn together again at some spot in some hour.... Destiny had woven a strand between Andree and Kendall....

CHAPTER V

Kendall Ware and Bert Stanley went early to *petit déjeuner* in the dining-room of the Union, for they had decided to move before the day's work began. The waitress laid her order-slips on the table, and as she did so Kendall noticed that her eyes were red and swollen with weeping and that it was with difficulty that she restrained her sobs.

"Mademoiselle is sad this morning," he said, sympathetically.

"*Oui, monsieur*, very sad.... Oh, it is my brother! The word came in the night. The *boches* have killed him...."

"Poor kid!" said Kendall. It was his first direct contact with the sadness of war, and it affected him strongly. Evidences of this sort had been all about him, but this was so close!

"He was the last," she said, finding comfort in his sympathy. "There were three brothers ..."

"It's rotten," Kendall said when she moved away. "Rotten. These poor women!..."

Bert made no reply. He was not the sort to voice sympathy if he felt it, nor was he the sort to be moved as Kendall was moved. He was more objective, less emotional—a trifle boisterous and swanking and not given to peering below the surface of events. It was his motto to take what came and make the best of it. On the whole, he was a careless, buoyant, thoughtless young American whose two great objects in life were to get on in the world and to have a good time. He had none of the scruples and inhibitions that made Kendall Ware more complex—not that he was unscrupulous; not that he was not an ordinarily square, able, decent sort of boy, but there did not reside in him that meticulous ethical sense that Kendall had inherited from his mother, and which had been softened and made finer by inheritances from his father.

"Four sons out of one family," said Kendall, "and there are thousands of such cases, I suppose." He stopped. "And every man killed is not a loss to his mother and sisters alone—but to the girl he was going to marry or had just married. After this war, Bert, where in thunder are the girls of France going to find enough husbands to go around?"

"They aren't," Bert said, and then he grinned. "That's why the American Army is so popular with them. Every one of us is a possible husband, so look out, young fellow."

"A million—maybe two million—girls with nobody to marry.... It's hell!"

"It's up to us to do our best to keep them from worrying about it," said Bert, characteristically. "Come on, we've got to hustle."

They loaded down a taxicab with their trunks and rolls and were driven to their new home. The *concierge*, naïvely proud of having two American officers as her tenants, bustled about them in genuine, motherly welcome. Kendall liked the brightness of her smile, it was so brisk, so alert; he liked her looks as a whole.... Why, she might have been his aunt, he thought. She had the look of an aunt, the sort a nephew would delight to visit.

"I have your *cuisinière*," she said. "I recommend her. She will please messieurs.... But she is large, *une bonne femme*. She comes to-morrow and she is called Arlette. All things may be left to her, do you understand? Yes, yes, Arlette will see to all, to the marketing and the accounts—if *messieurs les officiers* desire. Shall you dine at home to-morrow evening?"

Bert looked at Kendall.

"I had an engagement with Madeleine. Don't see why we shouldn't dine here, though."

"Why," Kendall said, hesitatingly, "Andree said she wanted to meet you and Madeleine—and to see the apartment. We might—" He was still reluctant.

But Bert settled the thing for him out of hand. "Dinner for four, if you please. At seventy-thirty."

"A nice dinner," Kendall added, rather apprehensively. "There will be ladies."

He watched the *concierge's* face to see how this news would affect her. Apparently it did not affect her at all.

"Of a surety," she said, "Arlette shall be notified."

The young men disposed of their traps temporarily and walked to their offices.

"I heard of a bully place to eat," said Bert. He was always finding new and excellent and quaint cafés. "Up on the rue de Richelieu. Marty's they call it. A French officer told me about it—says it's mostly patronized by actors from the Comédie and artists and newspaper men. Suppose we take a look."

"Suits me," said Kendall. "Meet you in the Union at seven."

Kendall was more anxious to see Marty's than he would have admitted to Bert; as soon as Bert mentioned the fact that its *habitués* were actors he wanted to go to the place very badly. He wanted to see what French actors were like—and actresses. In his whole life he had never seen an actor off the stage, had never been especially curious about them, but now it was different. Andree was going to be an actress if she could, and he wanted to see for himself what sort of creature she would be when she came to be one.

Since he left Andree the night before he had been filled with uneasiness. Again and again he reviewed his conversation with her and found it disturbing. He had rather lost his head, he perceived. He had told her he loved her when, so he declared to himself, he did not love her in the least, and the fact that she had made light of his declaration and had refused to believe in the possibility of a so-sudden affection helped the situation very little. What troubled him most was that he had made a start of some kind, to travel some sort of path. He didn't know what sort of path it was nor whither it led, but he was vaguely apprehensive of it. He fancied that half-meant declaration of his had altered the status of himself and Andree altogether, and placed them on a different basis. But he was wrong…. He remembered that he wanted to kiss her, but was not inclined to take himself to task for that. What could be more natural than to want to kiss Andree? He never saw anybody who was more kissable…. Again and again he consoled himself by conjuring up her face and studying it, and by remembering her modesty, her reserve, her sweetness and goodness. Of course it was all right. There wasn't the slightest danger with a girl like Andree—if, of course, they didn't actually fall in love with each other. He didn't want to do that. Andree was a *foreigner*. She was not American, but of another race, speaking another language. This may sound droll, but how many Americans are there who would have felt exactly as Kendall felt!

Therefore the idea of marriage did not occur to him as of the possibilities. He could not imagine himself marrying a foreigner. Here his mother functioned without hindrance. She had been against all foreigners. To her a foreigner had been a sort of freak of nature, a distressing accident. Anybody who was not English had been guilty of some sort of obscure offense against nature. Of course there were degrees of foreignness—some, as the Chinese, were more guilty than others—but it was a difference in degree and that was all. This was a basic *fact* to her, a part of her, and, without consciously instructing Kendall, she had impressed her way of thinking upon him until it was his own. He did not think of marriage with Andree any more than he would have thought of eating a rose....

As a matter of fact, he didn't know just what he did think of in connection with her. He had no definite hopes. She had occurred in his life and now he was drifting along, letting matters take care of themselves. He simply was without intentions of any sort.... But he was vaguely uneasy.

At seven-thirty Kendall and Bert entered Marty's a bit diffidently, as young men do who go to a place where they are uncertain of just how to behave. It was a dingy little café, poorly lighted and rather crowded with things. One passed a sort of bar upon which were piled *langoustes* and melons, and behind which was madame, very fat and capable, surrounded by bottles of various kinds, and keeping an efficient eye on her patrons and upon the finances of the institution. A half-partition of glass separated the bar from the rest of the room, which was filled with tables in parallel rows, with a narrow aisle down the middle. When filled to capacity the café might contain as many as thirty persons.

Madame bade them welcome with a smile and a *bon soir*, and motioned them to proceed to a table. They seated themselves and looked about. Only a few persons were present, but before a stout waitress dressed in black had taken their order a considerable party entered and took seats directly opposite. There were four men and two women. Almost simultaneously a fifth young man entered noisily. He waved his cane in the air as he hobbled in, for he had an artificial leg, and shouted greetings to everybody. He was rather tall and very thin and pale, but exceedingly jaunty. His felt hat, a disreputable affair, was askew on his head, and there was something rakish about even his limp. With many gestures and apparent great excitement he rushed from one table to the other, shaking hands with everybody, and once in a while stooping to kiss a girl on the cheek. Everybody laughed with him and at him. At last his eyes perceived Kendall and Bert and he came lunging across to them.

"Ha!" he shouted, throatily. "Americans! Welcome! I shall sit at your table and we shall be acquainted, is it not? You see I spik Engleesh ver' fine. Behol'! I shall sit here."

"Have nothing to do with him," a handsome young man called to Kendall in French. "He thinks you have sugar." And everybody laughed.

The young man leaped to his feet, waved his arms above his head, and glared at his accuser. "*Bah!*" he shouted, explosively. "You are nothing ..." and sat down very suddenly, apparently forgetting the whole incident, for he leaned over the table to Kendall and said: "It is an argument—yes. You shall decide, is it not? A foolish argument. Behol'—if there is a king in Siam—eh, you observe?—and he is rich, oh, ver', ver' rich. You onderstand? Yes? Also, if there is a—what you call—a electric button here"—he turned wildly and shoved his thumb against the partition as if he were ringing an electric bell—"if I could press this button—do you understand?—and thees king in Siam is dead—oh, queek, sudden, like thees"—he caught a long thumb-nail against his upper teeth and snapped it—"so.... Now, then, if I can so to push the button and thees king is dead, and all his money is mine—the argument, messieurs, is—shall I do it. *Voilà!*..." He leaned back and regarded them gravely.

"Give it a push," said Bert.

"Ah, you theenk!..." He leaped again to his feet and extended his hand across the table to Bert, who took it and shook hands rather embarrassedly.

"I am Jacques," said the young man. "We must to know one another. You are named—ah, Monsieur Bert.... Monsieur Ken-dall. Ha!... All my friends there, regard. Messieurs Bert and Ken-dall—my frien's.... My frien's—Messieurs Bert and Ken-dall. Now we are acquaint', is it not? So.... You see that yo'ng man who spill soup on his coat. He is Monsieur Robert, great comedian at the Comédie Française. *Oui*, he make the first prize at the *Académie* one year ago.... That other, with the hair *so*.... He is *espagnol*.... *Oui*. Also an actor, but not a comedian. He does *so*." Jacques illustrated by scowling horribly in imitation of the tragic method. "He also make the first prize at the *Académie* before two year.... They are ver' clever." Both young men so described got to their feet and came across to shake hands. "Those others," continued Jacques, in full voice, "are jus' boys an' girl. You onderstand? Not anybody.... That one who look so jealous at hees girl—he make the dress for ladies. *Oui*. He have much money, but no brains." At this *mot* everybody shouted with laughter, and the girl who accompanied the maker of dresses disentangled herself from him and came across to sit down by Kendall, putting her cheek up to him.

"She wants you should kees," said Jacques, and Kendall shamefacedly planted a hurried kiss on her cheek. "And now you shall see—thees yo'ng man with her, he is ver' jealous. Perhaps he shall beat her w'en they arrive at home.... *Oui*...."

Kendall proffered a cigarette to Jacques, and then extended his case toward the young actors across the aisle. They were real American cigarettes, one of which will do more to carry you into the good graces of a *poilu* than many bottles of *vin ordinaire*. Both young men came across, not too eagerly, and helped themselves. Monsieur Robert, the younger, and a very handsome, boyish, pleasing young man, seated himself in the chair the dressmaker's companion had just vacated. He understood a word of English, but dared not venture an attempt to speak it; however, he was exceedingly cordial in French. Kendall managed to understand most that he said. It was a very laughable, but somewhat *risqué*, account of a conversation he had essayed with an Englishwoman during a recent engagement in London, carried on through the agency of a dictionary. Purely through accident the young man's finger had pointed to a certain word when it should have been directed to quite another—with the result that he received a sound box on the ear. He told the thing with such boyish delight, and with such naïve joy in the outraged prudery of the Englishwoman, that Kendall laughed as he had laughed at nothing for months. This pleased the young actor. If Kendall had been diplomatically angling for Monsieur Robert's friendship, he could not have contrived better.

Suddenly he remembered Andree. "You must know a famous actor," she had commanded him. Andree desired the good offices of an actor in her effort to enter the *Académie*—and this young gentleman had carried off the first prize in that national institution but a year before.... He regarded Monsieur Robert with new interest.

While Kendall and Monsieur Robert made merry, if difficult, conversational progress, Bert was instructing Jacques in colloquial American in a manner to which his rather grotesque sense of humor was peculiarly adapted. "If you meet a lady," he was saying, "and she bids you good afternoon, the thing to say, if you want to be really polite, is, 'Go jump in the lake.' Of course you don't say this to a lady the first time you meet her, because it is rather friendly, but possibly the second time. Do you understand?"

"But surely.... Go jump in the lake.... Ah, it has a sound, has it not? I like that." He stood up, placed his hand on his heart and bowed to Bert profoundly. "Ah, madame," he said, in honeyed tones, "you should go to jump in the lake.... Is it so you say it? It is a phrase. I shall remember it. And what does one say if—"

Kendall lost the next lesson, for Monsieur Robert arose and shook hands warmly. "I hope you shall dine here often," he said. "Me, I always dine here.... So we shall become better acquainted."

Others of the company took their departure to their theaters or with their actor companions, or to write their criticisms, and as they went out, laughing and jostling, each stopped at the table of the Americans to shake hands and to say good evening. It was all very genial and companionable—a sort of family affair—but very un-American and droll.

Kendall and Bert took their departure soon afterward. The evening was rather hot, but they determined to walk home, a distance of a couple of miles. As they were passing the Hôtel Wagram, Kendall glanced inside and saw, standing just within the lobby, the Miss Knox who had been his playmate on the voyage across the Atlantic.

"Wait a minute. Here's a girl I know," he said to Bert, and led his companion inside.

"Well, Captain Ware!" she exclaimed. "I was wondering if I should ever see you again. What have you been doing? Have you been to the front?"

"No. I'm anchored in Paris. And you?"

"I've been down at Tours, but now I've been ordered to report at headquarters here. I don't know where I shall be sent."

"Better get assigned to Paris," he said, rashly, "then we can play around together."

"I don't know.... I'd rather be nearer things. It's more interesting."

"Anyhow, you'll be here a day or two. Can't you take dinner with me to-morrow"——he stopped, hesitated, got a bit red, and finished, lamely—"soon?"

"It looks as if I might have competition as a playmate," she said, dryly. "Is she nice? Who is she? Red Cross or Y. M. C. A.?"

"Neither."

She laughed. "And your French is so miserable," she said. "How do you talk to her?"

"She speaks some English," said Kendall, falling into a trap which had not been set for him, and Bert and Maude Knox laughed as he reddened with embarrassment.

"Is she pretty?" Miss Knox demanded of Bert.

"I don't think so," Bert said, solemnly. "He keeps her under cover. She must be homely or he'd let her be seen."

"Now I won't buy you a dinner," Kendall said.

"When I am so hungry!" she said, dolefully.

"Don't blame Ken," Bert said. "She hardly lets him have an evening to himself."

"Well," said Miss Knox, "if you do get a night off I'll be glad to see you. Probably I won't be here but a couple of days, though. You come, too, Captain Stanley, if you like."

"And pay for half of the dinner," said Bert. "That's fair. Half the young lady, half the dinner-check. Simple justice."

"Now I've got to run up to my room. I think—mind, I only think—I'm going to have a bath. If the bathtub is still there, and if the water hasn't stopped running, and if a few other things haven't happened to the plumbing—Good night.... Don't think of coming, Captain Ware, if it will make any trouble with your friend."

The two young officers walked on up the street. Kendall did not feel like talking. He was thinking about Andree and comparing her with Maude Knox. He was wondering what Andree would think of Maude, and what Maude would think of Andree. Also he wondered a bit what Maude thought about *him* and what sort of an affair she believed him to be carrying on with Andree.... Not that it mattered to him in the least what she thought, but—

At last they stood before the building in which their apartment was located. Bert pulled the bell and presently the lock clicked. They pushed open the huge door and stepped into the blackness of the court, lighting matches to find the light-button. It was a climb of four flights of stairs to their rooms, which they entered with some pride of possession and sat down to have a final smoke before going to bed.

"I wonder what the *concierge* will say to our bringing the girls here for dinner to-morrow night?" Kendall said, for the point still worried him.

"Young man," said Bert, drowsily, "you aren't in Detroit. Go to the window and reassure yourself. This is Paris...."

CHAPTER VI

Kendall was awakened next morning by the sound of some one shuffling about his room. It was a woman, and she was moving toward the door with his shoes in her hand, and for an instant he wondered if he were in the presence of some new sort of burglar. The woman was short and very fat, with a large head scantily covered by that colored hair which does not turn white at sixty. Her face was broad, her nose was broad and had a peculiar and laughable up-tilt, her mouth was broad, and her eyes were very large and kindly. She had one generous double chin and a quite respectable growth of whiskers. Her eyes and her nose were the most notable features. One liked her eyes and one could not help laughing at her nose. As a complete figure she was droll.

She saw that he was awake and grinned timidly.

"*Bon jour, monsieur,*" she said, and then, waggling his shoes, followed her greeting by a torrent of French in which the word "*chaussers*" occurred frequently. She spoke very rapidly and was unintelligible to Kendall.

"Arlette?" he asked.

"*Oui, je suis Arlette,*" she said, with a broad grin of delight, and then scudded through the door suddenly, as if she had been overtaken by a fit of embarrassment.

Kendall got out of bed and called Bert, who was still asleep.

"Hey, somebody's swiped my shoes!" came presently in a voice of complaint.

"Shut up!" said Kendall, going into his friend's room. "It's Arlette. I saw her sneaking out with mine when I woke up."

"Arlette? ... Oh, *she's* here, eh? What's she want with my shoes? I've heard these French cooks could —"

But just then Arlette pushed the door open, regardless of the state of her young employers' toilets, and deposited the shoes on the floor, carefully cleaned and polished.

The boys looked at each other, weighing this event in the light of their experience with American domestics. It was so surprising as to be upsetting.

"Seventy francs a month—including shines," said Bert.

"And seventy francs is fourteen dollars."

"And my mother pays her cook twelve a week—and hires another girl to wait on the cook! ... Come to France to solve the domestic-servant problem! ... I wonder if she bathes us."

They hurried into their clothes and went to the dining-room, where a great pitcher of chocolate stood in the center of the table, flanked by a pot of jam and a basket of rolls. On each plate was a bowl—not a cup. Arlette entered and stood with her stomach against the table's edge, whence she looked first at the food and then at her employers. She pointed accusingly at the confiture and said, "*Abricot!*"

"Apricot, eh? *Très-bien.*"

"*Mais non, messieurs.... Mais non.* It is not well.... Oh, the price—it is terrific, it is wicked. Of a surety, you are robbed. We shall have no more. *Messieurs les officiers* shall not so be robbed. I shall see well to it. But I was directed to procure confiture!" She crossed her pudgy hands on her ample stomach and rolled her eyes to heaven, calling upon Divinity to witness that apricot jam at four francs a jar was a thing to excite horror in any well-regulated and economical mind.

Kendall strove to comfort her, but it was impossible. No quantity of assurances that it was *très-bien* could remove her mind from the enormity of the cost of that delicacy, and she went out shaking her head and muttering and sniffling a trifle. In a moment she re-entered to ask what was desired for dinner. It was the first and the last time she made such an inquiry. In the future she made suggestions herself, but never did she ask outright what these strange young savages would have to eat.

"*Poulet,*" said Bert. "Chicken."

Arlette rested her hands on her hips and stared at him aghast. She repeated the word after him as if unwilling to believe such a thing had been mentioned in her presence. "*Poulet? ... Poulet? ... Non, non, non.* But no. It is too dear. The cost, consider the cost! Veal, perhaps, but never pullet."

"Young ladies are coming and we wish a suitable dinner," said Bert.

"But pullet—oh no. There shall be a suitable dinner, but there shall not be pullet. It is a thing unthinkable—at the price. Before the war—yes, but now! *Mon Dieu!* do the American officers consider what price is demanded for pullet?"

The American officers did not, nor did Arlette enlighten them, but she continued stubbornly to refuse to procure it.

Ken shrugged his shoulders. "It looks as if we were going to be henpecked," he said, ruefully.

Bert laughed. "Anyhow we get no chicken. I wonder if we can have a salad?"

Yes, a salad was thinkable, and even string-beans or cauliflower or peas—but pullet! Arlette's mind refused to be diverted from pullet.

"Very well, then," Bert said. "Whatever you want, Arlette. You're the boss. But get enough for four."

Arlette turned around and made for the door again, but paused on the threshold to turn and stare at them unbelievingly and to utter in a voice of anguish the word, *"Poulet."* She said it as one might say bubonic plague.

As Kendall left the dining-room and went for his cap he saw a tiny, big-eyed face suddenly whisk out of sight around the corner of the hall which led to the kitchen. It had been the merest glimpse, such as a believing mortal might hope some day to catch of a fairy.

"Hey, there!" he called in English, for he had a way with children and children had a way with him. There was no response, so he gave chase. The fairy had scudded into the kitchen, and was standing close to Arlette, concealing herself in the old woman's ample skirts. Arlette gazed at him with some apprehension as he came into the little kitchen, wondering, doubtless, what these barbarians would do to her for bringing a child into their lair, but a sight of his face reassured her, and she smiled a bit dubiously and placed her pudgy hand on the little girl's head.

Kendall got down on one knee and held out his hand gravely. *"Bon jour, mademoiselle,"* he said.

"Bon jour, monsieur," she said, with the cunningest little lisp, her face very sober and a little frightened, and she shook hands with him primly.

"How is your husband and all the family?" Ken asked.

Her eyes opened wide—blue and sweet they were—and she looked up at Arlette before replying. "But, monsieur, I have not yet a husband."

"No.... That is bad. You must find a husband. What, at your age? Oh *là, là, là, là!* And what is mademoiselle's age?"

"Eight years, monsieur."

He shook his head. "And no husband.... Would you like an American husband, mademoiselle?"

"Oh yes, monsieur. The Americans they are very nice."

She was the tiniest of mites with such a creamy-pink complexion as Ken had never seen. Her face was oval and beautiful, with a fairy-like childish beauty that deserved to be immortalized by some master of the brush and canvas. He looked from her to Arlette and was unwilling to admit a relationship between them or the possibility that this sprite could ever grow with the weight of years and labor to resemble the old woman. He wanted to kiss her; he wanted to kiss her on those little lips, parted a trifle now in her interest, but usually resting so lightly the one upon the other with the merest pursing which seemed to say they were made for kisses. He drew her to him, and she came diffidently, but not bashfully, and he lifted her to his knee. She seemed almost to be without weight.

"How do you name yourself?" he asked.

"Arlette," she said.

"My granddaughter," Arlette explained. "Her father is a prisoner of war in Germany—in consequence of which her mother is dead...."

"*Pauvre Mignonne,*" he said, and drew her close to him.

She looked up into his face briefly, and then, for the first time, she smiled.

"You will come often to see me," he said. "We must be friends—and then, who knows, but I may have to take you to America with me. You have no husband; I have no wife. I shall, perhaps, ask your grandmother for your hand."

"Yes, monsieur, I shall come often if monsieur permits.... And I shall sing for monsieur."

"I shall like that. And now let me see your hand. Something is the matter with it." He examined her palm gravely, then placed a franc upon it and closed her fingers tightly. "There, that will cure it, I think.... And you will not forget me—and you will think about going back to America with me?"

"Yes, monsieur," she said, very gravely.

Kendall rejoined Bert and they walked together to the Étoile and down the Champs Élysées to the hotel which sheltered the huge office staff of the American Expeditionary Force in Paris.

"I hope everything goes off right to-night," said Kendall, who was still a trifle dubious despite Andree's expressed desire to meet Bert and his friend.

"Sure. We'll make it a regular party," Bert said, confidently. "What's worrying you?"

"You never can tell how strange girls will get on together."

"Fiddlesticks!... Madeleine will get on with anybody. See you at the house at seven."

Promptly at seven Kendall was awaiting Andree at the entrance to the Metro in the Place de la Concorde, and promptly at the hour she appeared, walking leisurely, as she always seemed to do, and with an air of not seeing him at all until she was very close to him, an air which he came to associate with their meetings. There was something diffident about it, something modest and maidenly that he liked.... Then she would pause, always hesitatingly, as if she rather doubted her welcome, and look up into his face without the vestige of a smile, expecting him to extend his hand, and then she would shake hands very gravely. It was always so.

"You have made much work to-day?... You are *fatigué*?" she asked.

"But, no.... And you?"

"I have been—what do you say?—*ennuyée*?"

"Bored."

"Yes, yes, bored.... Have you thought of me?"

He had intended to be most circumspect, to make no repetitions of his half-joking declaration of their last meeting, but with her delightful presence beside him, with that half-veiled, appealing glance from her darkly shadowed eyes, good resolutions were forgotten.

"I've thought of nothing else," he said, and was near to the truth.

"But no"—she shook her head childishly—"you have not thought of me at all. It is not possible."

"I thought of you when I got up, I thought of you all the morning, I thought of you at noon and all the afternoon—and I am thinking of you now."

She laughed quietly. The drollery of his protestation pleased her and made her gay. Thereafter it became a formula, a sort of ritual. She would ask him if he had thought of her, and he would recite, "When I got up, all the morning, at noon, all the afternoon," and always she would laugh as if it were very new and very funny and very delightful.

"Where do we go?" she said, as he took his place by her side.

"To dine with Arlette."

"With Arlette!... Who is thees Arlette?"

"My cook," he said.

"At your apartment?"

"Yes."

"I do not know...."

"Bert and Madeleine are coming, too. You said you wanted to know them."

"Yes.... Yes.... I will know them. And this yo'ng girl, this Madeleine, does your friend love her?"

He spread his hands and shrugged his shoulders. "How should I know?"

"He has not told you?... He is your friend and he has not told you?"

"No."

"Have you told him about me?"

"A little; not much."

"*Pourquoi?*"

"Mademoiselle Pourquoi!... Oh, because you were none of his business."

"Oh, I do not onderstan', I do not onderstan'." She clasped hands together with mock despair, and with the cunningest expression of bafflement on her face. "I do not onderstan'.... It ees ver' difficult, ver' difficult."

"Shall we take the Metro or a taxi?"

"The Metro, of a certainty. It arrives, does it not? And the taxi—oh, it is very dear."

"You're a great little economist," he said, laughingly, but nevertheless wonderingly. American girls had never been so careful to choose the less expensive of two methods.

As they were descending into the Metro they came suddenly face to face with Maude Knox, and Kendall felt himself blushing hotly, and was ashamed of himself for it, so he blushed even more hotly than before. He stopped determinedly, and held Andree's arm.

"Miss Knox," he said, "I want you to meet Mademoiselle—" He hesitated, for he did not know Andree's family name. This piece of ignorance had never presented itself to him before. She had been Andree to him, and nothing more. She had needed no other name. "I want you to meet Mademoiselle Andree," he finished, rather defiantly.

The girls looked at each other, Miss Knox with a humorous twinkle in her eye, but nevertheless with a glint of keen appraisal; Andree rather timidly, as if she would like to hide behind Kendall as little Arlette had hidden behind her grandmother's skirts that morning, and peer out big-eyed at this woman of another race.

Maude Knox extended her hand. "Delighted," she said, and smiled.

"Mademoiselle is very agreeable," said Andree, but she did not smile; instead she studied Miss Knox's face intently and very gravely.

"There's our train," said Kendall, at a loss how otherwise to proceed with the conversation, and he snatched Andree away before another word could be exchanged. Maude Knox stood looking after them with a smile that had in it a hint of something that was not humor, that mingled curiosity with pique.

Andree and Kendall alighted from the Metro at the Étoile and walked to the apartment. He was rather taken aback to see the *concierge* sweeping the walk in front of the entrance, for he had hoped subconsciously to smuggle Andree in without being seen. He could hardly have explained this had he been asked. But he need not have been apprehensive. The *concierge* stopped, peered at Andree keenly for a second, then smiled and bade them good day. Kendall did not know it, but Andree had been inspected and had passed the inspection handsomely. Andree, however, was well aware of it.

Bert and Madeleine had not arrived, and Kendall showed Andree into their *salon* with something of a flourish. She stood looking about her at the massive gilt furniture, at the large bronze statue of Diana with a bent arrow in her hand which stood on a pedestal in a corner, and at a bronze monstrosity depicting Ceres which, half life size, overweighted the mantel. Her little nose was curling.

"Oh," she said in disappointment, "thees is not good. No, no. It is ver' bad."

"It is sort of fussy," said Kendall, more than half afraid that she would take fright at so much wretched taste on exhibition and refuse to remain. She seemed of a mind to beat a retreat. "But don't blame me for it," he hastened to say. "It isn't my furniture, you know. This is a furnished apartment—*meublé*, you know. I don't like these gimcracks any better than you do, but I couldn't help it."

She continued to shake her head dolefully; then her eyes spied a sort of throne between the windows, a fearful example of what a piece of furniture can be, and clapped her hands with childish delight. "Oh, it ees for me. See!" She ran to it and seated herself on the threadbare seat, her tiny feet dangling above the floor. "Behold!... Regard me!... I am a queen, is it not? You have not the manners. It is that you should kneel. Here ... at once."

Laughingly he humored her whim and, dropping on one knee, he lifted her hand to his lips. She laughed delightedly. Then she stepped down. "Come. I shall see the rest. You shall show me." And she insisted upon being shown over the apartment, making little sounds of approval or disapproval as she went, and finally they reached the kitchen where Arlette was busy over the stove.

"*Bon soir, madame,*" said Andree.

"*Bon soir, mademoiselle,*" Arlette replied, and swiftly scrutinized this young woman whom her master was bringing into his home. It was a frank appraisal, for Arlette felt a sort of responsibility for these strange, rather boisterous, difficult-to-understand, but kindly young savages of whom she had taken charge. Then she smiled and released a flood of French upon Andree, who smiled and chattered back at her. Kendall caught only a word here and there, so rapidly did they speak, but it was evident to him that they approved of each other, and there was something very pleasing to him in that. He felt that Arlette would not have approved of everybody.

Presently they returned to the *salon* and Andree said, seriously: "She is well. I am satisfied. She is of a trustworthiness. Yes...."

"I don't know what I'd do if she hadn't suited you," said Kendall, with a chuckle.

"Oh, I do not onderstan'.... I do not onderstan'. And why does your left eye laugh when your right does not? It ees ver' fonny." She pointed. "Oh, see! It is laugh! It is laugh!"

He wrinkled his nose at her, so bold and familiar had he become, and she pretended anger.

"You make *grimace* at me. It is not good. Why do you make *grimace?*" Then her mood changed. "Thees American girl—she is your friend?"

"An acquaintance."

"You love *her*. I know it.... You love her."

"Nonsense!"

"You see her often—and you love her."

"I didn't know she was in Paris until last night, and I certainly don't love her." She had withdrawn into herself and become a stranger to him. It startled him, frightened him, not so much because she had withdrawn herself from him, for he guessed that it was mostly pretense, but because he had a glimpse of what it would mean to him if she should withdraw herself utterly. "I don't love anybody but you," he said, and he said it without wishing or intending to say it.

"No," she said, decidedly. "It ees not possible. You mock me."

Before he could enter upon protestations Bert opened the outer door and handed a young woman into the apartment. Kendall could see that she was tall and rather slight, but that was all. He was anxious for her to appear, first out of curiosity, but principally to be reassured as to Andree's reception of the stranger.

In a moment Bert appeared in the door with the girl at his side, both laughing as at some joke which had just been uttered.

"Hello, children!" Bert said, a trifle noisily. "Mademoiselle Andree, is it not?" He advanced and took the hand which she held out to him primly while she studied his face with a calm, inscrutable expression. "Mademoiselle Andree, Monsieur Ken, this is Mademoiselle Madeleine."

Both shook hands with the laughing girl, Andree still with that restraint which was always hers at a first meeting, Kendall with relief, for he liked Madeleine's looks. She was taller than Andree by inches, and not at all beautiful as Andree was beautiful. The key-note of her character at first glance seemed to be joyousness, a lightness of heart, good nature. Her mouth was rather broad, but not displeasingly so, for it was always showing her white teeth through a smile that seemed to be the commencement of a laugh. She was always laughing, always moving her body or her hands as if the young life that was in her could not be still.... And yet there was a shrewd look about her eyes which advertised that here was no empty head, but a capable young person indeed.... She was a distinct blonde, with hair which seemed always just on the point of being disordered, yet which never seemed to lose control of itself and become disordered. Later Kendall wondered if Madeleine and her hair were not very much alike in character.

"All right, eh?" said Bert, proudly, patting Madeleine's shoulder.

She threw him a laughing, affectionate glance, and in another instant she and Andree were chattering to each other with a rapidity which was not only astonishing, but utterly unintelligible to the boys. If Andree spoke with bewildering rapidity, what could one say of Madeleine? Kendall laughed.

"Mademoiselle Mitrailleuse," he said, and it was a name that clung, for it was so apt. She was a veritable machine-gun, shooting out words with a rapidity almost incredible.

Arlette appeared in the door of the dining-room and announced that dinner was served. The quartet of young people took their places at table, and Kendall began serving a wonderful pea soup from a big bowl while Arlette stood in the door with hands folded across her stomach, watching anxiously and shooting quick glances at Madeleine.

"It is soup," she said, suddenly, and then darted out of sight with startling abruptness.

The soup was followed by meat, which Arlette placed on the table with something like a flourish, then stepped back and addressed Andree.

"Veal," she said. "Oh, mademoiselle, the meats are too dear. It is not my fault.... Perhaps this will be tough. Who knows?" She paused anxiously to look first at Bert and then at Ken, who was carving.

"It's all right, Arlette," he assured her, but she was not satisfied, remaining as close to the table as she could press and watching with an expression of the most comical anxiety while Ken cut off a morsel and put it in his mouth. She then, apparently, calculated the difficulty he encountered in mastication, her jaws working a trifle as if to aid in the process, and presently uttered a deep sigh of relief. According to her judgment, Ken had not chewed too laboriously and the meat was satisfactory. Only then did she retreat to the kitchen.

"She is very droll," said Madeleine, restraining her laughter with difficulty.

"She is very *well*," said Andree, nodding her head prettily, "but also she is droll."

"Monsieur Bert also is droll," said Madeleine, reaching out to bestow a little pat upon Bert's hand.

"All Americans are droll," said Andree, solemnly.

"*Tous les Américains sont fous*," said Ken, quoting a saying of Paris, which adored Americans at the moment and delighted in their peculiarities and their absurdities, and laughed at them as one laughs at the antics of children, deciding, as its dictum had it, that all the Americans were mad.

The *viande* was served alone, as is the French custom, without a vegetable, but with a delicious sauce which the girls, disdaining butter, sopped from their plates with their bread—not at all a manifestation of ill-breeding, but the proper and natural and habitual method of eating.

Ken turned to Andree. "I met your actor for you last night," he said.

"You have known an actor?... What actor?"

"Monsieur Robert, of the Comédie Française. Do you know him?"

"I have seen him. He is a very good actor—and very handsome, *n'est-ce pas*? Have you spoke of me?"

"No, my dear. Give a fellow time."

"But you must, you must.... It is ver' *nécessaire*—oh, you do not know how ver' *nécessaire*. It is my need to enter into the *Académie*, and he must help me. You will know him better." It was a command. "You will then make me to know him."

"I should say *not*.... He's too handsome. I'm not going to take any such chance as that—I should say *not*."

"*Pourquoi?*"

"Because I should be jealous," he said.

"*Non, non, non!*... You do not care. You only *say*...."

"How am I going to convince you?"

"I do not know. It is not possible.... I will not believe."

Ken turned despairingly to Madeleine. "She refuses to believe that I love her. How shall I make her believe?"

Madeleine laughed at him. "How should I know?... It is for you to do. It is a thing easy of accomplishment."

"Is it easy to make her love me, too?"

"French girls are not cold," she said, in the most matter-of-fact way imaginable.

"He loves an American girl.... I have seen her this night—yes. She is not beautiful. American girls do not know how to dress." Andree shook her head and frowned at Ken.

Arlette appeared presently with the vegetable, which she named and waited to see approved, and afterward with the salad and a like procedure. When the fruit appeared she made no observation, but asked, calmly, as if it were the most natural question in the world, "*Petit déjeuner* for four?"

Breakfast for four! It was dropping a thunderbolt on Kendall's plate. He was shocked. He was frightened, and shot a quick glance at Andree and Madeleine. Andree was sipping her wine and appeared not to have heard; if she had heard she was not disturbed nor shocked nor angered. Madeleine was laughing.

"*Arlette est très-méchante*—Arlette is very naughty," she said.

Bert shouted with laughter as at some superlative witticism, and both the girls looked at him rather surprised. Then Madeleine laughed a bit, as one laughs who does not quite see the point. Kendall watched Andree in consternation. What would she do? What would she say? What would she think?... She did nothing, said nothing, apparently thought nothing, but pared a banana with quaint intensity as if a banana were a strange and interesting fruit. She seemed always to be interested in her food with a sort of naïve curiosity and a very real appetite. Her appetite seemed to Kendall to be the only material thing about her. The rest was mystery, dainty, rather elfin, mystery.... And here was a new mystery—her attitude of unconcern in face of Arlette's *faux pas*. Why, the question had not touched her at all! It might as well not have been asked.... Or, in this strange country, was it possible that the *cuisinière* always expected her master's feminine guests to remain for breakfast as well as dinner? He wondered....

"Will they take Paris—the *boches*?" Andree asked, suddenly.

The Germans had broken across the Chemin des Dames and were rushing headlong toward the Marne. News was filtering through only in driblets. Paris was uneasy. One saw nondescript vehicles, piled with trunks and hampers, making haste for the railroad stations, as frightened inhabitants betook themselves to the country. Nobody knew what would happen, but for months the fortune had been bad—and Paris was asking if it had reached its worst.

"Of course not," said Bert, dogmatically.

"But they are very strong—they have great numbers."

"There are the Americans," said Madeleine.

"To be sure—the Americans. But they are in Lorraine. The journals say they are in Lorraine."

"You will see," said Madeleine, for she had more than her share of Paris's enthusiasm for its newest ally.

"Don't you worry. The *boches* are going to get themselves thrashed.... Paris!..." Bert shrugged his shoulders disdainfully.

"You really think they can be beaten?"

"Just wait."

"And the war will end?... When will it end?"

"In a year." Bert was very confident.

"Oh, a year—so long.... Monsieur Bert, it is terrible, this war. One hardly remembers when it was not. We are so tired of it. The women are so tired of it.... It makes me sad—sad. Everybody suffers." Andree's eyes grew bigger and blacker, and her wistful mouth became more wistful.

"It is true," said Madeleine. "I have an aunt who lives in the country— in a very little village. Before the war were thirty families and fifty men. I was there two years ago. The men were all at the front—all.... But the fields were planted and the harvests reaped. It was the women. They labored for the men.... I was there again—it was a month ago.... The fields were not planted. Matters were bad. It was not beautiful, and all was neglected.... The women no longer worked. And why? Ah, it was because there was no longer a reason for them to work.... There were no men to come home to those fields.... Of the fifty who went to the war, fifty were dead.... Forever it will be a village without men!..."

There was a silence. Every one was feeling the weight of the calamities of war.... Then Madeleine laughed, but it was a laugh without her customary gay, careless ring. "This is the last generation of the French," she said, half mockingly. "Our men are gone.... You shall see. The next generation will be what? Look you. It will be English, Belgian, Italian, American, Moroccan, Chinese...."

"For example!" exclaimed Andree.

"It is so," affirmed Madeleine.

"Already the government offers one five hundred francs for a son.... I think the government is satisfied if it is half French, is it not?"

"A son is a son," said Andree.

"To become a soldier when he is a man—and fight the *boches*!"

"There will be no more wars," said Bert. "When we are through with this one nobody will ever have to fight the *boches* again."

"If one could believe," Andree said, in a low voice.

Kendall was disturbed. It was within his power to be sympathetic, to feel deeply, to know pain because another was suffering pain. He wished this subject had not arisen and he wanted to have it changed ... because the plight of the women—especially the young women, the marriageable girls of France—was making itself apparent to him. Millions of them, and no men to marry them! It was appalling. It was appalling that they should realize it, and the consequences of their realization were appalling.... Life was denied them; the fullness and beauty and the joys and sufferings of womanhood were denied them. He wondered, with his Middle-Western conscience, if one could really blame them for snatching what little minutes of living came in their way. He wondered if the conventional—in these terrible circumstances—could be the *right*. Would the morals of Plymouth Rock answer in this emergency?... And then came the inevitable question, What are morals?... His mother could not answer this question for him to his satisfaction, nor could his father—with all his father's leniency. One had to see the thing to comprehend it, and neither of his parents had seen. For the first time he asked himself if the conventions, the cut-and-dried rules of living under which he had grown to manhood, really sprang, full-armed, from the will of Deity, or if they were evolved by expediency.... It was deep speculation for one of his equipment, and dangerous speculation for a young man set down as he was set down among manners strange and customs so divergent—and in such an emergency.

He moved back his chair. "Let's go in the other room," he said, "and—and suppose we talk about something besides the war."

"It makes you sad?" Andree said, and looked at him with a strange expression of sympathy, of understanding—of—of something that made her seem nearer to him, less mysterious, more human than she had ever seemed before. "Come ... we shall talk awhile and then I must go to my house, because it is ver' *nécessaire* for me to lift up at an early hour."

Kendall laughed. "Lift up?...." The literal translation uttered so soberly was exquisitely funny, made more so by Andree's solemn little face.

"It is fonnee? For example! And what should one say?"

"Get up," said Ken.

"It is not well.... I shall say lift up."

"You may say whatever you want to—*mignonne*," he said, with a sudden access of tenderness.

"*Mignonne!*...." She looked up at him and smiled timidly. "It is ver' pretty—for you to call me so. It is ver' well."

Madeleine was singing now. She always sang, Kendall discovered, mostly popular *chansons*. And Andree joined. It was that song dear to the *poilu*—"*Madelon*"—with its catchy air, its characteristic Frenchness. Madeleine sang gaily, carelessly, Andree seriously and without a smile.... Then the girls chattered with each other, becoming acquainted, while the young men smoked and tried to edge into the conversation, or to catch a stray word here and there. At last Andree rose.

"You must take me to my house." she said.

"So early?"

"It is ver' *nécessaire*."

"Coming?" Ken said to Bert, who cast a sidewise glance at Madeleine, and said: "No. We don't go your way, anyhow.... See you later."

So Kendall and Andree said good night and went down the stairs, counting the flights gaily, he offering to become an elevator to carry her down if she became tired, and she demanding that he do so at once, without delay. "Your friend, he is a high yo'ng man," she said, suddenly.

And that became a joke between them. Ever after that they referred to Bert, not by name, but as the "high yo'ng man." When people begin to have private jokes between just themselves they are getting on very well indeed....

Once more he took her to the Place St.-Michel and a little way up the Boulevard. There she dismissed him, but they lingered with their good nights. She seemed very gentle, very desirable, very sweet.... He was not afraid of her as he had been before. Some sort of message had traveled between them.... Kendall took the hand she extended, then he drew her to him and kissed her. She submitted, but did not return his kiss.

"When?" he asked.

"The day following to-morrow. Place de la Concorde. Metro. *Sept heures.*"

It was becoming a part of their ritual. And then she disappeared into the darkness—whither, he did not know; back into that mystery which was her life, from which she emerged from time to time as mysteriously as she disappeared.... He was impressed by this mystery tonight. He did not know her name—only Andree. She was a sort of apparition that manifested itself daintily, primly, conducted itself bewitchingly, and withdrew itself into the unknown....

He took the Metro back to the Étoile and walked home. The light was burning in the hall. When he hung his hat on the hall tree he found it still encumbered by Madeleine's hat and jacket....

Kendall went to bed in a frame of mind.... Madeleine had seemed such a *nice* girl. She *was* a nice girl. Why, Andree had liked her.... His mother in him was shocked, affronted. Yet, somehow, Kendall was not so shocked as he expected himself to be. He didn't know how he felt ... his thoughts were a turmoil, and he kept repeating to himself, "She *is* a nice girl ... she is a nice girl,..." as one who is bewildered in the presence of some incomprehensible phenomenon....

CHAPTER VII

Kendall dressed and went in to breakfast feeling no slight awkwardness. He was apprehensive, too, apprehensive of the *concierge*. The affair had upset him in a complex sort of way. It had startled him, yet it had not shocked him especially, and he was inclined to take himself to task for not being shocked. He was disappointed, and yet he was not disappointed in Madeleine. Anyhow, he was reluctant to meet her, for fear that the meeting would set him against her irrevocably and so cause trouble between himself and Bert.... And yet he was enjoying the experience as an experience, though he did not quite appreciate that he was enjoying it. Half a dozen times he said to himself, as if carrying on a subconscious argument: "But she's a *nice* girl.... Darn it all, she's a nice girl...." He was afraid a meeting with her would dispel this impression of her niceness.

Bert and Madeleine were already at table, waiting for him. Bert said good morning nonchalantly, and Madeleine smiled brightly and wished him *"bon jour"* without the least hint of embarrassment or self-consciousness. He was conscious of a feeling of relief. "By Jove! she is a nice girl," he said to himself, and took the hand which she arose and offered.

Then Arlette came in with the pitcher of chocolate, and Kendall scrutinized her and then shook his head rather bewildered. Arlette might have been serving breakfast to the most circumspect of families. The only thing one could say of Arlette was that she served breakfast. She was normal, everything was normal. Kendall's bewilderment increased.

"Mademoiselle Andree? Where is she?" Madeleine asked, presently.

"At home," said Kendall.

"Ah...." Madeleine's eyes twinkled.

"Now listen here," Kendall said, "Andree and I are friends, just friends. We—how do you say it?—*camarades*. That is all."

"And you do not love thees Mademoiselle Andree? Not at all?"

"I—" Kendall hesitated and did not answer, and Madeleine's eyes twinkled as she went on with her cross-examination.

"And thees Mademoiselle Andree—she do not love you?"

"I tell you we are just friends...."

"For example!... I understand. You are just friends. Oh yes. It is possible, because the French girl she is so col'."

Kendall applied himself to his chocolate and confiture industriously, while Madeleine looked at him with twinkling eyes. If he failed to understand her or her system of life and philosophy, she was equally unable to understand him. If he found the present situation bewildering, she, for her part, regarded him as a strange phenomenon that bordered on the impossible. As a final conclusion she did not believe him in the least, but thought of him as absurdly discreet. No other solution was possible to her.

They finished breakfast and went down the four flights of stairs, Bert and Madeleine chatting gaily, Kendall following apprehensively, for they must pass the omniscient eye of the *concierge*. He was inclined to make an excuse to go back to the apartment so that he would not be compelled to take part in the scene he feared.

Bert and Madeleine passed out of the big doors into the concrete-floored passageway that led to the street, and Kendall drew himself together as he saw the *concierge* busily sweeping between them and the outer doors. She looked up and nodded and smiled. Madeleine stopped and they chatted! Actually chatted as if—why, as if there was no reason why they should not chat. And that *concierge* was a gray-haired, motherly soul who in Detroit would have gone to foreign missionary meetings! Kendall could not follow the conversation, but he caught fragments of it. It was just casual chatter, with here and there a question dropped in to make for a better acquaintance. Then they bade each other good-by in the most friendly way imaginable and the trio went out to the street.

Kendall was suspended in mid-air, feet off the ground, nothing solid within reach. He was in an element that was not his, in a universe where two solids could occupy the same place at the same time, or where the shortest distance between two points was a curve. All his rules and axioms were useless.... He began to realize that the years he had lived were more or less useless to him, and that if he wished to judge his present life and the people among whom he lived he must start at the beginning with an open mind. As an American he could never comprehend them; he could not think their thoughts nor understand their mental language. The part of him inherited from his mother could never get into *rapport* with France; the part inherited from his father never could quite comprehend, though it might tolerate with a kindly toleration, and say: "Well, I don't understand this way of doing things at all.... But maybe it's all right—for the French."

He kept glancing at Madeleine. Every glance reassured him. She was a *nice* girl. He liked her. There was nothing reprehensible about her, but, on the contrary, she was charming as he liked to see a girl charming, and modest, and *good*. He felt instinctively that she was good, just as he had felt that Andree was good.... Somewhere there must be an explanation. Somehow the thing was reconcilable.

They left Madeleine at the Metro and walked to their offices. Neither boy referred to the situation; Bert, because he saw no reason for it; Kendall, because he dared not. Strangely, it was not Madeleine and Bert that troubled him; it was himself. He was not accustomed to studying himself, but he was doing so now. He had rather fancied himself a man capable of thought and understanding, a man who could look at the world and comprehend it. He had regarded himself as wise in his generation, not blatantly so, but with a certainty born of inherited dogmas and local dogmas. For the first time he saw dimly that one may understand the world from the Detroit point of view and be utterly at a loss in New York; that he may understand life from the American point of view and be grossly ignorant of the French. He even asked himself this question:

"Is one who lives up to his code of ethics, his moral conceptions, good and moral, even if those ethics and conceptions are utterly at variance with some other code of behavior?"

Could it be that a thing abominable in America because America's code was set against it could be perfectly proper in Persia because Persia's code permitted it? That there was an abstract *good* he believed, and that there was an abstract *evil*. But could a definite act be made universally evil by legislation or by the custom of only a part of the world? It was deeper reasoning than he had ever essayed before, and he limped sadly as he traveled toward no conclusion at all. The result was multiplied bewilderment....

One conclusion he reached: If Madeleine had been an American girl he would have been shocked, outraged.... This led him to think of Maude Knox, and suddenly he wanted to see her, to talk to her, to be with her because she was American as he was American. He wanted to get his feet on solid earth and to tread accustomed paths for a while. He determined he would see her.

At noon he told Bert he would not be at home for dinner, and then at six o'clock he hurried to the Hôtel Wagram and telephoned Miss Knox's room. She was in, and would be delighted to dine with him if he would wait twenty minutes. He sat down in the spacious lobby and smoked and waited.

She came down the stairs very trim and American and pleasing to the eye. He noted the little swagger—the rather charming swagger—to her walk. It was accentuated by the fact that she carried her hands in the side pockets of her coat. She was not in uniform; had left it off for the evening as the women in the various services love to do. He arose and walked to the stairway to meet her, and they shook hands in the frank American way.

"Well?" she said, with a humorous twinkle in her eye.

"I got to wanting to see you this morning," he said, "and it grew. So I just came along and took a chance."

"To-morrow would be too late. I've got a job with a combat division and I'm going out to-morrow. Maybe I'll get close to the front."

"Congratulations. You're luckier than I.... We'll make this a celebration. Where would you like to eat?"

"Any place.... I don't care—somewhere where we won't see an American.... Have you seen the papers?"

"No. I've been grubbing all day, but a hint of the news has dribbled in to me."

"Then you've heard that the Hun is stopped! And that we did it. Isn't that glorious? We—Americans—saved Paris. I wonder if it can be true."

They bought a *Herald* from a kiosk and found a brief, unsatisfactory, much-censored story, but it was a confirmation. The marines had been in it. Apparently they had been thrown in to stop a gap, and had stopped it effectively. Kendall knew that this meant the second division, comprising two regiments of marines and some of the old Regular Army. They had been thrown across the Paris-Metz road—and the *boches* had been halted abruptly. It was glorious, thrilling news.

"How would you like to go to a little restaurant where I eat once in a while? It's very Parisian. There will be no Americans there, and while it doesn't look much, the food is bully and the crowd amusing."

"Fine!" she said, and he stopped a passing taxicab. By dint of many repetitions he was able to make the chauffeur comprehend that he wanted to be driven to Marty's on the rue de Richelieu.

They were a trifle early. Few of the regular *habitués de maison* were present yet, and they had their choice of tables. Ken selected the one at which he had sat the other evening. One by one the regulars appeared and, recognizing Kendall, smiled and nodded. Monsieur Robert appeared with the Spanish tragedian, and Monsieur Robert came over to shake hands and be very cordial. Ken presented him to Maude and watched her face with amusement when the handsome young actor bent over her hand and kissed it. Then entered the elderly critic with the pointed white beard who was invariably accompanied by a beautiful girl—a new beautiful girl every evening. And then appeared Monsieur Jacques, swinging his artificial leg hilariously, waving his cane, and with his hat awry, as was its custom. He shouted greetings to all, then, espying Kendall, he rushed to his chair, clapped the captain on the back, and, turning, harangued the room. His subject was Americans. The Americans were heroic. They had appeared in France's hour of need. They were shedding their blood in France's quarrel, and France should proclaim her gratitude. Had not these so-much-to-be-loved Americans saved Paris from the *boche*. But certainly! That very day.... *Vive l'Amérique!*... Suddenly, in a transport of enthusiasm, he threw his arm about Kendall's neck and kissed him resoundingly on both cheeks....

Kendall was frightfully embarrassed, especially when he heard the room laugh until the dishes rocked. He was angry, but before he could give vent to his anger his eye encountered Maude Knox, mirthful tears rolling down her cheeks. Then he himself laughed, if a bit ruefully. Jacques threw himself into a seat across the table and began talking in his wild way to Maude Knox, who spoke French very well indeed. There was no need for introductions here. Jacques never thought of such a thing and Maude appeared perfectly willing to forgo the ceremony. Kendall was rather out of it temporarily. He looked across at Monsieur Robert, who was bobbing his head and laughing and writing on the back of a *carte de jour*.... Then he arose and handed it to Kendall.

Monsieur had a trifle of English of which he was very proud, and this communication, relating to Jacques, was couched in that language. Ken read it and then laughed in real earnest, for it made this rather amazing announcement:

"It is not a bad boy, but he is a few mad!"

What more could one ask of a single sentence?

"If you are looking for something un-American you get it here," he said to Maude.

"I like it.... I'm enjoying every second of it," she said, delightedly. "They're just like children."

"But Jacques here has an artificial leg, a silver plate in the crown of his head, the Médaille Militaire and the Croix de Guerre," he said.

Jacques, meantime, had possessed himself of Monsieur Robert's note and, leaping to his feet, was heaping scorn and derision on the young actor's head, while Monsieur Robert feigned terror and made as though he would hide under the table.

"Are they always like this," Maude asked, "or is it relief—now that Paris seems to be safe?"

"They are always so," he said.

"I envy them.... But it couldn't happen in America, could it? Imagine this in Cleveland or Detroit. Why, everybody would be put out by the management, or the police would be called in! And why?... I'm learning a lot since I came to France.... There's something in the very air here. One could do things never dreamed of at home.... I don't know what it is, but that's the way I feel. Maybe it is the freedom from restraint, maybe it's the example, maybe it is that the war is so tremendous that nothing a single individual can do is of the least importance.... But the feeling is there. Other girls have told me the same thing."

"Paris does get you," said Ken.

"Things don't seem to matter," she said, thoughtfully. "It's like being in a different world where none of the old rules hold good.... I can't imagine myself talking like this or feeling like this. I couldn't have a month ago.... I think," she said, with a little laugh, "that I shall have to keep my head very level."

Ken was astonished. So the thing was getting Maude Knox, too! She saw a difference, felt a difference, felt the challenge of a difference! "It gets you.... It gets you," he said, helplessly.

"Sometimes I have a feeling that I'd like to throw up the whole show and live here forever—be a lotus-eater," she said, with more seriousness. "If I were a man—"

"Yes?"

She shrugged her shoulders. "What's the use?... But I'll say this—I'm never going to see things with the same eyes again. I think I'll be able to understand that there are two sides to a story."

This was the same Maude Knox he had known on the vessel crossing the ocean—a Maude Knox who quite typified his ideas of the *nice* American girl, the sheltered, protected, almost prudish creature of his experience! She had traveled far—and yet she was not less nice because she had seen more of the life that inhabits the planet, nor because she had acquired a certain tolerance for manners and customs that were impossible for herself. It seemed as if she were passing through much the same mental conflict as himself. Perhaps it was not so pronounced with her because her experiences had not been so pronounced. But she seemed to have reached a surer conclusion than he. However, she had never had his mother. Her inheritances were different, and her upbringing by her philosopher father had, perhaps, made it possible for her to progress more rapidly in understanding and clear seeing than himself.

"For instance," she said, "if I had met you with that little French girl a month ago I should probably have cut you.... Especially when you wore such a guilty look...."

"It wasn't a guilty look. I—Andree is a mighty nice girl. I introduced her to you, didn't I?... Well?"

Her eyes twinkled. He could not decide whether it were derision or unbelief, and he felt very uncomfortable in consequence. "Just because she's French ..." he commenced.

"The young man doth protest too much," she said. "But what I was going to say was that it didn't seem to matter in the least. I suppose it ought to, but it didn't.... She looked like such a nice, sweet little thing."

"She is."

"And that's why the life here in Paris is so bewildering. It upsets all one's preconceived notions. It makes one wonder...."

"It does," he said, emphatically.

"I presume I should be just as intolerant back home as I ever was."

"It's different back home."

"Extremely," she said, dryly.

Jacques turned suddenly to Maude as the male dressmaker came in with his pink-cheeked companion of the other night. "You see her," he said, as one about to make a statement of distinct interest to the one addressed. "She ees his girl—yes.... I theenk she look for anozzer boy. Bicause thees dressmaker, he is ver' selfish. He make mooch money, but he theenk only of himself. It ees so.... For example!... He make that yo'ng girl do *so*—how you say?" He went through the pantomime of shining his shoes. "That ees not pleasant. *N'est-ce pas?*... So I theenk she look about for anozzer boy...."

Kendall felt his ears growing hot, and was on the point of committing an indiscretion when Maude answered with a quaver of mirth in her voice, and not the least of the anger and shocked indignation Kendall expected. "I should think she would...."

Presently Kendall called for the check and they went out, Jacques insisting on shaking hands with both of them, and appearing to be on the point of kissing Ken all over again.

"How shall we keep up the celebration?" Ken asked when they were out on the dark, narrow street.

"Let's walk," she said. "Paris fascinates me at night. I love to stroll about, but usually I have to go in so early. Are you too tired to walk up the Champs Élysées and possibly on to the Bois de Boulogne?"

"Indeed not!" he said, and they started off with good American strides, dodging taxicabs that came charging down upon them out of the darkness with lights so dim as to be scarcely visible, and almost bumping into pedestrians who loomed up suddenly out of the blackness ahead. In a few moments they emerged upon the broader thoroughfares where visibility was higher, and presently were walking up the rue de Rivoli toward the Étoile.

Kendall was feeling a new and different interest in Maude Knox. He had been attracted to her casually on the boat, for she had been very pleasant to look at, and a charming companion. But she had not impressed him other than with a mild pleasantness, calling forth a temporary friendliness. To-night he felt that he really *liked* her; that there was something to her. She had disclosed that there was a certain kinship between their mental processes and their reactions to the new life that surrounded them, but most of all she had shown herself adaptable and *sensible*. Sensible covered a multitude of meanings for Ken. His idea of girls was that they were creatures full of peculiar concealments and inhibitions who had a habit of looking at facts obliquely and interpreting them without frankness. Somehow they never seemed exactly sincere to him, but rather as if they felt compelled to certain pretenses as a measure of self-protection. His impression was that American girls were always conscious of the necessity for protecting themselves, and this destroyed comradeship and good understanding.... It was his notion that they were constantly on their guard against a danger which they rather feared did not exist....

But to-night Maude Knox seemed very different from all this; she seemed frank and fearless. She had seen more than her sisters back home, and it had not shocked her especially. She was capable of entering into the spirit of the life—at least theoretically—and she treated him, Kendall, as an equal and a friend rather than as a male to be kept in his place lest he pounce upon her with dire consequences.... He liked it. He liked the way she talked, and he liked the air with which she carried herself.

Half an hour later they were seated on uncomfortable iron chairs beside the Avenue du Bois de Boulogne, watching a string of American ambulances whiz by from the hospital beyond, on their way to one of the stations to meet a train bearing wounded from the front.

"It makes one realize that we're in it," Maude said, gravely. "It hardly seems possible that those ambulances will be back in an hour filled with American boys—wounded in France by the Germans. There's something unreal about it.... To think that those boys have crossed the ocean to be wounded and mutilated over here!... I wonder if they are sending any of the wounded home."

"I don't know."

"The folks won't realize this war till they see boys on crutches...."

Before them the promenaders straggled, dim forms in the dusk, only to be distinguished when they passed within reach of the arm. There were parties of three or four girls of the working-class hurrying home with packages under their arms; there were other parties who dawdled and laughed and jostled one another and giggled—young shop or factory girls out to enjoy the evening. There were young men and young women who walked very close to each other, sometimes holding hands. There were single young men and young men in pairs out for walk and adventure. There were officers of all armies and a sprinkling of American doughboys ready for whatever might happen, often three or four of them with a single girl, all jolly and laughing and having the most enjoyable sort of time trying to make themselves understood to one another. At a little distance two neat-looking girls were seriously giving a French lesson to a group of American soldiers.... It was such a company of strollers and dawdlers as the concerns of the world had never brought together before, drawn from all habitable quarters of the globe because the Hun, in his ruthless ambition, had thought to spread his *Kultur* over the face of the planet....

There were long lapses in the conversation, for both Maude and Kendall found a gripping interest in the passers-by.

"Just think," said Maude, presently, "almost every girl we see has lost a father or a brother or a sweetheart or a husband. Almost every one.... A waitress in our hotel told me this morning that eleven men of her family were dead."

"Yes," he said.

"But somehow the thing that—that *frightens* me most is not to think of the women who have lost fathers and brothers, or even husbands.... It is the girls who have lost sweethearts. It is the thought of the boys who are dead and who were to have been the husbands of these girls.... Think of the hundreds of them who have lost husbands whom, perhaps, they have never met ... whom they can never meet.... It's awful to think of a million girls who have *got* to be old maids! They don't want to be, but they've *got* to be.... War has taken from them the husbands they never had."

"I've thought of that," he said.

"It means these girls have lost more than life—they have had killed for them the possibility of living.... They can never have homes and families.... The future is nothing but a stretch of years for them—lonesome years without happiness and without sorrow."

"I suppose it is as hard to be deprived of sorrow as it is of happiness," said Kendall, slowly.

She paused before replying. "Yes," she said, "I can understand that—if the sorrow is brought because you love. Sorrow is a necessary experience of life. Emerson's essay on compensation is all about that...." She paused again and then broke out with a vehemence foreign to her. "I don't blame them—I don't blame them a bit. Everybody is entitled to live and to have the experiences of life. I never thought I should feel this way, but it is so.... If you can have a life full of living you are entitled to snatch your little moments of happiness—just as these French girls are doing. It is their right, because it is the best life has to offer them.... It isn't France alone—it might happen in America. Suppose half the girls at home were deprived of the possibility of marriage.... It's awful."

The little moments of happiness! Kendall's mind seized on that phrase and held it.... It was the essence of the whole matter. These women, shut out from the Banquet of Life, were seizing hungrily the crumbs of happiness that were brushed from the table.

In the pause that followed an American soldier and a French girl sat down in the chairs at the right of Maude and Kendall and talked jerkily, half in French, half in English. They tried so hard to talk to each other, because each was lonesome.... And then, as Kendall and Maude eavesdropped shamelessly, the siren sounded—the *Gothas* were coming!

People started to their feet and began scurrying away to seek for shelter, but Maude and Kendall did not move, nor did the boy and girl next them. Presently Kendall heard the boy ask, "Ain't you afraid of the bombs, mademoiselle?"

"*Non.... Non....*" She shrugged her shoulders and then said, in a hopeless voice, a pitiful voice: "I have not the fear, because what does it matter?... There is nothing in life for me. If I am kill—*pouf!... So....* There is an end, and it will be well...."

Kendall felt Maude's fingers on his arm, felt their sudden pressure. "There," she whispered. "There it is.... She *knows*. They all know.... Who has a right to say they sha'n't have their little moments?..."

Kendall stood up. It seemed as if movement were necessary, any sort of movement, of physical action. This sudden, close contact with terrible reality had seared through to his consciousness with a terrible, burning depression.... The thing was unbearable.... And this, he thought, is what war means!...

"Come," he said, almost roughly.

She arose obediently and they walked rapidly toward the Étoile.

"We have fifteen minutes," he said. "If we walk fast we can almost make your hotel."

As they walked the now almost deserted streets, deserted except for stragglers and for taxicabs which went scurrying about as they always do, not oblivious to bomb raids, but in defiance of them, they saw huge, mysterious bodies arising from the shrubbery, great grub-shapes that appeared from nowhere and mounted high into the heavens—the sausage balloons which in time of raid stretch in interminable line across the sky down the path of the Avenue du Bois de Boulogne and the Champs Élysées and the Jardin des Tuileries. They were so silent, so mysterious, such ghostly-gray blots against the sky!

They reached the Place de la Concorde before the first gun of the barrage sounded, and in a moment were safely under the arches of the buildings that face the rue de Rivoli.... And then the storm broke in all its fury.

Kendall waited for Maude's reactions. It was a sort of test. There was danger, real danger, even under those huge stone arches—if a bomb should strike directly above them or in the street without. He wanted to see how she would behave in presence of danger.

She satisfied him. She exhibited, not fear, but curiosity and a childlike interest, as if it were some sort of spectacle, and she were disappointed at not having a better seat. It was impossible to keep her back from the curb, for she insisted on standing in the very mouth of the arch to see all that was to be seen.... She had courage as well as frankness and understanding. His admiration for her grew amazingly.

In an hour the raid was over and they continued their way to the Hôtel Wagram.

"Good night," she said, extending her hand and giving him a pressure of real friendship. "I've enjoyed this evening—more than any other since I've been here."

"It has been bully," he said. "I feel as if I were just getting acquainted with you.... It's hard luck you're going so soon—but you'll be back."

She laughed. "You won't be lonesome," she said, gaily. "There's that cunning little French girl of yours—who doesn't seem to have any last name.... Mademoiselle Andree." She laughed again. "What is her last name? You know it isn't usual to introduce strangers by their given names, as you did."

He laughed ruefully. "I'm darned if I know," he said. "I always forget to ask her." It was a reply that would have been impossible for him to make to Maude Knox six hours before.

Her face grew serious and she touched his arm with her fingers lightly. "She had a sweet face," Maude said. "Don't be unkind to her.... Now good night. To-morrow I'll be where I can hear the guns."

"Good night," he said, and turned away.

He was repeating to himself what Maude had said: "Don't be unkind to her.... Don't be unkind to her." What was he to do? How was he to deal with that quaint little person who appeared out of mystery to assume such an important place in his life?... Was not merely knowing her being unkind to her?... Or was he giving her her little moment of happiness?...

CHAPTER VIII

All day Kendall had been comparing Maude Knox with Andree. When he left the American girl and went home to his apartment he had been under the spell of her American manner, of her frankness, of the undefinable something which one finds in all American girls of the college type, of the cultured type, which is to be found in no other women the world over. When you have called it the American manner you have done your best at description.... It was the old story of like calling to like, of that to which one is accustomed seeming to be more desirable than even the most delightful of novelties. It was the call of home, the call of race, a thing that can never be negligible in the affairs of mankind.

A night of sleep rounded the sharp peaks of his impressions. When he awoke in the morning he did not see Maude Knox so distinctly, but an impression remained with him that would be permanent—that she was splendid, desirable, the sort of girl a fellow would like to be very well acquainted with. He went no farther than that. He was not so near to being in love with her as he was with Andree, or, if he were, he failed to recognize it.... He did recognize that Andree had become an important personage in his life, so important that he could not think of another girl without thinking immediately of her.

She was everything that Maude Knox was not and Maude Knox seemed to be everything that Andree was not. There was no single point at which their characters converged and ran parallel—except that both were "nice".... And even their "niceness" was different. Kendall understood Maude's niceness perfectly; Andree's was a mystery to him; it was something he felt, but could not set down in any known terms.

One could readily imagine Maude playing golf or swimming or driving a car furiously and capably; it was impossible to imagine Andree doing any of these things. Andree was utterly feminine. One could be pals with Maude; with Andree, Kendall felt one could be bare acquaintance or sweetheart—nothing else.... One felt that Andree would give and give and give, asking only love in return: Maude would give and give, but would demand, as American women do, a like amount of giving in return.

Also, in the attraction which Andree exercised were the elements of mystery and of danger. It was something that he knew nothing about her; that she appeared as out of nothingness, and then disappeared into black night again—and that he was apprehensive as to where his acquaintance with her was leading him. To a young man of some imagination these two factors were compelling.... The more he thought of the girls that day the stronger grew his desire to be with Andree—to taste the charm of her presence and to sense the mystery that surrounded her, the mystery of herself and the mystery of a great race, apparent in her, and not understandable by him.

He was at the place of meeting early and there paced back and forth before the entrance to subterranean Paris, watching the crowds and waiting with impatience. The crowd was an old story to him now, but it never quite lost its fascination, never quite laid aside that air of unreality, of *foreignness*, of eventfulness that made the Paris throng of those days what it was— foreign in the eyes of the foreigner and foreign in the eyes of the Parisian.... He saw a slender girl—she seemed not more than twenty—bidding farewell to a youthful soldier. Their good-by was unrestrained and affecting. He was going to the north—to the battle-line—and always was the possibility that he might never return. It spoke eloquently in the fervor of that farewell.... They stood, locked in each other's arms while their lips met again and again—with all the world to see. But none pointed or smiled. The world understood, and the heart of the world moved in sympathy.... Here was another girl who might never know the joys of wife or mother. If that young man did not return, she, fortunate in the possession of a sweetheart, might descend from her high place of happiness and security to the drab, hopeless level of her million sisters.... It was no ordinary parting—it was a parting with more than a loved one, for it was a possible parting with the right to live....

Then Andree appeared, in white once more, walking with tiny, demure little steps, unsmiling, apparently unconscious that she was not alone on that crowded corner. So she always came. At one moment she was not there; the next moment she appeared—from her mystery—appeared so modestly, so diffidently. Kendall said to himself that she came like some fairy, afraid lest a hostile glance or a human touch might send her back all too soon to the fairyland whence she came....

He advanced to meet her and, as she always did, she stopped as if startled, raised her eyes to his gravely, as if she had never seen him before, and then smiled that little smile which seemed to say that she was uncertain of her welcome, but hoped she would find it warm. Her slender hand was in his, with quaint formality, and she said in French: "Good-day, monsieur. How carry you yourself?"

"Very well. Very well. And you?"

"Oh, I have been bored! I have had to make a visit of duty. It was very tiresome...."

Then came the short, awkward pause while they adjusted themselves to each other and sought for words in languages strange with which to begin conversation. It was always so—that they spoke little for the first five minutes after a meeting. Neither seemed to find words to begin. Then she said, looking at him sidewise, with the merest hint of a smile in her lovely eyes, "Have you thought of me?"

"When I lifted up." He laughed at this quotation of her literal translation of the French for *arise*. "In the morning, at noon, all the afternoon—always."

"It is well," she said. "I also have thought of you."

"Where shall we eat?"

"I do not care.... It makes nothing.... Is Arlette well?" She laughed a little at recollection of Arlette.

For a few moments they walked along undecided, and then Kendall looked up to see Monsieur Robert approaching.

"Here's your actor," he said.

"What actor, monsieur?"

"Monsieur Robert."

"You know heem?"

"I told you about him."

"Yes.... Yes.... That was well."

Monsieur Robert recognized Kendall, and looked quickly at Andree; then he smiled and waggled his head in the charming, boyish way he had, and lifted his hat.

"Good night," he said, making a display of his English and extending his hand.

"Monsieur Robert, permit me, Mademoiselle Andree."

The young actor took her hand and, with a smile that was half a laugh, bowed over it and made some response in French which was not intelligible to Kendall.

"Mademoiselle wishes to enter your profession," Kendall said, with a twinkle in his eye. "She is going to the *Académie* in September."

"Ah...." Monsieur Robert looked at her more carefully. "You enter the *Académie*?"

"I do not know—I hope.... I am working very hard."

"And you wish to be an actress?... It is well. But why?"

"So she can come to New York, *à la* Madame Bernhardt, and bring home much money, and be too proud to know an old friend like myself when I sit in the front row and applaud."

She smiled up at him. "When I come in New York you will go to see me?... But I shall be very great and famous. Oh yes. But I shall remember you, of a surety.... I shall remember you—a little." There was an infinity of subdued roguishness about her.

Monsieur Robert was studying Andree with interest. "You will be ver' pretty actress," he said, haltingly, speaking in English so that Kendall would share in the compliment.

"You bet," said Ken, spontaneously, and then, with characteristic American directness: "What's this about the necessity for having some actor speak for her? She says she cannot enter unless some actor says a good word for her."

"It makes the matter with more facility," said Monsieur Robert.

Andree looked from Kendall to the young actor timidly, almost with the shyness of a child.

"Why not come and dine with us?" said Ken.

"I should be delighted, but it is not possible for me to-night. I am—how you say?—*très-occupé*.... But some other night—very soon.... With mademoiselle." He waggled his head again and laughed his pleasing, boyish laugh.

"Shall we say to-morrow?"

"Oh, very well."

"If it is possible for mademoiselle," and Kendall looked at Andree.

"Yes," she said, "to-morrow."

"At Marty's," said Monsieur Robert.

"Seven o'clock?"

"It is well.... *Au revoir, mademoiselle et monsieur.* Until to-morrow."

Presently Kendall stopped. "By Jove!" he said, "I forgot to tell Arlette I wouldn't be home to dinner. She will have it ready. Shall we dine with her?"

"As you like."

"And afterward we can sit and talk."

"Oh, if only you can speak more French.... There are so many things we could speak of. I should like to talk of many things to you—and to read you poems.... You know French poets?"

Ken shook his head. "You like poetry, don't you?... I'll bet you're a poet yourself? Don't you make poems?"

"One leetle book," she said, with a rueful shake of the head. "One leetle, small book.... But it was not good—oh no. In it are only two poems that are good. The rest are bad, ver', ver' bad."

"I don't believe a word of it. I'll bet they're great."

"*Non ... non!...* I will bring them to you and you shall see.... But no. It is not possible for you to read. I am so sad ... so sad." She laughed a little to show that she was not sad at all, and tripped along by his side, almost instantly returning to that quaint gravity which always baffled Kendall. He never could tell whether it was real gravity or a sort of protective coloring such as birds use to make themselves invisible to the hostile eye.

As they descended into the Metro they met, coming up the stairs, a handsomely dressed young woman, exquisitely shod, but so painted as to cheeks that one could not possibly imagine what her natural complexion might have been. She looked at Kendall boldly.

"Camouflage," said Andree, serenely, when the young woman had passed. "I do not like ..."

It was not the first time Kendall had heard that Parisian term applied to the painted face, but he laughed now as if it were a fresh witticism to him. Andree made it fresh, for any sort of slang sounded so unnatural from her lips as to be irresistibly ludicrous ... like the harmless precocity of a child.

"*Vous êtes très-jolie,*" he said, with decision.

"No.... I am not pretty. You do not theenk. You make mock of me." And then, as he wrinkled his nose: "Oh, why do you make *grimace*?... It is not nice for make *grimace* at me.... And now—oh, I see—your left eye it laughs, and the other it does not. Why is that? Why does your left eye laugh?" She pointed accusingly at the offending eye and stopped still, shaking her head. "Oh, you are ver' bad. I do not like you.... No.... No.... I do not like you." And then she laughed with that sudden change from mock gravity to delicious merriment of which she alone, of all the people Kendall knew, was capable.

When she did that she was so alluring, so cunning, that Kendall had to hold his arms stiff at his sides to prevent them from picking her up and cuddling her and kissing her.... It seemed that humor of hers was given her to tempt kisses. Yet there was nothing deliberately provocative about her, nothing. Quite the contrary. It seemed rather her desire to suppress such things as demonstrations of affection than to provoke them.

At the apartment the *concierge* bowed and smiled to them, and wished them a good evening. Up-stairs Arlette was manifestly upset by the appearance of an unexpected guest, but Andree disappeared into the kitchen, whence emerged a whirlwind of chatter, and all was well.... Berṭ was just finishing shaving.

"Andree, eh?" he said. "Why didn't you tip me off, and I'd have gathered up Madeleine."

"I don't know.... I—" Kendall was thinking about the other night.

"Piffle!" said Bert. Then, "Do you mean to tell me—"

"I certainly do mean to tell you," Ken said, belligerently.

"You get me, young fellow. You sure do...."

"Oh, dry up, and come to dinner—and behave if you can manage it." Kendall went into the *salon* to rejoin Andree, more than a little apprehensive of the future if it should throw Andree and Madeleine together.

Andree was looking about the room with humorous toleration from a seat in the outrageous piece of furniture which she had claimed as her throne. "Mademoiselle Madeleine—she is not here?"

"No."

"It is not well. Go and fetch her.... Now.... At once. Or I shall go away." She shook her head and made stiff little gestures with her hand, but when he stood in front of her she twinkled at him and placed both hands in his when he held them out toward her. He retained them a moment and then raised them to his lips.

"You're a sweet child," he said.

"Oh, I do not onderstan'....I do not know.... Where is the *dictionnaire*?"

"No matter.... There's Arlette announcing dinner." It was Arlette's custom to poke her head through the door when dinner was ready and to stare into the room silently and a little affrightedly. She never spoke. It was necessary to watch for the appearance of her head if one wanted to know when the meal was served.

Bert came in and Andree asked after Madeleine's health as if she considered Bert personally responsible for it, demanding why she was not present.

"Ken's afraid you don't like her," Bert said, mischievously.

"*Mais oui.... Mais oui.* I do like. I like ver' much. Why you theenk?" She turned to Ken with the question.

"Don't pay any attention to Bert. He thinks he has a sense of humor," Ken said, but his ears were red, nevertheless, a circumstance which did not escape Andree's sharp eyes. She let the matter pass and addressed herself to her food with that detachment from all other matters which always brought a smile to Kendall's face. There were so many quaint, delightful attributes in her....

Toward the end of the dinner the diners heard a subdued whispering and giggling without, and then appeared little Arlette, bearing a dessert—a wonderful dessert. It was a pudding with a white frothiness of beaten egg covering it. It was a real dessert—the first, if one excepts fruit and ices without authority, that Ken had seen since he came to France. Little Arlette carried it to the table, and stood, big-eyed, mouth pursed, waiting for the astonishment which the miracle was to cause.... Arlette herself, wiping her chin on the back of her hand and grinning with delight, allowed her head to be seen through the door.

"It is from the *concierge*," she said, very rapidly. "She sends it to messieurs with her compliments."

"Now that's mighty nice. You thank her, Arlette, and we'll thank her when we go down.... I guess we haven't made a hit with madame, eh?... And, *mignonne*! We must have another place, Arlette, and a spoon. But *mignonne* does not like pudding, eh?"

"*Oui*," said little Arlette, her eyes growing even bigger, and the pucker turning into a smile.

Kendall settled the child at table and then gravely introduced her to Andree.

"She goes to America with me, you are to understand. I am about to ask Arlette for this young lady's hand. But yes. We are very fond of each other. Is it not so, mademoiselle?"

"Yes, monsieur," replied little Arlette, very gravely.

"Oh!... Oh!... You are ver' naughty. I am jealous. I shall not stay. I shall go away."

Little Arlette observed her gravely. "Monsieur will be my husband," she said. "It is arranged."

"Poor myself!... I am sad. I shall to weep."

Arlette looked at Andree interestedly and expectantly and cheerfully, not displeased to have caused this frightful storm of jealousy and well prepared to rejoice in the tears of her defeated rival.

Kendall carried the mite into the other room and placed her on the sofa between himself and Andree, where she snuggled up to him with a charming little air of proprietorship. Andree bent suddenly to kiss the child, and then turned her head away and gazed out of the window....

"Now you shall sing for me," said Kendall.

Little Arlette stood very erect and sang in a sweet little voice that carried the airs very accurately, sang the songs of the street and the music-halls and of the *poilus*, while her grandmother stood just within the dining-room, wrapping and unwrapping her pudgy hands in her apron and grinning and nodding her head with enormous pride. The child sang with great seriousness, her head a little back, looking for all the world like a bird on the nest opening its beak for the mother bird to drop in a worm.... When she was through, and both Andree and Arlette laughed at some of the songs especially, though Ken could not understand a word, he put a franc in her hand and kissed her. Andree snatched her up and held her close and murmured in her ear.

"Come now," said Arlette, and the baby shook hands ceremoniously.

"You must begin to get ready to go to America," Kendall said.

"Yes, monsieur," she responded, and went out, turning at every step to wave her hand in farewell.

Bert came back into the room, cap in hand, and said good night.

"And what shall we do?" Kendall asked when he was gone.

"We shall sit and talk," she replied.

"About what?"

"You shall tell to me many things.... If there really is a building of fifty stories high in New York, and when the war will finish, and if actors make much money in America, and also dancers.... Here the dancers do not make much money. Even the best.... *Non*.... A few—yes. Madame Duncan.... But in *Amérique*—is it not the same?"

"They earn lots of money—heaps."

"*Pourquoi?*"

"I don't know. They just do. People go to see them. Why don't they make much money here?"

She shook her head. "I do not know. The people they do not go for see a dancer.... Maybe, if I cannot enter into the *Conservatoire*, I shall become a dancer and take myself to *Amérique*. But that is very hard.... One must start in the music-halls, and I do not like."

"I should say *not*." Kendall thought of her in the atmosphere of the Paris music-hall and his soul revolted.

"*Pourquoi?*" she asked again.

"Mademoiselle Pourquoi.... Because you are a nice child, and the music-halls are not nice."

She smiled at him. "You theenk I am nice?"

"I think so many things about you..."

"Oh, I do not onderstan'." Her mock despair was very pathetic until her sudden laughter changed it to delight. In revenge she discharged a volley of rapid French at him for two minutes. "You see?... It is not nice to not onderstan'. You must *es*-tudy French ver' hard, and I will *es*-tudy English so w'en I go to New York..."

Her mood changed. "I am sad—ver' sad.... Life, it is not good.... No."

"Life is mighty confusing," he said. "Why are you sad?"

"Because I am *solitaire*—and because there is so much miserable. *Oui*.... There is little happiness—only *les petites minutes*.... But all the time life is not well."

The *petites minutes*!... The little minutes! There it was again, the same thought that Maude Knox had put into words. The little moments of happiness. Andree searched for them, too. She felt that the best life had to offer her were rare and transitory moments of joy.

"*Pauvre petite!*" he said, and took her hand. "You should be always glad. It isn't right for you to be sad. You weren't built to be sad.... It's rotten."

"Yes," she said, pensively, not understanding all his words, but comprehending their meaning from his tone.

It filled him with anger to think of this child whom sorrow had no right to touch for years—to think of her life as clouded at the moment when it should have been filled with joys. It was unfair.... Life had no right to treat her so. Sympathy and tenderness moved him, and he placed his arm about her and drew her to him. She did not resist, nor did she respond, even when he turned her face upward and kissed her. Her lips were cold.... If nothing but little minutes of happiness were possible for her, he vowed in his heart that he would make them more numerous.

He continued to hold her, and she lay in his arms unresisting while he whispered to her as he would have whispered to an unhappy child—yet not as he would have whispered to a child. The touch of her, her nearness, her sweet fragility mounted to his head.

"I want you to be very happy ... because I love you," he said, and, saying it, he believed it. There was room in his thoughts for nothing but her in that moment. Inhibitions were forgotten, apprehensions laid aside—the youth in his heart cried out to the youth in her heart—nothing remained but youth and love and a great sympathy. He did not look to the future. The sharp voice of conscience, suspicious, narrow, inherited from his mother, was silenced. Not that he was consciously running counter to the demands of that conscience! He was living that minute with no thought of what the next minute might bring....

Andree freed herself and looked at him gravely, with a sad scrutiny. "No," she said. "You do not love me.... It is not possible."

"But I do.... I do.... Don't you love me a little—just a little?"

"Oh," she said in a little voice, "I am afraid...."

"Afraid? ... Of what?"

"I do not know.... I am so *solitaire*—so lonely—and I am afraid."

"If you love me—"

"*Non!... Non!...* You do not love me. You only say. And if I love you—in a week, in two week, you go away to *Amérique* and leave me to be more *solitaire*.... I should be more sad...."

"No," he declared, and was about to expostulate and to declare that he would never leave her, but the words would not come. His mother had stepped in. "You will love me," he declared, in spite of his mother. "We will love each other—and there will be happiness.... If the best we can have is little moments of happiness, let us have all we can of them." He was honest, thought he was being honest in his sophistry.

"You would go away—in a week, in a month...."

"No, no!"

He saw that she was crying, and suddenly she turned from him to bury her face in her arms and to sob quietly, not unrestrainedly, but with such a quietness as went with powerful impulse to his heart, and he gathered her to him again and tried to comfort her.

"Why do you cry? What is it, *mignonne*?"

She shook her head. "I do not know," she said, but he knew that she did know and would not tell. "I will go home now.... I am sad, and you will not like me when I am sad."

"I like you any way you choose to be," he said, holding her close. She did not respond to his caresses, neither did she repulse them. She was simply negative, as if they were not happening to her at all. "I love you," he repeated, insistently.

"No...." She wiped her eyes and got to her feet. "I must go to my house. Will you come?" she asked, shyly.

"Of course.... But—"

"No.... No.... You do not love me. You cannot. I do not believe—and I am afraid."

They walked down the street in silence. Kendall tried to talk, but grew discouraged, for Andree was intent, thinking, thinking, thinking, and would not talk.... He wondered if it were the end of matters between them, if he had been too impetuous and had frightened her away. The thought frightened him, and he tried to reassure her, but could find no words. He did not know how to reassure her, because he did not know what she feared or what she was thinking.... How was he to understand? His eyes were not clear to see into her world, or his intelligence to understand it. He had declared his love to her as he would have declared it to an American girl—that and nothing more. And she—what was she thinking? What was going on inside that dainty, that sad little head? He spoke of love in American; she understood him in French. How was he to know that?

They spoke hardly a word as the Metro carried them to the Place St.-Michel, nor was the silence broken as they walked slowly up the darkened Boulevard, so dark that at times they had actually to feel their way through a spot of blackness. There was an occasional dim blue street light, but no lights were visible from any interior.... The shining out of the feeblest of lights would have brought next day a summons to appear before the police to explain the matter. Paris was severe in the matter of lights. Kendall had seen the people stone an automobile at night because the driver had neglected to dim his lamps! The city had no humor in its appreciation of air raids.

Andree did not make him turn back at the usual spot. She seemed to have forgotten him, though she clung to his arm, and they went on to broad rue Soufflot, which leads off the Boulevard at right angles to the Panthéon. In the middle of the first block Andree paused.

"It is necessary to go back now," she said, turning her face to him, and he bent over so that he might see its expression.

"Why did you cry?" he asked

"Because I was afraid," she said.

"You are not afraid now?"

"I—I have said I shall not have fear."

He took both her hands and drew her close to him. There were none to see. The street was deserted. Even the tables and chairs of the café at the corner were piled in close to the wall.

"You love me a little?" he insisted.

There was a tiny pause. "Yes," she said. It was a queer, decided little syllable, uttered as after mature deliberation. She was looking up into his face.

"Mignonne!" he said, softly, and kissed her. This time her lips were not cold, his caress was not tolerated, but returned. She returned his kiss. It was not the first girl Kendall had kissed, but it opened his eyes to the possibilities of a kiss. It went to his head, and he snatched her up in his arms as if she had been a baby. "You love me?... You will always love me?"

"Yes," she said, in that same voice of calm decision. "And you?"

"Always.... Always," he said.

"Non.... I know. For a week, for a month.... That is all. You are not *fidèle....* You will go away and I shall be sad. I know, but I am lonely." She kissed him. "But we shall be glad," she said, wistfully. "We shall have happiness—many little minutes of happiness. I shall pretend that you never go away to leave me *solitaire....*"

What could he say? He protested and asserted, but she smiled a grave smile of knowledge and of resignation. She knew what she knew. "To-morrow," she said. "Place de la Concorde. *Sept heures.*"

"And you love me?"

"Do you not believe?" she asked, sweetly.

"Yes."

"It is well.... Good night, monsieur. To-morrow."

She kissed him again and freed herself. In another moment her daintiness had been engulfed in the mysterious blackness. Once more she had vanished into her fairy-land.... Each time he wondered if it could be possible that there should be another visitation.

Kendall, young, inexperienced in serious thought as he was, realized that some sort of crisis in his life had arrived; events impended which were to modify him, which were to affect him and to continue to affect him so long as life should last. He did not know what. He did not realize what had just happened to him and to Andree, and yet he wondered ... wondered. And he loved her; he was sure of it. Just as he was sure she was worthy of his love!

He was exalted, yet he was troubled, perplexed, worried, so he walked. At the Boulevard St.-Germain he turned off to the eastward, crossing the Seine upon the Pont Sully, and swinging to the left on the Quai Henri IV until he reached the Boulevard de la Bastille, and so to the place forever marked in the annals of time as the spot, not where the Bastille had stood, but as the spot where it had been *destroyed....* The great column uprose blackly before him. At his left was a Metro station, its entrance surrounded by people, who elbowed and surged, or stood or sat wearily near to that place of subterranean refuge.... For so had the *Gothas* affected the imagination of the poor of Paris! Their nights were nights of terror, for the Hun in his malignant ingenuity sought to drop his bombs in this quarter of Paris, near the Bastille, in the Faubourg St.-Antoine—St.-Antoine, mother of revolutions! If these people could be terrorized, they might be driven to a fresh revolution, reasoned Berlin.... They were in terror, but there was no fresh revolution.... And so they cowered about the subway entrances, men, women, boys, girls, wailing children in arms, ready to descend into the cold dampness of the tube at the first note of the *alerte*.

It was the first time Kendall had seen this thing, and it went to his heart. He felt an uprush of rage against the Hun who wrought thus inhumanly, thus without that sportsmanship which has lifted war from its mire of blood and horror and degradation, to paint it with the glamour of chivalry and heroism.... Chivalry was dead, slain by the *boche*, who made frightful war upon defenseless populations, stark naked, hideous, savage war stripped of glamour and of glory. The Hun pictured war not as a St. Michael clad in shining armor and mounted upon a glorious charger, but as a skeleton from which the decaying flesh had not completely fallen, riding upon a wolf....

Kendall walked on, turning now toward home. He felt that he could not sleep unless he walked himself to exhaustion, so he continued on and on and on. His consciousness was the ground of a battle between the inheritances that came from his mother and those which came from his gentle father—in which his own individual, peculiar reason sought to intervene.

"Look out," said his mother. "She's French, and she must be bad. She's getting you into her clutches...."

"Now, now," said his father, "she's a sweet little thing, perty as a picture. I don't see how there can be harm in her, and if there should be, it wouldn't be wilful harm."

"She's nice," said Kendall himself. "She's a nice girl, and nothing's going to happen. Why—I tell you, she's a *nice* girl!"

And so it went, suspicion, accusation, argument, defense, until his brain whirled and he was miserable, but always his intelligence, lighted by meager experience, emerged triumphant with the declaration that she was a nice girl, and no harm could come of it....

Kendall forgot that he was a guest in a strange world; that his mode of thought, his code of ethics, his purview of life and of the affairs of life were foreign, were not of the currency of this land. It was more than a mere difference between races; it was a difference between those elements which make *life*.... But one thing he was given to see, and that was, that whatever came to Andree and himself could not be evil, could not be mean or squalid or wicked—and, in his limited vocabulary, it all came back to the comforting assertion, "But she's a nice girl." That persisted, no matter what other paths of speculation his thoughts might follow. Andree was good. There was something about her that proclaimed that she would continue to be *good*, and it was comforting to him.... And he believed he loved her....

He went to bed and fell asleep with the remembrance of Andree's kiss upon his lips....

CHAPTER IX

In the morning Kendall was given orders to leave that night for the headquarters of the Second Division, which lay not distant from Meaux—that splendid body of old Regulars and Marines who had but a few weeks before proved the worth of the American soldier to the Hun and to the Allied armies by its splendidly achieved defense of the Paris-Metz highway—and there to gather certain information on shoes and ships and sealing-wax and cabbages and cooties and morale and crops and transport. He was to acquire this information with all possible despatch and accuracy, and to return to Paris with his report. An army automobile, carrying certain other officers, would leave 10 rue Ste.-Anne at nine o'clock that evening.

So he was going to the front. He was actually to penetrate to those not distant battle-lines and to hear the sound of guns and himself to come under hostile fire.... He was not, then, to rest safely in Paris for the duration of the war; was not to return to America a veteran of the roll-top desk and the ink-well! It was only for a space of days, but he would actually have been there, actually have set his feet in a trench—to be a part of a combat division. He was delighted.... He hoped something would happen, that his days at the front might not be uneventful, that he might see and take part in some manifestation of real war. His sentiments were very boyish. Why, he might actually be wounded, and so entitled to wear on his sleeve a golden wound chevron! He found himself close to hoping it would be so, and, with a sudden assertion of common sense, laughed at himself when he discovered he was actually selecting the part of his anatomy in which he preferred to receive his wound. He had decided on a leg, the fleshy part of the leg. That would not be serious, would not incapacitate him for more than a few days or weeks. It was really a glowing prospect.... And it would make him a veteran!

However, going to the front that night was unhandy. He had a *rendez-vous* with Andree and an appointment to dine with Monsieur Robert.... But that would be possible. Number 10 rue Ste.-Anne was just around the corner from Marty's. He could dine and then hasten to be where his orders called him.... Andree was eclipsed by the adventure.

At noon he packed such things as were necessary and whisked them by taxicab to rue Ste.-Anne where he left them in charge of a sergeant in the Assistant Provost Marshal's office. This left him free until nine o'clock.... He was proud that his equipment contained a steel helmet and gas-mask.

It was an exultant and excited young man who waited for Andree at the Metro station in the Place de la Concorde that evening. He wanted to tell her. He wanted to impress her with the fact that he was a real soldier and was going into danger. He even rehearsed the nonchalant speech which would announce it to her.... And at last she appeared—again in white, again with that quaint air of detachment and concentration, and still very lovely in her fragile, slender way.... Suddenly he was sorry he was going, because it meant an absence from her.

Now she was recognizing him in that delightfully timid way of hers—doubting her welcome until he reassured her.

"Good evening, monsieur," she said in French. She was always formal in those first few moments.

"I've wanted to see you—wanted to see you ever since you left me last night," he said, rather unexpectedly to himself, especially unexpected in its truth, for it was true, though he realized it only then.

"That is well," she said, and looked up at him quickly, smilingly, with something shining in her eyes that had never been there before. "And I have thought of you."

"It has been a long day.... All the days are long because you are not with me."

"It is true?" She paused, demanding to be assured that he was speaking in earnest, and he took her arm and pressed it to his side. "That is nice," she said. "You should miss me at all times. Oh yes. Ver', ver' much.... And I shall also miss you."

"My dear," he said, bending close to her ear, "do you love me?"

"Yes," she said, simply.

And then he knew that his great news had turned to aloes in his mouth. The thing he had longed to tell her—a little boastfully—he could not bear to tell her now, and he wondered vaguely why it should be so. But he must tell her. He started to do so, and stopped. No—it would do as well after dinner.

"And you?" she said, after a little pause.

"Very much.... Very much...."

"No, no.... I am afraid. It cannot be so. You only say—that is all. You have make me love you—and soon you will go away and leave me to cry.... Yes...."

"And if I do," he said, striving to tease her, "you will soon find another American. Sure you will.... *Vous êtes très-méchante.... Pas fidèle.*"

"How can you say? It is not kind. Oh, I am *fidèle*. You believe? Yes, yes. You believe?"

"Of course, child," he said, repentantly. "I was only joking."

"And you—are you *fidèle*? On the nights when I do not meet with you—what then? Do you see some other girl?... Men are not *fidèle*.... You see other girl—lots of other girl."

"Now look here, you mustn't say that. You're the only girl in the world I give a snap of my finger for.... Just you."

"It is well," she said, contentedly; and then, "We dine with thees yo'ng actor thees evening?"

"Yes."

"Oh, I am glad.... It is ver' important. He must like me, and then he will speak for me at the *Conservatoire*. You must be ver' good friend to him so that he will speak for me."

"No, young lady, you keep away from that young actor. He's too darned handsome. I don't want him stealing you away from me."

"*Non.... Non....* I do not care for him, only that he speak for me. You must not be afraid."

"Shall we take a taxi?"

"No. There is much time. A taxi is much expensive. I must not make you spend all your money."

"That wouldn't be such a hard job. I haven't much to spend."

"It is no matter.... If you had much—that is different—then I would spend.... It is not for money that I know you—oh no. At first—then I do not know what kind of yo'ng man you are.... I take you to that expensive café. It is to punish you because you speak to me as you did.... I did not know you. But now I know you ver' well. You have been kind." She nodded her head in punctuation. "You have been always nice and ver' gentle, and so I see you ver' often."

"Nobody could help being gentle with you, *mignonne.*"

"I do not know," she said. "The worl' it is not nice." She shook her head disapprovingly. "All men are not nice.... It is ver' hard, and sometimes I am most unhappy. It is so."

"But you are happy now?"

She pointed her finger down at the sidewalk. "Now—thees minute— yes. In one hour in four hours it may not be so. Who can say?"

It brought him again to his going away, and a real dread of making the announcement to her seized upon him. He was afraid she would cry or do some other equally distressing thing. But that was selfish. He dreaded her crying because it would be unpleasant for himself and was rather ashamed of it. He even fancied he could understand something of how she would actually feel, but he was wrong. He was groping in the darkness, wandering in the darkness of a strange mansion with many rooms and devious passages, and it was inevitable that he should miss his way....

They entered Marty's and Monsieur Robert came forward to greet them with that delicious, boyish smile of his.

"I am glad you come," he said, bobbing his head. "My friends they shall be jealous to see me wit' such pretty girl."

Andree was very prim and quiet with that quaint attractive quietness that always made Kendall wonder, because he had never seen anything like it. It was a sort of waiting quietness, a kind of recess that Andree retired into to await events, and from which she would emerge impish or girlish or serious, like a child or like a weary woman. One felt she was not present bodily, but was staring at one expectantly to read one's mood, or, possibly, to read one into the future and to foretell if good or ill were to come out of it. Now she watched Monsieur Robert when he was not looking at her, but the instant his eyes turned toward her her own eyes would hide behind their lashes diffidently.

"What shall we eat?" Monsieur Robert asked, in French. "*Potage? Poulet rôti, cresson? Haricots verts? Salade?...* Eh?"

"Sounds good," said Kendall, but monsieur was looking expectantly to Andree.

"That is well," she said.

"Pommard?... The *vin ordinaire* is not for us to-night?"

She was not interested in the wine, and Kendall trusted to the young actor's judgment. So they gave their order, and were only commencing on the soup when a commotion at the door apprised Kendall that Jacques was coming. Andree had started at the noise.

"It is Jacques," he said to her. "I told you about him."

"Yes," she said, but did not turn her head.

In a moment Jacques paused at the table and stared, drew himself to his full height, threw back his hair from his brow with a flamboyant gesture, and shouted: "A-ah!... A-ah!..."

Kendall was embarrassed. There was no telling what Jacques might say or do, for the man had a rather terrible, if delicious, frankness, and discussed with openness and noise what Kendall was accustomed to hear spoken of in whispers by men alone—and by them in corners.... He had heard Jacques one evening going from table to table—demanding of friends and strangers alike their judgment on a certain phase of the art of making love. Kendall had really been shocked and had looked for somebody to stand up and smite Jacques mightily, but everybody had laughed and answered according to their kind with a frankness equal to Jacques's.... So now Kendall was apprehensive.

"A-ah!..." said Jacques again, and pointed at Andree. "I ask you if I should not find for you a girl, and you say *no*. Now I know why.... A-ah!..." He frowned at Andree and waggled his head. "She is nice," he said, approvingly. Then he appeared to notice Monsieur Robert for the first time and glared at him, glared and poked a long finger under his nose. "*He* dines with you," he said, tragically. "You—you make introduce your girl to him.... *Oh, là là!* What is this? Do you not know that this man steals little girls?... He is ver' bad. Look you out or he will steal her from you. It is I, Jacques, your friend, who make the warning." Then suddenly he turned away and flew across the room to kiss a young woman who had just entered with the elderly critic.

Ken was at a loss to know if the fellow had been in earnest or were merely up to his usual capers....

The three at the table chatted, Andree always maintaining that queer reserve, not emerging from her hiding-place, speaking only when directly addressed, and then briefly. Monsieur Robert looked at her frequently, and ever more frequently, for she was a charming picture, and more than once spoke to her in French. She always replied in English.

"I think mademoiselle look ver' nice on the stage," he said to Ken. "If only she have the talent." He shrugged his shoulders. "Pretty eyes and talent for act not always are together," he said.

"You can't tell till you try," said Kendall, colloquially.

"I should like for hear mademoiselle recite one day. Mademoiselle studies Racine?"

"Already I know many parts," said Andree.

"That is well. Some day you and Capitaine Ware shall come and you shall recite for me, *n'est-ce pas*?"

"*Oui, monsieur*," she said, primly.

"There is but one way to enter into the stage," he continued. "It is the *Conservatoire*. Then, if one make the success, there is the Comédie Française.... But it is not easy to enter into the *Conservatoire*."

"*Mais non*.... It is ver' difficult," she said, despairingly.

"Ah.... But if some one speak for you? Then it ees not the same—it ees differen'.... But we shall see. Capitaine Ware ees my frien'. I would oblige him. Also I would oblige mademoiselle." He looked at her rather intently. "We shall see."

The roast chicken arrived, surrounded by cress and swimming in a delicious sauce. Conversation languished. From time to time Kendall turned to look at Andree, for it always delighted him to see her eat, she was so intent about it. She went about it as if eating were an intricate problem requiring concentration.... And presently they fell to chatting in fragmentary fashion, Andree translating for both Kendall and Monsieur Robert, and it was very jolly and pleasant.... Kendall did not notice how often the young actor glanced at Andree....

Presently they were through and monsieur was compelled to hurry away because he had a part in the piece that was playing that evening. "I mus' see you ver' soon," he said to them both, but with his eyes intently upon Andree's—which dropped before his gaze. "I mus' hear mademoiselle recite."

"We'll fix it up," said Ken. "Good night." They shook hands and Monsieur Robert bent to kiss Andree's hand, bent gracefully, with a charming air that was half joking, half serious. It set upon him well. "Good night," he said, and hastened toward the theater.

"I like him," said Kendall.

Andree looked at him quickly, her face expressionless. "Yes?" she said.

"Don't you?"

"How can I say? I do not know him.... He is ver' handsome."

"It doesn't matter whether you like him or not—so long as he gets you into that *Conservatoire* thing."

She did not reply.

They walked the best part of a block before she spoke. "It is ver' *nécessaire* for me to enter into the Conservatoire.... Oh, ver' *nécessaire*.... I mus' earn money. I have no money. I mus' earn it for myself, because there is no one to earn it for me.... You do not onderstan'.... Sometime, before the war, yo'ng girls say they do not need to earn money, because they marry. All will be wives and the husbands they will earn.... Now it ees not so—*non*—it ees differen'.... You onderstan'? Many, many yo'ng girl mus' learn to earn money, and because they will always be alone.... There can be no one...."

"It does mean a lot to you, doesn't it? I'll be mighty happy if I can help."

She was silent again for a time and then said, suddenly, as if thinking aloud, "I theenk I can enter into the *Conservatoire* if I want to...."

"Eh?"

"It was not anything."

He scarcely heard her; his mind was not on what she said, for he was thinking to himself, "I must tell her.... I must tell her now," and was nerving himself up to make the announcement of his departure.

"Andree," he said, and stopped.

"Yes?"

"Do you love me?" he said, procrastinating. It was not what he had intended to say.

"Yes." She spoke very sweetly. "And you?" The question sounded so charming from her lips, the tone and the manner of it were rare and lovely; they seemed to say, "I know you love me, but it is sweet—very sweet—to hear you say so." The street was dark and he drew her close to him, and so they walked, his arm about her waist, she responding to his touch so deliciously.

"I love you—I do love you," he said.

"It is well.... I am ver' happy."

"But, Andree—"

"Yes?"

"I—I've got to go away.... Only for a day or two," he hastened to say. "It's just a little trip."

"When?"

"Now—to-night."

"*To-night?*" Her tone was so strange, so startled, so shocked. "*To-night?*"

"Orders," he said. "Nothing could take me away from you but orders."

She had drawn away from him, and was striving to peer into his face, but the darkness prevented. She was striving to read from his eyes if he were telling the truth. She had feared his going—this young man from strange America. The possibility of his going had become a nightmare to her—always present in the profound recesses of her thoughts.

"Where?" she asked.

"To the front."

"O-oh!..." It was not an exclamation, it was a suppressed cry. It was one of the things she had feared, that this young soldier would be sent from her to the hell of battle, and that he would not return, as the brothers and the husbands and the sweethearts of her acquaintances had gone—to be swallowed up and to be seen no more on earth.... He was going.... The thing was going to happen to her.... Her man—the man she loved—was going to become a sacrifice as those millions of other men had become sacrifices.

He had feared that she would cry, that she would cling to him with sobs and beg him not to go, that she might make some sort of regrettable scene, but she did not. But she was very still with the stillness of the stricken.

"*C'est la guerre,*" she said in a whisper.

It is the war—that phrase so often heard, which excuses everything, accounts for everything. But now it had a deeper meaning. *This* was the war! This parting was the war—this giving of a loved one to death, and this remaining behind in an agony of fear and of loneliness—this was indeed the war!... To men war is one thing—it is a grim fight, it is suffering and wounds, it is bravery and glory.... To man war, at its most, can mean only death. But to a woman who sends her man it means more, infinitely, terribly more. It means that she may be deprived of all that makes life desirable. It means that she must remain behind to fear and to suffer, and then, when the feared news arrives, to face a life that is not life, a life without love, without companionship.... A life with the smile snatched away and with the heart robbed of laughter! It means that from her the one, the great, the vital thing is to be forever missing, and that the future is to be nothing but day following day.... War means that men must die.... War means that women must continue to live!

"You mustn't worry.... I—I sha'n't be in the fighting. I'm just going to get certain information." He had looked forward to boasting to her about how he would stand under fire. He would have done it in such a way that it would not have sounded like boasting, but in a mock-modest way. He had wanted to show her that he was actually going into it to take his chance with the rest.... Now he had no thought but to reassure her; he had no desire to take unto himself the heroic. "I promise you to come back," he said. "I sha'n't be hurt.... It is only a day or two, and you mustn't be afraid.... Why"—here he lied—"I may not even be near to danger."

She shook her head. "I know," she said. And then: "I shall not let you be hurt.... I shall prevent it." Like a little Spartan, she was herself again, speaking like her own self, almost gaily. "Do you theenk I should let you be hurt?... Oh no! Not in the least." She was being brave and calm—for him!

"I will be back surely in four days—the fourth day from to-day.... Then I shall see you. We will make the engagement now."

"Yes."

"Where?"

"I shall dine with Arlette," she said, with a little laugh. "I will come there—it is easier—*sept heures*."

"And—"

"Yes," she said, quietly.

"I—by gad!—I *do* love you."

She touched his cheek gently with her finger. "And there will be many *petites minutes*," she said. "We shall have much happiness."

"I hope so."

"And you will be *fidèle*—when you go away from me? You will not find a yo'ng girl at the front—in the trenches? Promise me?" She was laughing gaily now.

"If I find a girl in the trenches," he said, "I will give her to the *boche*."

"It is well," she said, and clapped her hands merrily.

They were close to the Metro station at the Palais Royal now, and, for their parting, paused in the blackness of a recess.

"I can't go home with you—do you mind?"

"Ver' much."

"Good-by, *mignonne*...."

For a moment she clung to him, the fear that was upon her manifest in the trembling of her little body. "Not good-by," she said. "We must not say good-by."

"Four days from to-day—without fail."

"I shall not fail—I shall come, *certainement*."

Again their lips met. "Now you must go," he said, and she turned away slowly and walked in that dainty way of hers toward the entrance to the Metro. He stood watching her, expecting her to turn back, but she did not turn back.... In a moment she disappeared down the stairs. He was miserable....

But he did not understand—or if he did understand he hid the truth from himself—what this parting on this evening was to Andree.... Last night she had confessed that she loved him, and had made him a promise, a promise that he half understood, but which he pretended to himself he did not understand at all.... Perhaps he did not really grasp the extent of her surrender, for young men, American young men of such upbringing as his, and such code of ethics as he knew, are not equipped to understand—and sometimes nature has made them very dull.... He had drifted along with Andree until he was beyond his depth. To drift had been so easy, for his heart had told him Andree was good—was *nice*.... Now he hid from himself that he was apprehensive of what might come, just as he tried to hide from himself that his own viewpoint was changed, and that a thing which had seemed very wrong and squalid and unthinkable was not, perhaps, so evil as his mother might assert.

At any rate, he had arrived at this point—he would not draw back. Andree was good, and he loved and respected Andree. And ... it was very confusing ... he was young and decent and as clean of mind as a man may be.... But—he was seeing and learning. Plymouth Rock could not legislate for the world nor impose its prudery and falsity—a prudery and falsity that made it a punishable offense for a husband to kiss his wife on the Sabbath day—upon an older world well able to legislate for itself. America was America. Well and good! Let America live according to the code it had chosen.... France was France. Who, save only Deity Itself, could assert that France was less virtuous, less in accord with the wishes of the Supreme Composer of Ethical Systems, because the ethics of France were not the ethics of Plymouth, Massachusetts, or of Detroit, Michigan?

But Kendall did not realize—how could he realize it?—that to Andree, after her promise of the night before, this parting had been in all its essentials as if she had been deserted upon her bridal night....

CHAPTER X

It was nearly eleven o'clock when Kendall and his companions arrived in the old cathedral town of Meaux and found accommodations in the Hôtel Sirène, that rather quaint and down-at-heel hostelry which hides in a courtyard behind huge gates that close at an hour so early as to astonish Americans. Kendall was to discover that this was the universal custom in the smaller towns of the country—that the hotels closed themselves to guests in the early evening, and that to effect an entrance thereafter was an achievement.

They contrived, however, to find huddled accommodations, but Kendall did not find sleep for a long hour. Events were imminent, events both of the soul and material, and his imagination insisted upon handling them and scrutinizing them. Speculations upon the proximity of war mingled with anticipations and apprehensions of his relations with Andree.... He fancied she, too, was suffering a wakeful night....

In the morning he awoke and breakfasted in a dining-room filled with American newspaper correspondents, for Meaux was at that date one of their headquarters, with French and American officers and a few English Red Cross nurses.... Presently he was in his car again and moving through the narrow, crowded streets toward Montreuil. The open country, rolling, beautiful, rich, lay before him.

Here, indeed, were indications of war. The roads were crowded with the traffic of warfare, with vehicles of all sorts and descriptions moving toward the front or returning from the front. The greater part of them were huge French camions driven by *poilus* who looked out upon the world with eyes that had seen such sights as alter the fabric of a man's soul during the four years that were drawing to a close. They were all in haste. American camions and camionettes and side-cars were rumbling or whizzing by. Refugees driving cows, urging on weary horses that dragged enormous two-wheeled carts heaped high with household treasures, appeared now and then.... These seemed to Kendall to savor more of the thing that was war than even such jolting, bumping pieces of artillery as he encountered now and then....

The Little Moment Of Happiness | 117

Kendall was within hearing of the big guns on the battle-line, yet all about him, spread in peaceful beauty, was a country apparently secure, apparently untouched by the devastation of an invading army. Yet, a few weeks before, German cavalry patrols had penetrated almost to this point. The fields were green and beautiful, promising abundant crops. Children were entering a little school-house just as children enter school-houses in America. Farmers were working in their fields.... If it had not been for the mass of military vehicles upon the roads and for an occasional distant rumble that might have been thunder, but was not the thunder of heaven, Kendall could not have sensed the proximity of war.

French soldiers on bicycles were frequent. Now a Frenchman on a bicycle is one of the sights of the war. Somehow he never seems to master the contrivance in all its intricacies. He can ride furiously in a straight line, coattails standing out straight behind, eyes fixed and determined, jaws set. So long as he follows a bee-line all is well, but you can read on his face that he realizes the uncertainty of life. Let him be compelled to swerve from his course, to turn a corner, or even to stop the machine to alight, and there is none so rash as to prophesy what will be forthcoming. Kendall saw one stocky poilu attempt to turn around. It was amazing! The man ricochetted off a camion against a stone pile, off the stone pile into a donkey-cart, off the donkey-cart into the arms of a troop of his marching comrades, scattering them like chickens, thence through the *poilus* in zigzag to a ditch, from which he presently rebounded, facing in the direction in which he had originally traveled. He did not turn. He had had enough of turning. Now he would keep on his way without meddling with Providence, doubtless intending to reach his destination by circumnavigating the globe....

Now Ken was passing long mule-teams driven by American boys whose faces were so incrusted in dust as to give them the appearance of figures carved out of ghastly rock. Ken could see the dust in drifts on their eyebrows, and their eyelashes had a strange albino-look. Again his car edged over to give space to a truck carrying to the rear the remnants of a destroyed German avion. This moved by to disclose a long column of Italian troops, armed not with rifles, but with picks and shovels—each man wearing on his cap a vivid red star. Not a hundred yards beyond was visible the gray rump of an observation balloon, kneeling on the ground in the midst of a cluster of trees like some unbelievably monstrous elephant, its back incrusted with something that might have been the green moss of great age. This was the camouflage to make it indistinguishable from the foliage of the trees.... Presently Kendall was passing groups of hangars, aeroplanes standing before them in the fields. Now it was a huge howitzer grunting and straining to be at its business farther ahead and lumberingly eager to join its voice with the roars of its companions. Once in a while by the roadside nestled a little plot of graves above which waved the tricolor of France....

An hour's drive brought them to Montreuil and Kendall's car descended the steep and crooked road that led into the valley where the tiny village, teeming with American soldiers, lay in all its morning charm.... It was not quiet. There sounded, every minute or so, the sharp crack of the marvelous little seventy-five sending its word of defiance to the German army which crouched behind the hills, making ready for another leap at the throat of France.

There was no stopping here. On they went along roads whose wooded sides concealed American artillerymen and artillery. Here was the edge of the front. Guns were actually firing over Kendall's head at the distant and invisible enemy. He thrilled to this realization.... In a few moments they passed on their left a beautiful château, historic because it had been occupied by von Kluck as headquarters when his armies were rushing onward to meet their defeat at the Marne. The car passed through Bezu, where was an American field hospital occupying a tiny church, its operating-room now in the adjoining building, which had been, a few weeks before, the school crowded with urchins.... But there was neither priest nor school-boy now. All were gone; all had fled before the Hun and were scattered, God knew where, over the face of France.

Now Kendall's driver turned off the main road and shortly another hamlet lay before them—the remnants of the place that had been Domptin. Here a military policeman halted them, demanded credentials and destination.

"You walk from here," he said. "No cars pass over this road by day."

"You know the way?" Ken asked his driver.

"Yes."

So they alighted and trudged along the road. Ken observed many little craters by the roadside and in the fields, and, without asking, knew they had been caused by hostile shells.... It was very noisy—or so Kendall fancied. Artillery was at work on all sides of him, but it was only the desultory fire of the quiet day. Though the voices of the guns were audible, neither guns nor the men who served them were to be seen. Kendall's pulse increased; he felt in the pit of his stomach that electric sensation which always came to him while he stood waiting for the referee's whistle at the start of a football game.

They walked on. Even here, where the affairs of war were unmistakable, there was that exotic sense of peace. The woods were still green, the bushes thick and covered with foliage, the crops, almost ready for the reaper, waving and undulating as the breezes crossed the fields.... No human being was visible. Yet here ahead, to the right and to the left, was the locale of one of the most savage struggles of the war; here it was that the American Second Division was thrown into the line to stop the German as he marched, victory-flushed, upon Paris.... And here the German had stopped.... Just beyond were fields of wheat and woodlands tenanted by no living being, but nevertheless tenanted. In their depths, concealed from the eye, not reachable by any human hand, were the unburied bodies of American dead....

"Here we are," said Kendall's driver, pointing to a gray rectangular mass of buildings just ahead. "Paris Farms. Regimental headquarters of the Ninth Infantry."

They entered the gates, passed the saluting sentry, and found themselves in a square courtyard surrounded by barns and farm buildings, with the old farm-house at the opposite end. Groups of men in khaki sat close to the walls. None were in the middle of the courtyard, and Kendall's driver, instead of leading him up the path that ran directly to the door, conducted him in a round-about way, his shoulder rubbing the wall.... In the air above was the intermittent throb of a German aeroplane reconnoitering, and it was the duty as well as the desire of all men to remain invisible....

Life, for the most part, is made up of small matters, of small joys and small griefs, of little pleasurable surprises and minor catastrophes. In the ratio as the little joys outnumber the little sorrows we are happy. Tremendous events, crashing climaxes, occur in few lives. But we like to fancy ourselves participants in astonishing doings, and as the victims of beneficiaries of amazing coincidences. We are so constituted that we can be amazed at the slightest deviation from the normal, and the arrival of a genuine surprise can set us all by the ears with excitement.... A benevolent surprise awaited Kendall inside the door of the ancient farm-house. It was of not the least importance in the scheme of the universe and would not modify Kendall's life by the breadth of a hair, yet it was potent to overshadow everything else in his mind for hours and to make him feel that he had been singled out by the powers for especial grace.

There was a broad hallway, cluttered with bedding rolls and occupied by a group of lounging soldiers. At the right was a room occupied as the office of the adjutant, which Kendall entered a trifle diffidently as a stranger, wondering what manner of men he would be required to have dealings with.... And then....

"Ken Ware!" shouted a voice, and a young second lieutenant with the most pitiable of mustaches—a yellow and yearning mustache—leaped from a desk at his right to greet him. "Where did you rain down from, and where did you get all those bars on your shoulders?"

It was Jimmy Martin, whom Kendall had last known as a newspaper man in Detroit, with whom he had been familiar in those affairs of young manhood which make for friendships to be looked back upon with longing and regret when the days and the affairs of young manhood have been engulfed in the past.

"What are you doing? What are you doing *here*?" Jimmy demanded.

"I'm in the Intelligence. And you—?"

"Intelligence officer of this regiment.... And only a second lieutenant. Ought to be a captain. Doing a captain's work. Say"—he was a sudden young man—"wait till I get my tin lid and cane and we'll go to see the sights. How long are you here?"

"Bring on your sights," said Kendall. "While you are exhibiting I can get from you what I came for."

"Wish you could stay. We've got a darn good mess. Not as good as we had the first few days, but good."

"Why the first few days?"

"We went out and gathered up stuff to eat—to save it from the *boche*."

"Foraging, eh?"

"Not exactly. We gathered it in and ate it to prevent its giving aid and comfort to the enemy. One day we got a pig at eleven-thirty and had chops for lunch at one. The colonel said that pork was too close to being pig for him. Next day we had rabbits. Speared them with pitchforks. There was a bully strawberry-patch up the line and we had plenty until a regiment of Senegalese moved in and looted it. There's a patch of gooseberries in No Man's Land, and we have the devil's own time keeping the men from going out after them."

As they passed out and through the barn into the woods Kendall explained his errand, and the conversation became technical. Whatever else he might have been, Jimmy Martin was engrossed in his particular job and, apparently, was admirably efficient. The greater part of the data Kendall wanted was at Jimmy's tongue's end; the rest would be readily obtainable from available records of Martin's work.

By this time they had traversed a plainly marked road which led along the end of a field bordering the woods, and Jimmy complained bitterly of its evidence. "We've made that road since we came here. It'll show up plain on their photographs and show a lot of circulation here.... You can see they've been droppin' shells on it now."

They entered the denseness of the woods to find it teeming with American soldiery who occupied the quiet of the day in enlarging and making more comfortable the makeshift dugouts they inhabited.... These were not such dugouts as Kendall had seen described in books about the war; they were such affairs as he had made himself when he was a boy and called "coojees," where he had played robber and baked potatoes. They were hastily dug and as hastily covered with a mat of boughs and a layer of earth—flimsy sanctuaries, able to shelter from spraying shrapnel, but of no effect whatever against explosive shell.

Suddenly an invisible seventy-five was discharged almost at Kendall's elbow, and Jimmy laughed to see his friend's reaction to the unexpected sound. They parted the bushes and examined the beautiful little gun—that weapon which one may almost say has been the salvation of France!

A captain of artillery issued belligerently from a timbered dugout and confronted Martin. "Say," he demanded, "you're the ding-donged Intelligence officer that had me pinched the other night. Ain't you?"

"Oh, was it you? Sorry. The boys are sort of stirred up about spies. They didn't savvy you. When a strange officer comes poking around these woods looking for a place to light and asking oodles of questions about whether there's artillery here and such like, somethin's goin' to happen. A couple of boys came rushin' up to me to ask what to do, and I told them to pinch you. This place is full of spy rumors. Everybody's seein' them. The doughboy that hasn't seen somethin' darn mysterious and suspicious in the last twenty-four hours is hard to find."

"Forget it. I was some lost. Should have reported before I came down."

"Where was it they got Lieutenant Small last night?"

"Down this path about a hundred yards. His horse is there yet."

Kendall and Martin walked that way. Under a shelter of boughs stood the handsome horse of which the dead lieutenant had been so fond; he stood quietly switching his tail and nibbling the leaves about him, all unconscious that his back would never again bear the weight of a gentle master.... And thirty feet away was the spot where Small had met his death, met it because he had scorned the shelter of a dugout, but with his French orderly had slept on the surface of the earth, with no shelter except a lean-to of brushwood.... On the surrounding bushes were gruesome shreds....

So this was war at last! On this spot a man had been killed by the enemy and the blood of him was not yet dry!... Somehow it convinced Kendall that he was at the front, that there was actual danger where he stood. He was experiencing the thing he had come to France hoping to experience.... And yet it was difficult to feel the fact. He had fancied the line of battle to be a constant tumult, horrible with tremendous showers of bursting shells and glorious with charges and defenses. In its stark actuality it was quite different. Affairs were gone about nonchalantly and methodically. Even the artillerymen who sent a shell now and then at some target they could not see served their guns in a bored manner.

It was only by a certain tingling of the nerves that he, a tenderfoot in this business, sensed the presence of war; that war was here about him, within reach of his arm. Those seventy-fives which spoke with such a vicious, through-the-teeth bark were sending lethal shells across the sunlit landscape, causing death and wounds. Possibly that very shell which he could hear as it sped on its way might kill an enemy.... And these boys killed with an air of detachment and *ennui*....

And the infantrymen! Scattered through the woods about their rabbit-warren of dugouts, they looked and acted like boys on holiday, on some camping excursion. They chatted and frolicked, and grumbled about the food, and because they were not relieved and sent to rest billets, and because the enemy did not try to advance, and because they themselves were not sent against the enemy. Kendall absorbed a feeling that they rather liked the whole thing, that it was just the life they were born to and were fitted to live—and that they knew it.

It was a picture, there in the *bois*, a picture that touched the imagination of that young man from the peaceful Middle West and would not soon be erased from his memory. The trees grew closely, admitting only patches of sunlight here and there, with an effect of peaceful, lazy, restful shade.

One saw dimly. The scene was soothing to the eyes, alive as it was with movement. The brown of uniforms blended with the yellow-green of the foliage and with the red-yellow of the upturned soil where it had been broken by hundreds of shovels in the fashioning of shelters.... Kendall stood and watched and knew that he was beholding a sight which, in the years of his age, he would see again and describe again, and live again in the telling.... It excited him, yet he wondered why it should excite him more than it had done when he had seen other khaki-clad boys in camps in America.... It was because these boys slept with death for a blanket-mate. It was because no man of them knew what minute might call him with awful suddenness over the threshold of life and into the mysteries of death....

There had been no fire from the enemy. Since the dawn their guns had been silent, but now, without warning, the air was filled with a threat, with a sound which Kendall had never heard before, but which he recognized by the instinct of self-preservation which resided in him. It was the rushing, shrieking, rending, express-train rush of a big shell—not of a shell going, but of one coming. It startled Kendall. For an instant he was blind and deaf to everything in the universe but the approach of that shell, and it seemed to him to be directing itself exactly at the small of his back. He wanted to dodge, to run, to obliterate himself from that portion of the earth, but there was no place to betake himself. It was a matter of seconds, of parts of a second. The shell screeched over their heads and detonated over toward the farm-house.... And Ken became fully conscious again, a bit surprised that he was still in the same spot and that he had not made himself ridiculous.

And now pictures came to him that he had seen in that interval, pictures seen but registering now for the first time. He laughed.... The woods had resolved itself into a prairie-dog village at the first instant of alarm. The air had been full of diving legs as soldiers plunged headlong into the earth. Everywhere Ken's eyes had looked they had seen an American soldier disappearing with comical haste into the bowels of the earth.

"It was about time for them to start," said Martin. "We'd better get back to headquarters. I may be wanted."

They walked back hurriedly while shell after shell screamed down at them as it rushed over their heads. Ken was silent. He was thinking: "I'm under fire. I'm really under fire. The enemy is shooting at *me*.... They are trying to kill *me*." It was not easy to convince his mind.

As they entered the farm-house the shells were coming in rapid succession and exploding in the vicinity with tremendous detonations.

Young Martin cocked his ear and hazarded an opinion as to their caliber.... A jagged fragment, hurtled from an explosion a hundred feet away, crashed through the roof and came to rest on the second floor. Young Martin was delighted; he rushed up-stairs after the bit, carrying it down gingerly wrapped in a cloth, for it was still hot, and then with joy applied gauges and calipers to it so that he might identify it exactly.... He was happy. The gauge was as he had named it.

"Say," he said over his shoulder to several officers who were gathered in the room, "listen here: now comes this man with orders for us to report on the crops of the neighborhood. Kind of crops. Quantity. Quality. How many kernels of wheat to the head.... My business is collecting information about the Germans...."

"Huh!" grunted the lieutenant-colonel, who evidently in civilian life had been acquainted with market reports, "snails weak to medium. Frogs strong. Give it to 'em, boy. Full particulars."

"Say, colonel, you know that woods we were talking about." Martin pointed to a map on the wall. "The boches are using it. My men have reported circulation there, and they've been putting up camouflage. How many shells will it take to gas 'em out? I'd like to get 'em out of there."

"Have to have brigade orders to use gas...."

Blammm! came a detonation unpleasantly near, but still beyond the headquarters. The colonel cocked his ear. "Boy, don't you make them no shorter," he drawled.

The adjutant entered. "General's here. Come to mess. He and the colonel are coming down-stairs now. All in."

All filed into the mess-room. The younger officers had been full of boyish spirits and pranks, but decorum settled on them as they entered the door. They seemed suddenly to grow up and to acquire the demeanor of maturity, and stood erect in stately manner while Kendall was presented to the general and the colonel.... And then the meal proceeded. Kendall wondered where the food came from, but asked no embarrassing questions about the source of supplies. There was chicken, there were potatoes, there was fresh asparagus, there was custard pudding, there were cheese and coffee and cherries—and then cigars.

"Don't get the idea we pass cigars at every mess," whispered a daring lieutenant in Kendall's ear. "Just throwin' ourselves in honor of the general...."

The bombardment had increased in violence during the meal, had increased to such a degree that Kendall thought rather more of falling shells than of food.... There was absolutely no protection. A shell might crash down upon them through the frail structure at will.... But nobody appeared to mind. Kendall reflected that he, perhaps, did not appear to mind, and wondered if the others were experiencing the same sensations as he. He did not see how it could be otherwise. Or had they found some magic philosophy which rendered them immune to reflections upon sudden death?... The general told the colonel a humorous anecdote, and the colonel replied to it with another equally pointless to Kendall's way of thinking. Why in thunder, he wondered, didn't they get through with this meal and go to a place a bit more sheltered?... But the seniors chatted on, apparently with placid enjoyment of Philippine and Cuban reminiscences, all to the accompaniment of bursting high-explosive shells, one of which could have obliterated that farm-house and all the men it contained.

But an end arrived. The general and the colonel arose, and it became etiquette for the juniors to arise as well. The dignitaries disappeared to the colonel's quarters up the stairs, and a few of the younger officers went to the adjutant's office across the hall, Kendall and Jimmy with them. The telephone on Martin's desk buzzed and Jimmy lifted the receiver. He looked up with a frown.

"This nut down the road wants to know if the general's killed yet."

"Did he say *general* over that 'phone?"

"Yes."

"Then we can sit down and expect to get really shelled now."

It was then that Kendall learned that the general theory was that the enemy had found means to tap all our telephone wires and to listen in to our conversations—a theory which has given rise to much quaint telephone conversation, couched in a language not hitherto known on this or any other planet.

Darkness was falling without, and with the darkness came a multiplication of the shells designed by the enemy for the discomfort of the regiment.... Kendall, to his surprise, was growing accustomed to the shells. He was conscious of them, but had lost something of his consciousness of the danger that was in them.... He was interested. It was an interesting spot and an interesting moment, and he sat quiet and wide of eye to miss no thrill that might be there for him.... Telephones were busy with messages coming and going, messages camouflaged by strange words and code numbers and weird names. When plain English was necessary the longest and most erudite words in the dictionary were sought, doubtless on the theory that the German was not educated to the point of comprehending them.

Everybody had his job, and everybody seemed to believe his especial piece of work to be the most important in the army. A lieutenant came in with a scowl of tremendous ferocity.

"Colonel," he said, "we've got a damn bad situation. It's that doctor. He refuses to give some of my wounded men wound chevrons. Says they aren't wounded enough.... How bad has a man got to be shot before he's wounded, anyhow?"

"My understanding," said the lieutenant-colonel, "is that any man who is hurt enough to require medical attention is entitled to a chevron.... It doesn't make any difference if he's hurt by high explosive or hooked by a bull."

The din was now terrific. French and American artillery had opened fire all along the line. So quickly did report follow explosion and explosion report that the whole mingled into one continuous and mighty sound. And during it all the young Intelligence officer quarreled with a sergeant who was his draftsman, as they tried to reconcile maps drawn from observers' sketches with photographs taken from aeroplanes.

"Aw, hell!" growled the draftsman, "this guy's made a conventionalized design. What we're lookin' for is what's on the ground, not some guy's pretty ideas. You want me to make a map to send up to the general, and what the devil have I got to make it from? I'm S.O.L.... There hain't no damn woods like that."

"Here," declared Jimmy, indicating on maps and photographs, "this woods is supposed to be that woods, and this trench is supposed to be that trench."

"*Supposed!*"

"Yes."

"Expect me to send a map to the general and label it 'Supposed?...' That map's pretty, all right, but it hain't worth a hoot in Hoboken. Call him up and ask him what the blazes—"

Kendall laughed, and was surprised to discover that he could laugh, that anything would seem humor in this place with death showering down on all sides.

Now the attentions of the enemy seemed to take on the aspect of a serious effort, for the officers of experience began to gather and to hold consultations and to listen with marked interest.

"Gas!" somebody said. "Listen! Hear it?"

Kendall listened, but could not distinguish the bursting of the gas-shell, so easily to be identified by the practised ear.

"Gas-masks at *alerte,*" was the order.

The telephone rang. "Shrapnel and gas here," said an observer some place out in the darkness.

"Got your mask on?" demanded Jimmy.

"No. It ain't bad yet."

"You get that mask on and keep it on. Now. While I'm waiting.... Is it on? ... There. You can telephone as well through a mask as without it. Try it.... All right."

There was a moment of comparative inactivity, then the telephone again. "Mustard gas to the right," was reported, and after a few moments a call from a certain company of infantry which had become unhappy in its position: "Say, we want a retaliatory barrage. We're getting everything here—big, little, and gas."

"They want a barrage," reported Jimmy.

"Where do they want it?" asked the lieutenant-colonel.

"I don't know. Wake George up; that's *his* business.... Say, let's notify the gas officer; we're beginning to get it pretty close here."

Jimmy called the person designated as George. "Hey!" he said, irreverently. "Get your pants on and come down. The adjutant wants you."

It was very chilly. Ken shivered with the cold, and was rather thankful it was cold, because it gave him honest reason for shivering. He was keyed to a high pitch, nerves taut, imagination straining its leash, but he was enjoying himself after a strange fashion, reveling in this experience, in the sensations of peril, in the fact that he was at the very center of things. The artillery activity continued to increase, and the ear-shattering, sweeping, rolling gusts of infernal clamor seemed to reach a very climax of sound.... Again and again he could feel upon his own body the shock of adjacent explosions. It required but a few feet difference in the fall of one of those shells to mean all that stood between life and death for him.... And yet he was not afraid. He was not conscious of fear, only of that queer electric sensation, and of an elevation of spirits due to intense excitement.

The telephone insisted with a new insistence each moment. "Gas reported to the right.... Gas reported to the left...."

"What shall we do about it?" Jimmy asked the lieutenant-colonel.

"How about a little interdiction?" They spoke casually, as one would say, "The road is dusty," and the other reply, "It might be well to sprinkle it."

"It'll be all right if we can get enough.... I'll call up and ask for it."

Then: "Hello!... Hello! Is this Hoboken?... They're giving us more gas than we like ... at right and left and in front.... Yes.... Been coming twenty minutes.... Is it worth while to retaliate?... Orders to use gas have to come from you."

"We're in for *beaucoup* casualties," somebody said out of a moment's pause.

"Say, you were too mild with Hoboken. I'd 'a' told him we was gettin' gas to beat the devil, and we had to have some doin's of our own. Them birds don't worry about what *we're* gettin' unless we holler loud." This from the draftsman-sergeant.

"There!" The adjutant looked up at the ceiling. "Listen!... *Boche* aeroplane. I've heard it quite a spell. Directing their fire by the flash of our batteries.... Gawd! Why don't we get more aeroplanes of our own!"

The telephone again, and Jimmy reported with what Kendall conceived to be relief, "He says he'll have the hundred and fifty-fives and gas going in ten minutes."

"Say," somebody complained, "that *boche* aeroplane must be mired in a cloud. It sounds like it was standing still in one spot."

"Stuck or not, she's up there without any friendly intentions.... Say, we ought to go over to the States and shoot them peace-talkin' pups." It was the sergeant speaking again. "Anybody that wants to make peace with the *boche*!... They hain't got no right pollutin' the atmosphere...."

There came a pause while all waited hopefully for the "big stuff" that had been promised them—and presently it came. Kendall had believed the ultimate in sound had been achieved before, but this—this was impossible. Such an extreme from silence could not be. It was cosmic. It was awful. He seemed to be standing in the very center of such an upheaval as might have created worlds.... It upreared to a very ultimate climax of sound, to a single note made up of a multitude of gigantic sub-tones. It was amazing, it was terrifying, it was gratifying....

"Fritz is gettin' his good," said the sergeant, with profound satisfaction.

This continued an hour, and then gradually subsided. The German fire had become desultory—and then ceased. They had drawn upon themselves more than they liked by their evening's strafing.... The silence that ensued was startlingly loud. One could hear it....

"I'm for some grub if we can rustle it," said a raw-boned lieutenant.

The lieutenant-colonel yawned and stretched his arms high over his head. "Oh-hum!... Darn these quiet nights," he said, with sincerity. "I thought for a while there was going to be something stirring."

"Oh, I'm willing to have a rest once in a while," said Jimmy. "I'm going to sleep. Gimme all these quiet nights you want to...."

Kendall looked at his watch. It was half past two in the morning.... Quiet nights! He wondered if they were making game of him, but as he looked back on the conduct of these young men during that night he was persuaded of their sincerity.... And he—he had fancied himself present at the unloosing of Inferno....

Presently he was lying on a bundle of hay on a stone floor, wrapped in his blankets.... A sentence, a scrap from the talk of the night, repeated itself to him, "We're in for casualties." He pondered it. Casualties—that meant wounded and dead; men mangled and men in the horrible agonies that follow the breathing of mustard gas.... Some of those boys he had seen a few hours ago down in the woods—only a few hundred feet away—were dead ... *dead*! He had been near to death—had sat for hours where death might reach out and touch him upon the shoulder.... So this was war ... this was how the thing was done!

It seemed so futile. What had been accomplished by this night's slaughter? Neither side had advanced a foot; nothing had been won or lost.... But hundreds of lives had been wasted, hundreds of thousands of dollars' worth of munitions had been expended—and why? For nothing that he could see, for no purpose except the desire of each side to make the other side uncomfortable.... That night could have been erased from the history of the war, and its absence would never have been noticed. Its activities had no more effect upon the course of the war than the barking of a dog would have had—and yet hundreds of bodies were tenantless, and hundreds of mothers would mourn their sons.

"War is scientific waste," he said to himself, and repeated the phrase. He hated war because it was waste.... He wondered how many men had given their lives on just such futile nights as this during the years since August, 1914. Thousands upon thousands, doubtless.... How many of those girls he had seen in Paris had been deprived of husbands—of the men who would some day have been their husbands—in just such affairs? It was wrong—*wrong*.... War was a horrid disease, or was it the German nation which was a horrid disease? He could not think clearly.... He had thought little of mankind in the mass, but now he considered it, and his sympathy attached to it. It was futile to pity an individual, any individual, but one's heart might bleed for mankind.... And most of all it might bleed for that portion of mankind whose duty it is to be the mothers of forthcoming generations—who were deprived by war of the right to fulfil that duty.

Then he found himself repeating over and over a phrase: "Little moments of happiness.... Little moments of happiness...." If men were to be wasted as they had been wasted this night, and if God could sit quiescent in His heaven, tolerating such wastage, then could that God deny to women their little moments of happiness as a partial, an infinitesimal, balm for the agony He permitted? Could He frown upon those little moments, or decree them to be evil?... He wondered how God stood on this question of morals. In a moment came an answer, but Kendall could not assert it to be a true answer. It was this: "*God demands another generation of mankind.*"

CHAPTER XI

Kendall awoke refreshed, but with those sensations which a man experiences after an exceedingly circumstantial and vivid dream. The reality of last night's events had vanished, to be remembered only as something lived through in that subconscious land of dreams. The morning was bright, cheerful, and he breakfasted with enthusiasm. Directly afterward Jimmy was summoned to brigade headquarters, and Kendall, having finished his work at that point, set out with his chauffeur to walk back to Domptin.

On the way they paused on the road to watch the shelling out of a corner of the woods by a German battery. The high-explosive shells fell with beautiful precision and at regular intervals of about a minute. The scream of the shells could be heard during an interval in which one could count up to six slowly, and then would come the explosion. By counting so and keeping his eyes on that wooded angle Kendall could watch the work of the shells with exact timing of his vision. Somehow the processes of the explosion reminded him of an enormously powerful man heaving upward a weight with his shoulders. First would come a small surge of smoke, as if the giant were testing his load, and then an uprush of black smoke and debris in geyser form, regular until it had spent its force, then breaking into irregular billows at the top and dissipating through the air…. Shell after shell dropped precisely, neatly, not varying in their placing by more than a couple of score of feet…. About the corner was no sign of life, no hurrying figures stumbling headlong away from the peril, and Kendall wondered if life were present there, if life had been there, or if it had wholly ceased to exist.

They walked on down the road to their car and returned to Montreuil, where Kendall had business with the Assistant Provost Marshal, who occupied a house on the edge of town, midway down the winding hill. As Ken's car drew up at the house a gray camion stopped at an adjoining cottage, and Kendall saw a girl leap briskly down from the seat and run up the bank. She wore the uniform of the Y. M. C. A…. He recognized Maude Knox.

His first impulse was to hasten to her, for he was as much delighted as astonished to see her in such a place, but something stopped him—call it curiosity. He was conscious of wanting to see how she acted, what she was doing, how she did it.... An American girl alone in a French hamlet deserted by its civil population! A girl alone with an army! Here was indeed a situation; here was romance; here was something to excite the imagination! Kendall leaned forward eagerly and watched.

She entered the open door of the little cottage and looked within; then she turned about in the most matter-of-fact way and called something to the man who drove the truck. He dismounted and began unloading cases and crates—and a cook-stove. These he carried up the bank and placed in the house. Maude shook hands with the man; he climbed on his camion again and drove away. She was alone!... She, an American girl, had been set down casually in a matter-of-course manner here within range of hostile guns, and abandoned to her own devices! She seemed not in the least excited or disturbed. It was amazing. This sort of thing might have been happening to her every day or so for years, and yet Kendall knew she had never, probably, spent a night alone in a house before in her life.... And here she was more than alone in a house. There was not another woman within miles.... He saw her attempting to fasten a sign to the wall beside the door, and, failing, turn and look about her for the first time.... Seventy-fives were being discharged every few minutes from points not a quarter of a mile away from her. He saw that she was gazing toward the sound.... He shook his head, for the thing was beyond his comprehension. Did American girls do this sort of thing? Was this expected of them? Were they all capable of such adaptations of themselves, or was Maude Knox a remarkable exception? He wondered....

There was nothing more to be seen. Maude had gone inside, and Kendall stepped from his car and walked up to her door, on whose threshold he paused, not speaking, and peered inside. She was standing in the middle of a rubbish-littered room, looking about her, not with bewilderment or with uncertainty, but calculatingly. She seemed the embodiment of capability.... She nodded her head as much as to say, "This will do nicely," and reached for a broom that was among the boxes that had accompanied her.

"Good morning," said Kendall.

She turned and looked at him, smiling even before she recognized him, and then exclaimed, "Kendall Ware, of all people!"

"Of all people, indeed! How about yourself? I presume you are a natural and normal part of the scenery."

She nodded. "Of course. This is what I came to France to do."

"To—to be set down on a pile of filth like this"—his arm swept the room—"alone—in the middle of an army—within a couple of miles of No Man's Land?"

"Of course.... Why not?"

"Aren't you—afraid?"

She was actually surprised; there was no pretense about it. "Of what?" she asked.

He shrugged his shoulders. "I'll bet you never slept alone in a house before in your life."

"Never."

"You wouldn't do it at home."

"I suppose not."

He waggled his head. "You'd have been afraid to stay alone in a house in a civilized town.... Now, wouldn't you?"

"I—I guess I would. Yes, I would."

"But here—with nothing to protect you, without even a decent lock—and not a woman within half a dozen kilometers!... It isn't right. They hadn't any business sending you to such a place."

"Rubbish!... I'm safer than I would be in my own home with a policeman standing in front of the door. Why, I've never even thought of being nervous! Really.... I suppose it is queer." She stopped a moment to speculate on its queerness. "If I were back home and somebody should describe this to me I couldn't understand any girl doing it.... But I'm here—and it's all different.... I never felt so—so *safe*."

"But an army—even our army—is made up of all sorts of men."

She laughed with sincerity. "Fiddlesticks!... What do you suppose would happen to a man who offended me? Why, Kendall"—it was the first time she had used his given name, but it appeared perfectly natural—"I've got a whole division to look after me."

It was true. He knew it was true. These American boys—lonely for a familiar American face, hungry for the sound of the voice and laughter of an American woman—would idolize her. They would be her slaves. Safe?... There never had been such safety as was hers—and yet he was troubled. It was so unconventional—so off the beaten track of the ordinary movement of life. He did not quite like it.... That was his mother speaking in him. His mother would have declared such conduct to be unwomanly, to be not nice, and she would have condemned Maude Knox unheard.... Because Maude Knox was doing a thing *she* had never done and had never seen done by a respectable member of her sex!... Kendall realized this to be absurd.

"We're surely in a different world," he said, tritely.

"The Epworth Sewing Circle wouldn't approve," she said, with a twinkle, "but the Epworth Sewing Circle doesn't count over here, does it?... I wonder if it will ever count again anywhere—for us who have been here?"

Kendall wondered, too. What was going to become of the home conventions when these young women, who had adventured to France to aid as they found opportunity in the winning of the war, got home? What ideas would they bring with them and disseminate? What would happen to America?... America could never be the same, for, not only would these thousands of girls return, having seen the world with opened eyes—and lived undreamable lives—but two millions of young men would be going home, too.... Each one of them would take something of France and of the war to his home—and what would come of it?...

"You're—you're *bully*!" he said, with sudden conviction. "By Jove! you're *bully*!"

"Fiddlesticks!"

"What are you here for?... What do you expect to do?"

"Talk, mostly," she said, merrily. "I guess that's what I'm wanted for more than anything else—to let the boys talk to me. Incidentally I'll make hot chocolate and sell cigarettes and safety razors and jam and cookies.... I'll just be here."

"Just be here," he repeated after her. "Just be here...." And in a flash as of lightning he saw what her just being here would mean to those men.... He saw what a lofty height they would set her upon, and how they would worship her beauty, and how they would delight in her every word.... It would be good for them, good for them as soldiers and good for them as men!... What a war it was that produced this!...

"Look!" she said, and laughed aloud.

Kendall turned. The doorway was closed by a rapidly augmenting crowd of boys in khaki, curious, eager, delighted, grinning.

"How do you do?" Maude said, with perfect calm. She walked toward them and extended her hand, which boy after boy seized bashfully. "I'm

Miss Knox—and if you ever expect to get any hot chocolate, somebody's got to put up the stove. It isn't much of a stove."

"Say, miss," blurted out a sergeant, "if you'll—er—git out of here a spell we'll fix things up.... Say, was you calc'latin' on stayin'?"

"I'm a permanent improvement," she said.

From that instant Kendall had no doubts, conjured up no violated proprieties. Maude Knox was *right* to be there; there was no other spot in the world where it was so right for her to be....

"I'll clear out," she said, and, pausing as she passed through the door, "I could use some sort of a counter...."

"You bet, miss."

"There," said Maude to Kendall, presently.

"I see," he said, soberly. "I'm seeing lots of things."

"That weren't visible in Detroit," she added for him. Then, after a pause, "And so am I.... There's something in the air—here—in Paris—wherever one goes in this country. It *gets* you.... I could do things. Yes, I could.... You have a feeling that nothing you do as an individual counts—nothing matters. Everything we've ever been used to seems so far away and insignificant. Don't you feel that way?"

"Yes."

"As if you could be very good or very, very bad—and it wouldn't make a cent's worth of difference to anybody?"

"Yes."

"Other girls are feeling it. I think they are all feeling it. There are plenty of signs.... *C'est la guerre.* I suppose that's it.... No, it can't be explained by a phrase of the streets; it's deeper than that.... With one half of the world trying to slaughter the other half.... Every little while I have a feeling that right and wrong have grown to be too big to apply to individuals—they're for *nations.* Does that express what I mean? And then I've thought more than once that this is the end of the world—the end of the old world and the starting-place of a new one.... Temporarily we're without a set of rules because the old ones won't do any more, and we've got to build up an altogether new code."

"I've felt something like that, but I didn't have a philosopher for a father, so I didn't know just what I was feeling or how to say it."

"We're being a sort of spiritual Bolsheviki, I suppose, going through a transition period of confusion and lawlessness and wild thinking.... But, just as something better than the old Russian Empire with its czars and grand dukes and Siberias and its—its *Rasputins*—is bound to follow Bolsheviki-ism, so something better than the narrowness of the sewing-circles and the Pilgrims and the viciousness of blindly accepted conventions and codes.... This has turned into something bigger than a World War—it is turning into a Greater Reformation.... Not the reformation of a religion, but a reformation in the basic *thought* of the world—surely of America...."

"Whew!" exclaimed Kendall. "I follow you, I guess, but my feet are off the bottom ... and I can't swim."

"You can think, can't you?" she said, a trifle tartly.

"I guess I *feel* more than I *think*," he said.

"We all do.... We have to feel in order to think, and we have to feel in order to understand. Cold logic isn't worth a snap of the fingers—really.... You've been getting something out of Paris, haven't you? Feeling something? I think you get it there more than any place else.... I love Paris."

"My mother wouldn't love it," he said, gravely.

"And you're like her—sometimes—aren't you?... But aren't you growing more tolerant—more able to see the other person's point of view?"

"I—hang it all!—I can't get away from the notion that good is good and bad is bad."

She shook her head. "But you are beginning to see that America hasn't the right to legislate for the world, and to define what is good and what is evil.... I know you are.... Now don't be shocked, please. I'm American, of course, and the American code is for me—until it is altered. Whatever I may think about it, still it is the code and accepted by the majority. That binds me to a degree.... But I can still believe we are narrow and prudish.... It doesn't take much imagination to understand that eating pork may be a sin to an orthodox Jew. It is a sin because he believes it is a sin. It is no sin for you because you think it is nonsense.... When you get down to essentials, the thing that is a *sin* is doing a thing you *think* to be a sin. It isn't the *thing*, but the thinking...."

"I suppose that's it."

"Of course it is.... And that's enough of this sort of talk, isn't it? I don't always talk this way, really. I'm quite pleasant and frivolous most of the time.... You're not to be stationed here by any chance?"

"No such luck."

She laughed. "I wouldn't have time to bother with you, anyhow, if you were meaning that as a compliment.... I've got at least a regiment of young men, and I sha'n't be partial.... Besides, there's that pretty little French girl.... I liked her looks.... Tell the truth, you'd be heartbroken if you were sent away from Paris and her."

Andree!... He had scarcely remembered her existence for twenty-four hours. And only the night before last he had been telling her that he loved her, and kissing her good-by! He felt ashamed of himself. He felt ashamed because he felt that he was not being true to the love he professed for her—in his thoughts and in the pleasure which he found in the presence of Maude Knox.... He *was* in love with Andree, but—confound it all!—was it possible he could be falling in love with Maude Knox, too? He had heard that people and books asserted a man could be in love with two women at once.... If this were so, he said to himself, it would create a devilish unpleasant situation ... and a situation not without an element to cause laughter. If a man loved two girls, he would have to choose one of them. In which case he would be, at the same instant, in a state of bliss because he had won a sweetheart and in a state of heartbreak because he had been thwarted in love!...

"I wish you could know Andree," he said. "She—she's educating me, I guess. I don't understand her, of course. She is constantly startling me. I never knew anybody who in the least resembled her."

"Of course not.... She's French. She's a war-time Parisienne."

"But she's good," said Kendall, as if Maude had brought some charge against Andree.

"Why not?" Maude smiled a trifle.

"You mustn't think—" he began.

"I'm thinking nothing. It's none of my business." She paused. "Frankly, I don't care.... Now don't misunderstand that. I like you, Kendall. I'm interested in you. There was a time when, if I suspected of a man what you seem to think I suspect of you, I would have cut him in a hurry.... And the girl—I would have been horrified.... But now—I don't quite understand myself—I wouldn't in the least object to knowing your Andree."

"But I tell you—"

"Of course you do—and I don't believe you. So there!"

Kendall was embarrassed and a trifle angry. "I don't see why you should suspect anything—just because Andree is French!"

"And because you are American? And because lots of things?" She shrugged her shoulders.

"Would you marry a man you knew had been having an—an affair with a girl like Andree?"

"It would depend. There are affairs and affairs.... Somehow I don't think I should marry a man who had an affair with an American woman, one of these squalid, scandalous things we hear about in New York or Detroit.... But in war conditions—with a girl like Andree, as you say, why, if I loved the man of course I would marry him.... I think I would—if I loved him."

"Where is the difference?"

"I don't know.... It gets back to a sin being a sin because you think it is. It's a feeling. I've seen these women in France, women I knew were having affairs, and they were sweet and modest—and natural. An American woman can't seem to have an affair and still be sweet and modest—and natural. She feels she is doing something wicked and degrading, and consequently is degraded. She is being deliberately bad.... Don't you see?"

"I—I think so.... There's something. I have the same notion about it as you, but I couldn't explain it. I guess you're right.... Do you think a man can be in love with two girls at once?" He asked the question suddenly.

She laughed joyously. "Now, you aren't going to tell me you are in love with me, too?... Please don't. I suppose a lot of these boys will fancy they're in love with me just because I happen to be moderately neat and clean and good-looking and because I'm out here alone like this.... I'll stand to them for their sweethearts back home, and all that, but they won't be in love with me in the least—and neither are you."

This frankness was truly American, modern American. Kendall could not imagine Andree saying or thinking such things; he could not imagine his mother saying or thinking such things. And why? To Andree love was love—the great business of life. Everything else was subordinate to it. To his mother love was—was just a little bit off color, because there was sex in it. His mother could love her son frankly, but she could not love her husband frankly nor talk with frankness about it.... Original sin clung to love in her mind. It was the thing that had cast man out of Paradise, and while one married and bore children, and marital relations were necessary, nevertheless there was something squalid and indecent about them. Andree saw nothing indecent in sex, as she saw nothing indecent in eating her dinner.... Maude Knox was more like Andree than like his mother, but even there there was a vast difference. There was the difference of race and of racial philosophy.

Maude placed her hand on Kendall's arm. "Be nice to that little girl," she said. "Don't hurt her.... Be fair."

"What do you mean?... Do you mean I should marry her?"

She hesitated. "I don't know.... Marriage!..."

Her own inherited prejudices were lifting their heads now. Marriage!... Marriage with a French girl with whom one was having relations! That was different. She hesitated and did not give him a frank answer.

"Well?" he said.

"You mustn't ask me.... I can't answer that. It is a thing you'll have to decide."

"I guess you have answered," he said, gloomily.

"Perhaps—and perhaps I'm ashamed of myself for answering so.... But I was born in America and brought up in a surrounding of sewing-circles."

There was a pause. Then he said, almost as if to himself, "You're the sort of girl I'd like to be in love with."

"That's a very nice thing to say—but you're not."

"I don't know.... I'm not sure. I could be very easily if I were to see much of you."

"And Andree?..."

He was really depressed, worried, and she perceived it with genuine sympathy. She saw that this young man was facing a problem whose correct solution would be vital to his happiness and to his future peace of mind. She was able to realize that he was approaching one of those climaxes of the soul which are infinitely more trying and infinitely more potent to modify than could any climax in which the physical predominated. She fancied she knew Kendall rather well and understood him. She fancied he was not complex, but rather simple and straightforward—just a young man—but she was wrong. There were such elements of complexity in him as made for the sharpest of suffering, which would have defied the analysis of the most expert psychologist. She did not perceive the overwhelming importance of his inheritances from mother and father, those beliefs and those sensations and those reactions which were almost a physical part of him as his arms and legs were a physical part of him. She could not know that his body was in constant use as an arena in which Puritanism and dogmas and blind faiths and intolerances of the unknown were battling with that mild toleration derived from his father, that desire to see good in everything, that sweetness which held fast to its faith in mankind, even when it could not understand what mankind was about.... Nor could she know that Kendall himself stood between these adversaries with a mind better equipped than either to see and to appraise, striving with a great hunger for the right, to be modified by the adversaries only as it was right to be modified by them. Youth and the desires of youth for life and pleasure and the knowledge that comes by experiencing was also there with its immature carelessness of consequences.... There was no simplicity here, rather such a complexity as seemed destined to defy solution and to make a decent peace of the soul a thing possible to attain....

A young captain ran down the bank to meet them. "You are Miss Knox?" he asked, cordially.

"Yes."

"I'm Captain Morris, A.P.M. here—and I'm mighty glad to see you. You don't mean you're really going to stay?"

"Really."

"*No!*... By Jove!... Say!..." He was inarticulate, but there was no doubting of his delight.

"Captain Ware—Captain Morris," said Maude, and the two young men shook hands.

"I've got some business with you," Kendall said, "as soon as we can get Miss Ware settled."

"What do you want? What do you need?..." This to Maude: "I'll give you details of men till the cows come home. Just ask for it, and—if it's in this sector—we'll get it for you.... By Jove!... Think of it! Going to stay!... Oh, say!"

Maude laughed. "You'll have me thinking I'm doing something unusual in a minute."

"Unusual! Miss Knox, if you knew what it will mean to these boys to have an American girl here—just to know she's around! It's wonderful, that's what it is! Do you realize that some of the men haven't seen an American woman in a year—haven't talked to a woman?... By Jove!..." Every time he thought about it he became boyishly inarticulate again.

"They're fixing up my canteen for me," she said.

"Good! I'll run up and see they do it right."

"I—I wouldn't, if I were you," said Maude, gently. "They seem to like it—to want to do it themselves. They shooed me away. Don't you think it would be better to let them go ahead by themselves—if it pleases them?"

Kendall was conscious of a pride in her, in her understanding and her beautiful tact. So was Captain Morris, who could only stare at her unbelievingly and utter, "By Jove!..."

In half an hour they three walked back to the canteen.

"Here she comes!" yelled a boy in the door, and a sergeant with a smudge on his nose, his sleeves rolled up, and a hammer in his hand, poked his nose out of the door.

"Shoo her off ag'in," he said, in a rumble that was distinctly audible, though not intended for Maude's ears. "We hain't done yet."

Maude turned away with a laugh. "I guess we'd better walk some more. If you men are busy I can look after myself."

"Busy!..." exclaimed Captain Morris. "By Jove!" And they all laughed, even the captain, who had a faint perception of his own state of mind.

In another half-hour they returned again to the little cottage. This time a dozen boys were standing about with a great pretense of carelessness, but with an embarrassed eagerness which set her eyes to twinkling.

"May I go in now?" she asked.

"Yes, ma'am.... You bet!"

They crowded in after her to watch her every movement and expression and to assure themselves that they had pleased her. There was a serviceable counter. Behind it were rough shelves for her wares. The stove was set up, and such utensils as she possessed hung precisely on nails. There was a comfortable chair, rather dilapidated, but foraged at some expense of trouble.... And the cleanliness of the place was nothing short of amazing. It had been swept and dusted and scoured until not a trace of its former filth remained.

"Oh, boys," said Maude, after a moment's silence, "isn't it fine!... Haven't you made a nice place of it! I wouldn't have thought it was possible.... And the counter and shelving!... I don't know how to thank you."

The soldiers were in a dreadful state of embarrassment, blushing and giggling and nudging one another like schoolboys detected in a prank. They seemed to have a feeling that something ought to be said, for they kept jostling and pushing the sergeant, who growled back at them, savagely. "Lemme be, doggone you!" Maude heard him mutter. But they pushed him out into consciousness. "Go on, Hank.... Open up. Git it off your chest," he was abjured.

Hank scowled terribly at Maude, opened his mouth and closed it again, hunched his broad shoulders and felt of his prominent Adam's apple. "Aw—" he began, and then, "Aw—hell!..." With which well-chosen remark he burst through his comrades and fled headlong.

Maude again did the one tactful thing, the one thing that, in those circumstances, not only saved the face of the vanished Hank, but raised her to an elevation in the minds of the soldiers from which she would never descend.... She simply sat down on that scoured floor and laughed and laughed until her cheeks were wet with tears of mirth. So infectious was her laugh that there was not a man but laughed with her.

"By Jove!..." exclaimed Captain Morris. "She's a wonder."

"She is," said Kendall, soberly.

Maude looked up at them. "You officers go away," she said, severely. "I'm going to be very busy.... No, you boys needn't go—just the officers...."

"I may come back to say good-by?" Kendall asked. "I'll be leaving in an hour."

"Of course."

When Kendall finished his business with the Assistant Provost Marshal he returned to the canteen.

"I'm going," he said from the door.

Maude issued from behind her counter and made her way through a knot of soldiers who had crowded about it.

"Good-by," she said, extending her hand. "It's been nice to see you."

"It—it has been wonderful to see you," he said. "I don't think I shall ever forget this." He waved his hand around the room. "It isn't possible." He smiled whimsically. "I know I'm dreaming the whole thing. You're really back in Ohio somewhere, probably playing bridge."

"Not bridge—I don't like bridge. Tennis, maybe."

"And I'm going to wake up in a little while and tell folks what a queer dream I've had."

She pinched herself. "See, I'm awake—and you don't know how glad I am that I am awake—that I am here, seeing this, being a part of this...."

"But it isn't done, you know. There's nothing in the rules to cover it.... No, Miss Knox, I'm dreaming it—and I'm glad I am dreaming it. If it were real—" His face grew serious.

"Perhaps," she said, "this is the first time you've ever seen anything real ... since you came to France. That is it.... France is real, the war is real, Andree is real, I am real.... The only things that aren't real are the habits and thoughts we were busy with sixty days ago.... Sixty days!..."

"Good-by—and don't forget me."

"I sha'n't do that. I like you.... Good-by."

Kendall leaned far back in his car and smoked and found his thoughts disturbing company. He was not used to facing questions of big importance, but he saw now that for weeks he had been drifting toward a day when he would have to meet and reply to the first soul-modifying question that had ever been propounded to him.... The thing was inevitable. He was moving toward facts that could not be brushed aside.... Strangely enough, though he was heavy with apprehension, nevertheless there was a certain exultation.... This was living—living not in a circumscribed area, but in the unbounded world. This was *life*—this was *experience*—something big, worthy of the consideration of a man. There were happiness and misery in it.... He was beginning to see that he could not win through with happiness intact; it was his hope to win through with happiness preponderant.... The day he landed in France he had been a boy; less than two months had passed—and he had become a man.... France had done that for him.

CHAPTER XII

On the fourth evening after his departure from Paris Captain Ware stood at the entrance to the Metro on the Place de la Concorde, just across the road from the headquarters of the American Red Cross, waiting for Andree. At his left the Obelisk arose like a great needle; he could see the Metz and Strasburg statues green with wreaths, and beyond other pieces of sculpture deemed of sufficient artistic value to protect with sandbags from the menace of German bombs. Somehow this made him feel that he had not seen Paris, that it would be necessary for him to come back again when the base of the Vendôme Column should not be concealed by sand and concrete, when the carvings on the Arc de Triomphe should not be hidden under scaffoldings and stacked sandbags, when the once despised and criticized statue at the extreme right of the face of the Opéra—now the single piece of sculpture of all that adorned the building considered worth careful protection—should be exposed to view.

There was an analogy between the hooded statues and the spirit of the city. He wanted to see both when they were as they had been before August, 1914. He wanted to see Paris when it was gay, beautiful, carefree, buoyant, volatile. How much more it would mean to see it so after having seen it as it was now.... Just across from him was a wall upon which was a poster exclaiming, "*Abri, 40 places.*" He wanted to see Paris without that fear riding its shoulders. He wanted to see it when every fourth or fifth shop had not its shutters down in permanence, explained by a sign which gave notice that the closing was by reason of the mobilization.... And yet it was beautiful, compellingly beautiful. Suddenly the certainty came upon him that a people whose genius could have created such a city could not be *wrong*. He had been told that the genius of the French was rotten at the core, its morals corrupt. He knew in this moment that it was a lie.... Such a city could not have been produced by a people who were decadent, who were not of the greatest, the worthiest of the earth....

In a moment Andree appeared, in a flimsy dress of light material this time, a dress that came just to her shoe-tops. It made her look even slenderer than he had remembered her to be, and more childish.... He waited for her to speak. She approached almost to his side before she seemed to see him, then she raised her eyes quickly, searchingly, to his face and let them fall again. But he had read anxiety and relief in that flickering glance. She shook hands, giving him a trusting little pressure of her fingers.

"You see," he said, "I promised to come back safe. The *boches* didn't get me."

"It is ver' well. If the *boches* keel you I am ver' angry—me."

"Have you been lonely for me?"

"Oh!..." she said, and raised her eyes again for an instant. "And you— do you think of me? But, no. You have been *très-occupé*—ver' busy.... And you have seen other girls."

She asked no questions about the front, showed no desire to hear about the affairs of war. Poor child! Like the great multitude of her sisters, she was tired of war, bored with war. In her mind was only one question about the war—when would it end?

"Bert and Madeleine are going to dine with us," he said.

"That is well.... Monsieur Bert—is he well? And Madeleine? Have you seen her?"

"No."

"That high yo'ng man!" she said, and laughed. "Oh, it is not nice for you to make fon of me. High.... Tall.... How shall one tell them apart?"

"Don't try," Kendall said. Then he laughed at his recollections of her blunders in a strange language. "At what hour do you lift up?" he mimicked her.

"I have study English since you have gone away. I know that now. It is not *lift up*; it is raise up. At what hour do you raise up in the morning. *N'est-ce pas?*"

"You *have* studied!" he exclaimed. "I'm proud of you. But you speak English better than I do now."

"Better than you do French," she said, with a little grimace.

"What have you been doing while I was away?" he asked, and asked because he was really curious. He wanted to know something about her life away from him, about her regular routine life. To him now she was a creature that appeared as out of a fog, to disappear again into a fog, untraceable, strange, mysterious. She must do something. She must have a family. She must live in a house and sleep in a bed and take her meals at a table. It must be that she had her friends and her little every-day affairs, different, perhaps, from the every-day affairs of the American girl, but nevertheless taking up the greater part of her life.... He wished he could have the history of one of her days from waking to sleeping, could be present to oversee one of her days.

"I have been lonely," she said. So she always answered, and, it seemed to him, not from any conscious effort to hide her life from him, but rather because when she was with him it was her belief that nothing was of interest to them but each other. It was as if she wanted to shut all the rest of the world out, forget all the world and its business, and remember only themselves and their little moments of happiness together. No, it was not concealment, it was the exclusiveness of love. "I—many times—I thought you would not come.... And I was sad." She pressed his arm gently.

They boarded the red car—first class—of the Metro, and it started its rather leisurely journey westward under the Place de la Concorde and the Champs Élysées. Kendall always insisted on riding first class on the subway, though Andree urged it was a scandalous waste of money. One could ride as comfortably second class, or, if the trip were very short, the saving by taking third class was worth one's while. The car was crowded—women, a few old men in civilian clothes, *poilus*, officers (one with four medals on his breast), Belgians with little gold tassels dangling from the fronts of their caps, two English soldiers in an advanced state of intoxication who recognized Kendall as belonging to a kindred race and shouted joyously to him from afar.

"Hey, matey, does this 'ere car git us to the Gare St.-Nizaire?"

Kendall shook his head.

"Needn't be so dam' close-mouthed. Speak up like you was a officer and a gen'lman! 'Urrah for America, says I. 'Ear me, Jock? Wi' a will, Jock.... 'Urrah for America."

With enthusiasm they cheered for their newest ally, while Kendall blushed with the embarrassment of finding himself thus elevated to a place of prominence. The car laughed joyfully and in sympathy with the Britishers. Andree looked up into Kendall's face and, finding it forbidding, pressed his arm and smiled.

"*Beaucoup* de zigzag," she said, philosophically, as if that explained all and excused all.

It was not until they alighted at the Étoile that Kendall was rid of the attentions of his friends, and even there one of them leaned out of the front door as Ken descended from the rear and shouted: "Give me love to your lidy friend, ol' top.... 'Urrah for President Wilson...."

Kendall did not regain his equanimity until they were nearing the apartment; it was the more difficult to regain because he had a feeling that Andree was laughing at him a bit, notwithstanding her grave face. He felt, somehow, that the necessity for maintaining dignity at all times—a foible of American youth—was not to be understood by Andree, and fell under that category of actions which she described as "*C'est drôle.*"

Madame the *concierge* greeted them with affability; the big glass door slammed behind them as it always did when Kendall forgot to hold it carefully, and the sound of its slamming echoed hollowly up the stairs.

At the first floor Andree paused and clung to the banister. "Oh, you must have—what you call—?" She made a lifting motion with her hands.

"An elevator?"

"Yes, yes.... Now. At once. Go. Run quickly and fetch an elevator. I shall stay here."

He made pretense of lifting her in his arms.

"No.... No.... I must have an elevator. Oh, you do not get me an elevator." There was awful despair in her voice. "You do not love me.... No.... Then I shall go away. You are not kind."

"I'll get you two elevators. I'll get you half a dozen, but the elevator-store is closed for the night. You'll have to wait till morning."

"Oh, I do not onderstan'. You speak *trop vite*—much fast. So I shall ron away from you...." And she danced away from him up the stairs, not at all like a young woman, but wholly like a child, with the glee of a child. "Behol'!" she cried, presently. "The *clef* it is under the mat. I find it. I know where it is hidden. Now I shall come by night and rob you.... I shall carry away everything—everything."

She handed him the huge key and he opened the door for her and allowed her to pass into the narrow hall. She stopped timidly, waiting for him to enter, peering about as if some danger might lurk behind any of the doors. She was very sweet, very dainty....

"*Mignonne*," he said, and took both her hands—and then she was in his arms, her lips to his ... and he knew that he loved her, that she had charmed his heart into her keeping—and that he was very glad to have it there.

"You love me?" she whispered.

"Much.... Much.... And you?"

"Oh yes.... I am not *solitaire* now. *Je suis très-joyeuse.*"

"You must always be glad. You must always be happy."

"As long as you love me."

"I shall always love you."

"*Non!... Non!...* It ees not possible. In a day, in a week—I do not know when—you will go away, and I will be sad."

"I don't know when I shall have to go, nor where I shall have to go.... It is the war.... But whenever and wherever, I shall love you."

"It is well—but—but I do not believe you.... Oh, life it is not well! It is our *besoin*—our need—to find many little minutes. That is the best of life. I know.... Much sadness, much loneliness ... but now and then the little minutes of happiness."

He was hanging her tam-o'-shanter on the hall tree, then he led her into the *salon* with its bronze statues and its gilded furniture, at which she did not wrinkle her nose this time, for she was in serious mood.

"Are you always happy?" she asked.

"I'm not often unhappy."

"That is ver' well—yes.... It is not so well as to be happy, but it is better than to be sad.... Me, I am often sad."

"I'll put a stop to that. From now on you must be happy."

"Come—you must sit close to me—ver' close—so...." She had seated herself by the table and was looking at a magazine, a French periodical filled with pictures of young women in one-piece bathing-suits. "They are ver' beautiful," she said, slipping her arm about his neck and pressing her cheek to his. "I should like to be beautiful—yes. That would be well."

"*Vous étes très-jolie,*" he protested.

She laughed. "No, but I like you to tell me.... You theenk I am pretty?"

"You bet I do."

"It is well. Then for you I am pretty, and I am glad.... Also I am ver' nice, and ver' wise, n'est-ce pas?"

"You are the cunningest little person that ever lived."

"Hush!... There is some one. Listen."

"Bert and Madeleine," he said, as he heard a key fumbling in the door.

"Then I mus' be ver' *sérieuse*—so." She sat erect, very primly, her hands folded in her lap—a very image of gravity and circumspection. Presently Bert and Madeleine entered the room. The girls shook hands gravely and exchanged a few words. Then Madeleine shook hands with Kendall and Bert with Andree. Everybody must shake hands before matters could proceed. Once disposed of, formality relaxed; the girls chattered in French, Madeleine with laughing vivacity and many gestures, Andree rather as if she were a bit embarrassed, always searching Madeleine with her eyes as she studied every new-comer into her acquaintance. Her eyes were always studying, studying, but she never disclosed what they told her.

Arlette opened the door of the dining-room very softly and allowed her head to project into the room. She did so very discreetly and silently, as if she were afraid of being detected in the act of announcing dinner. She uttered no word, but allowed her head to remain, round and big-eyed, until it should be seen—like the sign of a restaurant making its silent announcement. Kendall caught her eye, and in a twinkling she disappeared with comical haste—a pudgy jack-in-a-box.

"Dinner is served," Kendall said, "and I'm hungry."

A fine, thick soup steamed in a huge bowl in the middle of the table, and Arlette watched with big-eyed anxiety while Bert served it. Before any one could taste a spoonful her impatience overcame her; she could contain herself no longer.

"It is pea soup," she said, explosively.

Madeleine laughed, showing her fine white teeth. "It is very good," she said in French.

"Monsieur Kendall does not like," exclaimed Arlette, in heartrending accents as she perceived that Ken did not at once address himself to the *potage*, but sat regarding Andree, forgetful of everything else.

"Oh yes, he does," said Bert, "but Monsieur Kendall is in love. Presently if he does not eat I shall feed him.... Arlette," he demanded, severely, "are you in love with some young man?"

"Ho!..." she exclaimed, and, overcome with embarrassed giggles, scurried out of the room.

"*C'est drôle*," said Andree, judgmatically.

"Is red wine or white wine desired?" Arlette asked from the door.

"Suppose we try a bottle of that Anjou Rose," said Ken. "I like the color of it."

"Anjou!" exclaimed Madeleine. "Ah, that is my country. I am born there.... The wine of Anjou it is ver' well.... I shall go soon to visit in that country—to, if possible, sell a house. Yes. Oh, it is mos' beautiful."

Andree regarded her speculatively, gravely.

"Before the war my father owns the store of the shoes there. There is a yo'ng man work in thees store, and I am ver' yo'ng. I do not know theengs. *Mais non*. I am marry thees yo'ng man, but he ees no good—him. My father die, my mother die, and I am *orpheline*. It ees ver' bad for me, bicause my *oncle* and thees yo'ng man they take away the store of the shoes and I have not'ing only thees house. It ees so. Thees yo'ng man he ees ver' bad; he is not *fidèle*; also he is mos' unkind. Then he go to the war, and I never see him since. I theenk he is dead.... It ees ver' well. But my oncle he lives—but I have not'ing. It is ver' necessary I mus' eat, so I come to Paris and work in the store of the shoes.... Now, ver' soon I go to my country for sell thees house and to have a leetle money." She shrugged her shoulders and laughed. "I do not cry—no, I laugh. Much time I laugh, bicause why not? It is ver' *nécessaire* to laugh and be happy. Is it not so, my Bert?"

"Laugh all you like, my dear."

Andree raised her eyes to Madeleine's face. "Oh, it ees too bad," she said. "Thees husban' and thees *oncle* they are ver' wicked."

Thus encouraged, Madeleine amplified her autobiography in an avalanche of headlong French, while Andree listened unsmilingly and nodded her head now and then, or waggled it a trifle in sympathy or condemnation of some related atrocity.

"You see," she said to Kendall, "no one is happy. It is so. Life it is not nice—for yo'ng girls."

"One mus' theenk not about the sad theengs," said Madeleine, sententiously. "One mus' be happy. That ees best. Me—I take what comes.... See, I am ver' ol'. *Oui*.... I am twenty-four. So ol' am I that no man ever want to marry me.... *Tiens!* I am *passée*. But still I laugh.... I love Monsieur Bert, and

I am happy. One day Monsieur Bert love me no more...." She shrugged her shoulders. "Then I am sad for leetle w'ile.... But another yo'ng man he will love me, perhaps. It ees so. What would you?... If one does not love and is not loved, then there is no happiness, *n'est-ce pas?*..."

Andree nodded. "When there is no love it is terrible," she said.

Bert laughed and looked at Kendall. "Aha!" he said. "But, mademoiselle, Ken says you and he do not love each other—that you are just *camarades*...."

"It was so," she said, "but now"—she looked at Kendall gravely—"it is so no longer. No.... We love."

"I said to you," Madeleine addressed Kendall, "that French girls are not cold. Did I not?"

"But—" Kendall began to expostulate and to explain.

But Madeleine would have none of it. "You are ver' *sérieux*, monsieur. Doubtless you are also *un religieux!*"

"*Religieux?* What is that?"

"She means in English a monk," said Andree, her eyes twinkling. "To wear a brown robe—*oui!*—and also bare feet and sandals."

"It must be." Madeleine laughed delightedly. "For heem to look at a yo'ng girl ees a sin.... See!... See!... He makes to blush. Regard his ear!..."

Andree laughed quietly, meantime studying Kendall's face with kindly, twinkling eye. She did not deride him, but one could see that she loved to tease him—this incomprehensible foreigner who was so *drôle!*

Kendall laughed, too, a bit ruefully, but while he laughed he was thinking, fumbling for Madeleine's point of view. It was clear to him that the man who was not eager for love could be no man at all—but a monk. It was the only possible explanation. Love was for men and women; continence was for monks. Well, then? To love might be a sin for a monk, but even on this point she doubtless was lenient; for a man not to love was a sin. He was not realizing his duty to achieve happiness. Love was love. It was good. It carried no burden of evil.

"The good God—He make the yo'ng man and the yo'ng girl, and He tell them to love.... It is true. Then one must obey the good God," she said, seriously.

Here was rather a new religion to Kendall, but, somehow, it did not seem absurd, nor did her utterance of it touch upon the sacrilegious. She made the statement simply, out of her heart, with simple belief.... He turned to Andree.

"Is that what you think?" he asked.

"Of a certainty—or why did the good God create men and women and love?... I theenk God is happy when He sees a yo'ng man and a yo'ng girl who love each other much."

"Some philosophy!" said Bert. "I'm for it."

"But the love—it ees *nécessaire*...."

"By Jove!..." Kendall exclaimed. "My dear, you're a nice child.... Bert, she's *good*! Get that? *Good!*... Maybe she's right, and we're all wrong.... Morals are a devil of a mix-up. They're beyond me.... But I know this, and nobody can argue me out of it—these girls are *good*."

He spoke in English and rapidly. Neither girl could follow him.

Bert laughed. "You take it mighty seriously. What's the matter with you, anyhow?"

"Nothing's the matter.... But a fellow can think. It's a big question. We've been taught one way—these girls have been taught, or have learned and seen, another way.... Who is right and who is wrong?..."

"Fiddlesticks!" said Bert. "Why worry about it? We're having the time of our young lives."

"They're good," Kendall repeated to himself.

"Who said they weren't?"

"All of America.... All the world that we know. And it must be wrong—it must be."

"Suits me—it's wrong, then."

"But—but the way America thinks is right in America. That's what I can't understand. Right is right there, and what America thinks is wrong seems to be right over here...."

"What do you speak?... Oh, you speak *trop vite*. I cannot onderstan'." Andree made a little face of distress.

"I was saying that you are a dear child and I love you."

"It is ver' well." She stretched out her tiny hand and patted Kendall's hand.

Arlette entered with the meat, depositing it on the table and standing by with her usual apprehension. "It is beef," she said. "Perhaps it is tough!..."

"It is ver' well," said Andree.

Arlette sighed with relief and waggled her head.

"But the price, mademoiselle—I ask you to regard the price. One is frightened. It is so. For this so small piece of meat! But messieurs demand the meat. They spend much money, and I am alarmed. I shall be blamed. It is I who make the purchases.... Also the cheese ... and butter. *Mon Dieu!* The cost! It is frightful! It is because these American soldiers arrive in France with great wealth in their pockets and spend with the so great freedom that prices rise.... Oh yes. They do not care. They have no regard for money—and in consequence the poor must pay. Can nothing be done to prevent these Americans from making the prices to rise?"

"*C'est la guerre,*" said Madeleine.

"It is the Americans," said Arlette, dogmatically. "But one must admit they are generous and of a kindness. I regard messieurs highly. *Oui. Ils sont très-gentils.*"

"Arlette likes you much," said Andree. "I theenk she fall in love weeth you, and I am jealous—oh, so jealous. You shall send her away. I will not have her. She is bad—bad. She take you away from me." And then she laughed low, with a charm that found its way to Kendall's heart. She was so cunning, so full of little humors and tricks of manner, of moods and delightful graces—at one moment grave and wise, at the next playful and gay. One instant she was a woman made wise by sorrow, the next moment she was a child, untouched by anything but joy.... She was wonderful, thought Kendall, there was no one in the world to compare with her....

"We're going to the Casino de Paris to-night. Coming along?" asked Bert.

Kendall turned to Andree. "Shall we?"

"No. We shall stay here." She pointed downward at the floor with a gesture that was peculiarly her own. "I have not seen you for long.... We shall talk of many theengs."

"Keep your dictionary handy, Ken," jeered Bert. "There are lots of useful words in it.... Comme ça: You take the lady's hand. 'Mademoiselle, vous êtes—' Quick the dictionary! Find the first word that fits.... Here it is—look! '*Charmante.*' Fine! Thus we have a compliment with only a slight interruption. A compliment doesn't get cold like a dish of soup. It is still good even if we have to look in the dictionary twice. In the course of an evening we can get through a dozen sentences.... You shall talk of many theengs," he finished, mimicking Andree.

"Monsieur Bert—he does not need to speak," laughed Madeleine. "He is ver' fonny. *Écoutez!* He says, *'Je no' désirez de la potage.' Oui.* Always. One understands what he is about, but it is awful. But yes.... I cannot teach him. No. Past or present, number, person, it is all one for him. He jus' make words and expects one to understand.... But when he does not speak at all—then he does much better."

Arlette served the vegetable and the salad, and finally cheese and confiture. "*Abricot* for Mademoiselle Andree," she explained, remembering Andree's preference. Presently they went into the *salon* where the boys lighted cigarettes. Kendall tendered his case to Andree, who selected one and lighted it daintily.

"I thought you didn't smoke," he said, with surprise.

"Only in the house. Nevaire outside," she said.

Madeleine did not smoke at all. Madeleine began to walk about the room and sing "Madelon," while Andree looked out of the window and speculated on the characters and peculiarities of the occupants of the apartments across the avenue.

The four turned toward the door upon hearing a shuffling and a subdued giggling in the hall. It was Arlette and little Arlette. The child hung back bashfully, while her grandmother shooed her ahead with her apron.

"I have brought her to see Mademoiselle Madeleine," she said. "I have told her, and she desires to see."

The child had seen Andree, but it was necessary that she become acquainted with the entire family, it seemed. It was another shock for Kendall—the idea that fat, respectable, motherly Arlette should take delight in bringing this baby to make the acquaintance of Madeleine!... It was impossible. In America grandmothers would have shut their grandchildren in locked rooms to prevent any contact with a girl about whom they had the knowledge Arlette possessed of Madeleine.... Why, Arlette had gotten breakfast for Madeleine in that apartment! Yet she brought the baby to see her, and fairly wriggled with delight when Madeleine caught little Arlette up in her arms and kissed her and called her endearing names. The old woman could scarcely contain her pride and delight when Madeleine turned to tell her how pretty the child was!... It was bewildering.

"You must sing," Madeleine said to Arlette. "I know you can sing many songs. Oh, I have heard. See. Stand you so, and sing."

So little Arlette stood erect and lifted her little chin without embarrassment and sang, while her grandmother, in the door, waggled her head and kept time by a ponderous swaying of her body.... Little Arlette ran to Kendall, always her favorite, and crawled between him and Andree, who had seated herself beside him. She insinuated her arm about his neck and pressed her cheek to his, while she intrusted a hand to Andree to be held.

"*Mignonne!*" said Andree, tremulously.

"Good efening, sirr," said little Arlette, suddenly, and her grandmother giggled in the very great pride of hearing this English spoken.

"Aha!" said Kendall, "you study English.... She is getting ready to go back to America with me. Yes, indeed. I have asked for her hand. We are sweethearts, aren't we, Arlette?"

"Yes, monsieur," she said, very seriously.

"You love me very much?"

"Yes, monsieur."

"You learn to cook and to sew and all the things a wife should know?"

"Yes, monsieur.... When shall we go to this America? Is it America of the North or of the South?"

"Of the North, *petite*...."

"Oh, my uncle was once in America of the South."

"It is not quite the same. But it is just as nice. Really. Shall we take grandma with us when we go?"

"If monsieur desires."

She was very serious and grown-up in her manner; even then there was something feminine, something of the woman in her, for she turned her face toward Andree with eyes that seemed to say: "You see. He is mine. It is no use for you to try to steal him from me."

Andree made pretense to draw away from her and to cry. "You are ver' naughty," she said from between her fingers. "You steal away my sweetheart. Oh, what shall I do?... What shall I do?"

Little Arlette smiled out of a great satisfaction at this discomfiture of a rival, and openly kissed Kendall.

"Now, come," called Arlette. "You must not bother monsieur. Say good night."

So little Arlette shook hands all around, and backed out of the door, throwing kisses and waving her tiny hand, a dainty little fairy, a very breath of sweetness and purity.... And her grandmother had not thought it amiss to bring her to see Madeleine—for whom she had gotten breakfast....

"If we're going to the Casino—" said Bert to Madeleine, and got to his feet. "Sure you won't come?" he said to Andree.

"*Merci*," said Andree, positively.

"See you later, then.... Good night."

In a moment the door closed behind Bert, and Madeleine and Kendall were alone with Andree.... Somehow he had never felt the sensation of being alone with her as he felt it now. On other occasions he had been alone merely with a girl he knew, was somewhat interested in; now he was alone with Andree, whom he loved, who loved him.... He was alone with her as a man would be alone with his wife in his home. It was very sweet, wonderful, and yet he was disquieted. There were things he did not understand. Chief of all he did not know what Andree was thinking, what she was intending. Second in importance, he did not know what he himself was intending.... He put the thought away from him, even though he realized that their relations had reached some sort of climax.... He would allow that climax to approach unurged. When it arrived he would meet it....

"The sun puts itself to bed," Andree said, using the French locution.

"I'll light the lights," he replied, and, walking to the windows, closed the heavy iron shutters and drew the curtains as the law required him to do before he illuminated the room. He was glad of something to do to cover the awkwardness he felt in those first moments.

"Sit by me," she said, softly.

She was not embarrassed, was, indeed, perfectly normal, unexcited, at ease; her manner was very gentle, very sweet. Her every look, every gesture, seemed to declare her love and her joy in his love. There was a quiet assurance in her manner; the sure trace of present happiness which would not tolerate a shadow on this night.... She was her own self, dainty, genuine, wonderfully appealing. It seemed as if she had lived all her life for this moment so that she could unfold under the touch of the marvel of love and become wholly admirable.... She was beautiful, as was fitting, beautiful with the loveliness that can come only from a soul not warring with the laws of God. Untroubled by doubt or question, she reassured him, gave him renewed confidence in her goodness, her rightness, her purity.... Her moment of happiness had come to her, and she looked into the brightness of it with unwavering eyes that saw nothing to fear, nothing to conceal—saw only love.

He sat beside her and she nestled close to him, touching his hand, lifting her deep-shadowed eyes to his—and then she smiled.

"*Mignonne!*" he whispered, tenderly.

"Tell me," she said. "Say it—quickly."

"I love you," he responded, and she sighed softly, closing her eyes, and was silent. So still was she that he might have fancied her asleep but for the pressure of her fingers upon his own. After a time she spoke again:

"It *is* well—ver' well—to love."

"Yes.... But—you are not afraid. Do you remember the last time you were here you cried? You were afraid."

"I have not fear—no. Then I cried because I was not certain.... I was making up my mind. I have made up my mind, and so I have no fear.... Oh, I was ver' *solitaire*.... But we mus' not theenk of that now—only of ourselves. Is it not?... And be happy. We must be ver' happy—every little second we must be happy ... while it lasts."

"While it lasts? What do you mean?"

"Nothing. We mus' speak of that—not at all. We mus' speak only of love and happiness—and of how sweet is the world and to be alive—together."

"It *is* sweet," he said, unevenly, moved as he had never been moved before. "You are sweet ... and *good*."

Doubt, self-accusations, uneasiness, inhibitions, were swept from him by a flood of tenderness. The world was right; Andree was right; love was right. Nothing mattered but Andree and himself. It was their universe, of which they were masters, with none to forbid. Happiness was their right; it might not be denied them. The future was the future, but to-night was to-night, and little moments of happiness were the gift of Heaven....

"You love me?" he demanded.

"I am here," she said, simply.

His arms were about her, her lips were upon his lips; he knew his own moment of happiness. "You are here ..." he whispered. "You are here...."

CHAPTER XIII

Kendall Ware had set foot on the French liner bound for France early in May; he had landed at Bordeaux, May 19th. It was now the last of June. Less than two months had passed over his head, but the Kendall Ware who paced the Avenue du Bois de Boulogne this evening was years removed from the boy who walked the decks of the *Rochambeau* with Maude Knox. He was altered as only years of experience could have altered him in the times when men went about their business after the manner of rational human beings, when death was not a profession which engaged the world, when the dollar was the measure of success, when one day was like another, and meat could be eaten seven days in the week. The great modification in him was that he had learned it to be true that man is a thinking animal and that the brain may be used for something besides adding a column of figures or as a storage-house for the thoughts of a past generation. He had perceived that different theories of life existed in the world. He had been seized by events and forcibly fed with something which might crystallize into knowledge, and he had arrived at that unpleasant junction in the railroad system of life where he must choose between trains—whether he would board the one which went ahead swiftly through the Country of Responsible Individual Thought or the one which lagged backward through the Land of Swallowed Dogmas.... He was not happy.

He was making another discovery—namely, that one can theorize very comfortably, but that when one transmutes theory into accomplished fact, theory has become practice, and speculations upon its results may be exceedingly unpleasant. Within the last twenty-four hours Kendall had translated one theory into a fact, and another fact had arrived, needing no transmutation. The theory was the little-moment-of-happiness theory, and the fact was a letter from his mother.

That morning after he had left Andree he was rather disappointed to find that he suffered no remorse, experienced no sense of having done what he should have left undone. Andree was Andree, sweet, good, lovable. Because she was so, and because of his certainty of her cleanness of soul, he felt no sense of degradation or of having transgressed. He was even happy, rejoicing, boylike, in the sweetness of the gift of her love.... He found his mother's letter at the office and, having read it, his romance was smirched with sordidness, its beauty was dulled by the intrusion of harsh, unsparing, cold convention. The Middle West had intruded upon Paris, and he was discovering that there was much Middle West remaining alive in him.

His mother's letter had said, and he could visualize her face as she wrote, severe, unyielding, harsh, forbidding:

> I am sorry to hear that you are stationed in Paris. They say that Paris is a wicked city. Everybody says the French are loose and immoral, which makes me worry about all our young men who are thrown with them. Your letter says that Paris is beautiful. It is not a good beauty, I have heard. Some one told me there were statues of naked women all over in the parks. I cannot understand how they allow such things; they must be bad, passionate men to allow it. I hope you will be very careful. You are young, and sometimes you are like your father, who is easily taken in. I am glad you do not speak that language, because you cannot get acquainted with French people. Those women have no morals; they are nasty creatures who just want to get hold of every penny you get. Some day you will want to marry a nice, clean American girl, and you have got to think about that. I don't see why the war couldn't have been some place else. Don't ever look at one of them. They're all atheists and that accounts for it....

There was more to the same effect. It reflected his mother perfectly, and the sentiments of the people among whom his mother lived; it represented, in extreme terms, the sentiment of his home community.... And over against it all stood Andree! That such words should be used to apply to her was sacrilege!... Yet ... yet ... she was—no matter what he might argue in her favor—in the language of his people, Andree was not an honest woman....

The effect of the letter upon him, however, had been uncanny. While he read he was again in Detroit. His sensations were almost exactly those which he always felt as he entered the Presbyterian church with his father and mother—not as he sat down in the accustomed pew, but as he passed through the crowded little vestibule where bald, smug elders and bearded, smug deacons and severe-faced chairwomen of missionary boards held their court before the service, shaking hands with all who entered with that religious affability, that hushed and somber and severe welcome, which strove to counterfeit open-heartedness.... It was that vestibule, and not the church, not the sermon, not the hymns nor the songs, which personified Kendall's religion and what his religion meant.... He had grown up among those elders and deacons and chairwomen, and he knew them—in the church. It was incomprehensible to him that they could have any interests or activities outside the church. The practice of religion in that place seemed to him to be the sole occupations of their lives, and when he met one of them in the secular world of a week-day in the act of selling goods, or of handling money in a bank, or of anything else which savored of business and earning a living, Ken had the sort of feeling one has when he detects a person in something unusual and a bit discreditable. Why, those persons *were* the church!... And the thoughts of those persons were the thoughts of Kendall's home world, thoughts among which he had been raised from babyhood.... So, as he read, he was transported to that vestibule—and that vestibule's occupants smugly set the stain of guilt upon him and rolled eyes of horror at Andree.... He had been seeing Paris with something that approximated the eyes of Paris—now he was seeing it with the eyes of the vestibule of the Presbyterian church.

Before him stretched the magnificent avenue, crowded, as dusk descended, with pleasure-seeking Parisians: he regarded it—regarded it as a spectator, an utter outsider. It was as if he looked at the scene from a window in the Presbyterian church. The two worlds stood starkly facing each other, challenging each other—the civilization that was Paris and the civilization that had its expression in the occupants of the church vestibule. Kendall saw, with something very like to fear, that they could not be reconciled, that neither contained a starting-point which would lead to understanding of the other.... And yet he, springing from the one, felt that he understood both. He was drawn to the one while the other clung to him tenaciously.

It was not that his mother's letter made him feel guilt; it was rather that it made him feel as if he *ought* to be conscious of wrong-doing. He ought to feel wicked and degraded, but he could not, and the fact that he could not seemed in itself to convict him of sin.... It was only when he thought of Andree that any semblance of stability came upon his thinking. There could be no argument about Andree. He had studied her, known her, loved her— and she was good. No church vestibule, no dogmatic elder, not even his mother, should say Andree was anything but good. He got some happiness out of that thought; Andree was an oasis of safety for him. He was capable of distinguishing between evil and virtue, he thought, and he had studied Andree as he had never studied any other living being. From the first moment of their acquaintance he had not perceived in her one quality, one emotion, one tendency that was not sweet, womanly, kindly, lovable, springing from a heart of purity.... How could a girl, proved to his intelligence to be good, be otherwise than good? How was it that any act of hers might be brought into question? Why was he questioning *his* righteousness because of his relations with her when her righteousness because of her relations with him were not open to question? It was very confusing. Could two individuals share an act and one of them be good and the other bad because of it? That sounded like a violation of some natural law as, for instance, that two solids cannot occupy the same space at the same instant.... Or was he wholly wrong? Could his judgment of her and of Paris and of the whole French nation be mistaken?... It might even be that Paris was not beautiful, as he had seen it beautiful, or that the French nation was not really sturdy, glowing with virility, heroic, as its deeds had seemed to prove it to be, but squalid, decadent....

He began to walk rapidly, as was his custom when in mental difficulty, and as he walked he knew the keen discomfort of a soul in turmoil.... He tried not to think about it, to put it out of his mind, and to find pleasure in the evening and in the dusk-softened beauties of the city, but his mind would not obey. He had a sensation of being terribly awake, of the blinding glow as of a tremendously powerful white light inside his head. His thoughts seemed to function independently of him, and himself to be an audience present to observe and listen to their activities. There was something ghastly about it, something unreal....

He strode around the Arc de Triomphe and thence down the Champs Élysées until he reached the Palais des Beaux-Arts, and there he turned to his right, crossing the Pont Alexandre III, marvelously beautiful in the half-light. He did not pause to admire the river and the city's sky-line as he had so often done, but turned again, this time to his left, and followed the Quai d'Orsay, clinging to the bank of the Seine until he was opposite the Cité and in the familiar open space of the Place St.-Michel.

Again he turned and followed the broad boulevard up which he had walked again and again with Andree. Perhaps that was why he had come to the locality, drawn subconsciously into a region of such associations. Perhaps there had been hidden in some recess of his mind the hope that he might encounter her, and so feel her presence and sense her goodness and verify his judgment.

At the corner of the Boulevard St.-Michel and the equally broad rue Soufflot is a café whose tables and chairs crowded the sidewalk. It was still light enough to distinguish the crowd of people who patronized the place, sipping coffee from small goblets or drinking wine or that strange beverage kept in bottles which Paris believes to be lemonade.... He glanced carelessly at the café, then he stopped, peered again intently with a sudden up-leap of the pulse, for at a table near the end sat a girl in white, wearing a white tam-o'-shanter. This alone would not have halted Kendall, rather it would have urged him forward with eager haste, but the girl was not alone. A man occupied the chair at her side, bending over her with that eagerness which is not to be mistaken in a young man, that eagerness which apprises all the watching world that he is in the act of making love....

At the end of the café were a number of small potted trees reaching almost to the awning above. Kendall, unconscious that it was jealousy that dictated his movements, drew near cautiously to peer over the foliage at that adjacent table, to assure himself if it were Andree or not.... It was Andree, and her companion was Monsieur Robert, of the Comédie Française....

Quick suspicion is a natural result of the thing that the vestibule of the Presbyterian church, as Kendall knew it, stood for. Intolerance has for its favorite child Suspicion, Acute Suspicion, which convicts without trial and, if subsequent trial goes against it, asserts that the jury was tampered with. It was one of Kendall's inheritances. He had been raised under the influence of constant suspicion. He himself had been suspected; he was used to seeing the most trivial events suspected. His mother, for instance, knew instantly that any happening which came under her eye and about which she was not fully informed meant something bad. It was never the way of that body of society in which he had been brought up to think the best when a trifle of imagination would enable it to think the worst—and to-night Kendall was peculiarly under the influence of his inheritances.... He suspected. A natural jealousy deepened his suspicion. Monsieur Robert's profession deepened it further, and Andree's often stated ambition to become an actress carried it to more profound depths. Suspicion may own a specious logic: Andree declared it was necessary for her to undertake a stage career. To do so it was necessary to enter the *Académie*. To enter the *Académie* it was necessary to interest the influence of some actor of prominence, and she had more than once hoped for this intervention. Ken himself had introduced her to this Monsieur Robert with that end in view.... And Jacques, perhaps in jest, perhaps in earnest, had warned him to beware of Monsieur Robert, or that handsome young actor would steal Andree from him. Hence Robert must have that sort of reputation.... And, therefore, Robert was with Andree at this moment for that purpose.... Again, what more natural and logical than that Andree should be willing to purchase her career, and that, even at this very moment, the agreement was being made.... Or, perhaps, had been made before, and he had been deceived already! Undoubtedly that was it....

The part of him inherited from his mother was in complete control now; he was narrow, certain in suspicion, hard, willing to be cruel. All that was worst in Roundhead, Puritan, Pilgrim Father was apparent in him. He had seen, and, in the instant of seeing, the pendulum of his character had swung to the uppermost point of its arc on the side opposed to tolerance, a reasonable philosophy, and the wider things toward which he had been growing since he came to France....

"Mother was right," he said to himself, "they were all right. I've been fooled and I've been a fool.... And I thought she was *good!*... This damn, miserable country—if ever I can get out of it back to where decent people live...."

Almost exactly twenty-four hours ago he had held Andree in his arms, loving her and believing in her love. He remembered it, recalled the sweetness of last evening, Andree's tender sweetness, which could have been nothing but designing and duplicity.... And now *this*.... He despised her and he despised himself. A beautiful dream had become a sordid reality....

How much of all this was due to a sudden perception of right and how much to boyish jealousy and a sharp hurt to a boyish heart he did not know. It did not occur to him to ask.... He had been made a fool of. He was furious with what he took to be righteous anger; what he did not know was that as soon as she passed there would come the most poignant grief he had ever known; the grief that comes only when a beautiful something has crept into one's life to be snatched away brutally, leaving in its nest something squalid, unsightly, disgusting.

For a moment he was on the point of confronting Andree and Monsieur Robert, but he restrained himself. There would be a scene; probably he would thrash Robert—and to what good?... He glared at them a moment longer, then turned away and almost ran down the boulevard.... He was not thinking now, only suffering.

Presently he found himself repeating over and over to himself: "Andree, how could you?... Andree, how could you?..." Rage was departing, grief and disillusionment were taking its place. Presently he came to a Metro station and plunged downward. The train would carry him home faster than he could walk, and he wanted to be home, to shut himself up, to be alone. He wanted to feel that doors and walls were between him and all the world.... It was the sort of feeling which, long continued, drives men into religious orders, makes of them Trappists, Cistercians.... Shelter and silence were what Kendall wanted—to crawl away into some hiding-place where he might make the most of his suffering.

He ran up the stairs of the apartment, snatched the key from under the rug, and threw open the door. The apartment was lighted. He paused. Madeleine and Bert were in the *salon*, and both appeared in the door to greet him. They called to him gaily, but Kendall did not reply. He scowled at them and flung himself past them without a word, to disappear in his room and slam the door.

"*Qu'est-ce que c'est?*" exclaimed Madeleine, and then laughed. "*Beaucoup zigzag!*"

"No," said Bert, staring after his friend, "he doesn't drink. Something's up. Something's happened."

"It is Andree," Madeleine said, with a shake of her head. "I know. *Oui*.... It is plain to read. *Jaloux*. Oh yes. I know the signs. *Pauvre enfant!* He is ver' jealous. There is no other anger like it—none."

"What had I better do?"

"Not anything. That is best.... He mus' be lef' alone—him.... But I do not theenk—Andree love heem. I could see. He is not glad.... But what would you? It is not nice to be jealous. One suffers. But I theenk he make the mistake—yes."

"Anyhow, he's in an awful stew. Seems like I ought to do something."

"No—he would behave like one *sauvage*. It is to make to leave him alone. To-morrow, perhaps...."

CHAPTER XIV

Andree glanced at her watch as she emerged from the Metro at the St.-Michel station that evening and noticed that it was almost exactly seven o'clock. With quaint, almost stiff little steps she proceeded across the Place, her eyes lowered with that charmingly unconscious demureness which was a part of her, her thoughts directed inward, as they always seemed to be. She had a gift of detachment; it was possible for her to be in the midst of a crowd, and yet to seem and to be unconscious of the crowd's proximity or existence. She always seemed grave, with a tiny hint of apprehension, and when, as she rarely did, she raised her eyes to regard some passing individual, it was with a sort of naïve wonder to discover that there was another human being in her neighborhood.... That is how she impressed one. What she was really thinking, how much she saw of what went on about her, nobody ever knew. Kendall, who had studied her every mood, had not the least idea of what her little head busied itself with. She was a dainty mystery to him. She was a dainty mystery to everybody who felt an interest in her.

"Good evening, Mademoiselle Andree," said a voice in her own language, and she looked up with that childishly startled air which was hers alone. It was Monsieur Robert, smiling with handsome boyishness and with a twinkle of mischief in his eye. She regarded him gravely.

"Good evening, monsieur," she replied, timidly.

"I have good fortune," he said. "I have thought of you so often; I have wished to meet you, and, behold! here you are."

She made no reply, but stood looking at him questioningly.

"Is it permitted to say that mademoiselle is very pretty this evening—as always?... Ah, we were to be friends, do you remember? It was agreed, was it not? And some day we were to talk of many things ... of the *Académie* and the Comédie and of yourself. Was it not so?"

"Yes, monsieur."

"It is well." He laughed gaily. "Then shall we talk this evening? You shall dine with me, then.... It is impossible that you are much occupied.

Fortune could not be so unkind. You will dine with me and we will talk of those plans of yours?"

She considered a moment unsmilingly, and Monsieur Robert wondered what were her thoughts. It was impossible to guess.

"Yes," she said, presently.

"There is a café at the corner of the rue Soufflot. Does that please you?"

"Yes."

He took his place at her side and they continued up the boulevard, Andree silent and apparently preoccupied; Monsieur Robert laughing, gay, exerting all his great charm and displaying his high abilities in droll humor. Occasionally Andree looked up at him a moment and smiled, but for the most part she was serious and gave what answers were required of her in monosyllables. They found a table on the sidewalk of the café and gave their orders.

"Mademoiselle desires to enter the *Académie*?" said he.

"Yes."

"It is not easy to gain admission, which is correct. It is not every one who is fit.... There are the examinations, which are difficult."

"I have not fear of the examinations, for I have studied very much. It is that—" She hesitated.

"That you have not an influential friend to make the recommendation. Is that it?"

"Yes."

He laughed easily. "Why do you wish to become an actress?"

"Because I must do something—I must find a career, because it is necessary to eat. The stage is very well. I think I can do it; I have always felt I was for the stage."

"That is very well. One must feel so.... You have the beauty that appeals, yes. You have the youth. You have the intelligence, that is clear. Now, if only you have the talent, the genius—"

"One does not know."

"Until one makes the attempt, it is true.... But I have a feeling it is there, mademoiselle. Something tells me so. I am sure of it."

"You are very amiable."

"No.... No.... It is but the truth.... But there is much hard work. In the *Académie* one must work until one is ready to drop with fatigue."

"It is nothing—if one succeeds."

"True.... And the success is very good. Ah, mademoiselle, I can see the success of you. Behold!... To-day you are not rich, is it not so? You have no fame. But the future—what possibilities are there!... You succeed in entering the *Académie*. That is possible. You work, you study, you learn.... The teachers see that you have beauty, and they search for the talent.... That is their way, and when they see it to be present they make you work the harder and bestow upon you the extra pains. Oh yes.... I can see it. Then, with good fortune, you take the first prize of all the women, and that makes a place for you on the stage of the Comédie Française. You shall be a *comédienne*—that is for you.... And then—one day will come the great success...." He stopped suddenly and regarded her.

"Can you not see it? To-day you—you are very charming, but you are merely you. You have nothing, you are nothing. You have a room, perhaps, for which you pay seventy francs a month. Am I not right? You are not happy. You are hidden.... But then comes a wonderful night. You make the great success. Paris is at your feet. Paris adores you.... What does it mean? Ah, mademoiselle, one can scarcely imagine it. It means a career, a great success in life. It means to be adored, to have all that a beautiful woman can desire.... It means applause and the envy of all the world—everything! everything!... What a change! What a wonderful change!"

"Yes," she said, her eyes glowing.

"It means that famous men will compete for your favor. You will be pointed out everywhere, received everywhere.... The papers will speak of your every movement.... You will be happy."

"Yes," she said.

Then his manner changed, his enthusiasm seemed to die, and he looked steadily into her face.

"But before it all comes one must enter the *Académie*."

"It is so."

"Mademoiselle, do you want very much to do so?"

"Oh, greatly! greatly!"

"Then it shall be. I guarantee it."

"Oh, monsieur!"

He leaned over the table, his face serious now, his handsome eyes eager. "If mademoiselle will be kind," he said.

She looked at him an instant and let her eyes fall.

"Ah," she said.

"I love you.... I adore you."

"No," she replied, with the merest hint of a smile. "It is not so. You do not love me."

"You are very lovely.... You are poor—you shall be rich. You are unknown—you shall be famous.... And I love you."

She did not lift her eyes now, but sat very still and looked at her plate. Her face told him nothing; it had not altered its expression of detached gravity—and it intrigued him, made her the more desirable because he could not understand her. Her lips quivered, she closed her eyes and drew a little breath which was almost a sigh.

"It cannot be, monsieur."

He sat erect, astonished, really astonished.

"You—you refuse?"

"Yes, monsieur."

"You refuse fame and wealth and all that may be yours?"

"It is necessary, monsieur."

"And why? Why?"

"Because, monsieur, I love, and I am happy.... I am faithful.... I am very happy."

He stared, unbelieving. Then, "It is the American officer—this Capitaine Ware?"

"Yes, monsieur."

"You—you throw it all away for him—for this foreigner? You throw away your chance—your career?... It is absurd, impossible!... But look, mademoiselle. These Americans they do not remain. There is the war. To-morrow, the next day, he may be ordered away—he may be sent back to America.... He will go away from you and leave you lonely.... For a week, a month, will you throw away your life? Oh, mademoiselle, think! It would be terrible."

She smiled. "It is the first happiness I have known.... I love him, monsieur, and he loves me. We are very happy.... Life is not good. It is very bad, but there may be the little moments of happiness, and they are most sweet. Does monsieur understand? There may be grief and loneliness to follow, but those little moments—they are all of life.... Nothing else is to be considered. It is as you say.... It may be a week, a month, but I would not lose it, not for all you promise me.... And I am constant, I am faithful.... If I must buy my little moments with this career, then I shall pay—oh, so happily. Do you not understand? At all events, one can remember them while life lasts.... They will make a long life sweet.... And so, monsieur, it cannot be. I have considered and I have chosen...."

It was at this moment, the moment when Andree was surrendering her future, passing by the call of Fame and closing her ears to the knock of Opportunity, that Kendall Ware glared at her above the bushes that shut in the front of the café.... It was this moment that he saw—a wonderful, a glowing, a superb moment. He saw a miracle, and his eyes were shut so that it was not apparent to him....

Monsieur Robert was silent for a space, during which one might have told the numbers to twenty, and then he arose, very gravely, dignified now, courtly. He lifted Andree's hand and bowed over it and his lips touched it in token of respect and of honor.

"Mademoiselle," he said, quietly, "I have said that I love you.... It is true.... I have seen a great thing, a beautiful thing.... I am proud that I have kissed your hand. From this moment I revere two women—my mother and yourself...."

She smiled up at him with that quaint smile of hers, that smile which was half lost child, half banished fairy. "It is nothing ..." she said.

"May I walk on with you?" he asked.

She shook her head, and then extended her hand. "Good-by, monsieur," she said.

He accompanied her to the open walk. "Good-by, mademoiselle," he said, softly, and stood looking after her until she reached the distant Panthéon and turned the corner. Then he sighed and smiled and shook his head and walked away. "The women of France!..." he said aloud, and there was a hushed wonder in his voice.

CHAPTER XV

Despite Bert Stanley's crudities and carelessness and boisterousness, he had no mean capacity for friendship. He was fond of Kendall Ware with that sort of friendship which one so often finds in men of his character for others of finer fiber. He did not understand Kendall, nor did he try overly hard to understand him; it was enough that he liked him and rather admired him. Sometimes his attitude toward his friend was of humorous tolerance. He laughed to himself when Ken took some slight affair with gravity and seriousness. He thought Ken was a bit queer and moody. As for himself, he took things as they presented themselves and made the best of it, not inquiring into causes and not caring about results unless there was a possibility of their presenting themselves in too unpleasant fashion.

For instance, he had seen Kendall thrown into somber mood by a discussion of the unhappy future of hundreds of thousands of French girls deprived of men with whom to marry. Of course it did look a bit tough on the women, Bert thought, but what can you expect? And what could one do about it? He put this thought into words.

"Do about it?" Kendall replied, gloomily. "That's the devil of it—there's nothing that can be done about it. They're just up against it.... Poor devils!"

"Oh, it'll come out all right somehow," Bert said, with a shrug. "They'll find men somewhere."

"Find men!... There aren't any men. You can't take a stick and whittle out men."

"Then what in thunder is the use worrying about it? It's so, and that's all there is to it. No use getting gloomy."

"But it makes me gloomy. It's so rotten unfair. It's horrible. Just think of what it means to them!..."

"Just don't think about it and you'll be better off."

It was this sort of thing that Bert failed to understand. He could imagine a man worrying because he was out of a job, or because he had broken his leg, or because his house was on fire; but why anybody should go out of his way to fuss over something that seemed to him like a rather distant abstraction, he failed to comprehend. But Ken always did it.

Bert could never understand the effect of the sight of Paris on his friend. Of course it was a regular city, different from New York and Chicago, but there was no use to rave about it or to stand on a bridge mooning and looking at a row of buildings. Paris meant a good time of an exotic sort to Bert—and that was all. He was willing to agree that the town was beautiful if anybody insisted, but what was the use of insisting? A town was a town. It wasn't what a town looked like that made it a good place to be; it was the business opportunities of the town and the opportunities for pleasure when business was over for the day. He went with Kendall to see Notre Dame, and wondered why in the dickens anybody had ever gone to the trouble to hew all those ugly carvings out of stone, or why they should run fringes of them around a church. It was a sort of dingy old place, anyhow.... Now for a regular building, give him the Hôtel de Ville. That was something like, because it might have been the post-office or a railroad station in New York. He would have traded his chance to see all the ramshackle cathedrals in France for one sight of the Woolworth Building. Now there was something! There was some use in going to see that structure! It was capable of astonishing him—but only because it was so lofty. To see it of a spring morning with the hazy sun tipping its golden peak meant nothing to him except looking at a tall building early in the day.... There wasn't a high building in Paris! But Ken wanted to poke around to see such things as Notre Dame, and if he got pleasure out of it, that was his business.

Nevertheless, Bert saw dimly that Kendall had something admirable which was denied to him. Not that he wanted it especially! He was very well satisfied, but somehow he admired Ken for having it and liked him the better for it.... And Ken was always philosophizing about things, and advancing theories, and worrying about morals, and splitting hairs of right and wrong. To Bert certain things were wrong, and the rest didn't matter. It was wrong to murder and to steal or to kick a child or to cheat at cards or in any other game. As for the bulk of the rest of the possible acts of man, he saw them as neuter, and not mattering much.... But Ken could get up a moral argument over the way he spread his bread! And these arguments had the power to upset his friend completely, to make him gloomy, to worry him.... It was utter nonsense, but it was a part of Ken and Ken was his friend.

He felt a sort of duty to look after Ken, a responsibility for him. He was actually troubled sometimes by one of Ken's moods and deliberately thought up means to cheer him.... And now he was really worried. He had never seen Kendall as he had appeared last night. Something out of the ordinary had happened. Most likely it was nothing that the ordinary fellow would think twice about, but the Lord only knew how it would affect Ken. Anyhow, Ken thought he was in some sort of trouble, and Bert was really disturbed. He had wanted to do something about it last night, but Madeleine had prevented, and now he felt rather guilty. Putting on his bathrobe and slippers, he went to Ken's door and opened it softly. Ken was sitting up in bed, staring out of the window.

"Morning," said Bert, affably.

"Morning," replied Kendall, shortly.

"Um!... Cheerful, ain't you? Say, what's eating you, anyhow?"

"Nothing."

"Nothing, my aunt's knee-cap! Come through. What's carried off your goat?"

Kendall did not reply.

"Get up and have breakfast. I hear Arlette in the kitchen. You'll feel better after you've had a bowl of chocolate warming up your tummy."

"I don't want any breakfast."

"Huh?..." Bert was beginning now to be seriously troubled. "Say, what's the matter, anyhow? Is it Andree?"

"I've just been a damn fool, that's all."

"Ought to be used to it," said Bert, flippantly, and then, more seriously, "Say, you don't mean to say that you've gone and went and fallen in love with her, or anything like that?"

"Look here," Ken said, morosely, "I don't want to talk about it."

"I do," said Bert, with a grin, "so we're going to talk. I'm the biggest, and I can doggone well hold you while we thrash it out. Now tell it to your uncle. Are you in love with Andree?"

"I—I don't know."

"That means you are.... What about it? Say, you don't mean you're worrying about *marrying* her, do you?"

Ken laughed unpleasantly. "I wouldn't marry her if she was the last woman on earth. I never want to see her again. I never want to think about her again."

"Huh! Had a row, eh?"

"No."

Bert glowered at his friend a minute. "I don't know whether you are interested or not, but you give me an acute pain. Why in blazes can't you go along and have a good time like a fellow ought to without always landing into the middle of something that fusses you all up? You think too darn much.... Now there's Madeleine and I—you don't see me doing any worrying or scrapping, do you? Well!... Nor falling in love. You bet you don't! When I fall in love it will be with some American girl, and then I'll settle down and raise a family and wear slippers in the evening. But now I'm out to have what fun is going before I get my style cramped. I like Madeleine and she likes me.... That's all. I'm giving her a good time, and she's a good fellow—but that's all there is to it. She knows it and I know it, and there you are. I saw to that right at the start-off. I told her. You bet I did! I said to her, 'Now look here, young lady, we're just playing, understand. There's nothing serious about this. I'm going back to America some day, and when I do, it's good-by.' And she feels the same way about it.... And that's the only system."

Arlette came shuffling into the room after Kendall's shoes and responded to Bert's greeting with a grin and a bob of her head.

"Arlette," said Bert, "Monsieur Ken's in love. You've had experience, eh? What's to be done about it?"

"Eh?... In love!... *Mon Dieu!* What does one do about it? One makes nothing. Either one is in love or one is not.... I have been in love." She wagged her head sagely.

"I knew it. I could tell it just by looking at you. What did you do?"

"I married ... and now I have grandchildren, and love is no more for me.... But I remember it, messieurs.... Yes, yes, I often think of it. Is that not droll?" Again she waggled her head.

"But Monsieur Ken is in love and he doesn't seem to like it."

"It happens so," she said. "There is both joy and sorrow. But monsieur is loved in return. I have perceived it. Why, then, is he not joyous?"

"You tell the answer. I don't know."

"He loves Mademoiselle Andree; Mademoiselle Andree loves him. She is very pretty, very sweet.... Well, then?" She made a gesture with her arms as if to say that the thing was beyond human comprehension.

"All the Americans are mad," said Bert in French, employing the phrase of the streets.

"It is true," said Arlette, nodding. "I have seen it."

"And when they are in love they are madder than ever."

"It may well be believed."

"Oh, get out and leave me alone, both of you," Ken said, morosely.

"Nothing of the sort. Explain carefully the difficulty to Arlette and me. We are the council of experts."

"It's nothing—except that I was a fool to get mixed up in this kind of a thing. It's rotten."

"It's his conscience, Arlette," said Bert, with mock impressiveness.

"When the conscience makes to interfere in a matter of love," said Arlette, "it means either that one is not in love at all or that one is jealous. Love, messieurs, is its own conscience."

"Madeleine said you were jealous last night. Two experts agree.... Jealous! Um!..."

"I'm not jealous, you gibbering idiot. I—It's just that I thought Andree was something and find she's not.... It's the whole idea over here. I thought it was right—and it's rotten. I was losing my balance. I thought wrong could be right."

"It never can be when the other fellow does it," said Bert, with more acuteness than usual. "Then you're not worrying about marrying Andree? And you have discovered that you're being very wicked, and so you're in the dumps, and you're figuring on calling the whole thing off and living a noble and austere life. Huh!... What happened last night? You can't fool your uncle. You got a letter from home, and then something happened. What was it?"

"I saw Andree with that actor."

"*Mon Dieu!*" exclaimed Arlette, and she passed off, as though frightened, to her kitchen.

"You saw them together? Where?"

"In a café?"

"Yes—go on."

"That's all."

"And you—Oh, say—all this cat-fit is because you saw Andree in a café with another man! Get out!"

"With that particular man. You know what Jacques said about him.... You know Andree wants to get into the *Conservatoire* and on the stage. I introduced them—"

"More fool you," said Bert, succinctly.

"It was plain enough. She could use him. She needed his influence—so—Oh, what's the use? I don't want to talk about it."

Bert thought that Ken's view was altogether likely. And why not? But he conceived it to be his duty to argue against it in his friend's interest. "Just a case of plain, or garden, jealousy. Nothing to it. You see them together in a café and jump to conclusions. Didn't hang around to see where they went?"

"Certainly not."

"Made up your mind with a snap—and then, because you were jealous, and it looked as if your nose was out of joint, you hollered sour grapes. In a second it all got to be immoral and naughty—and you're worked up to a state of mind.... If this actor had never come along, and if Andree had loved you alone and all that, would it have been wrong?... Of course not, and you know it."

Ken did not reply, but he had an uncomfortable feeling that Bert was right.

"You'd better give her a chance to explain—or did you burst in on the party and rear and tear all over the place?"

"They never knew I saw them."

"Then, old son, you'd better let Andree tell you about it. Madeleine says she loves you and Arlette says she loves you—and, believe me, they're experts."

"If she loves me, and then would do such a thing, it's all the worse.... I'll never see her again."

"Well, if your mind's made up, there's the end of the whole thing. Get up and eat and forget it.... The river's full of fish."

"You don't think I'd try it again. Never!... I've been a fool, and a rotten fool.... I fooled myself into thinking one could do this kind of thing and not be wrong. I got it into my head that our ideas of morals in America were old-fashioned and narrow and absurd, and that the French were right."

"Of course you'd have to philosophize about it."

"Well, I'm through now. I've got what was coming to me—and right on top of it there was a letter from mother."

"I'll bet I know the kind. I've stayed at your house, you know."

"Do you think—" Ken bit his lips and stopped.

"No, and I'm not going to. I'm satisfied. What's the use wasting energy thinking when it doesn't earn you anything? You got a jolt and a sermon, and between them they've given you a mental twister.... After we've walked down to the office you'll feel better, son.... Get up before I haul you out."

Kendall got heavily out of bed while Bert returned to his own room to dress. When one is Kendall Ware's age the morning should be the pleasantest part of the day, and usually it is so. One does not arise weary and irritable, but joyously, looking forward to the day that is coming.... This morning Ken left his bed like a man of sixty whose digestion has become the primary consideration of his life, and who is not fit to enter human society before noon. He had not slept well, his head was heavy—and he despised himself. At any rate, he fancied he despised himself, which makes for the same result. There was the sharp grief of youth as well, and one does not wisely who belittles the griefs of youth. It seems to be true that the energies which make youth wonderful give of their strength to the pain that youth can feel.... Now he was certain he had loved Andree and he had never experienced anything that compared with the distress and chagrin at his discovery that he had loved an unworthy object. He had idealized Andree, had made of her something more than human, something above the laws of humanity, mystic, of the stuff of which fairies are made, and she had been proved dross and himself a self-deluded fool.... He was bitter against himself and her. His thoughts made him well worthy to accept a high place in the company of those who gathered in the vestibule of his church at home....

He approached the table without appetite, and Arlette, when she brought in the pitcher of chocolate, eyed him sidewise and askance, and waddled out, shaking her head uneasily. He could hear her muttering to herself, and it annoyed him, because he knew she was troubled about him.

Bert had chosen to leave him alone and to let the thing run its course, so the breakfast was a silent one. They put on their overseas caps and descended the stairs without a word.

In the passageway the *concierge* was waiting for them with the friendly smile which had always made his returnings to the apartment seem more like homecomings. She rested on her broom and wished them good morning.

"Your national *fête* is but a few days away," she said. "It is made a national *fête* for us also—this fourth day of July. All Paris—all France will make it a day the like of which has not been seen. I hear this on all sides.... It is a pleasure to me to have American officers in this house. I am envied. I speak only the truth. Therefore I hope messieurs the American officers will procure for me flags of their country to hang from their windows. It will be an honor. Will messieurs see to this matter?"

"Yes, indeed," said Bert. "I'll get them for you to-day."

"Many thanks," she said, and returned to her sweeping.

"Nice old lady," said Bert. "They're all nice. Cordial lot—these French people.... I wonder how we would act in America if we had a couple of millions of foreign soldiers planted down on us. Mostly we're disagreeable to strangers."

Ken did not answer. He was staring straight before him and thinking, thinking, thinking. His thoughts were intolerant thoughts, uncharitable, narrow. It was of thoughts such as his, persisted in until they become habitual, that are born the hanging of witches and the burning of martyrs.... They were not natural to him, and they filled him with discomfort and restlessness. He had a vague sense that he was being not altogether fair, and that he was condemning the whole because of a fault in a part. All France must not necessarily be evil because Andree had proved to be faithless, but he was declaring it to be evil. There was no good in it; there was no good in anything except the ruthless bigotry which had taken possession of him. There was no God but Puritanism, and Narrowness was its prophet....

They reached the Élysées Palace Hotel in which were their offices. He had not enjoyed his walk; there had been none of that pleasure which always before he derived from the great open stretches and wide boulevards of Paris. Beauty had ceased to exist or to signify.... He had a sensation of being shriveled up and dried—of lifelessness, and his thoughts seemed to rub against one another like sand-paper.... He saw it all as the unpleasant process of a moral awakening; it was not that; it was the disgruntlement of a youth over a love-affair gone awry....

"Hope it wears off during the day," said Bert.

Ken only grunted, and turned up the stairs.

It was a futile day and he was glad when it came to an end. It was not until he was hanging his cap on the hall tree that he remembered Andree was to come—to come there to dine this evening. He paused with hand in mid-air as he recalled how they had made the plan. Hereafter she was not to meet him at the Metro, but would come directly to the apartment. It would be better, and there was something exquisitely attractive about it. He had been very happy. Her lips had been close to his as she had given her promise to come there to him; the perfume of her had been in his nostrils, and in that maddening way of perfumes it returned now unasked and undesired. It was almost as if she were there, close to him, but invisible. He remembered that she had lain in his arms at the moment, smiling, sweet, a marvelous creature to be treasured with a great tenderness.... And she had gone from that to a meeting with another man—to purchase material success at the price of spurious love!...

What should he do? He did not want to see her, felt that he could not undergo the ordeal of seeing her.... He snatched his cap and turned to the door, only to replace it again on the hall tree and to stand wavering, undecided.... He did not know it, would not admit it, but his heart cried out to see her, to feel the delight of her presence.... He despised her, but he loved her.... As one does at such moments, he sought refuge in sophistry. It was necessary for him to see her this last single time. He must tell her that he had detected her infamy and, with harsh words, cast her out of his life. He told himself that this was both appropriate and essential.... Yes, he would allow her to come and would admit her—and then—and then she should hear the truth, the bald truth. She should hear what a decent man thought of such behavior as hers.... Not that it would benefit her or change a character that could be guilty of the thing of which she was guilty.... But he had to accuse her.... It was the desire, the cruel desire, which comes to every man at some moment, for some cause, to inflict agony on the one he most loves....

Kendall glanced at his watch. It wanted fifteen minutes to seven, the hour at which Andree would arrive, so he went into the *salon*, there to pace up and down, restlessly composing dignified but biting speeches one after the other and forgetting them as soon as composed.... Bert entered and spoke to him, but Kendall only growled, and Bert passed into his own room with a shrug. From the door to the window Kendall paced, and from the window to the door, to and fro, with rapid, excited stride. As the moment of Andree's arrival neared, his thoughts became less coherent and himself more apprehensive. He felt that it was his duty to be very angry, so he worked himself up to anger.... Then came a soft, timid rap at the door.

He strode into the hall and flung the door open savagely. There stood Andree, fragile, lovely, appealing, her face turned up to his with that wistful question which it always wore when they first met. She looked so dainty, so small, so sweet!... Her eyes met his and waited a moment for his smile of welcome before they smiled. Always she seemed to be afraid—afraid that she would not read welcome in his eyes. He remembered it, and her look accused him. He stood silent, staring. Her lips parted at the strangeness of his manner and he saw astonishment grow in her dark-shaded eyes.... He found the rage up to which he had worked himself slipping away from him; as he looked down at her it even seemed impossible to believe that she was not all he had thought her to be. There was an innocence, a trustfulness about her.

"Come in, mademoiselle," he said, coldly, stepping back to permit her to pass.

She entered slowly, diffidently. He could see that she was surprised, hurt by his manner, and a feeling of guilt overtook him. She stopped near him and turned expectantly.... He understood. He was expected to act the lover; she was awaiting his lover-like greeting.... He discovered how much bolder and more resolute one may be in anticipation than at the required moment.

"Do not take off your things," he said, striving to keep his voice steady and emotionless. "Will you come in here?"

She obeyed silently, with a silence that came from sudden apprehension. He followed her and stood before her, searching for words with which to begin, and she, her face grave and a little sad, as was its custom, stood very still, but once or twice her eyes turned upward quickly to read his face. The speeches he had prepared against this moment had hidden themselves away, and he was left with an uncomfortable feeling of inadequacy to the event. He hesitated; the silence became unsupportable, and he began with sudden harshness, a harshness that a little frightened himself when he heard it.

"I never intended to see you again," he said, "but I forgot you were coming here to-night." He spoke in English, rapidly, but she understood him, for her eyes lifted now and remained fixed on his own, dark, frightened, appealing. He looked into them and turned hastily away. There was a magic in them that he feared; they seemed so pure, so honest.... Her lips parted a little, but she did not speak.

"I loved you," he said, hoarsely, "and I trusted you.... I thought you were good and honest. I trusted you, do you understand? Trusted you and believed in you." Words were coming more easily now, and with facility in speech returned what he fancied to be his righteous anger. "I was a fool.... I thought that you, even brought up in this city, in this way of life, could be good and faithful.... You fooled me—I should have known better. It was my own fault.... But I've got my lesson. I've seen. I know now.... I loved you—I was all ready to love you—but I despise you.... Do you understand? I despise you. You are bad—bad. You said you loved me and you gave me your love—and it was all a lie.... How many other men are you telling the same thing? Is every day given to somebody?" He was bitter now, cruelly bitter.

She did not speak, but stared up at him as though she did not believe, at least as if she did not understand. Her face was pitiful in its surprise and pain. Motionless, without movement or gesture, she stood and looked up into his face as a dog might look into the face of his master, knowing that master is about to shoot him to death.

"I never want to see you again. I want to forget you. I wish I could forget that I ever saw you and all that has happened. Probably it doesn't matter to you. Maybe you don't see any harm in what you've done—but it was squalid and contemptible."

His voice rose with his anger and she shrank back from him. Bert, startled, came hurrying into the room and stopped with amazement.

"Ken," he exclaimed, "easy ... easy. What's all this?"

"Please go away, Bert.... I'm telling her what I think of her.... Go away."

Bert looked curiously at Andree, who did not move her eyes from Kendall's face, and then he shook his head.

"No need to shout," he said. "You're excited, old man." He turned to Andree. "You mustn't mind him. He's wrought up about something."

Andree did not appear to notice that Bert was present.

He laid his hand on Kendall's arm. "Come along," he said. "Don't say something you'll be sorry for.... If you want Andree to go away, I'll take her.... Come on into your room." He was really apprehensive, for Kendall's eyes glowed somberly, his face was convulsed with toxic emotion.

Ken shook off his friend's hand. "Leave me be.... This is my affair." He pointed to the door. "Go!..." he said to Andree, his voice quivering. "You don't know what you've done—what miserable thing you've done.... I despise you.... I despise you...."

Bert stepped forward and touched her arm. "You'd better go, I guess," he said in a low tone. "Ken's pretty excited. Let me take you down." His voice was sympathetic.

Andree did not move. "Oh, I do not onderstan'.... I do not onderstan' ..." she said, like a frightened child.

"Don't lie," said Kendall, furiously. "Go!... And never come back.... I'll never see you again."

She stood an instant more, her eyes seeking his, demanding of his. Then, very slowly, very quietly, without sob or even a quiver of her dainty lips, she turned and walked to the door. There she paused and turned to look at him again, rather drooping, hopeless, appealing.... "Oh, it is not well.... I do not onderstan'," she said.

Kendall turned his back.... In another instant the door had opened and closed and Andree was gone. He stood with hands clenched, experiencing a certain unholy satisfaction. He had done the thing thoroughly. He had finished it. He had told her what he thought of her, and he was rid of her forever.

Presently Bert returned. He walked up to his friend with a grim look upon his usually nonchalant face. "That was pretty average brutal," he said. "Maybe it's good Presbyterian to do that sort of thing.... If it is, I thank God I'm a heathen.... That poor little kid! Did you see her face?..."

CHAPTER XVI

Arlette stood in the dining-room door, making her silent announcement that dinner was served. Her round eyes, which usually wore an expression of surprise, were now frightened, and she stared at Kendall as if he were some sort of explosive that was likely to go off at any moment with a tremendous explosion. Then she withdrew her head and could be heard padding out to the kitchen.

"Come on," said Bert. "Dinner's on."

"I don't want any dinner."

"You don't deserve any dinner," said Bert, hotly, "but you've got to eat." He pushed Ken toward the dining-room. "In with you."

Kendall obeyed apathetically, took his chair and began to eat automatically, without interest in his food. He had anticipated a sort of barbarous pleasure from his harshness toward Andree, but found it ashes in his mouth. He was ashamed of himself, and then ashamed of himself again for being ashamed. He had done right, exactly right, he insisted. She had deserved what he had given her, but nevertheless he was ashamed of himself. There are two identities in every man, the emotional, the sentimental, the natural—and the intellectual. Either of these identities may perform actions satisfactory to itself but abhorrent to the other. Kendall's intellectual and logical self was content; his emotional self accused him.... If one would be happy, if he would gain and retain affection, if he would have the best gifts of life for himself and those with whom he comes in contact, he should place confidence in his emotional self rather than his intellectual. The emotions are natural and for the most part kindly. They do not operate by rule and precept, but spontaneously; intellect is artificial and logic is without the warmth of life.... Even the law recognizes a distinction, for it does not punish a crime of emotion with the severity that it metes out to the crime of cold reason. Peter was emotional, he denied his Master, yet was forgiven and stands chief of the companions of Christ; Judas took logical thought and betrayed. He committed the unforgivable sin. The difference was not so much in kind as in cause....

"What would you have done?" he demanded, suddenly, of Bert.

"I wouldn't have been so infernally brutal.... You and I have been friends a long time, haven't we?... Well, right now I'm nearer to wanting to give you a thrashing than I thought I could ever come. It was rotten!... Poor kid!... And the way she took it! Without a word or a whimper!... But did you see her face?... I came darn near blubbing."

"She deserved it.... She did. She did a rotten thing—and anybody would think it was I who was to blame. I won't be put in the wrong."

"I'm not going to quarrel with you. You asked me what I thought, and I told you.... I wouldn't have the confounded conscience you have to live with for a million dollars. I'm no angel. I suppose I do a lot of things the righteous folks back home would think were pretty bad. I'm not much on religion, either. But, all the same, if there is a God, I'll bet He's a lot more apt to take a liking to the fellow who is a bit off color, but tries to be sort of kind and tolerant, and not to hurt folks, than He is to the man who lives up to every letter and punctuation mark of the law, and does it like a brute.... From what I've seen of you stiff-necked, righteous folks, if I were God I'd be pretty average sore to think I had to have heaven crowded with you. You'd irritate me till I let in a bunch of sinners just to get some decent company...."

"Right is right and wrong is wrong."

"Huh!... Maybe! But who knows what is right and what is wrong? It's a guess, and everybody does his own guessing.... There are your Ten Commandments, sure enough, but you can't regulate the whole world and all it does with ten little rules.... Let's see! Wasn't there an eleventh commandment later on? I used to go to Sunday-school myself. Something to the effect that you ought to love your neighbor as yourself? A God that could make that sort of a commandment isn't going to be too stiff-backed about the other ten. No, sir.... Things are too mixed up for *anything* to be all wrong or all right. Everything's a mixture—and the more of that love-your-neighbor stuff there is in it, why, my notion is, the nearer it is to what is really good."

Ken was surprised. He had never accused Bert of so much abstract speculation, and perhaps Bert had not been speculating consciously before. It was rather that these ideas had been taking root in him and growing spontaneously. Possibly Bert was himself astonished to find himself uttering such ideas.

"It's over now," Bert said, presently, "so let's shut up about it. You're in a devil of a state of mind, and the only thing to get rid of *that* is to walk it off. As soon as I finish this cheese I'm going to take you out and walk you till you're human again—or till you drop."

"I'll walk.... I'll do anything. I want to get outdoors and move."

"Come on, then, sonny, but be genial—be genial. It's a walk we're going for, not a march to the grave."

They walked over to the rue du Faubourg St.-Honoré, which presented to them a face of little second-class shops, dairy products, bakeries, locksmiths, antiques, wine-shops, variety-stores, in front of every second one of which was its cat—a huge, sleek Thomas or a matronly old Tabby keeping an eye on two or three adventurous kittens. The street seemed to have a special leaning toward the feline in pets. But, then, all Paris is a sanctuary for cats, which is remarkable when one takes into account the number of dogs, and even jackals and young foxes, the latter affected by the ladies. It may be that there is a permanent truce between the dogs and cats in Paris. Bert remarked that he had never seen a cat chased by a dog there. Possibly, he declared, it might be the system. American dogs chased cats. It was their moral code to do so; Parisian dogs left cats alone, for a similar reason.

"It's all a matter of where you live," he said, in an effort to arouse Kendall. "Maybe there's a place in the world where they put deacons in jail and look up reverently to burglars. You can't tell. I suppose folks could agree among themselves to almost anything."

"Except to alter a natural law," said Ken, harshly.

"Natural law, eh? What's a natural law? To be sure, I get you. The shortest distance between two points, and gravitation, and that sort of thing. I guess nobody could change them, but, so far as I can see, they're the only settled things in the world. Natural laws—pretty good name for them. Means they come right from nature without people's tinkering with them at all, doesn't it?"

"Yes."

"That's the kind of law for me—the sort you can't disobey and so get in wrong.... But the other kind—what'll we call 'em—that's something else again, Mawrus. The kind of law that has to be agreed upon by a majority before it goes to work isn't such a serious matter in the long run. I mean, it is important only to the majority that agrees on it. Some other majority in the next county might agree to its exact opposite. Like local option. It's a sin to sell liquor on one side of a fence and a legitimate business on the other.... Huh!... I never got to thinking how funny it all was before."

How curious it was, thought Kendall, with quickened interest, that Bert should rather clumsily be following a line of reasoning that he himself had followed with deeper study and more particularity during the past weeks!... Could there really be something in it, after all? He had been sure of it yesterday, but yesterday was gone forever, and that had happened since which made the affairs and reasonings of yesterday repulsive to him.... But—the dogmatism, the harsh, uncompromising, puritanical attitude he had chosen to take quivered a very little on its foundations....

They proceeded onward past the Ministry of the Interior on their left, and on their right the building with its great central court, and its archway through which could be seen broad, red-carpeted steps, which was the French White House—the residence of France's President. Now small cafés and wine-shops became more numerous, and the shops to partake of a better quality.

"Hey!" said Bert, stopping, "want to introduce you to a friend." He stepped into a little wine-shop and spoke to the young woman behind the bar, who lifted her voice loudly, calling a name that Kendall could not catch. In a moment a rather dirty, but very bright-eyed, bull-terrier appeared from the rear and stood looking at Bert expectantly. Bert selected a copper from his pocket and put it in the dog's mouth. The creature waggled his tail violently and trotted out into the street.

"Watch him," Bert urged.

The dog trotted into the adjoining baker's shop, barked once sharply with a note of command. A young woman leaned far over the counter, holding out her hand, into which the dog dropped his coin and stood expectant while she selected a roll and handed it to him. Then, in the most dignified manner, he paced back to Bert, waggled his tail in thanks, waited to be patted, and withdrew under a table to eat his dainty.

"There!" said Bert. "Finest dog in Paris. Wish I could buy him. Say, wasn't that great?"

"Huh!..." grunted Kendall, rather astonished that anybody could be interested in dogs when the world was coming down in awful ruin as his world was coming down.

Bert was offended. To him that dog was one of the sights of Paris, and, when he returned to America, it would be that animal and his little piece of cleverness that he would describe rather than anything else he had seen in Paris. The dog was worth coming to see.... Notre Dame was just a dingy pile of stones.... Yet, somewhere in him was a strain that was able to speculate on the attitude of God toward Pharisees and sinners....

They continued in silence until they reached the Place du Théâtre Français, with the Palais Royal before them and the Comédie Française, and with the magnificent breadth of the Avenue de l'Opéra angling sharply to the left. Across the open space was the University Union, and Bert suggested dropping in to see if any acquaintances were lounging about, when suddenly they were hailed from a distance, and, turning, saw Jacques, wooden leg grotesquely swinging at an angle from his body, hat swinging about his head, and cane describing enthusiastic circles. Jacques was trying to run to catch them. His method was to take two hops with his sound leg and then one lurch with the artificial one. There was a devil-may-care jauntiness about this unusual gait and a good-fellowship about his eccentric salutations that, somehow, always gained him a welcome.

"Ah," he shouted, when yet he was thirty feet away, "I have find you! I have surround you—eh? Where 'ave you been? I have not seen you for *longtemps*.... And Monsieur Kendall. It ees well. We are friends and *camarades*.... I have speak about you thees evening—you, Monsieur Kendall. Ho! you have the great good fortune, *n'est-ce pas*? I give you my felicitations. I salute you.... Ah, messieurs, eet was *magnifique, splendide!*..."

"What was magnificent, Jacques? Take a breath and start in fresh," Bert admonished.

Jacques patted Ken on the back. "Oh, he ees a good boy, thees Monsieur Kendall. He deserve the good fortune, *mais*, messieurs, it ees of a grandeur. Again I make the congratulations."

"Why? Why? Why?"

"Bicause," said Jacques, becoming preternaturally solemn, "bicause monsieur ees loved." He paused. "*Oui*, he ees loved ver' well by beautiful yo'ng girl who ees ver' *fidèle*. It ees one beautiful theeng. I make to weep w'en it ees tol' to me. *Vraiment!* The tear she stand in my eyes. *Sacré nom d'une pipe!* but it ees the theme for a poem."

"What in thunder are you talking about? Light on a bough, little bird, light." Bert grasped Jacques by the shoulder and pretended to hold him down to earth. "Now, little man, come clean. Tell the story and don't bubble over."

"It ees the leetle sweetheart of Monsieur Kendall—thees so graceful and beautiful yo'ng girl that has for her name Andree. She weesh for enter into the *Académie* and *après* to be an actress. It is so.... To do this is ver' *difficile*. It is necessary first to have much influence. Monsieur Kendall know thees. Yes. *Alors*, Monsieur Kendall introduce thees yo'ng girl to Monsieur Robert. I am present and see. Also I warn monsieur that thees Robert loves all young girl.... What would you? The theeng befalls yesterday. As Monsieur Robert emerges from the Metro near the Place St.-Michel he see bifore him thees Mademoiselle Andree, walking weeth her eyes so careful upon the sidewalk—so." Jacques imitated Andree's demure glance. "She do not see Robert until he address her. She is startle'—ver' much startle', but Monsieur Robert he is polite, *oui*, he is *très-gentil*. He ask mademoiselle will she promenade weeth heem, and she cannot refuse. Next he ask will she dine weeth heem, and she ees too sweet and gentle to hurt hees feeling, so she consent...."

Bert felt Kendall grasp his arm with fingers that gripped to the bone.

"Then they eat, this Mademoiselle Andree and Monsieur Robert, and he say to her if she will be kind to heem he make her to enter into the *Académie*, and give her hees influence, which is much, that she bicome a success, weeth all Paris at her feet.... It was wonderful chance for poor yo'ng girl, *n'est-ce pas*? One million girl they jump at it. Truly.... But thees mademoiselle she shake her head and say no—and why, messieurs?... Bicause she love thees yo'ng man here ver' true and is *fidèle*. It ees the truth, and it ees ver' beautiful.... Monsieur Robert say thees yo'ng man make himself to go away and leave her *solitaire*. Mademoiselle makes to him the reply that it does not matter—for weeth Monsieur Kendall she have the wonderful little moment of happiness w'ich is more splendid, more magnificent, more to be desired than any other theeng in the worl' ... bicause it ees the great love.... Yes, she say thees theeng to Robert, who admire so much he kees her hand, and now he tells me and others, and as he tell the tear stands in his eyes. He theenk Mademoiselle Andree she has make the great success, to which nothing can compare, a success much times greater than fame or than glory—bicause it is a success of the soul.... So I make many compliments to Monsieur Kendall—many compliments...."

"Bert ..." said Ken, in a voice that was little more than a whisper. "Bert...."

"Ees monsieur ill?" asked Jacques.

"No, Jacques. Just out of sorts—worried," said Bert. "I'm walking it out of him.... Mighty glad to have met you, old man."

Kendall turned to Jacques. "What you say about Andree—is it true? You are sure?..."

"*Certainement.*"

"Of course," Ken answered, slowly. "I didn't doubt it.... It sounded like the truth.... I thank you, Jacques. Some day I'll thank you better." He held out his hand. "Good night, Jacques."

He turned away, and Bert, after shaking hands with the exuberant little Frenchman, followed. Jacques stood for a moment staring after them, then waved his cane in the air for no purpose whatever, and said, perplexedly, "*Tous les Américains sont fous....*"

Ken walked rapidly, as one in haste to reach a definite destination; he did not speak. Bert, keeping pace with him, watched his friend's face covertly; it was a gray mask without expression, a mask that seemed to tell a tale of years double that which made the total of Kendall's life.

They diagonaled across the Place Marengo and at a more acute angle through the Place du Louvre to the Quai du Louvre and crossed the Pont Neuf, which carried them over the broader arm of the Seine, the upper point of the Cité, where to their left arose the dark mass of the Palais de Justice, and across the narrower branch of the river to the Quai des Augustins. Presently the Place St.-Michel opened before them, and, as Kendall turned into it Bert stopped to demand where they were going.

"To find her," said Kendall.

Bert nodded. "I thought so."

It was like Kendall—to start upon a search for her immediately. Just as jealousy, made more vicious by an attack of Puritan conscience, had caused him to drive Andree out of his life, so now that same conscience demanded that immediate reparation be made. If Bert knew his friend, then Kendall would be unable to rest until he had seen Andree, until he had debased himself before her and begged her forgiveness....

"Does she live here?" he asked.

"Near the Panthéon some place.... I don't know. I haven't her address.... Bert, I don't even know her last name!"

The Little Moment Of Happiness | 189

"Eh? What's that?"

"I don't know her name.... Somehow that was a part of it—the mystery—not knowing. It—I can't explain it to you—but she seemed like something dainty and lovely that appeared out of nothingness. I never asked, because I didn't want to know. She appeared and disappeared—like a fairy.... It was as if she were immaterial and only materialized herself for me—do you understand?"

"I'm darned if I do."

"I always left her a little ways beyond—on the rue Soufflot. She went on alone toward the Panthéon. That's all I know. Just that her name was Andree—and that she could appear and disappear. It was that unreality that made the whole thing possible."

"A few practical details would make the whole thing a lot more possible now.... What do you aim to do?"

"Wait for her."

"Huh!... Where?"

"At the corner of the rue Soufflot.... She may pass to-night."

"And she may not pass for a month."

"Then I'll wait a month," said Kendall, and Bert knew that his friend meant what he said.

They walked on up the boulevard and took seats at a table in that very café where Kendall had seen Andree and Monsieur Robert the night before. He could see that table, occupied now by a *poilu* and his sweetheart.... Bert ordered coffee for them, which came in thick glasses accompanied by a bottle of *saccharin* for the sweetening. Kendall left his glass untouched while his eyes fixed themselves on the street, now becoming ever more rapidly hidden by the dusk. Many people were passing, *habitués* of the Quartier Latin; young men in uniform with girls on their arms, skylarking, humming the chorus of "Madelon"; old women making a last effort of the day to sell bright-colored Rintintins and Ninettes fabricated out of worsteds, those quaint little charms which were all the rage in Paris, and which were supposed to make one safe from Big Bertha and the bomb of the air raid. One young girl passed clinging to the arm of a youth in a broad hat, baggy corduroy trousers, paint-daubed coat, and flowing tie—a figure who might have stepped out of the pages of Henri Mürger. He seemed the very genius of the Latin Quarter, a hungry *peintre* with canvas under his arm, and his gay-hearted little mistress who cooked his meals and shared his hunger and poverty brightly.... Kendall watched them go and envied them the thing that was theirs. Now and then a gendarme, wearing his short sword, passed stiffly.... It became darker and darker, and the crowd in the café thinned itself away until nobody remained but himself and Bert. Impatient waiters began piling up chairs and moving tables against the wall. Dim, hooded, blue street-lights glowed in the distance, making the boulevard ghastly and somber.... The darkness became impenetrable, but still Kendall lingered, hoping, demanding that Andree's dainty little figure appear.

"No use, Ken," Bert said. "She won't come now, and if she did you wouldn't be able to see her."

"I can't go till I'm sure," Ken answered.

"Let's walk, then. More chance of seeing her out on the sidewalk."

They arose and sauntered slowly toward the Panthéon, crossing the very spot where Andree had given Kendall that first kiss.... They retraced their steps. The streets were now all but deserted; only here and there was a hurrying figure, or upon some bench along the curb a pair of lovers sitting close and whispering in each other's ears.

"It's eleven o'clock," said Bert. "Come on home."

"Yes," said Ken. "It is too late now. She won't come to-night...."

Suddenly the air was rent by the wail of the siren; the avions were coming! One heard cries of anger or fright, saw dark blots resolve into hurried action as loiterers sought places of refuge.... A fire-engine swept by with gnome-like black figures clinging to it, and that voice like some horrid wail from the pit rising from it as a fireman turned the handle of the siren.... It was a voice that matched Kendall's humor—a voice of despair, a voice that made audible a thing which described to his ear all that was evil and squalid and treacherous and unforgivable that lurked in the black and stealthy warrens of the world....

"Let's get out of this," said Bert.

Kendall did not want to go, and the less so now that there was danger.... Andree was in danger and, somehow, he felt that his place, if it could not be with her, was as near to her as he could station himself. He was alarmed. People were killed in these air raids. There were always casualties.... What if a bomb—what if he should never be able to see Andree again to make matters right with her? How if he should be prevented from entreating her pardon for the ugly wrong he had done her and for his brutality—he could recognize it as brutality now.

Yet, mixed with all his self-accusation, his bitter heartache and wretchedness, there ran a vein of relief—actual relief, and of something like comfort. The pendulum of his subconscious self was swaying downward, preparatory to the upward sweep in the opposite direction.... The world was good, there was good in the world. All was not suspicion and sin; one might have faith in humanity.... The vestibule of the home church with its crowd of bigots seemed cold and untrue now, though they had appeared the one safe and living thing in the world so short a time ago.... Andree was good. He had not been mistaken in her; and if Andree was good, then other things and people must be good likewise.... Even Paris....

They descended into the Metro whose underground platforms were crowded with refuge-seekers of all classes and ages, who clustered together and railed against the *boche*. It was impossible to find a seat.... In half an hour many were sitting on the concrete floor: mothers with children sleeping in their laps; youths supporting the heads of sweethearts on willing shoulders; sleepy and frowsy old men and slatternly old women with hair that hung gray and unpleasant before their eyes. A gendarme prevented any from ascending the stairs to the open air.

It seemed hours, though it was only a trifle more than an hour before the "all clear" was sounded. The mighty clamor of the barrage and of falling bombs had penetrated only as a dim rumble to that depth. There had been no excitement, no exhilaration, only damp, cold discomfort. The refugees made their way stiffly to the out-of-doors, Kendall and Bert in their midst.

"If I should never find her—" Ken said, uneasily.

"You will."

"But if she should refuse to listen."

"Um.... I shouldn't blame her. But you know her, son, better than I. I saw her eyes to-night—and I shouldn't worry. They were the sort of eyes that forgive much."

"Yes," said Kendall, slowly. "But she will remember. She is that sort, too. She will never forget—and this thing will always be there, never to be gotten rid of.... She will look at me, and I will see it in her eyes, that she is wondering and that she is afraid—that I might do such a thing again...."

"The trouble with you is too darn much imagination," Bert said, disgustedly. "Let's get to bed. Work goes on to-morrow, whatever happens."

Work would go on and life would go on; death would continue to claim its own and births would replenish the races of the earth; there would be sorrow and joy, sin and repentance, squalor and luxury, in spite of anything that happened to him.... Kendall seized upon this thought. He was infinitely small, of less than negligible importance in the world's scheme.... Events would transpire as usual, and the story of mankind would continue adding to itself chapter by chapter. It was inevitable.... Just as it was inevitable that the *motif* of the story should be love, and that so long as it should continue to be love the good should predominate the evil, and the ending, though it might threaten to be tragic, must be happy for the majority. He saw, for the first time, that a world in which love is the first essential cannot be a lost world nor an unhappy world. He wondered if love, in whatever form it showed itself, was not merely the essence of *good* masquerading under another style. In that case to love was to be virtuous.... He inclined to believe it. The reflection made him easier of mind.

"I think I can sleep," he said to Bert, and they turned their faces homeward.

CHAPTER XVII

Kendall Ware woke up to a world which was not all straight lines and angles, which was not an uncompromising and rule-of-thumb world as it had seemed yesterday. To-day it was a world in which curves and even curlicues were permissible. Yesterday he was in sympathy with the Blue Laws and could have understood a God who frowned if a man were to kiss his wife of a Sabbath. To-day he could not comprehend the attitude of yesterday, hardly remembered it, in fact. He was young, and rapid changes of attitude were possible to him as the heart was heavy or light, as events were kind or harsh. It would not have been true to say that he was light of heart this morning, but his heart was in a condition to become light, needing only to find Andree and to receive Andree's forgiveness to make it so.

As was characteristic, the pendulum of his convictions had swung to the opposite and most remote point of its arc; where yesterday any deviation from orthodox rule and rigid form had been a sin, to-day he was inclined to err on the side of liberality. It seemed, rather, as if nothing could be wholly evil, and this simply because it had been shown to him that Andree was not evil and that his relations with her need not of necessity be degrading. Yesterday he had been possessed by his inheritances from his mother; to-day his father was in control. Just as the one had been exaggerated, so now the other was in extreme.... And therefore he could conceive happiness and stand upon the brink of happiness.... To be able to perceive virtue is to be happy. It is a perception which is its own reward....

Last night he had been afraid he would never find Andree; now he was certain she would be easy to find. It was the matter of forgiveness that caused his uneasiness. He had been brutal, harsh, presenting an unlovely spectacle. It was such a spectacle of a man's self as might prove fatal to love, for who can love the unlovely? And yet when he thought of Andree's gentleness, her sweetness, of all the many indications he had seen of a gracious and tender character, he even dared to hope that he had not offended past condoning.

He arose impatiently, eager for the day to commence so that it might end and enable him to take up his search.

"Bert!" he called. "Up yet?"

"Getting up," Bert answered, drowsily.

"Is Arlette here yet?"

"Haven't heard her."

"What in thunder's getting into her! Doesn't she know a fellow's got to have breakfast in the morning?"

"Huh—she isn't due for quarter of an hour. What's the sudden rush?"

Before he was fully clothed Arlette rapped on his closed door to demand his shoes, which he passed out to her, together with his puttees, and walked into Bert's room, wearing bedroom slippers.

"Some uniform," said Bert, eying the spectacle. "Ought to recommend it to the General Staff. Swagger, I call it. Now if you only wore red socks.... H'm! How you feeling this morning?"

"Hungry."

"Surprising, seeing you didn't eat anything all day yesterday." Bert studied his friend's face covertly and found reason for satisfaction. With more tact than his character warranted one to expect, he let the subject of yesterday rest there and did not again refer to it. He finished shaving in his usual leisurely manner, put on his blouse and belt, and was just in time to receive his shoes and leggings from Arlette.

"Mind having dinner late to-night?" Ken asked.

"No. Why?"

"I—I hope Andree will be here."

"H'm!... Want me to look up Madeleine?"

"Rather you didn't. We'll—Well, you can see yourself that we'll have a lot of talking to do.... I've got to square myself."

"I'll clear out altogether and let you have the place to yourselves."

"No need. I might not—it's possible I won't find her."

Bert thought that was highly probable, but he did not say so. "Just as you say," he said. "What time?"

"Eight o'clock. If I'm not here by that time, go ahead and eat."

"What about you?"

"I'm going to camp in that café on the corner there until I find her." Ken's jaws became prominent. "I'll stay there till I'm a permanent improvement."

Arlette came in, casting apprehensive glances at Kendall; she was unsmiling and had nothing to say beyond the greetings of the morning. Ken realized that he was in her disfavor.

"Arlette," he said.

She paused in the door and, glancing up to his face quickly, let her eyes shift to the carpet. "Yes, monsieur," she said.

"You're angry with me."

"*Non, monsieur.*"

"Yes you are. You should be. I've been a fool."

She looked up again, this time scrutinizing his face more carefully. "Monsieur did not conduct himself with wisdom," she said.

"What should I have done, Arlette?" He was really curious to know what she would answer.

"It is never wise to hurt where one is loved," she said. "Also one should be sure that no mistake is made—"

"But it was a mistake, Arlette.... If you loved as you told me you did once, and the man you loved behaved as I did, what would you do? Would you forgive him?"

"Me?" said Arlette. "Ah, who can say! It is many years, and love is only a thing to remember sometimes.... But I, monsieur, was not as Mademoiselle Andree is. Oh, no. There was weight to me, and a temper of the highest. Oh yes, and I spoke many words with great readiness. It is so.... What would you? Mademoiselle Andree is not at any point the same. She is gentle and sweet, monsieur, and it may be she is forgiving. As for me, I think if any man had so behaved to me he would have taken himself away with words in his ear that, I'll warrant, would have leaped through to his clumsy brain, *oui*, and with other reminders that I was not to be dealt with after such a manner.... But, as I have said, I was of a weight, and my temper was high."

"But you would have forgiven?"

Arlette waggled her head and wiped her chin on the back of her hand. "At least," she said, "I should have made him earn my forgiveness.... Oh, Monsieur Ken, it was not well for you to treat her so; it was of a cruelty.... But I believe she will forgive; her eyes were of the kind that forgive with too great readiness."

She turned and was about to disappear when she leaned far back to allow her face to present itself at a droll angle in the doorway. "Jealousy," she said, "is a disease that makes heavy hearts. In very truth, I have seen it.... It is much better if one is not jealous. One cannot at the same time be jealous and wise.... And always there are regrets."

"Will you have dinner at eight to-night? A nice dinner. I hope to find Mademoiselle Andree and bring her home again."

"Find her? But monsieur has but to go to her address. She has not gone away?"

"I do not know her address."

Arlette sighed and waggled her head ponderously.

"Then monsieur must apply to the police. All addresses are known to the police."

"But I don't know her name—only Andree."

"Name of God!... Can such things be? Oh, these Americans! Who has seen their like? Not know her name, not know her address. It is of an impossibility!... Does he speak truly, monsieur?" she demanded of Bert, who nodded in the affirmative.

"*Mon Dieu!... Mon Dieu!...*" she exclaimed, and waddled off to the kitchen as if she dared no longer trust her body in the presence of such a madman.

"There," said Bert, "now you know what a respectable body thinks of you. Apparently she thinks all Americans are in the habit of cutting up such capers. Most likely she believes addresses don't count with us because we live under trees like savages, and never go back to the same tree twice...."

"Anybody who doesn't do things exactly as you yourself do them is a savage. We think the French are barbarians, the French think we are barbarians, and the English consider both of us savages.... Come on, it's time we were starting."

When they reached the street Ken began to walk swiftly, as if by hurrying now he could make the day pass more quickly. At the office he plunged into his work, taking only the briefest period for lunch. At five o'clock he was on his way toward the Place St.-Michel to take up his sentry-go there. Somehow he was confident he would see Andree. What she did with her days he did not know, but he imagined she went into the city. Certainly she went somewhere, and to return she must traverse the square from the Metro station over at the left. He, therefore, took his station by the rim of the fountain and watched each passer-by. It was tiresome to watch and wait; the people did not interest him as they had always interested him before. Quaint couples passed unnoticed; children stopped to stare at him as he sat on the flat rim of the basin; venders of Rintintin and Ninette dangled their worsted dolls before him in vain. Once or twice he thought he saw her coming, and stood up eagerly, only to sink down again, disappointed.... And then he saw her coming; it was she unmistakably; there was no mistaking that tam, that flimsy little dress, that slender figure and her quaint, abstracted walk.

Long before she saw him he was groping for words, searching for the one thing to say, because he knew that there must be some single thought that should be put into words.... There must be some eloquent sentence which would explain all, gain forgiveness for all. But he could not find it. His French was gone; his English would not take form.

She crossed the square with little steps that seemed almost stiff, her body very erect, as always, and her eyes seeming to see nothing that went on about her. He fancied a shade of sadness was added to the gravity of her face.... She did not see him until he stood before her and spoke, and it was no eloquent sentence that he uttered, no wonderful thought that he put into words.

"*Mignonne!*..." he said.

She did not start, but merely stopped and raised her eyes to his face slowly. There was no surprise, no emotion of any sort to be seen, only that quaint gravity with which he was so familiar. She stopped and waited, as she always stopped and waited, ready, it seemed, to take her cue from what was about to happen. She might never have seen him before, but then, he thought, she always met him so—as if she had never seen him before.... She did not speak; only waited.

He was inarticulate, abashed, nonplussed. Suddenly it seemed to him that there was nothing to say, nothing that could be said. He had been guilty of conduct which removed him forever from her life, which was unforgivable. There was an impulse to turn and to hurry away from her, but he repressed it.... He must do something, say something.

"I'm ashamed," he said, clumsily. "I've been miserable.... I had to find you and tell you.... I—What can I say? It was wicked—wicked...."

He could go no farther, could only search her face with his eyes for some reflection of her thoughts, for some sign that he might hope for pardon. She did not reply; there was no change in her expression, only that unfathomable gravity and that air of suspended judgment.

"Last night I tried to find you.... I sat and waited, but you did not come. I couldn't go to sleep until I had begged you to forgive me.... I don't deserve to be forgiven. What I did—what I said, was unforgivable.... Oh, Andree!..."

There was a little pause, then she said, "You have been sad?"

"Yes."

"And I also," she said, not reproachfully.

"I—Never before have I known what it was to suffer—and I have suffered. It was right that I should. I deserved punishment." Even here the Puritan in him obtruded itself. "And you were so good, so sweet, so wonderful.... I know all about it now—and I was suspicious and brutal.... I was jealous, too. But I didn't know I was jealous.... When I thought you were not good, it seemed to me that nothing in the world could be good. Do you understand?... But there's no excuse for me. I should have known, and I should have trusted you.... I didn't even give you a chance to explain...."

"Oh, you speak ver' fast. I cannot onderstan' all.... But you have not been happy—no.... It is to be seen.... At first I do not onderstan', and I am ver' sad and hurt—oh, ver' sad. When I make to cross the *pont* I look down at the water—yes.... And then I say it is some mistake.... I say something have happen I do not know of and it makes you to be not like Monsieur Ken, but ver' hurt and miserable and—how you say?—upset? Yes. I say, also, that I love Monsieur Ken and always that I am *fidèle*.... So what could it be?... If, then, it is nothing, only some mistake, then I am much sorry.... Not sorry for me, monsieur, who have done no wrong, but for you, who are mos' unhappy.... It is so. My heart it makes to weep for you because you suffer...."

"Andree!..."

She nodded her head gravely. "I do not onderstan' *les Américains*.... *Non!... Non!* They are of a difference. But I onderstan' love which mus' be the same in America as in France, so I say Monsieur Ken he is ver' jealous and ver' mistaken, and I mus' be patient and not sad more than is *nécessaire*.... So I wait till thees mistake is not a mistake any more. And many times I mus' say to myself that you are jealous, and therefore you love me. Because if there is not love, then there is not to be jealous, *n'est-ce pas*? So I am almos' happy, but not quite ... because you love me."

"And you don't hate me? You can forgive me?"

"Oh, *mon bien cher ami*, there is nothing to forgive! It is so.... It is only that I cried sometimes for you, because you are mos' miserable.... I say to theenk how sad you are, and then I cry.... I would not have you to be sad."

"It isn't possible," Ken said, more than half to himself. "There's nobody like this in the world."

"Possible?... *Pourquoi?*"

"Mademoiselle Pourquoi—dear little Mademoiselle Pourquoi!" he said, softly.

"You are not angry with me any more—not jealous?"

"No.... No."

"It is well." She smiled for the first time and touched his arm with her little hand. "Then I am joyous."

"You ought to be joyous always.... You are wonderful. When I think what you were giving up for me—and that I could suspect you—I hate myself."

"But you are not sad now? There is not any mistake any more, and we are together. You are not sad?"

"Sad, *mignonne*!... Only when I think of what I said to you—things you can never forget—"

"Never forget?" She laughed a little. "Behol', already I have forgotten. It is as if nothing ever happen'. I do not remember. Now"—she made that old familiar gesture of pointing repeatedly to the sidewalk with her finger to indicate the identical present second—"now I remember nothing. I do not know what you talk about.... You are ver' droll, Monsieur Ken, to be speak so much about something I do not know ... about a something that have never happen'."

Kendall felt something that was almost reverence for her; it was more than wonder and little less than awe. Never until that moment had he conceived of the possibility that such greatness of heart, such forgetfulness of self, such *rightness* could exist in the world.... He felt himself incapable of appreciating, of appraising the gold of her heart. It was very sweet, very radiant, that moment. There must be a goodness in the world more marvelous, purer, worthier than he had been able to imagine, and Andree possessed it.... And, possessing that goodness, she could not in any particular be evil. She would see rightly, and evil that was truly evil would be abhorrent in her eyes. His last doubt, his last fear, his last self-accusation departed from him; in his elation he was unable to perceive that a thing virtuous in Andree and for Andree might be quite other for himself....

"You gave up everything for me—your chance to enter the *Académie*, to go on the stage ... to be famous, perhaps."

"Oh, that!..." She smiled up at him. "Nothing in the worl' is so good to have as love. It is so. It is a ver' great theeng. One leetle hour, one day of love—that is more great and more necessary to have than the mos' fame that can be."

"You do love me, Andree? Say it."

"I love you," she said, gently.

"I can never let you out of my sight again. You must be with me always—where I can see you and touch you."

She smiled up at him, but there was a shade of sadness, perhaps of apprehension, in her deep-shadowed black eyes. "It is not possible," she said.

"Arlette has dinner waiting for us."

"To-night? Now.... Oh, it is not possible...." She made a pretty gesture of dismay.

"It is necessary. To prove that you have forgiven me. I couldn't let you go now ... now that I've found you again. Come."

She looked down at the walk a moment with detached gravity, then put her fingers on his arm. "Ver' well," she said. "You mus' take me off like *prisonnier de guerre, n'est-ce pas?*... You have capture me, so what am I to do? I am ver' helpless.... You mus' say many sweet theengs to me so that I am not sad."

They crossed the street to the Metro station and descended to the crowded train in which they were compelled to stand until they reached the Châtelet station, where they changed to the line that runs under the rue de Rivoli and the Champs Élysées. It was impossible to talk except in occasional monosyllables, but every now and then Kendall would look down into Andree's face, always to find her looking up at him gravely, but happily. Then he would press her arm gently, and she would respond by nestling his fingers between her arm and her body. He was happy, boyishly happy. It was a new sort of happiness for him—a great, surging happiness which made the world lovely, which made even standing in a swaying subway car, jostled and elbowed by a tired crowd, a delectable thing.

He yearned toward Andree as he had never yearned toward her before. He wanted to hold her in his arms, not passionately, but gently. He was filled with a desire to show a great gentleness and consideration for her, to prove to her that he was kind. He wanted to protect her, to shield her, to deal with her as he would have dealt with a tired, trusting child, for she seemed very childlike to him, with all the purity and heart honesty of a child.... He magnified the thing she had done, and the beauty of her forgiveness, repeating over and over in his thoughts that she was good, wonderfully, miraculously good.

"*Mignonne!...*" he whispered in her ear, and she smiled up at him and pressed his hand.

At last they alighted and mounted to the street, and there he attempted to keep step with her tiny, severe strides until both of them laughed gaily at his efforts. She was all child now, laughing, roguish, teasing. She rattled French at him, well knowing he could not understand, and laughed at him for not understanding, and he pretended to believe she was telling him that he was ugly and cross-eyed and that she was ashamed to walk with him. Then they were at the apartment, and Ken greeted the *concierge* with a cordiality that left the old lady a little amazed and wondering if her American officer had not been dealing too liberally with the wines of the country.

"Oh, I shall not walk up these so many stairs," Andree said, with her pretty mock despair. "It is not possible. You have not made an *ascenseur*. It was a promise.... Oui. And until you fetch one I shall remain here, on this spot." She indicated the spot severely.

"I'll be the *ascenseur*," he volunteered, and made as if to lift her in his arms, but she slipped away and danced up the stairs before him, making believe, as she approached each floor, to be on the point of dropping from exhaustion, and counting each floor with dismay.

"So much have we climb' and it only is the *premier étage....* Oo là là.... For hours we mount, and arrive but at the secon'—what do you say?—secon' floor. It is ver' fonny. Secon' floor. *Mais, mon bien cher ami,* it sound' like nothing at all, on'y jus' sound.... Secon' floor!... Such a language is thees Engleesh!"

They arrived at the fourth floor honestly panting, and she sank into a chair while Kendall searched under the mat for the key.

"I will go no more," she said, firmly. "I am *blessée*. I am one *poilu* with the bad wound. It is not possible to proceed. Behol', I am one *poilu*."

She puffed out her cheeks and frowned. *"Sacré nom d'une pipe!...* It is so the *poilu* swears...."

He thrust open the door and, picking her slight form up as he might have lifted little Arlette, he carried her inside and set her down before the hall tree.... His hands rested on her shoulders and they both became grave, looking into each other's eyes.... And then he drew her close to him and pressed his lips to hers....

Arlette padded into the hall, attracted by the sound, observed what she observed, folded her pudgy hands on her stomach, and stared with amazement. *"Mon Dieu!... Mon Dieu!..."* she exclaimed, and padded away again in confusion.

Then they went into the *salon*, where Bert was reading the paper.

"I've found her," Ken said, gaily.

"So I observe." Bert's voice was dry.

"Your voice must not be so w'en you speak to Monsieur Ken," Andree said, severely. *"Non...* I will not have it so. Bicause he is ver' good, and nobody mus' be—w'at you say?—cross with him—so."

"Well," Bert said, "I'll be gentle with the child, mademoiselle, though it's contrary to my duty." He turned to Ken. "You seem to have put it over," he said.

"Bert, she's wonderful—she's—"

"I've heard just two hundred and seven men say that at one time and another. Seems to be a stock phrase in the language of young gentlemen in your state of mind.... Anyhow, I'm glad the rumpus is settled. I can get some sleep now."

"Does he scold you?" Andree asked.

"It doesn't matter what he does," Ken said, laughingly. "Nothing matters.... There's Arlette's head through the door. Let's eat."

Arlette served silently, but as she moved about the table she kept her eyes furtively upon Andree, and her lips moved constantly without uttering a sound. This continued until it was time to remove the meat, and then Arlette could contain herself no longer. She reached the door on her way to the kitchen with the platter, when, with startling suddenness, she turned, replaced the platter on the edge of the table, folded her hands across her stomach, rolled her eyes to heaven, and launched upon a harangue in such rapid French that it seemed one continuous word of mingled syllables.

Andree listened gravely, nodding her head the merest trifle every moment or so. Then Arlette paused expectantly and Andree replied with all the gravity of a Cabinet Minister facing a crisis. At the end of a sentence she got out of her chair and walked to Ken and put her arm about his neck and her cheek to his, continuing the reply thence. Arlette rolled her eyes and waggled her head and heaved great sighs.... Presently her set face relaxed and she smiled and wiped her chin on the back of her hand.

"*Mon Dieu!...*" she said. "*Mon Dieu!...*" and with a tremulous smile which, somehow, was not at all absurd on her heavy face—was almost tender—she retreated with suddenness to her kitchen.

"Well," said Ken, "what now, *mignonne*? What's it all about?"

Andree shook her head gaily. "No!... No!... It is not for you. I shall not speak it."

"Was it so terrible as that?... I'm afraid I have made an enemy of Arlette."

"But no. Well, dear friend, it is that she have much worry for you. Yes. She have much worry. She theenk you—oh, it is ver' fonny!—she theenk you are leetle child that is lost and also is mad! She theenk something happen to you if you have no one to take care of you. She tell me I mus' not be angry with you, but ver' nice and kind always, bicause it is not your fault you are a baby and mad.... Oh yes. She say she love you like she is your *marraine*, but she is powerless to make you to be protected.... And she theenk I mus' take you by the hand same theeng as you are blind.... So I have promise', and now she will not worry, but gives you to me to care for. She have been mos' unhappy. She say that only God can onderstan' a mad American who is in love!..."

"Arlette," said Bert, "is a woman of sound judgment."

"Where is Mademoiselle Madeleine?" Andree asked, with one of those sudden changes of subject which were characteristic of her.

"I haven't the least idea."

"Why is she not here? I want her to be here. I would speak of many things to her."

"Blame Ken there. I suggested having Madeleine, but he said he wanted you all by yourself with nobody else around."

She turned to look at Ken as if to satisfy herself if this were truth or jesting, and then she smiled the merest trifle. "It is well," she said, softly.

"I'm on my way," said Bert, arising. "Got a bridge game on at the Union.... *Bon soir, mademoiselle*.... And you, Ken, keep your feet on the ground."

"'Keep your feet on the groun',''' repeated Andree, when Bert was gone. "Oh, it mean nothing whatever. Thees English language, it is *très-drôle*. What is thees keep your feet on the groun'?"

"It means that Bert agrees with Arlette that I need somebody to look after me," he said, a bit ruefully.

"It is well. Here am I—here—here." She laughed that fairy laugh, and poked her finger toward the floor many times. "I am here, so he mus' not be afraid. I shall look after you. Oh yes, I shall be mos' firm and ver' stern. You shall see." And she made a tremendous face to show him what severity she was capable of.

They went into the *salon*, with its absurd bronze statues, its tasteless gilt furniture, and its absurd little throne between the windows. Andree must observe herself closely before the huge glass above the fireplace and do little unnecessary things to her hair and touch her nose with a powder-puff. Ken watched her delightedly, and then carried her to her throne, where she sat dangling her tiny feet while he closed the heavy iron shutters to make it lawful for him to turn on the lights.

Andree moved over to the sofa, looking up at him with that gravely curious expression which he saw so often on her face; she seemed to be wondering, always wondering, about something. Was it possible he was as strange, as unusual, as interesting to her as she was to him? He would have given much to know just what she was thinking, but, somehow, even then it was borne in upon him that he should never know—that she would always remain a sweet, bewildering, exotic mystery to him.

"Sit by me—ver' close," she said; and he sat by her and took her in his arms, while she snuggled against him with the contented sigh of a child.

"Do you love me?" he whispered.

She nodded emphatically, and then with an upward glance said, as she always said, "And you?"

"More than I can say.... *Toujours*—always. I shall always love you."

"It is well.... We shall make the pretense it is so—that you love me always. But the little moments, they are so sweet—well, dear friend, that they could not be always. Is it not so? If it could be always then I theenk God He would be jealous.... No.... But we mus' pretend. We mus' pretend there is no war, and that you shall never go to *Amérique* again ... and leave me *solitaire*."

He was silent. This was a thought that had been growing in his mind from day to day, a thought he had refused to face or to consider. What was to be the end of it all? Suppose he should be ordered home in a week or a month. What then?... He did not know, and he was unwilling to ask himself. Rather he would be contented with the little minutes and let each day care for each day's problems. When the day of his return arrived, then the thing must be faced and the question answered.... But to-night he loved her; wanted to think of nothing but love and the happiness that such a sweetheart could bestow.... She seemed to wait for some answer, for some assurance, but he had none to make, and presently she said, but not with the same happy note in her voice:

"It may be that love is so great a thing that it cannot live forever—as it is for us. Behol'—one has a mos' beautiful jewel, and it is ver' nice and there is much joy to have it. But consider—if everything one had is jewels, jewels, jewels, then the firs' jewel it is not so nice, so wonderful. *N'est-ce pas?* It may be it is the same theeng with love. Do you onderstan'? It is great and ver' beautiful bicause it is only for the leetle moments w'en one is yo'ng— and w'en the heart it is ready for love.... I theenk this is so. Then, what can matter, *bien cher ami*? Thees love of now is the mos' bes' theeng of all life ... bicause, maybe, it cannot live much long.... Yes, yes, I have seen many ol' man and ol' woman who say they remember thees love—but not one who say he has thees love still. You see I theenk of it much...."

"Yes, honey."

"And so I have not fear that you go.... I have only fear that something happen bifore our little moment of happiness is done—never to come back again. Do you onderstan'? One day, for all, thees love it begins to fade and be less lovely. It becomes less strong and not weeth such wonderfulness.... I have seen. At las' it is but a friendship and a memory. But it is a great and a fine friendship bicause of the memory. Is it not so?... And that is marriage, my friend ... that friendship. It is but a good regard of each for the other which comes like the bread after the beautiful growing wheat.... Am I ver' foolish?"

"No.... No...."

"Bicause of thees that I believe, then I am not sad, but ver' happy, and I do not fear. I have what is worth all other theengs—thees leetle moment of happiness which is love.... I would pay for it weeth ever'thing. It is worth to pay for weeth much sorrow and weeth much loneliness.... If you mus' go—well, dear friend, let it be bifore thees leetle moment fades.... But we mus' pretend it shall never fade and that we are together always as thees.... It is more better so."

She drew his lips down to hers, and he knew that blind, throbbing, winged happiness which has no language, no symbols, no words of description, which can never be remembered except as a mysterious, haunting ecstasy which once was living and real, which leaves behind but the dim outline of its spirit and an elusive something as of a sweet scent that once tingled the nostrils for an instant, to be wafted away forever....

CHAPTER XVIII

Now commenced a brief period which was, perhaps, to be the happiest of Kendall Ware's whole life. It was happy because it was free from doubts and questionings. From the depths he had mounted to the heights from which he looked upon a world bathed in sunshine, rich in harvest, beautiful as a world could be beautiful only when it was freed from all evil. He saw everything as good, and it contented him. He ate of the lotus of inexperienced youth, flavored with the pungent spice of sophistry, and the taste of it was sweet in his mouth. Plymouth Rock had sunk beneath its sands, the vestibule of the Presbyterian church had vanished behind the mists of an intervening ocean. He did not think; he only felt and acted—and was happy.

His work was interesting, and he could recognize its value, so he became less dissatisfied with the necessity that held him far behind the battle-line. Not that he was content, rather that he was resigned.... And at the end of the day there was Andree....

There were few evenings which they did not spend together, either by themselves or with Bert and Madeleine, dining at home, at Poccardi's, at Marty's, or in interesting, homelike little cafés across the river where excellent food could be had very cheaply. Sometimes they went to the theater or to the music-halls. Sometimes they strolled up and down the Avenue du Bois de Boulogne until they were tired and then sat and talked contentedly on springy iron chairs along the promenade. Once they walked out that street, so crowded of evenings—that street of the ever-changing names—Montmartre, Poissonnière, Nouvelle, St.-Denis, St.-Martin—as far as the Place de la République. It was interesting, if tiresome. More than once Kendall was impressed with the fact that Parisians of a certain class take their pleasures simply and childishly. More than one glaring palace, open at the front, showed rows upon rows of those devices, long extinct in America, before which one could sit or stand with the ends of a rubber tube in one's ears and listen to such tunes as found favor with him played by phonograph. The popularity of these places surprised him. They were always crowded.... It seemed to him that this was the most crowded thoroughfare in Paris, as well as one of the most questionable. The crowds impressed him as being questionable and bent on questionable errands.... And yet he did not know; he only guessed. So far as his knowledge went, these folk might be the most respectable in all France—all save the numerous soft-voice girls who threaded their way in and out.... And for a mere child, a girl who seemed hardly in her teens, who bit and struggled in the hands of two gendarmes, shrieking in a voice that remained long in Kendall's ears, "I have the age!... I have the age!... I have the age!..." over and over again....

Madeleine had laughed and shrugged her shoulders with some flippant word of comment, but Kendall looked down at Andree to see her eyes moist and big with pity.

"*Pauvre p'tite!... Pauvre p'tite!...* It is not she who should be punish'. She have made no wrong.... I theenk it is the crime of poverty. *N'est-ce pas?* Oh, to be *pauvre*—it is not well...."

"Yet *le bon Dieu* permits it," said Madeleine.

"*Non!... Non!...* It is not of God, ma'm'selle; it is of man—thees poverty and thees awful theengs.... It mus' be that tears come often to the eyes of the good God...."

Kendall was affected deeply. She spoke of the good God with such simplicity, with the sort of intimacy which children use. He felt almost a reverence for her.... There was a *rightness* about her, a simple, unaffected, unconscious *goodness*, that set her apart and made her different, to him, from all mankind.

"*Mignonne!*" he whispered, and pressed her arm, and she, looking up shyly into his face, gave answering pressure, and, perhaps, wondered a little.

She was always so, never changing, yet always possessed of that infinite variety of which Shakespeare speaks. But it was a variety which was always Andree. In no mood, in no manifestation, could she be anything but Andree. If she were sad, it was with a sadness peculiar to her, and very lovable; if she were gay, it was with her own gaiety; if she were mischievous, it was with a charming impishness which no other being could have managed. And always she was natural—as natural as the rain that falls or the sun that shines or the breezes that blow.... She was Andree.

"To-morrow is the great fête," said Andree. "There will be much to see."

"And I can't show it to you. I must work in the morning, and in the afternoon I am ordered to go to the front."

"How long?" she said, quickly.

"But one day. I shall be here again Sunday—and we shall play, eh? We shall have *déjeuner* together and do something in the afternoon, and find a place to dine...."

"It is well—but you mus' be ver' careful. You mus' not let the *boche* keel you.... Oh, I should be sad, sad."

Already Paris was dressing for the American fête-day, the Fourth of July, which, by methods of law, had been made her own national holiday this year. Everywhere were American flags. There was no house in Paris too poor to show some small copy of the Stars and Stripes, for just now Paris was mad about America and Americans ... as it had had its day of madness over the Belgians and then the English. Paris is given to such enthusiasms, and at the moment there were men in the service of the great god Propaganda who labored to bring it about that this latest passion should not die and become sudden ashes as the others had done, but rather to persuade it to subside slowly, unnoticeably, leaving a pleasant memory behind....

"The *boches* will pull something off to-morrow," said Bert. "You see. They'll do something to bust up the celebration."

This was the opinion of the Paris streets—that the Hun would, by some ingenious and disagreeable means, make the fête memorable in the history of the city.

"Maybe it's just as well I'm going away," laughed Ken. "So you, Ma'm'selle Pourquoi—you look out for yourself. Don't you let anything hurt you."

"Me—*pouf!*... It could not be. While there is you nothing can happen to me—nothing. I am ver' safe."

They tried in vain to persuade a *voiture* or a taxicab to take them home, but, with that perversity which belongs to the Paris cabby alone, none of them would go. One reason or another was given—the horse was tired, the gasolene supply was depleted, it was the wrong quarter of the city. A large volume, serious or comic, might be written on the habits and moods of these public conveyances of the most charming city in the world. Paris would not be the same without them. While they are one of the irritations, none the less they are of the quaint and pleasant memories of the city, and Kendall could often see himself, as he sat at some future day, retailing to audiences of less traveled Americans than he his adventures with the war-time taxi.

Finally they were obliged to descend to the Metro, which carried them to the Place de l'Opéra, to change there for the short ride to the Palais Royal, where another change was necessary to carry them to the Étoile. It was late and they were tired.

"Oh, we have make the *beaucoup travail*—the so great labor thees day," said Andree, shaking her head. "I have the *fatigue*.... But it is well to be weary. Are you weary, Monsieur Ken?"

"I am happy," he said.

"Yes.... Yes.... That is bes' of all—to be happy. Tell me, when you have gone to the front—will you theenk of me?"

"In the morning, at noon, in the afternoon—"

"Oh, oh!... It is not possible. But sometimes. Once, twice? For I shall be theenking of you always."

"Do you love me?"

"Yes," she nodded emphatically, and then—he would have missed it had she omitted it—"and you?"

"More than anybody in the world."

"More than thees yo'ng American girl?... I have seen her thees day. She is in Paris. Do you know?"

"You must be mistaken, *mignonne*. Miss Knox is out at the front."

"It is so.... It is so. I have seen her—thees day. Oh, do you theenk I do not know her? I am ver' *jalouse*—mos' *jalouse*. She come for take you away from me."

"Don't you let her do it," said Ken happily. "Don't you dare let her do it."

"I do not know," she said, becoming suddenly grave. "You are American—she is American.... Some day..." Then she laughed gaily, impishly. "*Mais* these American girl, they do not know how to dress. Oh, it is terrible!"

"You mustn't judge all American women by these uniforms you see in France," said Bert. "Just now it is the style in America for women to get into something they think are uniforms. I wonder who designed these Y. M. C. A. uniforms, anyhow?... But really, Mademoiselle Andree, our women do know how to dress."

"I have never seen," she said, stubbornly. "Also they do not always wear uniforms, but always they wear their feet. Their feet they cannot take off. *Mais non*. It is too bad. If only they could leave at home their feet."

Kendall suspected that American women were suffering for the sins of Maude Knox, so he did not rush to their defense. He did not want to think about Maude Knox to-night—he wanted to think of no woman but Andree.

"*Méchante!*" he whispered.

"It is so—what I say," she said, severely. "I do not like American women.... I do not like thees girl. She ees ver' wicked, for she wish to steal you from me."

The street was very dark. Kendall made youth's answer to youth's jealousy. He lifted her slight form in his arms and kissed her until she returned his kisses.

"There," he said, "you are punished."

"It ees ver' nice to be wicked," she said. "Thees punishment is ver' well."

Maude Knox was banished. They two found themselves the sole inhabitants of a brightly glowing world....

Next morning Kendall made his way through early assembling crowds to his office, where he was much occupied until noon, making preparations for his trip to the front. Then he was driven through the holiday-making streets crowded with a populace in holiday humor to the *barrière*, and thence into the country. On every building waved an American flag, in every buttonhole was a tiny American flag, and the appearance of an American military automobile was the signal for applause and lifting of hats. Small boys shouted as small boys of all countries shout; friendly old gentlemen waved their canes; young women smiled broadly or demurely, invitingly or shyly. Kendall felt as if he were enjoying some sort of a triumph, as if this celebration were for him. The frankness and open-heartedness and courtesy of it were delightful.

They drove rapidly through little villages, between rolling fields cultivated as only the French agriculturist seems to be able to cultivate. The villages, too, were in gala dress and the people in holiday attire. In one place a brief stop was made. Immediately the car was surrounded by children who shouted eagerly for "penny," for "gu-um," for "cigarette." So it was all over France. Let but an American soldier appear and the children of the neighborhood formed a group about him demanding tribute.

Soon the civil inhabitants disappeared. Whole villages were occupied by billeted troops, *poilus* and colonials, black-skinned men wearing red fezzes and speaking strange tongues who gave to the picture an exotic tint. The countryside swarmed with soldiers *en repos*, a zone miles deep crowded with the guardians of Paris and of the Channel ports.... Now came forests in whose depths could be caught fleeting glimpses of huge ammunition-dumps, skilfully camouflaged, then a wonderful woods, clean as the floor of a kitchen, a forest of magnificent trees, but as well kept as a Michigan peach-orchard.... Dusk descended, then darkness. The car seemed to be running into a black curtain upon a thread of white cloud. Kendall could not see the length of his nose to one side or the other, but ahead could be discerned that pale cloud avenue, a sort of milky way that disappeared itself into blackness a hundred feet away. He was now upon one of those roads of white chalk, deep with dust which arose in clouds and nestled in the hair and eyebrows and penetrated the very pores of the skin, giving to men the singular appearance of having been carved out of bronze.

Presently the horizon glowed for an instant, as with heat lightning, and glowed again and again. There was a mutter and a grumble ahead which was the distant voice of the guns.... Something burst into flower in the sky far ahead, a vivid rose-blossom, then another and another. It was shrapnel, either our own demanding toll of a prowling German aeroplane or the enemy searching the air for an Allied machine.... The heat lightning became continuous, the roar of the guns a rumble without break, almost a single, sustained note.

Ken was riding in the depths of a sea of blackness. To right and left the eyes encountered an *impasse*; ahead was only that dim milky way of road and those upsurging lights as the guns answered one another across the desert of No Man's Land. The car was traveling at breakneck speed. Suddenly came a tremendous snap almost in Ken's ears, a snap as of a mountain being cracked in twain by giant hands. There was a blinding flash across the road ahead and the air was usurped by the scream of a departing shell. A battery by the roadside had taken up its work of the night. Kendall was in the midst of it now. Guns on both sides cracked and roared; projectiles screamed over his head, and now and then would come that easily distinguishable sound, the bursting of a German shell....

Presently the road sank below the level of the fields. The car was running between irregular rows of barely discernible lights which appeared to issue from the ground—as indeed they did—glowing from the dugouts of French artillerymen who had burrowed into the banks at the side of the road. The moon began to climb so that objects became dimly visible. The scene was like that of some village of prehistoric cave-dwellers, save for those breaks in the line of dugouts, cunningly covered with nets of camouflage, under which lurked the cannon, muzzles directed toward the foe.

Now they stopped in a battered, deserted village which was headquarters of our Twenty-eighth Infantry, a component of that First Division made up of our old regulars—a body of troops whose name will be famous as long as the history of America shall endure. And there, in an enormous dugout entered through a narrow tunnel some fifty feet in length, Ken found shelter for the night. He traversed the tunnel, descended steps carved out of the stone to a level twenty feet below, and found himself in a warren. Here, notwithstanding the hour of the night, were bustle and activity. Here were offices where sounded the click of typewriters and the staccato of the telephone; here were passages, bedrooms, a dining-room—a veritable maze hewn out of the chalk formation. It was as if Ali Baba's forty thieves had turned systematic and were carrying on their trade according to modern business methods. Yet men worked here as casually and nonchalantly, accustomed by long habit, as they would have worked in their New York offices....

Kendall was provided with a cot, and, despite the sounds that penetrated here, the sounds of the Fourth of July celebration of the First Division, he slept....

Early in the morning he awoke, then, after some hours spent with the regimental intelligence officer, he walked abroad to see this historic countryside. Far off to the left the glasses showed him that spot which had been Montdidier; almost straight ahead was the grisly, silent crumble known now to the world by the name of Cantigny.

The day was beautiful. It seemed strange, unnatural that the country should be so beautiful as well. Even the gun-pits among which Kendall quickly found himself did not detract from the beauty, for they were almost invisible even at a distance of a few yards, only appearing as low mounds, scarcely differing in color from the surrounding fields. Yet the guns were there under their tents of chicken-wire covered with stained burlap and grasses. Everywhere he looked were these mounds which during the night that had just passed had been uncovered to the sky while shells filled with deadly gas had screamed through intervening miles of air to fall with deadly effect in the German lines.... It had been mustard gas, six thousand rounds of it, he had been told. He was also told it was the first time American gunners had been supplied with that devilishness of war—to celebrate the Fourth.... Now the gun-pits were neat as a New England parlor, guns were brightly polished. Nothing seemed to have happened there.

He stood above and looked down the slope of the valley, a valley of golden fields, a valley which was a miracle of color. Never had Kendall seen such color, acres upon acres of it, nor such a profusion of flowers. Gold and red and white and blue ... and *peace*! That valley had been spread there for some painter—not for a battle-field. It impressed the inherited mysticism in him—he saw a symbolism in it all. The fields blazed with gorgeous tints; rectangles acres in extent were red with poppies, not with a sprinkling of poppies here and there, but as with a snowfall of vivid red. Segregated in an adjoining field were cornflowers, a carpet of blue; and then another field glaring white with some flower that Kendall did not know.... Other fields there were in which the three flowers mingled. The panorama spoke of peace and beauty.... It was as if the war irritated God until He spread this, His own camouflage of peace, to hide the horrors from His down-gazing eyes.... Or perhaps, as of olden times He had set His rainbow in the sky as a promise to the sons of Noah, so now He planted this living rainbow in the fields as a new and more wonderful promise to all the sons of men ... a promise that His purposes should nevermore demand another war to devastate the earth....

Before him, knee-deep in poppies, moved half a dozen figures in khaki.

"The boys are gathering flowers for the funeral," he was told.

"The funeral?..."

"Of the men killed last night...."

Presently, his business completed, he was driving toward Paris, reached Paris in the darkness with a feeling of home-coming and pleasure.... But he was thoughtful, troubled. His sternly believing mother was awake in him, asserting that he had seen with his own eyes a movement of the finger of God—that he had read a sign from Omnipotence. It weighed him down, filled him not with joyous faith, but with Calvinistic gloom to have this assurance that God was actually taking an active interest in His world.... The weight of the knowledge of the existence of a Deity was upon him as it had been upon his stern forebears—the knowledge of the existence of a Deity, stern, forbidding, cruel in his revenges and implacable in his demands ... not of such a God as Andree knew—whose eyes might be wet with tears caused by the sufferings of His puppets to whom He had vouchsafed the dubious boon of freedom of action....

He awoke in the morning as one awakes from an impressive dream, with a feeling of heaviness upon him, a consciousness of his personal existence that made him dull company at breakfast. This humor did not pass away, it was rather laid aside for further reference and obscured by the events and anticipations of the day.

"Good trip?" asked Bert.

"Fine! Saw a lot."

"Wish I could get a crack at it sometime. I haven't heard a gun go off yet—except in an air raid.... Was anything stirring up there?"

Ken described his experiences of the day and night, and, strangely, from a different viewpoint than that from which he had beheld them. Yesterday the thing had been subjective, symbolical; to-day it was objective. He described the war he had seen as a tourist might describe some interesting scene in a foreign country—and he rather wondered at himself that he could think of it in that manner.

"When do you meet Andree?" Bert asked.

"Eleven o'clock—at the Place de la Concorde. You and Madeleine are coming along?"

"Sure! We'll pick you up there at eleven."

"Anything happen here yesterday?"

"Not a thing. The *boches* disappointed everybody. I went to one of those dinners the crowd at the Union are always piloting a fellow to—this Society of French Homes, or whatever they call it.... Four of us dined with a Madame Lefebvre."

"Good time?"

"Interesting. Played bridge with three French people, a deputy and two women. None of them spoke a word of English, but we made out pretty well. I won thirty francs.... They were rather upper crust in this town, I guess. Fine house and that sort of thing."

"I must go to one of those some day," said Ken, reflectively. "I've wondered if we were really seeing Paris—the way the French live."

"Not if that dinner last night was a sample. I had to lug out all my manners. And the women—they sort of made me feel uncomfortable. Dignified, you know, but very friendly. It was all the family. Old grandmother and her sons and daughters and a few grandchildren. Patriarchal affair."

"I want to see that sort of thing. People have told me that French family life is beautiful.... One wouldn't think it to judge from what we've seen."

"I don't know about the beautiful," said Bert, and Ken registered a thought that Bert would not be likely to notice domestic beauties, "but there was something fine about it. I liked it.... That old grandmother was bully.

They were all so doggone respectful.... And there was a young lieutenant, a grandson—had his face shot away. Nothing left but his mouth and one eye. Wore a big triangular patch over his face. He must have been quite a fellow, though. Had the Croix de Guerre and the Legion of Honor and the Médaille Militaire. Just been married, too—to a mighty nice little girl—one of these home bodies, looked as though. And, by Jove! she acted like she was a heap in love with him. It sort of got me—especially when everybody in the room took the opportunity at some time during the evening to tell me that she never met him until after he was mutilated.... I don't believe that sort of girl would pick up with a fellow, somehow. And I know mighty well her mother and grandmother never would have. I guess there are all kinds of French people, just the same as there are Americans...."

"Of course," said Ken, out of his abysmal ignorance. Then, defensively, "Maybe these aristocrats are different from the girls we know, but, I don't care how they live or how straitlaced they are, they're no better than Andree.... Andree's *good*."

"Sure," said Bert, "and you're dotty.... Meet you at eleven."

Ken wrote a few letters home, one to his mother in which he went rather to descriptions and very little to personal matters. He spoke little of France and the French, but rather made it appear that he was living in a Paris inhabited exclusively by American soldiers who were all so busy with the war that they had no time to do anything else but work and sleep. He did mention seeing Notre Dame ... which was a church, and of undoubted historic interest. It was a very circumspect letter, and not at all confidential.... But it is an undoubted fact that mothers and fathers have to earn by their conduct toward their children those confidences which they seem to fancy are theirs by right. Ken could have told his father anything—everything. But his mother—somehow it was difficult for him to compel himself to make the most trivial disclosure to her. Her attitude toward him and toward the world had created that difficulty. The young are naturally confidential....

Then he went to meet Andree.

One of the delights of Ken's acquaintance with Andree was that each meeting with her seemed a fresh adventure; there was a sameness about these meetings. Andree always appeared just so, and conducted herself just so. He could foretell with exactitude what her every movement and gesture and word would be when she did appear. But somehow, probably unconsciously, she was able to impart to every rendezvous a freshness, an air of mystery, something elusive and elfin that made them, no matter how often repeated, always alluring, exciting, delightful. Her sudden appearances out of a life of which he knew nothing and her disappearances back into that life lifted this affair above the level of all other affairs, imparting to it something of the occult, giving play to the imagination.... Ken cherished this illusion and, therefore, though often tempted, he asked no questions. Even now he did not know her name—only Andree.

Presently she appeared, just as he knew she would appear, walking very erect, with little steps that seemed almost stiff, her eyes cast downward or staring straight before her and seeming to see nothing whatever. He knew that she would approach within reach of his hand before she gave sign of recognition, and then she would regard him with grave query as if to ascertain if it were really he, and if, as she feared, she was not welcome. And then she would smile timidly, without taking her eyes from his, and shake hands with quaint formality, and ask how he carried himself. If she had changed any particular of it he would have been alarmed, would have felt a sense of loss.

"Bert and Madeleine will meet us here," he said.

"It is well." She smiled and nodded. "You have been at the front?"

"Yes."

"You are ver' *fatigué* perhaps?"

"No. I had a bully night's sleep, and I'm ready for anything. We must have a regular party to-day. We'll paint the town and all the suburbs."

"Oh, so ver' fast. I do not onderstan'.... I do not onderstan'. You mus' speak more slow.... Give me the *dictionnaire*."

"It was nothing.... Are you happy?"

"Are you not here?" she said, gravely.

There was something so timid, yet so confident about her, so gentle, so child-womanly, that the realization of it struck Kendall almost with the force of an accusation.... It was the forerunner of self-accusation which might have come then and there, had not Bert and Madeleine turned the corner and waved to them. Immediately the girls were chattering French, after their inevitable formal handshake.

"Where to, children?" asked Bert.

They turned to the girls. "Where are we going?" Ken asked.

"Oh, out of the city. Let us go to the Bois—for the long day."

"*Oui*," agreed Madeleine. "The Bois—every one—*tout le monde*—make themselves to go to the Bois."

So, after some difficulty, they persuaded the driver of a *voiture* to drive them up the Champs Élysées and the length of the Avenue du Bois de Boulogne to the gates of the park. There the *cocher* drew up to the curb inexorably and stopped without paying the least attention to the protests of the Americans.

"We must get down," said Andree. "He cannot go inside."

"But there are *voitures* inside—lots of them. Why can't he go in?"

She shrugged her shoulders, but arose, and Madeleine followed her. They knew the way of the Paris coachmen—or it may have been a rule, or an agreement for the division of patronage. At any rate, they got down and paid the absurdly low fare. Then, walking two by two, they entered the famous park.

The walks near the entrance were crowded, but as they penetrated the city's playground the congestion became less dense. But it did seem as if Madeleine were right, that all the world had come to the Bois that day. Every seat, and they were scattered about generously, was occupied. Back among the trees family parties had preempted shady glades and were spreading lunches. Buxom young women played battledore with *poilus* on permission, or engaged in what they seriously believed to be tennis with the most profound earnestness. This tennis delighted Bert, who insisted upon stopping to watch more than one game. The players had no nets— only rackets and a ball. With these they placed themselves sometimes as much as twenty feet apart and then lobbed the ball back and forth with such a seriousness and intensity that it seemed they were playing for life itself.... Children were everywhere, and stout old ladies who drowsed and lean old men who had taken off their coats and were tormented by insects.... Out on the pavements men and women and children rode furiously by on bicycles, all crouching apprehensively over their handlebars and pedaling for dear life.... Youths in French uniforms made vigorous and unashamed love to their sweethearts.... It was very hot.

A few minutes' walk brought them to the lake, steaming with the heat of the day, its surface churned by the unskilled oars of pleasure-seekers. On the opposite shore was a dense crowd packed about a booth, awaiting their turns to go upon the water and suffer. Two or three huge *bateaux* capable of seating a score of people made little voyages up and down, each propelled by one sweating, coatless individual who pulled the enormous weight at such terrific speed that a circuit of the pond might have been made in an hour. The passengers sat packed together in blissful enjoyment.... Those who took rowboats seemed to have a positive genius for loading them in such a way as to make them unmanageable. In the middle was an elderly man, very stout, with two young girls. One girl rowed while her companions sat as far into the bow as possible, lifting the stern high in the air, and making any progress except a sort of whirligig motion impossible. There were collisions, shouts, laughter, screams—and an intolerable heat. But the crowd was happy as only a Parisian crowd can be happy. They had not the least fear of making themselves appear absurd; they went about their pleasure in a determined, do-or-die spirit, and everybody was so satisfied, so happy, so charming that Ken was delighted and tried to tell Andree how pleased he was by aid of French, English, and the dictionary, but only succeeding in bewildering the young lady utterly.... He had a suspicion that both Andree and Madeleine looked at those boats longingly, but with characteristic American terror of making himself look ridiculous he would not have gone upon that water if they had fallen on their knees to plead with him....

After a time they managed by bribery and cajolery to persuade a *cocher* to drive them about the park and an hour or two later got down near to a toy railroad with a tiny engine which pulled crowded trains along a child's track. Bert, whose inhibitions were less pronounced than Ken's, insisted upon riding. The girls boarded the train as a matter of course, with no trace of self-consciousness, but as they bowled along past crowds that waved and pointed and laughed, Ken felt like the father of all idiots.... Finally they arrived at the zoo, which Andree insisted upon inspecting.

The cages in the zoo which attracted the crowds contained dogs! Indeed, dogs were the backbone and almost the sum total of the animals to be seen. They were caged like bears and ran around and around behind their iron bars with the ceaseless gait of wolves. It rather revolted Kendall, especially to see a beautiful English setter in such an environment. There were setters, Danes, bulls, fox-terriers—and the crowds stood and stared and gasped and exclaimed as if they gazed at the behemoth of Holy Writ....

But it was all fascinating to Ken, all different and strange. Here was France again! He was seeing something foreign, not of the Middle West, and it was droll and incomprehensible to him. He did not speculate on what your Frenchman might have thought of a Sunday crowd at Coney Island or the Bronx Zoo or in Belle Isle Park in his own Detroit.... He reveled in it, drinking in eagerly the sensation that he was in another world peopled by incomprehensible beings who functioned in an incomprehensible manner.

Here at least was none of the depression and woe of war.... Had it not been for the presence of uniforms, one would have forgotten war. Ken wondered if these people had been able to forget it—and then reflected that some of these that he saw might be killed before another dawn by bombs dropped upon their sleeping homes from ruthless German aeroplanes.... All was lightness and joyousness now; in a few hours every individual here might be cowering in a cellar, damp with the sweat of fear of imminent slaughter....

They dined expensively at a table under the trees and near to a fountain, and Andree exclaimed at the extravagance of it and declared that for days to come they must satisfy their hunger on bread and water.... They were very gay and very young. For that one day all cares and apprehensions had taken flight; they simply did what occurred to them, and the word *responsibility* was scratched from their vocabularies.

After a time they found a pleasant spot among the trees and sat down to rest, for such a day is very tiring.

"Thees day has been ver' well," said Andree, nodding her head three times by way of punctuation.

"I wish all days were like it," Madeleine said in French.

Andree regarded her gravely a moment, then shook her head emphatically. "No. It would not be well. The days like thees day are ver' nice bicause they are seldom. To-day is for nothing but only happiness— yes. But it is not possible to be so happy to-day if we are not ver' unhappy some other day."

"Do you think that unhappiness makes happiness?" said Bert, with a laugh.

"But yes, monsieur. If there is not sadness there is no joy. It is of a truthfulness. *Certainement.* How do you know you are happy? It is bicause you theenk of days when you are ver' miserable, and thees day is so different from that day. If all days shall be like to-day, then we shall be—how do you say?—we shall be bored."

"But if one is very miserable after he has been happy?" said Ken.

Andree looked at him quickly as if trying to penetrate to the thought that prompted the question.

"It is well," she said, softly. "On the unhappy day you theenk often of the happy day—it makes the unhappiness to be less. After many, many days one may forget the unhappiness. The good God has made it a law. The sorrow it becomes not so sharp. Even the ver' greatest grief becomes jus' a theeng to be remembered. But a happiness! Oh, my friend, that live forever. A happiness cannot be made to fade. Always it live and always it is ver' beautiful and makes itself to give other happiness.... That is why," she said, softly, to Ken, "that I have not great fear to love you. Do you see?... W'en it is ended, thees love of ours, it will be ver' sad, but the sadness it will become soft and make itself to fade after many year. The happiness, such happiness as thees ver' day, it will be always...."

"But," said Ken, suddenly depressed and thoughtful, "isn't there a sorrow so great that it cannot be endured?"

"Oh yes, yes! But that is terrible. I have thought many times of such a sorrow. There is only one like that. It is to love ver' much and trust ver' much and be ver' much happy, and then, one day, to know that one has been deceive' entirely. To know that the friend one love' was on'y making to pretend and did not himself love.... That one could not bear.... Then all the little moments of happiness with him would make themselves to be black and wicked ... and one must die...."

Kendall lifted her hand and touched it with his lips and looked into her eyes. "I do not know what will come, *mignonne* ... but whatever does come, it must not be that.... See, I am speaking the truth so that you may remember it always.... I love you."

For a moment she returned his gaze gravely, then into her dark-shadowed eyes came a glow that was real happiness, her lips smiled and she leaned a little toward him.

"I believe," she said, softly, "and it is ver' well...."

CHAPTER XIX

Kendall had paid little attention to Andree's assertion that she had seen Maude Knox in Paris, yet on Monday he received a *petit bleu* from her informing him that she was again at the Hôtel Wagram and would be delighted to have him call that evening if he were free. At his first reading of the note Maude Knox seemed to him an intrusion. Somehow be rather resented her existence because, subconsciously, he knew that association with her was going to be disquieting. It would give rise to argument within himself and to speculations upon the future which he would have liked to avoid. He was satisfied and as happy as he had ever been in his life—and Maude was a complication. If Maude Knox had been less important in his life he would have welcomed her more heartily.

However, as he thought more and more of her presence, he found himself desiring greatly to see her. There was something sympathetic and dependable about her, something that he could understand and approve. She was American, thoroughly American. Yes, by all means, he wished to see her, but he would hold himself in restraint. They should not become at all personal, and he would watch the conversation carefully to see that it did not turn any unexpected corners or wander down lanes ending in disagreeable obstacles to be cleared.

"There's no reason why I shouldn't be decent to her," he told himself, speciously. "She's probably lonesome, and we are both Americans...." He remembered the hour or so he had spent with her in Montreuil, and how he had come away from her in a state of perplexity, wondering if it were possible for a man to love two women at the same time.... "It isn't that," he told himself. "I love Andree and nobody but Andree ... but that's no reason I shouldn't see Maude. Anyhow, she'll be here only a day or so...."

The truth of the matter was that, without realizing it, Kendall did not trust himself. He was afraid that a thing might happen which he was in a queer sort of way half willing should happen—that he might fall in love with Maude Knox or that he might realize in her presence that he actually was in love with her. It was a singular position. Undoubtedly he loved Andree—but how? That he did not ask himself. He loved her, he had a sort of reverence for her, and he had besides a real friendship for her, but—He would inevitably have reached that *but* if he had allowed himself to analyze his love for her.... A man may have one child and love it with a love which he fancies is boundless and exclusive. He may believe that every fraction of the love he has to give belongs to that child, and he may resent the coming of a second child and look upon it as an interloper. But very shortly he finds himself loving the new-comer not one whit less than the first-born.... If love can become miraculous in this manner—inexhaustible like the loaves and fishes—with respect to children, cannot it be the same with respect to women? Kendall had seen the first develop in the case of a friend, had heard the friend speak in confidence before the coming of his second child, and had observed him after the passage of a few weeks. He took it as the basis of an argument and, using it as a stepping-stone, reached a conclusion which was disturbing ... but not lacking in a certain allurement.... And what of countries where there are plural marriages? How in the case of a man lawfully possessed of more than one wife? Does such a man love all, or only one, or none?...

It was in this uncertain frame of mind that he went to the Wagram and called Maude Knox's room on the rather difficult house telephone.

"Captain Ware!..." said her voice. "I hardly expected you, but it's good of you to have come. I'll be right down."

She appeared presently, not in her uniform, but in such a dress as she might have worn at home in America when going out for the evening with a young gentleman.

"What are you doing in Paris?" he demanded. "I thought you were busy being the queen of the doughboys."

"The division's being moved, I don't know where, and I was sent in to wait for orders. Some of our men marched on the Fourth."

"I suppose it seems good to get back into the world again."

"Anybody can be in Paris," she said. "I've been having the time of my life—and, really, I think I was some good. I believe I was. The men liked to have me there."

"Naturally."

She shrugged her shoulders. "Do I understand that you are taking me to dinner?"

"You do. Where shall it be?"

"Anywhere, so long as there is food I don't have to cook myself.... I've been living on things out of cans—except when the officers' mess had something particularly good and sent some over."

"It hasn't hurt you a bit.... You look mighty well." He was thinking that she did look very well, indeed. Not exactly beautiful, but satisfyingly good-looking—the way he liked to see a girl look. A fellow might be proud to be seen with her. She showed class....

"How about the Continental?" he asked.

"I'd like it. I've never eaten there."

They passed out of the hotel and strolled up the rue de Rivoli to the rue Royale, and then dodged careless taxi-cabs to cross the broad avenue which stretched with an air of pride to the face of the Madeleine. Two or three American officers were loitering about the entrance to the Continental, and Ken experienced a sense of satisfaction as he became conscious of their surreptitious stares of admiration at his companion.... They traversed the court and entered the big dining-room which stretched along the rue de Rivoli and through whose windows one may look out upon the Place de la Concorde and across the river to the Palais Legislatif. The occupants of the room were mostly Americans—officers, officials of the Red Cross, and women of that organization and the Y. M. C. A.

"What have you been doing? Tell me all the news," Maude said, as they seated themselves at a table close to the windows.

"I?... Working as usual, and there isn't any news. Never come to the war if you want news of the war. I knew a lot more about it when I was back in Detroit than I do in Paris."

"Our division was full of rumors of a big American offensive."

"And Paris is full of rumors of a big German offensive. It was to have started on the fourth of July, but now it has been postponed to the fourteenth—Bastille Day.... You can hear anything."

"I think something is going to happen. The Blue Devils are up the other side of Meaux. I've seen them. Everybody tells me their presence is a sign that something is going to happen."

"Frankly, I don't believe it. If anything comes I think it will be a German attack. I don't look for the Allies to do much before spring—"

"When our aeroplanes get here?" she interjected. "My! but our boys have grumbled about aeroplanes. It makes them irritable to see German planes buzzing around."

"Don't blame them. There are rumors about aeroplanes, too. A *poilu* asked me the other day if it was true that we had twenty thousand of them over here."

The conversation was following a matter-of-fact, commonplace, impersonal lane—just such a way as Ken had determined it should follow. Yet he was dissatisfied with it. He felt that it lacked something, and that, consequently, Maude and himself were not getting the most out of each other's company. He had resolved not to talk about himself nor about Maude nor about the sentiments they inspired in each other, but he found himself wanting to do so. The staple, as well as the most absorbing, topic for any young person is himself. It becomes doubly absorbing if two young persons can join and discuss *themselves* and their reactions to each other.... Maude seemed a trifle bored, he thought. Then, suddenly and with a touch of impatience, she said:

"What has been happening to *you*?... And that pretty little girl? What was her name?"

She, too, seemed to desire to alter the character of the conversation.

Nothing had been happening to him—at least that he could tell her about. He insisted that life had been a dull affair of work and sleep for him.

"Nonsense! I'm interested.... Oh, I remember her name—it was Andree. Tell me about Andree."

"She's a mighty nice little girl. I see her every now and then."

"Every now and then," she mocked. "When did you see her last?"

"Yesterday."

"And before that?"

"I was away for a few days."

"But you saw her the night before you went away?"

"Yes."

"And if I hadn't interfered you'd have seen her to-night."

"No—we had no engagement for to-night."

She laughed. "You're not especially subtle. Are you really in love with this girl?... Do tell me all about her. I know I'm prying and curious—but—Oh, I'm just curious about her."

"I—there's nothing to tell."

"There must be. How is she different from us American girls? She seemed very attractive—and sweet."

"She says the difference between French and American girls is that you don't know how to dress your feet," he said, with an uneasy laugh. It rather pleased him that Maude looked blank an instant and then made an evident effort to look at her footgear. "Do you want to go to the Casino or some other place to-night?"

"Not until I've found out more about your friend. You know I liked her looks very much.... Why can't I meet her? She wouldn't be jealous, would she? You did introduce her, you know. Can't we have a little party—the three of us?"

"No," he said, with flat finality in his voice.

"Why?"

He did not want to reply, did not know what to reply. The reason that he did not even want to put into definite thought was that Maude ought not to meet Andree—because Andree was to him what she was.... Maude was an American girl, a compatriot living under the laws of the Medes and the Persians, and it would not be proper for her to associate with Andree.

"Why?" she repeated. "You said she was *nice*." She accented the *nice*. "If you don't let me meet her I shall think she isn't nice at all—and a great many other things."

"She is nice," he said, sullenly. "She's good.... You wouldn't understand her. I don't think I've ever known anybody who was as good as Andree—really good.... But ..."

"I think I understand," she said, slowly. "It was really what I wanted to know." She frowned a trifle and became thoughtful. Then: "You know I said before that—that I didn't blame these girls.... It's the war—and their men being killed—and—Well, there's something in the air.... I don't suppose I shall ever understand them, or be able to see as they see—but I'm—well, I have a lot of sympathy.... A great many of us are going to look at things more broadly when we get home to America. We had never come into contact with other standards and other ways of trying for happiness.... I know I'm talking in a muddle, but I hope you understand. What I mean is that I wouldn't object to meeting Andree...."

"In Paris," said Ken.

"In Paris? What do you mean?"

"Would you be willing to meet her in New York or Cleveland or Chicago?"

She wrinkled her brows. "Honestly, I don't know."

"Here she would be just one of the sights of France—an experience. Well, I'm not going to have her on exhibition, like Notre Dame."

"It isn't that. It isn't curiosity.... Really, I don't know just what it is, but I want to be acquainted with her. I think it is so I can find out if it is really true that she—that she can live as she does and still be—*nice*."

"I tell you she is nice."

"But you are in love with her? Aren't you in love with her? Somehow that makes a difference. It would seem sordid and inexcusable if you weren't."

"I am very fond of her."

"Do you *love her*?"

"Yes," he said, desperately.

She was just picking up her fork. At his words it dropped and her lips compressed, but he did not notice. Perhaps he would have attached no significance to these signals if he had noticed, because he was fully occupied in thinking about himself. He had never taken time to consider Maude Knox's possible feelings toward himself, although he had more than once tried in an inconclusive way to assay his own sentiments toward Maude. Not that he was exceptionally selfish or self-centered. He was only at that stage in his relations with Maude when he was trying to make out what those relations might develop into. Until a young man is fairly sure he wants a young woman very much he does not start to worry about whether she will want him.

And Maude ... she had advanced a trifle farther than Ken, perhaps. Ken had attracted her from the first, and, peculiarly enough, the rather open mystery of his affair with Andree had made him a more striking figure, if not more desirable. It had accented him.... She had never confessed to herself that she wanted to establish proprietary rights in Ken, but she did realize that he was of some importance to her. He was the one individual in

Paris that she had been anxious to see. When she had been ordered to Paris her first thought had been that she would see Ken. These things were only indicative. They proved nothing to her.... But when she heard Ken baldly admit that he loved Andree she was close to proof. Undoubtedly it had been a shock and an unpleasant shock. Ken was more important to her than she had supposed. She was glad that the waiter appeared at that moment with the *viande*, for it gave her an excuse for silence and attention to her plate.

She wondered if this feeling were jealousy.... Then she repeated to herself, "He loves this girl," and refused to believe it, and then was doubtful, and then was afraid.... Other aspects of the affair did not present themselves to her then—only the fact that this man, who might have been, whom she wanted to be, something to her, was in love with another woman, an alien, a Frenchwoman. Then she asserted to herself, "It's only an affair...." There was some comfort and promise in this.

She looked up suddenly. "What are you going to do, Ken?" she asked. "Are you going to marry her?"

He stammered, hesitated. This was very disquieting. She had no right to ask such a question. "I—I've never thought about marriage—in connection with Andree," he said. He was almost honest in his statement. They two had been living in the present, had eaten of the lotus, and the future was only a vague time that might have to be faced when it arrived. He had been living in a world which was not a world of reality. It had been a species of imaginary world into which practical matters like marriage do not obtrude.

"You don't think of—of settling in France? I hear some of the men say they want to."

"No." He was certain of that. America was his home, and the homing instinct was strong in him. He was a citizen of the United States, and it seemed unnatural and impossible for him to give up that citizenship. To do so appeared to him to be in the same category as divorcing a wife, a thing which seemed incredible to him. But to leave America permanently, to become a citizen of some other country, seemed more impossible than divorce. It was simply an act so absurd as to be beyond consideration. This was not patriotism, but a habit of mind. He was an American, and it was a natural impossibility to become anything else—that was it.

"Then, if you married her, you would take her home?"

"Let's not talk about it," he said, uncomfortably, for this opened up a field of disagreeable apprehensions that he did not want to undertake. "We're talking too much about me. Let's talk about something else."

"But I want to talk about you.... I'm afraid—afraid you're getting into an entanglement that will be—a bad thing for you.... If you do marry this girl and take her home, what will your people say? How will your friends receive her?... Because the story would leak out. It would be sure to leak out. People know about you. Your chum knows, and others know...."

"Andree is good," he said, "and it doesn't make any difference what people think."

"Not in Paris. But in America it would make a lot of difference.... She would be whispered about and talked about—and people might—might refuse to receive her."

He was angry now. "People are rotten and narrow. Andree is better than all of them put together. What do I care for what they say or think?"

"You would care a great deal—and so would she. She would soon find out what people were thinking. Here she may be able to go along and believe that she is not doing anything wrong. Mind, I don't say she is bad. I'm almost able to sympathize with her. If I weren't your friend, if I didn't know you, and this were all happening to a stranger, I'm sure I should be able to understand and not to blame her.... As it is, I'm truly sorry for her.... But I do know you, and that makes it seem different. Things are always different when they strike close to home...."

"I suppose so."

"Well, she would find herself in a different world, a world that lives in a different way, and that world would make her feel as if she had done wrong, and she would be very unhappy...."

"I don't believe it. Not if I were with her."

"But you—when you get home *you* will think differently about this.... You wouldn't marry an American girl who had—done as Andree has done.... Would you?"

He thought briefly. "No," he said, honestly.

"So, if you married her, you would begin to think about that some day.... You would.... And you would wonder what she had done before she met you—if—if you had been the only man she ever loved. Don't you see?..."

"I don't see. I know her. You don't know her at all. You don't know how sweet and gentle and decent she is. You don't know how she thinks.... She is wonderful...." He was loyal, at least, and she could not help being glad of it. Loyalty was a quality she especially admired.

"She may be all of that, Ken, but it wouldn't matter. Other people wouldn't know it and wouldn't believe it.... Your mother ..."

His mother!... He knew what his mother would think and what his mother would do. If he took Andree home his mother would be suspicious of her because she was French. Then, if the story should leak out, or a hint of it should be sent to do its slinking work, his mother would hate Andree—no less. She would make it her business to eliminate Andree and to render her life unendurable.

With unconscious strategy he made a counterattack. "And you," he said, "would you marry a man who had—had that sort of an experience?"

She looked up at him suddenly to determine if there were anything personal in this question, but could not make up her mind.

"I—I don't know.... I—I've never imagined—"

"Of course not.... But you might have to imagine it. Suppose you were in love with a man—suppose you were in love with me"—she concealed a gasp at his clumsiness—"would you marry me?"

She tried to protect herself, and said, with a forced laugh, "Am I to consider this as a proposal?"

He disregarded her flippancy. "I suppose I shall marry some day, and if it isn't Andree—if it is some American girl like you—what will she think? I want to know. You have asked me a lot of questions, and that sort of gives me the right to ask you this one: Would you marry me?"

"I can't answer—now. I don't know.... I don't think so.... I should have to think...."

He regarded her. Mentally he paid her the compliment of thinking that she was a splendid type. He could not help thinking that she was just such a girl as he would like to marry and to live with always. She exerted an attraction that drew him toward her strongly.... A wife! She would be a splendid wife, a wife that his mother would receive joyfully, about whom there could not be the slightest question.... He wondered if she liked him at all—and that was a sign and a portent. Suddenly the answer to her question became of large importance to him. He leaned over the table and looked into her eyes—and saw her cheeks color under his gaze.

"I wish you would think," he said, slowly, "and tell me what you think—" Then he added something he had not at all intended to say: "And tell me if it is possible for a man to love two girls at the same time...."

CHAPTER XX

Kendall Ware leaned out of a window of the apartment, looking down at the avenue beneath. He had an unobstructed view of the sidewalk as far as the corner. It was time for Andree to arrive, and he was watching for her. Taxicabs rattled past, a huge *camion* manufactured in America and driven by an American rumbled along; a French officer, resplendent with gold braid and medals and red trousers, walked by gaily, a beautiful woman on each side; the *concierge* was sweeping the sidewalk in front of the entrance; a child or two in the inevitable black outer garment or smock played near a bench ... and then came Andree. She was all in white, as he loved to see her best. Perhaps it was because she had been all in white when he saw her for the first time. She looked very tiny from his place four stories above the street, and he watched her with something of the tender amusement with which one watches a child when it is unconscious of one's presence.

Andree approached in a determined, business-like manner. One could tell at once that she had a destination in view. The quaint stiffness of her gait was accentuated by the angle from which he looked at her, as was her slenderness. He watched to see if she would turn her head or allow her eyes to vary from that intent, straight-ahead gaze which seemed to see nothing. They did not vary. She was prim. Prim was the word, he thought.... The white tam was jaunty, but it did not give her an air of jauntiness; instead of doing so it gave quite another impression—that of inexperienced youth, youth untouched by the events of life, youth that had yet to come to a knowledge that there was evil in the world. That was a great deal for a tam-o'-shanter to tell, but somehow it managed to tell it. Ken leaned farther out to watch her as she came directly underneath, wondering if she would glance up at the windows.

She did glance upward, suddenly, as if something had fallen at her feet and startled her. She saw Ken, but she neither smiled nor waved, and dropped her eyes again as quickly as she had raised them. But there was about her then an air of relief, as if she had sighed audibly.... He was there waiting for her eagerly; she had seen it, and her apprehensions, if she had any, were quieted.

Ken listened for her step upon the stairs, but heard no sound until the door-bell rang with a sort of tentative, hesitating ring. It seemed as if she could touch nothing without imparting some character, something of her mood of the moment.... He opened the door and she raised her eyes to his and looked into his face a moment, her face perfectly immobile. She stood very straight and still, her arms stiffly at her sides.

"My dear," he said, and held out his arms to her.

She smiled shyly, diffidently, as she allowed him to take her in his arms and kiss her. She was not responsive, but seemed rather speculative.... As if she were allowing this thing to happen to see if it were really going to happen.... And then she returned his kiss gravely, as much as to say: "Yes, this can really happen. It is so. I am much relieved."

"You are *triste*," he said, anxiously.

"*Mais non.... Mais non....*"

"Then smile."

"When I have climb' many stairs I cannot smile.... But I am glad.... Who is here?"

"Nobody."

"Not Arlette?"

"Oh yes, of course. But Bert won't be home to dinner."

"It is well.... *Non, non*, you mus' not take my *sac*. It is ver' valuable—yes. I mus' watch it ver' careful. It has my tickets of the bread."

"I'll hang it right here, and your jacket, or whatever you call it.... What have you been doing?"

"I have work *beaucoup*. Oh, it is ver' tiresome to work! It is much better jus' to play all the days.... And you? Have you theenk of me?"

"Yes."

"I do not believe—no, no, not once have you theenk of me. You are ver' wicked—*très-méchante*. I shall to weep."

"I think of you when I wake up, all the morning, at noon, all the afternoon—"

"*Non, non, non!*..." She was laughing now. "Maybe one leetle theenk—only. But I—oh, I have theenk of you ver' much. I have theenk you are *pas fidèle*."

"I!... Not faithful!"

"Yes." She nodded her head decidedly.

"Why do you say that? You know I am *fidèle*."

"I have see' you."

"Seen me—where?"

"Oh, you are ver' wicked.... You deceive me mos' cruel." He could not tell if she were serious or if she were teasing him. "Also I am mos' *jalouse*. It is thees yo'ng girl—thees yo'ng American girl. I have see' you with her las' night."

"Oh yes. We had dinner together. She has just come back to Paris for a day or two."

"Oh yes," she mimicked. "I know thees leetle dinner. She tries to steal you away from me.... You like her more than me. It is so. I see it.... I shall take me a dagger and make her to die—so." She laughed gaily.

"You don't really believe I'm unfaithful at all. You're just making fun of me."

"Did you bring her *here*?"

"Eh?... What's that? Here? Maude Knox here?"

"And why not? Since you are not *fidèle*."

"But you don't understand. Maude Knox is an American girl. She wouldn't—I couldn't—"

"Oh, it is so?... Then these American girls, they do not love. They are stone or wood, is it so?... I do not onderstan' these American girls." She was delightfully disgusted. "Sometime I shall cross the ocean to observe these girls. It will be ver' droll. America mus' be a ver' droll, ver' serious country—where the girls do not love."

"They do love. Of course they love."

"Well, then, Why do you make such astonishment when I speak that she comes here?"

He waggled his hand helplessly, and she, perceiving that she was teasing him, put on greater pretense of seriousness.

"Ah, I see," she said. "The American girl she say, 'I love,' and then she enter into the convent.... She goes in the *jardin* and see the bud about to blossom, and she cover it weeth a veil. Is it not? Oh, such love as thees! It is the love of the ice for the snow."

"It's different, Andree. I can't explain it to you because I can't explain it to myself."

"*Pouf!* Different! Do you theenk I cannot perceive it is different? Oh yes, monsieur. I perceive ver' clearly ... the difference between alive and dead."

"You're wrong. American girls can love—"

"How do you know?" she interrupted, impishly.

"—can love," he persisted, "but all nice American girls marry—"

"To be sure. Ah, marriage—that is ver' well. There is nothing against marriage. Not in the least. Many people marry, and it is ver' well. Why not?..."

"I never can make you understand."

"Nevair.... I cannot to onderstan' what is not natural. Do you onderstan' if you see the river ron up the hill? *Mais non.* To love is to love; to marry is to marry. It is not the same theeng altogether...."

"America is different."

"You have say that bifore.... It mus' be the fault of the girls. *Oui....* So far as I observe the men they are willing enough.... Perhaps they are so willing bicause at America they are always denied. It is mos' fortunate for them they come to Paris. Otherwise they would die and not ever have been alive at all."

"You're a dear child and I love you and I almost understand what you're talking about. But you could never understand America—and sometimes I'm glad of it.... And America never will be able to understand you."

"What would Americans theenk of me if I come to New York?"

"They would think you were very lovely."

"I do not mean *that*. I am not lovely. I am ver' hideous. See, I cover my face bicause you are afraid."

"Let's not bother about America—just about us."

"But I am *jalouse*. I hate thees American yo'ng girl."

"Fiddlesticks!"

"For all you say, I theenk she come here las' night."

"Now, look here—"

She laughed gaily and ran to the window. "See, I shall jump down and die.... *Bon soir*, Arlette...."

"*Bon soir, mademoiselle. Dîner est servi.*"

"It is well.... How does your little granddaughter carry herself?"

"Very well, mademoiselle. Even now she is in the kitchen and very impatient to visit you and Monsieur Ken."

"She must dine weeth us, mus' she not, *cher ami*?"

"Of course. Set a place for her, Arlette. And tell her we shall have some American cakes that I got at the commissary store."

Arlette beamed with pride and satisfaction and padded about, setting a third place at the table, waggling her head and whispering to herself as she went. Ken and Andree seated themselves, and then Arlette appeared in the door with little Arlette concealed among her skirts. The tiny head, with its birdlike features, peeped out at them timorously.

"Enter, mademoiselle," said Andree. "See, she has eyes only for Monsieur Ken, is it not? She is my rival.... I shall not dine weeth her. She is ver' bad and wicked."

Arlette pushed her granddaughter ahead of her, muttering to her in French.

"*Bon soir, monsieur. Bon soir, mademoiselle*," she said in a tiny voice.

"Arlette!" prompted her grandmother, and set her head on one side and made her eyes very large and round while she awaited the result of her prompting. Little Arlette looked at her grandmother, then at Ken and Andree in turn, and said, with the most comical manner of pride in achievement, "Goo'-by, gent'men."

"Oh," exclaimed Andree, "she has learned English to make me sad! With these accomplishments she will make short work of me."

Ken lifted the child into her place and tilted her delicate, fragile, fairy face upward. "You shall give me a kiss and make her very jealous," he said, whereupon she kissed him, keeping one eye on Andree to observe results, and was much gratified to see her rival cover her face with her hands to hide her grief.

"I go to America with him," she said to Andree. "I do not know if it is America of the North or America of the South. It does not matter. I am to be his wife."

"Ah, already you are American," said Andree, slyly. "You theenk only of marry."

"And we shall live in a toy-shop and eat nothing but candy," said Ken.

"Americans are very rich," observed little Arlette. "My grandmother has told it to me—and that I must teach my husband that it is wicked to be careless with one's money.... We shall not dine upon pullet."

"You see what it is to marry," said Andree. "Already you are denied what you desire.... I theenk mademoiselle makes a marriage of money."

"It is not a marriage of money, is it, *mignonne*? No. It is for true love you marry me, is it not?"

"Oh yes, yes! I love monsieur very much."

"But what is to become of me? I, too, love monsieur ver' much," said Andree.

Arlette observed her gravely and pondered. "You, too, shall be his wife, mademoiselle," she said.

"Ah ... it seems I was wrong. After all, little Arlette is not wholly American."

The dinner was finished and Ken carried little Arlette into the *salon* on his shoulder. She cuddled between him and Andree on the sofa, insisted upon holding his hand, and looked at Andree with calculating eye.

"Have you no new *chansons*, *petite*?" asked Ken.

"*Oui, monsieur.*" And she stood up with a most serious air, taking her position just so and smoothing down her skirts. Then she tilted up her little chin and, with her eyes fixed gravely on Ken's face, she sang a song of many verses while her grandmother stood in the door and bobbed and grinned and made signs of a great satisfaction.... It was not like a child singing, Ken thought, but like some playfellow of elves and fairies. There were about her a daintiness, an ethereal quality, a purity which was something more than merely human and of the flesh.... He wondered what life held for her; wondered if Andree might not have been just such a child with just such characteristics as she. He thought it possible ... for Andree retained some of those characteristics even now.

He lifted the child in his arms and kissed her, and Arlette took her away.

"You must come often," Ken said, "because we are to be married."

"Yes, monsieur. That is understood.... It was America of the North, was it not?"

"It was."

"I shall remember.... *Bon soir, monsieur. Bon soir, mademoiselle.*" And she was gone.

"I have many rivals," said Andree. "It is not well."

"There is only one *you, mignonne.*"

"But yes, there is only one *me,* but there are many others. Little Arlette, thees yo'ng American girl.... I wish to know thees yo'ng American girl. I will meet her." She nodded her head several times. "You will have her come here or we shall dine together."

"Nothing doing!"

"Oh, what is thees you say? I do not onderstan'. Give me the *dictionnaire.*"

"The dictionary won't help. I mean I won't do it."

"*Pourquoi?*"

"There you are again. *Pourquoi.... Toujours pourquoi.*"

"It is well to ask why many times. If one does not ask why, then many unpleasant theengs may happen. If one asks why—then one knows and can weigh the results. *N'est-ce pas?* I like to know where I am marching."

"I don't want you to meet Miss Knox, because you would not understand each other at all."

"I theenk we would. But I shall meet her jus' the same. ... She is the kind of girl Americans marry. I wish to study why."

"She would be studying you, too."

She shrugged her shoulders. "Of course. One woman always studies another. It is natural.... I do not know why, unless it is to determine if the woman can take one's lover away, or if one can take the woman's lover away from her.... I theenk that is it."

"But suppose you didn't want the woman's lover?"

"That is of no importance. It is still ver' well to be able to say to oneself that it would be possible to take that woman's lover if it was desired."

"1 don't like to hear you talk like that!"

"*Pourquoi?*" Andree's eyes were big with surprise.

"It doesn't sound nice.... It sounds—oh, it doesn't sound like *you*."

She put her cheek against his. "Then I will not say it if you do not like.... I do not want any other man. I want only you.... Do you love me?"

"Yes."

"No, I do not believe. You love this yo'ng American girl because she theenks only of marry.... You will marry thees yo'ng girl."

"I'm not going to marry anybody."

"Americans always do. It is the law of the country. You have said it."

"You know I love you."

"I am afraid bicause of thees yo'ng girl."

"Nonsense. I can't marry anybody, Andree. All I have in the world is my captain's pay. Nobody can tell how long the war will last, nor how long I will be held in the service after it is over—and when I am discharged ... well, what then? I don't know. There's nothing to look forward to but war ... just this and nothing else."

She stroked his hand reflectively. "It is well," she said, after a moment. "While there is war you shall be here. We shall theenk of nothing else.... *Après la guerre*"—she made a little gesture with both hands—"then we shall see.... I theenk you will be *fidèle* w'ile it is that you remain in France. I am satisfy—for now."

"You don't believe I love you."

She mused, and then with that characteristic gesture of poking downward with her index finger she said: "I theenk many things. I theenk that I know jus' one kind of love, and it ees *love*, it ees for all time and for all thing'. It ees for marry or for not marry. But I theenk you have two kinds of love—*oui*. Perhaps it ees *américain*—the custom of the country. One love for pleasure and—how do you say?—one love for business.... Listen, my friend. Do the pleasure love and the business love never come at the same time and for the same yo'ng girl? Eh?"

"I have never loved anybody but you." He paused. "You know all about such things, *mignonne*. Is it possible for a woman to love two men at the same time—or for a man to love two women at the same time?"

She laughed. "It ees the las' half of the question you wish for to have answer.... I theenk it ees different weeth man and woman. The woman she love only one. She give all.... The man—maybe. It ees ver' difficult. But I theenk if there ees one large love that it ees all.... And I theenk, Monsieur Ken, that one day you go away and leave me *solitaire*. Oh, I shall to weep." She clenched her fists and dug them into her eyes, and then laughed up at him. "See, I am ver' *triste*.... You mus' make me to be joyous."

She was right, he thought. There could be but one love, one great love. How could he think otherwise, for was she not there, close beside him, her breath upon his cheek, her wonderful eyes turning up to his face every now and then with that inquiring, wondering, speculating glance that spoke to his heart? ... One love, marvelous, sweet, *good*. He could even pause to assert its virtue.... Maude Knox became very dim, intangible. Andree was here, present, living—in all the mystery of her and all the foreign allurement.... This was love. This was an amazing sweetness without which his life would be immeasurably the poorer. It was a permanent thing—could not be uprooted at a moment's notice. He knew that it had altered, was altering, his whole life, and he was glad. Whatever might come of it, he was glad.... Something had been given to him which would remain a miraculous possession so long as light entered his eyes or reason blossomed in his soul....

"Andree," he said, tremulously. "Andree...."

She sighed with content. "I am ver' happy," she replied. "Ever'thing is ver' well...."

CHAPTER XXI

Paris awoke to the 14th of July—Bastille Day—without knowing that, as it had marked the beginning of the end of the *ancien régime*, it was now to mark the last hour of the peril of France. It was fitting that this great national fête should bring to an end the days when the *boche* was to be feared, and that to-morrow was to see the beginning of the end. But Paris did not know. The air was heavy with portent; events impended.... There was present in every heart the apprehension that the unthinkable might happen, and that their beloved city might, within a period of days, fall into the hands of the enemy.... Bastille Day was the last day of the reign of fear.... The event was still on the knees of the gods; Paris could not read the future, but it could make holiday with destruction at its door. The heart of Paris was steadfast.... Its fortitude was on the eve of its reward.

Paris did not know that to-morrow the boche would lunge at its throat, throwing a weight into the thrust that it had never been able to throw before; nor did Paris know that its armies and its allies would receive that thrust without faltering, and would hurl upon it such rain of fire and steel as would crush it to the ground futile and staggering.... Paris did not know, nor did the brain of any human being know, that but three days must pass before that man of infinite patience and courage who was generalissimo of the forces which barred the path of the Hun would make his first mighty stride toward victory, a stride which should become a steady march, never flagging, never stopping, until his armies should have won the precious right to march with heads erect under that great pile which dominates their city—the Arc de Triomphe.

It was such events which impended on this 14th of July....

Kendall Ware and Andree had chosen the Place des Ternes as the most advantageous point from which to see the parade, and though it was raining a trifle when they started out, with skies which promised a drizzly day, they were not to be deterred. The little concrete oval which is the meeting-place of the Boulevard de Courcelles, the Avenue de Wagram, the Avenue des Ternes, and the rue du Faubourg St.-Honoré was already crowded. People splashed about in its shallow puddles and jostled one another between its flower-booths, which were doing a thriving business. The parade was already passing with martial music and amid much clapping of hands, but less shouting than would have obtained in an American city.

Ken edged Andree as near to the street as he could. For him it was easy to look over the heads of the people and to see the marching soldiers, but little Andree might as well have been at home across the river. She could see nothing, and there was no box nor chair to be had.

"Shall I lift you up?" he asked.

"*Mais non.* You cannot. I am of such a largeness!... But I shall see."

"I'll sit you on my shoulder and tell folks you are my granddaughter," he said.

"*Regardez!*" She took a small rectangular mirror from her *sac* and held it before his eyes. Then she turned her back on the parade and, holding the mirror at an angle above her head, looked into it with quaint intentness.

"Oh, I see!" she exclaimed. "Behol', the parade it marches in the glass."

Ken laughed, but he was a trifle annoyed and embarrassed. Andree herself, he thought, was so natural, so herself, that she would have not the least thought in the world of making herself ridiculous or conspicuous, but this absurd makeshift of hers would certainly attract the attention of the crowd—and nobody knew what a Parisian crowd might do. He hesitated, looked about him uncomfortably, and decided to hold his peace. It was well, for within a radius of thirty feet a dozen men and women were doing exactly as Andree did. They had come prepared. Each of them stood facing away from the procession, a mirror held above the heads of the crowd, and it was with difficulty Kendall restrained his laughter. Their expressions were all so eager, so interested. It was absurd. With all that was going on behind them, they peered as if bewitched into rectangles of glass, and shouted, or lowered their mirrors to clap their hands just as if they were seeing living soldiers instead of tiny reflections....

The crowd interested him more than the marching men. There was a good-natured simplicity, a lack of reserve, a childishness about them, yet there were a bigness, a pathos, and a grandeur in their bearing.... Boys and young men mounted into trees; couples carrying bouquets scurried up and down the line, seeking a point where they might penetrate to the street; here was a woman weeping and smiling at once. She was in black.... And everywhere flowers! Now and then a girl would run out from the curb to hand a blossom to some *poilu* or Italian or Englishman or Portuguese....

Every French soldier marched with a smile and with a posy nodding from the muzzle of his gun. The street was thick with flowers and the air rained flowers.

The Americans passed. In their guns were no blossoms, on their tunics were no bouquets. They marched very stiffly, erect, business-like, with eyes to the front. The French had shuffled by jovially with nods and smiles. One could tell they had seen the war and were marching men, but there was no stiffness, no rigidity. They were like the defense of their great general—elastic. The Italians grinned cheerfully; so did the Portuguese; even the English were somewhat relaxed—but all these had known four years of war.... The Americans, marching like one man, like a splendid machine, seemed, somehow, sterner, of more warlike stuff. They struck the eye and won the applause of the multitude.... But they were of no sterner stuff, nor would they have asserted themselves to be better fighting-men than the sturdy *poilus* or the wiry Tommies.... They were younger—that was what impressed one. Their youth cried aloud.... Amid those soldiers of France and England and Italy and Belgium they looked like boys—and yet their age might not have been greater than these others—for the others had seen four years of war.... But they were splendid, these young men from another world, and the heart of Paris went out to them....

A hand touched Kendall's arm and he turned.

"Why, Maude!" he exclaimed, and shot a startled glance toward Andree.

She had not seen, but was peering into her mirror.

"How glad you are to see me!" She laughed. "Really, I've nothing catching. What's the matter?..." She glanced about and saw Andree. "Oh!" she said. "I'm glad. I wanted to know her."

"I told you—" he began; but it was Andree who interrupted.

"*Bon jour*, Mademoiselle Knox," she said, gravely. "We have met one little time."

"Yes, indeed, and I have wanted so much to meet you again. I have told Mr. Ware...."

"And I, too, have wanted to know you. I have said it to him, yes, many times. I have said that I shall to know thees Miss Maude Knox—but"—she shrugged her shoulders—"*les Américains* are droll.... He would not."

"He can't help himself now, can he? Now that we know we want to be acquainted with each other, there's nothing he can do about it."

"Oh, I do not onderstan'. You speak *trop vite, mademoiselle*. My English it is of the worst."

"And my French is non-existent. But that doesn't matter in the least, does it? We shall get on."

For those girls there was now something of much greater importance than the parade, and they promptly forgot it. Maude moved over to Andree's side and they began the sort of conversation that women use when they are appraising each other with serious intention. Ken listened uneasily. There was nothing he could do. This thing that he had desired not to happen *had* happened, and that was all there was to it. He pretended to watch the parade, but his mind was concentrated on what the girls were saying. The girls appeared to have forgotten him as well as the marching men.

Ken was acutely apprehensive, but of what he was apprehensive he did not know. The thought that Andree and Maude were together, chatting, becoming acquainted, seemed to him very threatening. He had been in a holiday humor, but that humor was gone. He frowned and was conscious of both irritation and depression. It was not right for them to meet. Something was sure to come of it.

It was not at all that he felt that Andree was not a fit companion for Maude Knox. That was not it. He was not ashamed of Andree, and, strangely enough, when one considers his temperament and the hereditary impulses which stirred within him, he was not ashamed of his relations with her. It was an intangible apprehension, a feeling that one woman whom he knew he loved and another woman with whom he might be in love could not meet without unpleasant results to him.

There was curiosity, too, which grew stronger. More than once he had compared Andree with Maude Knox when neither was present, but now they were together, at his side, under his eyes.... He edged away a trifle with elaborate unconsciousness, and presently reached a point from which he could study the girls with covert glances.

It was not so much their appearances that he compared as it was their *selves* as he knew them, and as they were indicated by what met the eye. He was trying to arrive at a knowledge of what each girl meant in his life, what she could contribute to his life. Perhaps this was wholly selfish, but choice must ever be selfish. It is after choice is made that one may be generous and self-denying.

The contrast between Andree and Maude was so extreme that they seemed to have nothing in common but their sex, and as Ken considered he saw they had not even this in common. At least their conception of it and of its duties and possibilities and obligations and uses were as different as the color of their eyes or the expressions of their faces. One could not see Andree without being conscious that she was a woman, of the femininity of her, and that the chief business of her life was to be the complement of some man. The first emotion that Andree excited was tenderness.... As one looked at Maude Knox his first thought was comradeship, followed by a mental note that she would be reliable, capable of taking care of herself. Maude was not beautiful, but she was pretty, with a clean-cut, boyish prettiness that spoke of health of mind and of body. She was not the sort a man would fall in love with at first sight, but rather one who would first be admired and then loved.... Andree would be loved first, then admired as the sweetness of herself unfolded under the urging of love. Andree was fragile. Ken looked at her lips, perfectly drawn, delicate, sensitive—her most eloquent feature. They were lips to kiss, lips to give kisses. There, perhaps, stood the chief difference between these girls and their attitude toward life: that Andree would give, give, give—asked no other happiness but to give of herself and her sweetness and her tenderness and her love—while Maude would demand an exchange. She, too, could love, but always there would be inhibitions and reservations. She would take thought of practical matters, be efficient in love and marriage. Not that she would be selfish, Ken felt sure, but that she would see to it her relations with the man she loved would be well organized and stabilized. She would be a wife and a comrade to the man she married, and perhaps a dominant force; Andree would be wife and sweetheart, with no thought of dominating, but only of giving, of adding to the happiness of the man she loved.

If love were cruel to Andree, and the man she worshiped unkind, she would fade silently, withdraw into herself, and suffer; Maude would have suffered, but she would have faced the matter and held her own. It would be possible for Maude to go through life alone; that Andree should do so was utterly unthinkable. This was, perhaps, because Andree thought of herself only as a woman, and as a woman whose life must be bound up with the life of some man. Maude Knox thought of herself as an individual, a distinct entity with rights and purposes which must not be invaded or interfered with.

A man might expect help, encouragement, even dynamic career from Maude Knox. He might expect a wonderful fidelity from her. She would take an interest in his life and would want to have a finger in the shaping of his destiny. Andree would play her part in his life less obtrusively, but perhaps as powerfully by keeping alive his love and by lavishing her love upon him. She would ask nothing, demand nothing except a continuance of love and a lavishment of tenderness. So long as love endured she would follow him to the highest success without taking any great thought of that success, or she would have descended with him to the depths of failure without bewailing that failure—for success to her meant but one thing, and that thing was love.

Maude was the ideal wife in a partnership of man and wife as Americans have come to look upon that relation. The vestibule of the Presbyterian church would receive Maude with fulsome compliments and would congratulate Ken upon making a wise selection. Everybody would say that he had won a splendid wife ... and it would be true. She was a typical American wife—that is to say, she embodied those things which Americans have set as their ideals of wifehood.... He wondered what the vestibule would say of Andree, even granting that Andree's conception of virtue were the American conception. He could not imagine, though he could well imagine the stir she would create. She would be too beautiful— so beautiful as to excite righteous suspicion. She would be beautiful in a foreign sort of way, and therefore a sinful sort of way. The vestibule would never forgive her because she had lived in Paris and because she did not pronounce English as well as it did—through its nose. They would never be able to see into her heart nor to understand the marvel of her goodness.... She was as far outside their experience as she was actually outside Ken's experience, who studied her hourly, but never understood her and never would understand her.... She would always be a mystery and an anomaly to him. She would always be to him a creature who was guilty according to his inherited conscience and yet escaped the accusation or the stain of guilt. She was bad, yet she was wholly good.

He said this to himself, and then hotly denied it. She was not bad. In his heart he knew she was not bad, and he knew as well that he had never approached a soul which was as clean, as unselfish, as purely tender as hers.... Maude Knox was good, too, capable of unselfishness and fine tenderness. But she could never accomplish what Andree had accomplished. She could never do as Andree did and retain her purity.... He did not realize that this was because Maude herself would have believed herself to have lost her purity.

For Kendall the matter marched back to the attitude he had absorbed from his mother—that relations between the sexes were wicked in themselves and could never be anything else, but that by some miraculous quality belonging to a formula pronounced by a parson it became permissible for designated couples to practise wickedness without fear of punishment. The wickedness remained, but the formula remitted the punishment. That was his mother's belief.... She had been bitterly ashamed when Kendall became evident, because he was testimony to the world that she had been guilty....

Ken realized that he was getting himself into a state of mind, that he was reviving those disturbing thoughts which had such power to make him miserable ... and he had been very happy with Andree. He had loved his happiness, and now he wanted it to persist. It had been something new in his life, very precious, very wonderful ... and he was not willing that it should be dimmed.

He stepped behind the girls and spoke.

Andree turned and smiled. "You shall go away," she said. "We do not need you. You shall watch the parade while Miss Knox and myself make thees ver' interesting talk. Yes?"

"What are you and Miss Knox talking about?"

"What should we be talking about?" asked Maude. "About ourselves, of course."

"It is ver' nice subjec'," said Andree, with an impish twinkle.

"Let me come in. Talk about me, and I'll listen."

"*Pouf!*... You! If we talk about you, then you are ver' angry."

"Why?"

"Bicause we shall say the truth, and men want only to be praised. *N'est-ce pas?*... Oh, all men are greedy for praise. *Oh, là là là là.*"

"There, Captain Ware. Will you behave now?"

Ken laughed. "Andree is always very disagreeable. I don't see how I endure her."

She nodded. "Yes. I am mos' disagree-able." She accented the last syllable quaintly. "It is bicause I do not like you."

"Mademoiselle is very much interested in America," said Maude.

"And *Monsieur le capitaine* he tell me so ver' leetle."

"America is a large country. It has a hundred million of population. The Woolworth Building is sixty stories high. Everybody owns an automobile and goes to the movies. Baseball is the national game...."

"And ever' man ees marry and ees faithful to his wife," interrupted Andree, "and all are ver' *sérieux* and mos' religious, and they are asham' when they love. I know! I have study monsieur." She laughed with childish gaiety. "Oh, mademoiselle, it mus' be ver' droll.... Regard them—they are born, these Americans, they become ver' rich, they marry, they die—but they never live. It is that I believe they are afraid to live...."

"Yes, mademoiselle," said Maude, "you have hit on something there. We are afraid to live, all of us. We want to live. We want a great happiness, but we are afraid of it. You can't understand us better than we can understand you.... You have learned to live and be unafraid. We have not learned to get the best out of life, and our greatest terror is of our neighbors' tongues.... It has been wonderful for me to come to your country and to see...."

"And has mademoiselle really seen?" asked Andree, her eyes on Maude's face.

Maude hesitated. "I have tried to see, and I think I have understood a little. I have changed. I am not the same.... No, I am not the same girl at all who landed in France a few months ago."

"May one ask what mademoiselle have see'?"

Maude answered, speaking slowly and feeling her way: "When I left America I thought I was broad-minded and tolerant. My father had brought me up to be less narrow-minded than most girls.... He is a professor of philosophy. But I have found out that I was very narrow-minded indeed. I could see only one side, and that was the viewpoint of those among whom I was brought up. The thing I have come to see is that my home town was right in setting up its own standards and in maintaining them—because those standards were best for my home town.... But I have found out that other towns and countries have an equal right to set up their own standards and arrange their own modes of living. I think I can believe now that a thing which is very wrong in Terre Haute, Indiana, may be right in Paris or London or Rome, and that a thing which may be right in Terre Haute may be wrong in Venice."

"I onderstan'," said Andree, gravely. "The theeng you mean to say is thees, is it not? That an act it become' wrong when we theenk it is wrong? But if one city theenk it is right, then it is right for that city? *N'est-ce pas?*"

"Yes, something very like that."

"Is that an answer to the question I asked you at dinner a few days ago?" Ken asked.

Andree looked at him quickly.

Maude paused a moment before she replied; then she shook her head. "No," she said, "that is more complex.... If you were a Parisian I think I could answer, yes, without hesitation. But you are an American, who, possibly, should cling to American standards, no matter where you find yourself.... It is different.... No, I don't know what the answer is—yet."

"And thees question?" asked Andree, directly.

It was something like this that Kendall had feared from a meeting between Andree and Maude, that some subject such as this would spring up, that he would be subjected to embarrassment and discomfort. He was embarrassed now because he fancied Maude would be embarrassed and because he feared Andree, in her child-like frankness, might say something which would shock Maude's American prudery. He did not make use of the word *prudery*, but the state of mind for which it stood was in his thoughts. He flushed and was about to attempt some stammered diversion, but Maude answered, perfectly calm and without hesitation.

"Captain Ware asked me if I would ever marry a man who had had an affair with another girl."

"Ah...." said Andree. Then: "And why not, mademoiselle? What has that to do weeth the marriage? It was a silly question, was it not?"

Ken regarded her anxiously, but she gave no sign that she had attached any significance to his question other than a faint note in the long-drawn "Ah...." with which she had heard it stated.

"Yes, it was a ver' silly question," Andree repeated, "for if it ees not then there shall nevair be any marriages at all."

"I don't know...." said Maude.

"Perhaps it ees bicause mademoiselle ees ver' yo'ng and does not know the worl'," said Andree, with an air of age and wisdom.

"No. It is something in myself. I resent the idea."

"Then there is but one hope for mademoiselle.... She mus' marry the monk."

"Now, listen here," said Ken, bruskly. "This—this—Oh, darn it all, let's talk about something else."

Andree laughed gaily and pointed a finger of ridicule at him. "Oh, see! We have frighten' him.... He is ver' droll. Sometime' he is same theeng as yo'ng girl jus' from the convent.... But he is ver' good, mademoiselle," she said, suddenly and seriously. "He is mos' good and gentle and kind, and I love him ver' much."

Maude touched Andree's hand, and her eyes were not guiltless of moisture. "I am sure you do, dear," she said, "and he must love you very dearly, too."

Ken felt that the situation demanded something of him; that if he did not prove himself adequate to the demand he would sink in his own estimation and take a lower place in the regard of both the girls. It was awkward. No situation could be more awkward, but a thing was required of him if he desired to be true to himself and worthy of the love that Andree had given him.

"By God! I do!" he said, desperately, and had his reward in the depths of the smile which came into Andree's eyes....

There threatened to come an uncomfortable pause, but Andree averted it.

"Monsieur Ken and I go soon for the *déjeuner*. Mademoiselle, of course, comes also."

"I wish I might," said Maude, her voice a trifle dulled and her eyes not altogether happy. "But I promised to help out in the club on the Avenue Montaigne.... And I must be going." She looked at her wrist watch. "Indeed I must. I can cross the street now.... Good-by, Captain Ware. Good-by, mademoiselle."

"*Au revoir*," said Andree, holding out her hand. "We mus' meet again. There are many theengs we mus' speak of."

Maude looked down into Andree's dark-shadowed black eyes and smiled. "Yes," she said, "we must speak of many things...."

CHAPTER XXII

In the morning Paris stopped in groups to whisper and to point off to the northeastward. Paris was apprehensive. It had been awakened before dawn by the distant rumble of cannon, such a rumble as had never before come to its ears, and it wanted to know the reason for it. The guns had never sounded so loudly. Was it that the *boches* had made a fresh advance and were by that much nearer to the defenses of the city? Or had it been some huge air raid turned abortive before it reached its objective?... It was the 15th of July.

Slowly, by devious channels, the news spread. The enemy had struck again, had launched such a blow as warfare had not seen up to this period.... And Paris waited for the outcome. Then dull explosions were heard in various parts of the city at regular intervals.... Big Bertha was at her work again; the long-range cannon was once more bombarding Paris. As in the days past, one might see wagons loaded high with trunks and personal belongings moving toward a gate of the city or toward a railway station as the more apprehensive abandoned their homes for places of greater security. These were days when it was impossible to find tenants for the top floors of apartment-houses. There was a feeling that one was safer from Bertha and the bomb with at least one *étage* between him and the roof....

Papers were eagerly snatched from kiosks and from news-venders, who ran through the crowds with such speed that it was almost impossible to buy their wares—but the news was scanty. At least the guns were not heard again. After that first tremendous artillery preparation there was no sound from the direction of Château-Thierry and Reims. The silence, the pall which the censorship threw over events, was portentous, threatening. People recalled the inexorability of the last two German attacks. If this one proceeded as its predecessors had done, Paris would be made untenable. There would be a siege.... There was talk of complete evacuation.

Then tidings of a more encouraging nature filtered in. The *boches* had advanced a little here and there, had been checked at this and that point. There had been no breaking through, no headlong rush upon Paris, no marching down roads in columns of four with guns over shoulders.

On the 16th the apprehension was less, but the tension was still present. The 17th saw Paris again almost at the normal of war-times. It was reassured. It was rumored that Foch had given his word that Paris was safe. The magic of one man's name was potent to reassure the millions of citizens of the metropolis. If Foch said Paris was safe, then Paris was safe.

Then came the 18th, which dawned as other days dawn, with the same sun rising in the east, with the same blue skies above, and the same breezes moving over the surface of the same earth. But it was a day not like other days. History may well set it down as the Day of Days, for it marked the beginning of the end, the first note of the finale of the crashing, discordant Germanic opera.... The Allies had counterattacked, and fear was dead. That was the significant thing. The 18th of July, A.D., 1918, marked the death of fear in the heart of Paris. From that date onward there would be no news but good news. Terror of the Hun had become a thing which one remembered but would no more experience.

The Élysées Palace Hôtel knew by night that our First and Second divisions had struck at the base of the German salient about Reims and that our Twenty-sixth Division had battered the apex before Château-Thierry — and at last the American Expeditionary Force was in the war. The Americans had come! The Americans were ready! The Americans had started! Number 10 rue Ste.-Anne knew these things, as did the American censorship high up in the Bourse. It was a day of exultation for Americans in Paris....

In spite of censorships, in spite of military secrecy, in spite of minute precautions, rumors circulate through armies which have an undeniable basis of fact. On the 4th of July Kendall heard the soldiers of the First Division stating confidently that they would march through Paris streets on Bastille Day. No one had told them. Nobody knew how the rumor earned its life, but it was there, and the event proved its reliability. So an army rumor receives a degree of belief which does not seem to be warranted. Rumors were a plentiful harvest now; big rumors and little rumors ... and among them, circulating through the officers of the Intelligence Department in Paris, was the whisper that some officer or officers were to be sent back to America either on a mission or to undertake permanent work.

Ken heard this prophecy early in the morning, and it troubled him. He had no cause for imagining that he would be selected, yet he might be selected. The chances were, perhaps, minute, but, nevertheless, they were present, and it was far from his desire to be returned to America to run down German sympathizers in Hoboken or to take a desk in some crowded bureau in Washington. While he was in France there always was the hope that he might be transferred to active duty with some regiment at the front. Like all men in the American Expeditionary Force, he wanted to serve at the front, and he did not want to return to America—at least until the work was done. Man after man Kendall had heard to speak longingly of America, but to couple with his homesickness the quick statement that he did not want to return until the job was done. It was a sort of religion—the cleaning up of that job. Somehow each man seemed to feel that the success of the army depended on his presence, and that to be sent home before victory arrived would be to deprive him of something precious which he had earned.... It was so with Ken.

But he had a stronger motive than most for wishing to stay in France. It was Andree....

Suddenly and very poignantly he realized what it would mean if he were compelled to part from Andree. It seemed to him that she had become a part of him, an essential part without which he could not continue. She had brought an essence into his life which was sweet and desirable and wonderful. He knew that no other woman could bring to him what Andree had brought so unconsciously, yet so generously.... She was Andree!... Andree! The world could show but one.

What was to be the outcome? It was a question he had evaded time and again, well knowing that it must some day be faced. He did not face it now, though it urged itself upon his attention. He did not believe the world had seen a more precious thing than their love—and yet, because of his training and the imprint of heredity, that love was questionable, tainted with irregularity. It was good, sweet, pure, but it was irregular as the Middle West and Plymouth Rock perceived irregularity.

He had never known Andree to utter an immodest word or to think a thought that was not clean and good. He had wondered at a certain diffident loftiness in her thoughts. She was a woman whose soul was to be regarded with awe, as any virtuous soul is to be regarded with awe. He did not believe he saw her falsely, nor that love blinded him to defects which should be apparent. He knew he saw her truly, and that she was worthy of all his love.... And yet his friends, his neighbors—above all, his mother—would despise her as a woman of light virtue, as a thing of evil.... He could see the seething among the gossips if Andree were to be set down in their midst, and he despised them.... But—

The Little Moment Of Happiness | 253

Again he evaded. He had not the courage to ask himself what he would do when the moment for doing arrived.... He could not give her up. That was the thought that came now—that she was indispensable.... But would he have the courage to face the vestibule of the Presbyterian church with her? He did not ask.

One of those moods of depression to which he was liable when his reflections were troubled settled upon him. He was acutely unhappy. Those moods possessed a physical sensation, not a pain so much as a consciousness of the existence of his body, which was very disturbing. It was as if his arms and legs had suddenly become vivid. At such times he did not want companionship, could not have answered conversational advances. The life within him seemed to become as putty—a dead mass. The only relief was to walk and walk and walk.

He left the office to trudge to the apartment, meaning to eat lightly and to wander about Paris until the obsession was ejected.... At the entrance to the building the concierge was standing, waiting for him.

"Oh, monsieur ... monsieur," she said, and broke forth into weeping.

He was not surprised. Such scenes were to be expected in those days when every mail brought word that some loved one had been demanded of his country. He patted her shoulder awkwardly.

"You have had evil news, madame," he said. "I am so sorry."

Through her tears rage flared. "The *boches*," she exclaimed. "Why is it that the good God allows such creatures to be!... What good can it do them? But they would laugh and be joyous. It is so. I have read.... These killers of babies!"

"What is it, madame? Your son? Have you had the news?"

"My son, monsieur, is gone these two years," she said, not without a lift of the shoulders. "It would not be that. When one is a soldier one must march.... To kill the men—that is war. But the babies—the helpless little babies!... They are not men, monsieur, but monsters...."

"Yes.... Yes," he answered, not knowing what to say.

"And monsieur loved her, did he not? It was Arlette who declared it to be so. Always she spoke of the fondness of monsieur for the *petite fille*—the tiny Arlette."

"Little Arlette! What do you mean, madame? What has happened to little Arlette?"

"*La longue portée, monsieur.* Again it began to fire this day. It is that you have heard its explosions.... This Big Bertha of the boche that murders babies!... *La pauvre enfant!* She is playing in the street before her home. Out of the sky comes the shell of this so wicked cannon. There is a noise of great frightfulness." She covered her eyes. "When the smoke makes to lift itself and one can see—there lies little Arlette...."

"Killed!" Kendall felt something that was rage and grief clutch his throat. "Have they killed that child?"

"She still lives, monsieur, and asks for you. It is so.... But she will die. It is dreadful. Yes.... Both legs, monsieur, at the knee. They were swept from beneath her as with a scythe ... and she still lives—asking for monsieur."

"Where?"

She told him the hospital, and without a word he turned, running, to search for a taxicab. The thing was incredible. Little Arlette, that mite from fairyland, maimed and bleeding and dying. Such things could not be. This was not war.... He raged, though tears were wet upon his cheeks.... As he rode, the dainty figure of the child stood before him, chin upraised, mouth opened birdwise to sing. He saw her as if she were real.... And then he saw that scene in the street: children playing, the sun daring to shine.... A sudden rushing in the air above, a tremendous detonation. He saw it all, even to the most minute happening. He saw little Arlette standing erect, stricken with sudden fear, saw the burst of the explosion, saw the child diminish suddenly in stature as her little legs were flicked from under her and she dropped upon bleeding stumps before toppling to the pavement.... He uttered a hoarse groan of protest.... He cowered back into a corner of the taxicab and shut his eyes, as if that could shut out the pictures of his imagination.

And she had called for him!

It seemed he was expected at the hospital, for he was escorted immediately to the little bed upon which Arlette lay. He had dreaded to see her, flinching from a sight which he apprehended might be horrible. He forced himself to look ... and the horror passed. The little face upon the pillow was bloodless, her eyes closed. She seemed not alive, but a thing of fragile loveliness carved from some material brought into being by the fairies for this very purpose.... There was no trace of pain—only motionlessness, a mysterious gravity ... and peace. Old Arlette sat with eyes fixed unwaveringly on the little face; the child's mother cowered with her face against Arlette's ample shoulder.... Ken stood in silence.

The nurse touched his arm. "Speak to her," she whispered. "It will make no difference. She has asked many times for you."

"She is—alive?"

"And conscious."

"It will not—harm her to arouse her?"

"Nothing can harm her."

Kendall understood. Little Arlette was past hurt now, and he had been brought there to give to the child her last little moment of happiness.... He knelt by the cot.

"*Mignonne,*" he said, softly.

She opened her eyes and stared at him, and then smiled.

"He is come. Regard him. I said he would come." Her voice was so faint as to be almost no voice at all.

"Of a certainty I have come," he said. "What could keep me away from my little sweetheart?... Does—does it hurt?"

"Hurt?" She seemed vaguely surprised. "What should hurt, monsieur?" She did not know what had happened to her.

"May I kiss you?" he asked.

"But yes. Is it not that I am to be your wife? I wish you to kiss me."

"Do you love me very much, *mignonne*?"

"Oh, very much.... We shall be very happy, monsieur, in this America of the North. I am too little to be married now, is it not? But it will not be long.... My grandmother says I grow very fast."

"I have seen it myself."

She sighed. "I am glad. I had fear that you might grow tired of waiting...."

"I would wait for you forever, *mignonne*."

Again she smiled. "I shall sing for monsieur. One should stand up to sing ... but grandmother says I must not stand up to-day."

"Will it harm her?" Kendall asked, quickly, of the nurse.

"Nothing will harm her," she repeated.

"Then sing, dear ... sing 'Madelon.'"

The birdlike lips opened and the song came forth, faint as a morning breeze, that song of the little barmaid who stands to the *poilu* for the wife or sweetheart at home, the little barmaid whom he kisses in his loneliness, and in kissing her feels that he is touching the lips of one far away.... It was a song which, to Middle-Western ears, sounded strangely on the lips of a dying child, but it did not offend Kendall.... It sprang from the soul of France.

There ceased to be any semblance of an air to the song; it became a faint whisper, halting, coming now a word at a time. Arlette's eyes were closed.... Now her lips moved, but there was no sound.... Presently the lips ceased to move....

Kendall turned to the nurse, who nodded. He arose suddenly, looked down upon the child and then rushed from the room ... and as he traversed the corridor he found himself repeating again and again: "With a song on her lips.... With a song on her lips...."

For two months experiences had been jostling one another to enter Kendall Ware's life. It seemed as if there was a conspiracy among events to modify him, to change the fiber of him, and to break down the structure that had been himself when he landed in France. As compared with these past sixty days the previous ten thousand days of his life had been colorless and without life.... It had required twenty-seven years of personal existence and more than one generation of predecessors to make him what he was—and now a mere fraction of time, a handful of minutes, were striving to undo all that had been accomplished and to create a new being. The question to be answered was: Can the present overcome the past? Can events master the fiber growth of heredity? It seemed an experiment to determine if individuality is a fixed quantity or if it is subject to revolution.... So far it might be asserted that Kendall had been modified—but no more.

Little Arlette had been a bit of humor in his life—no more. He had been unconscious that she was anything more. But now in her catastrophe she loomed larger and assumed significance. His was a world of symbolisms, a religion of symbolisms. As his mother saw the hand of God in every event— the hand of God interposed with direct reference to herself—so Kendall, in a minor degree, and perhaps with something of unconsciousness, was subject to the same obsession. He looked for the lessons of events. He was apprehensive of the warnings of events. An implacable God regarded him under lowering brows and now and then caused an event to occur for his guidance.... So he looked for the significance of Arlette's murder.

He had an uncomfortable feeling that innocence had been caused to perish for his benefit—as a lesson to him. It made him a sort of accessory after the fact. He rebelled in a vague way, feeling dimly that God had no right to implicate him in such a crime. Old catch phrases came back to him as he walked toward his home, phrases such as that one must search for the divine purpose behind the event; that the ways of God pass human understanding; that it is all for the best!... There was no comfort in these. He could descry no divine purpose. For that matter, he could find no divine purpose back of the war.... Yet God permitted it, furthered it, as it were.... And because it was, because Divinity permitted it to occur, it followed indisputably that it must be right for it to occur.... He would not have dared to define his creed as stating that his God was one who committed wholesale crime that a remote benefit might accrue. Yet that was his creed and the creed of hundreds of thousands of his fellow-countrymen.... It was strange that he should remember Andree's attitude toward God at that moment— her saying that the eyes of the good God must be wet with tears to see a wickedness. But he did remember, and was grateful to her.

He wandered in a maze of gloomy theorizings, a maze which was nothing but a maze, which led to no desired center. It was the struggle between present and past, and it was a drawn battle. It only left him bewildered and gloomy, treading a bog and miring at every step.... Then he became aware that he wanted Andree, that she was necessary to him, because there was something simple and sure about her. She gave him a handhold to cling to. He felt that she knew, and he wanted the security and uplift of her knowledge. The universe was toppling, and Andree could stabilize it again—but Andree was not coming.... He felt he would never need her more than at this moment, but she was residing in her land of mystery, and he had neither her name nor address....

The stark fact was that little Arlette was dead—and with a song on her tiny lips. He would never again think of France without thinking of Arlette ... without seeing Arlette as a symbol of something at once pure and ruthless....

CHAPTER XXIII

Now began a phase of Kendall Ware's life which was to continue for a matter of six weeks, a period full of conflict between anomalies, of indecisions, of procrastinations. There stood out high moments of happiness, and there were dark descents into unlighted realms of self-distrust. He questioned everything, doubted everything, and most especially did he doubt his own ability to weigh events and to choose between the better and the worse. He almost doubted if he had the power of choice and felt a dour leaning toward predestination. Much of this was self-deception, and conscious self-deception. He was becoming increasingly aware of a day when he would have to make a choice and reach a decision, but he was afraid of that day. He knew the choice was his, and could belong to no other individual or force. *He* must choose. The event was in his keeping.

Three major questions presented themselves: First, what was he going to do about Andree? Second, what was he going to do about Maude Knox? And, third, which was interwoven with the first, what about the vestibule of the Presbyterian church?

Ken had not the least doubt that he loved Andree. That was the one sure fact in the whole confused mass. He loved Andree and Andree loved him. To many young men, perhaps to most, this alone would have answered all his questions. Perhaps the ordinary young man would have thought of nothing else, but, perceiving that Andree was essential to him, he would have taken her and made her his own in permanence with due forms of marriage. This would have been the natural step for youth to take—disregarding consequences and challenging the future. But Ken was not an ordinary young man. He was a young man who was afraid of the future, who had been brought up to know a lively fear of the opinion of the community among which he lived. "What will folks say?" was a question he had heard propounded from his earliest childhood, until the thing that "they" would say had assumed a place of importance in his affairs second to nothing. It had almost confused his perceptions of right and wrong, for, even as a small boy, it had been made to appear to him that his mother was not so much concerned with the righteousness of any given act as she was by the effect of that act upon her circle of neighbors. Undoubtedly this was a mistaken notion, but it had at least the color of truth.

He recalled vividly how a certain prominent member of his church had become an absconder and the coming of the news of it into his household. He remembered how his father had said: "Mother, we don't know all the ins and outs of it. Maybe he's more sinned against than sinning. We don't know...." His mother had rejected that view harshly. "Whatever will people say about him? It'll be terrible on his wife, and him so prominent in the church." She had not said, "What will God say about him?" but, "What will people say?" His sin, so it had seemed to Ken's young mind, had not been so much in absconding with money as it had been in creating adverse talk.... This attitude of mind had altered somewhat with years, but never had his fear of clacking tongues diminished. It stood for the supreme punishment of evil ... not hell, but gossip.

So his first and third questions stood together, and he dared not force himself to answer them. The second question could not be answered until he had satisfied the other two.... There came a fourth question, upon which, ultimately, must hang the answers to all, and that was, "Can a man marry a woman with whom he has had such a relation as I have had with Andree?" In other words, could he, by his own act, unfit Andree to become his own wife? This question did not present itself poignantly for some time, but it was beginning to formulate in the back of his mind. As yet he was considering only the expediency of matters; later he would find trouble with their moral and sociological aspects.

Matters further complicated themselves when Maude Knox informed him that she had been assigned permanently to an administrative position in Paris. He would be compelled to see her frequently. He would want to see her frequently. Somehow this seemed unfair to Andree, but he knew that Maude could not remain in the city without his seeing a great deal of her. Andree would discover this, and what would Andree do about it? With Maude Knox absent her importance receded, was held in abeyance; if she were here she would grow increasingly important—and what would come of it?

"You don't seem overjoyed," she said.

"I'm glad you're going to be here," he said, "but just the same, I wish you weren't."

"Why? You aren't compelled to have anything to do with me if you don't want to."

"That's it. I am compelled, and I don't know whether I want to or not."

"Well!..." She drew the word out to its full value. "I must say you're frank."

"Please don't be offended. I don't mean to be offensive, but things have gotten so rottenly complicated with me that I'm afraid of another complication."

"And I'm a complication?"

He nodded. "You know it," he said. "I think you know more about what a complication you are than I do."

"You are thinking Andree will be jealous."

"I'm thinking she may have cause to be jealous."

"And you don't want her to have?"

"That's just it. I don't know.... I don't want anything ever to happen to make her unhappy. You and I have talked pretty frankly, haven't we? Somehow you seem to understand things over here, though you are as American as I am—and you—well, you don't make a fuss. But even at that, you don't know how I feel about her.... Maybe I'm going to be in love with you, and maybe I'm in love with you already. I don't know.... But I do know that I love her."

"If you are by way of making love to me you've invented a new method."

"I'm not making love to you. I guess I'm trying to reason things out aloud."

"Using me as a wall to bounce your ball against."

He smiled without mirth. "Something like that. I know I love Andree, but yet I can see myself in love with you.... I've asked you before if a man can be in love with two girls at the same time."

"I don't know. Not in the same way, anyhow."

"It would be different. If I did love you I would be thinking about marriage all the time. It would mean marriage. I would want you for my wife.... But Andree—she doesn't mean that. At least marriage doesn't figure in it. I can't explain exactly, but it's as if there never had been such a thing in the world as marriage—only love."

"I'm not sure but that is better. Even if I am American I don't know but I'd rather have that kind."

"Andree isn't just an adventure, an incident. She's more important than that—the most important thing that ever happened to me.... I can't explain. I can feel it, but I can't express what it is. It isn't that I couldn't marry her, nor that I wouldn't be mighty lucky to have her for a wife.... It seems, somehow, that marriage doesn't signify—isn't necessary."

"I'm sure I don't know what you're trying to get at."

"I don't, either. I'm trying to find out.... But I do know that I don't want to hurt her or make her sorry she has loved me."

"How about me?" she asked, suddenly.

"You?"

"How about hurting me?" she asked. "You've made a weird sort of love to me. You've balanced on the fence and told me you might fall in love with me. You've carried on a sort of rubber-elastic courtship—ready to snap back out of reach if I seemed likely to catch you.... Have you thought about me at all? Really, I've some right to be considered."

She was right. Undoubtedly he had not been fair to her. He had thought only of himself and of his sentiments toward her, but scarcely at all of her sentiments toward him.

"Why," he said, "I don't believe I've thought of that side of it. It never occurred to me that you—that you might be in love with me."

"Well, I'm not." She spoke sharply.

"Do you mean you never could be?"

"There! Of all things!... You want me to tell you that if you make up your mind to condescend to love me I'll be ready to drop into your hands. You want to have your cake and eat it. I'd say you were the most completely selfish person I've ever encountered."

"Really I'm not. It isn't selfishness.... It's just that I am so confused by the whole situation that I don't know what to do.... You don't know how relieved and happy I would be if there was nobody but you, and we were going to be married. You are just the kind of wife—"

"That your neighbors would approve of," she interrupted. "I know. What I don't know is why I keep on talking to you like this. I ought to send you about your business and tell you never to come near me again ... but

I'm not going to. You've told me in effect that you would be in love with me if it weren't for somebody else, and that the only reason you are pleased to consider me as a candidate at all is because you are afraid your family and your neighbors would make a fuss if you took the other woman home. That's the truth, and you know it is."

"Well," he said, ruefully, and not wisely, "so long as you don't love me, what does it matter?"

"So long as I don't love you it doesn't matter in the least."

"But—"

She shook her head. "We sha'n't talk about my loving you. I'm not going to love you."

"Do you mean that?"

"Decidedly."

"You wouldn't marry me?"

"Of course not."

"Why?"

"Really, I think you're out of your mind. Even if I loved you—which I don't—do you think I'd sit and wait for you to reason out that you had better fall in love with me, and then grab you with wild eagerness—after you make up your mind to chuck another woman whom you have assured me that you do love?"

"But suppose I do love you? Would the fact of my—my affair with Andree prevent you from marrying me?"

"If you loved me and I loved you nothing in the world would stop me from marrying you."

"Anyhow, I've got that question answered."

"And much good may it do you."

"Why?"

"Because the condition doesn't exist. If it did exist I might answer differently. I might think then that I could never marry a man who had done such a thing."

This conversation took place at noon in a little café on the rue St.-Honoré not distant from the Y. M. C. A. headquarters. Kendall had met Maude Knox as he was seeking a place to lunch, and they had gone together. Now he wished he might sit and argue the question until his status with her was definitely settled, if it could be definitely settled, but she refused to pursue the subject.

"No, that's all we talk about that. You can pick out any subject you want to, but we are through talking about you and me.... And, besides, I've got to get back to work."

"When shall we have dinner together?"

"I don't know."

"You're angry with me."

"No, but I'm disgusted with myself because I'm not. If I had a spark of pride I'd never speak to you again."

"Why?"

"Ken Ware, you are a miracle of denseness. Don't you know that this whole conversation has been impossible—that it couldn't have happened? I never imagined such cool effrontery! But I'm not offended, and I don't know why.... I'll dine with you some evening soon—but not to touch this subject again. Don't ever mention it—never! I've got some rights to be thought about, and I'm going to think about them. There are just two things you may do: either propose to me out and out, so I can refuse you, or else treat me as a friend, and no trimmings. I mean it!"

"But I don't want to do either."

"You'll have to." She laughed, and slid deftly from behind the table. "Are you going to walk up the street with me?"

"Let me pay the check."

He called a waiter and asked for *l'addition* and then walked to the corner of the rue d'Aguesseau with Maude. She did not permit him to linger.

"Good-by," she said, turning abruptly away. "Drop me a note when you feel in a condescending mood."

That evening when he got home he found Bert and Madeleine there ahead of him.

"Andree's coming, too," said Bert. "I met her this afternoon and told her there was going to be a party.... This is a farewell. See Madeleine's tears?"

"Farewell?"

"Yes. I'm going away for a couple of weeks—some buildings to look after. I don't mind, but Madeleine's darn near heartbroken."

"Oh yes," said Madeleine, gaily. "My heart it break. I am so lonely.... You see, Monsieur Bert he is the on'y American *officier* in France. When he is gone, there is no other."

"You don't mean that," said Ken.

"Of course she does," Bert said, with a grin.

Ken shrugged his shoulders and went to his room to tidy up a bit for dinner. He heard them laugh, and Bert's voice said, "He thinks we are very naughty."

He did think so, but in spite of himself he liked Madeleine, indeed, felt a real friendship for her. She was not like Andree, but she possessed qualities which could not pass unnoticed. She was generous, kind, always concerned for Bert's comfort and financial welfare. There was not a mercenary hair in her head, if there was not a serious hair. Even though there was nothing deep and enduring and lofty in her relations with Bert, there was nothing sordid. She was seeking her little moments of happiness, seeking them lightly, gaily, carelessly.... Ken excused his own conduct because it was concerned with a great love and a beautiful fidelity. There were no such matters between Bert and Madeleine, yet Ken could not find it in his heart to denounce her as bad. According to all his standards she was bad—a light creature. But, somehow, he did not see her as a light woman nor as wicked.

It would have been difficult to find any one more different from Andree.... Ken had become used to accepting Andree's judgments in large measure, and Andree did not declare Madeleine *méchante*. She, too, liked the girl, accepted her as a friend and equal.... It was all a part of this strange world with its upsetting standards....

The bell interrupted his moral reflections and he hurried to the door with that thrill of anticipation which Andree's arrival always caused.... There she stood, very straight and still and grave, just as he knew she would be. She raised her eyes to his exactly as he knew she would raise them, and smiled appealingly. He drew her inside, into his arms.

"I've been needing you, *mignonne*," he said. "Everything goes wrong when you're not with me."

"I am here," she said, brightly. "Behol'! all is now well. I shall let nothing trouble you."

"Do you love me?"

"Yes.... And you?"

"You are very beautiful."

"That is well.... No, I am not beautiful, but it is well you theenk it is so. I am happy."

She regarded him solicitously. "You are ver' tired. Have you work' *beaucoup*? It is not that you have an illness?"

"No.... No. Everything is all right now that you are here. You are the only person who is *right* in the whole world."

"Oh!... Oh!... I am ver' wonderful! I do not know thees till I meet you. I theenk I am only a yo'ng girl, but behol'! I have ver' suddenly become— how do you say?—The *dictionnaire*—queek. The *dictionnaire*!" Laughing gaily, she searched with ludicrous haste for the word and could not find it. "Oh, it is terrible! W'at I am I cannot say. I am something that ees not in the *dictionnaire*. To be a thing that is not in the *dictionnaire* is mos' grand and étonnant—astonishing. I shall to be ver' vain."

Her eyes were dancing with an impish light. She seemed very young, a child, endowed with some magical quality which reassured him, dispelled the heaviness which rested on him.

"Have Monsieur Bert and Mademoiselle Madeleine yet arrive'?"

"They're in the *salon*."

"Come. We shall see them—now." Again that quaint gesture of poking downward at the floor with a slender finger. "Thees minute."

The girls shook hands formally and lapsed into an amazing splutter of French. Ken looked from one to the other, from Andree, tiny, fragile, dark, elfin, to Madeleine, tall, slender, fair of hair, always laughing. Madeleine seemed nothing but embodied laughter; Andree seemed to him now as she always seemed to him, a mystery, incomprehensible—a being come to him out of a land of wonders.

"Bert is going away," he said.

"For how long?"

"Three weeks."

"Oh, it ees a lifetime. Mademoiselle will be ver' sad."

"She says not," Ken said.

"It is not possible. She will be mos' sad."

"Not Madeleine," said Bert. "She's going to find another American officer to keep her happy while I'm gone."

"But she could not—*non, non!* You do not theenk!"

Madeleine laughed gaily.

"What would you do if I went away for three weeks?" Ken asked.

"You do not go!... It ees not true." Her eyes grew big and her lips parted as she waited for his answer.

"No, I'm not going any place.... But if I should go, what would you do?"

"I should be ver' *solitaire*. Ver' often I should weep. And I should work ver' hard at all times—to make the days go more fast."

"Would you find another American officer to help you pass the time?"

"You know," she said, simply.

"*Oh, là là!*" exclaimed Madeleine. "Regard these children. It ees the great love. *Toujours fidèle*. It ees mos' beautiful."

"It is ever'thing," said Andree. "You, mademoiselle, love a ver' little. So you are happy a ver' little. *N'est-ce pas?* I love ver' much, so I am happy ver' much. It is clear. You theenk you are mos' happy, but you do not know. It is not until you love, mademoiselle, until you love weeth all the love there is that you have the great happiness."

"It may be so.... But also the great sadness. Is it not so? Regard me. I love thees Monsieur Bert a leetle. He makes to go away, so I am sad a leetle. Yes? But, then, I love him so ver', ver' much and he makes to go away. And then?..." She shrugged her shoulders. "Behol'—then I am in despair. I theenk my way is more better. Not the great joy, but also not the great sadness."

"*Non!... Non!...* It ees not so. There is the great sadness, it is true. *Certainement!* But even that, mademoiselle, is sweet. Bicause one remembers the great love and the great joy. The so great happiness has been. It will nevair die. No. For so long as one lives the happiness will remain.... The grief—one must expect grief.... It is a part of the worl'."

"*Vous êtes un poète, mademoiselle*.... You write the poetry. Therefore you are different. The poet makes of sadness a great thing, a wonderful thing.... But I—I, mademoiselle, am cashier in a shop. I do not have the so beautiful thoughts. No, I am jus' a girl that loves to be happy always. I cannot think the wonderful thoughts like the poet—*non*. To me it seems that ver' many leetle happinesses without a sorrow are more better than one great, wonderful happiness of the poet—but also with the terrible grief that makes to kill.... So I love a little and laugh all the days and am ver' content."

"Would you not wish to love—to have forever one man and to love him weeth the great love?"

"Ah, that is another matter. Always to have one lover, one husband! It is different. Then I would love—yes. I would love as much as any one.... But it is not possible. Do I not know? Where do I get the husband? *Pouf!* There is no husband for me, and as for lovers—thees American lovers—they come, and it is a little while when they go. So I do not love. I make believe to love, and so I am happy.... But why, mademoiselle, give to one of them the great love when one knows well it is but for a day? It is to throw away the love, is it not?"

Andree was silent; all were silent. Madeleine had thrust the situation before Kendall and Andree baldly. Ken drew Andree to him, but she did not respond; she was cold, frightened.

"But for a day ..." she said.

"Monsieur Bert and I we do not deceive ourselves. We tell each other that thees is not for always.... It is play—so there is no cloud between us.... But you—oh, you are ver' wrong, mademoiselle. In your heart you know.... You love Monsieur Ken and he loves you—it is true. But—ask him the question, mademoiselle—does he stay forever? Or, when the day comes on which he mus' depart, will he take you weeth him to thees America?... Ask him, mademoiselle, and if he tell you you shall be weeth him always, then I am wrong." She looked at Ken. He was conscious that Andree was looking at him appealingly, and that even Bert was demanding something of him with his eyes.

He might have lied. He might have assured Andree that she should never leave him, but with her eyes upon him he could not lie.... He did not know. This was the thing that was making him miserable—the question of whether he should take Andree to America with him.... He did not know. Therefore he answered, lamely:

"I love you, *mignonne*."

"It ees not an answer," said Madeleine, inexorably.

"I can't answer.... I can't see the future.... I don't know. All I know, Andree, is that I do love you. Why can't we be satisfied with that until we have to decide?... The war will be long. I shall be here for years, perhaps.... Oh, my dear, I cannot think of a life without you—but I do not know...."

He was conscious that he was proving inadequate to the situation, that he was not measuring up to what Andree had a right to expect of him, and he was afraid of what she might do or say. Madeleine shrugged her shoulders expressively. He looked at Andree apprehensively, saw her eyes flash with anger, her little figure grow tense, her lips compress. It was the first time he had ever seen her angry.... He had offended her. She was in a rage with him, and rightly in a rage.... She stepped close to him and clasped his arm with both hands, turning her face toward Madeleine and Bert.

"See!" she exclaimed, and her black eyes flashed, "you have make him unhappy weeth your questions.... I shall not have questions asked of him.... *Non!* He shall not be troubled. It is not the affair of any one but himself and me.... I will not permit it.... What is it to you? It is for us alone. If it is *nécessaire* that he leave me one day—that is for him to say. Is it that I have ask or demand anything? *Non, non, non!*... He is ver' good, and I love him—jus' like he love' me.... I know that and I am satisfy.... You shall not make him to be unhappy weeth questions...."

She faced them, tense, breathing rapidly. Her hands clutched his arm and pressed it to her breast....

"Andree ..." he said, hoarsely. "Andree ..."

She smiled up at him, her face softening, her eyes becoming big and tender. "Ever'thing is well," she said.

Bert drew a long breath. "By Jupiter!" he said, and there was admiration in his eyes. "I'll tell you what, Andree, if you'll have me, if you can put up with a roughneck like me, I'll take you for keeps ... and to hell with the consequences."

Madeleine laughed and shook her head. "You see how *fidèle* thees Monsieur Bert is.... *Là là!* But you shall not have heem, mademoiselle, until I am through weeth him.... See, there is the head of Arlette.... Let us have the dinner and be gay!"

CHAPTER XXIV

There are persons who seem to have their emotions under the control of push-buttons, as it were. They are capable of friendship and anger and love and jealousy, but they have been given the faculty of suppressing these emotions until it is their desire to allow them freedom. Maude Knox was one of these. It would be unfair to say that she was coldly calculating, but she was careful. Many of the minor inhibitions which rule American girls did not signify to her; she was broader of mind, capable of perceptions of which her sisters were incapable. But she did not fly into passions, nor was she given to headlong tumbles into love.

Her condition with respect to Kendall Ware was noncommittal. As a matter of fact, she was not in love with him, because he had not committed himself. If Ken had come frankly to her, declaring his love, and had asked her to be his wife she would by this time have been as much in love with him as he could have desired. Nobody could deny that they were suited to each other, and nature has seen to it that young people who are suited to each other, and enjoy propinquity with each other, do fall in love. It seems to be the law that everybody must love somebody; it also seems to be the law that propinquity is nine-tenths of the matter.... So Maude was in a receptive mood. She was ready to let go and be very much in love with Ken when a suitable moment arrived—if it ever did arrive.

Once she had released her controls she would be tender, faithful, a wife such as any man might boast of. His life would be her life. His concerns would be her concerns. Her career would be to make him happy and to make a success of the family of which he would be the head.

Just how much she realized of this condition it would be difficult to say. Just how much she desired Kendall to fall in love with her she herself did not know; but she did like him, liked him a great deal. He was on her mind, and perhaps she even schemed a little to have him near her frequently and so to give him the opportunity to love her if such a thing were to happen. But at the same time she held a serious doubt if she would marry him in any event—because of Andree.

True, she was of broad mind, and her life abroad had enabled her to perceive and to understand many matters which are obscure in America.

These she could understand and condone or pronounce to be good and even virtuous—when they did not touch her directly. They were all right for others, but—but when they entered her own life that made of it another matter.

If she had been told that in a time past Kendall Ware had carried on an affair with a French girl—an affair that was wholly of the past—she might have dismissed it after small bitterness and have accepted him without more than a slight question. But this was present, going on under her eyes. She saw the workings of it, and saw that he actually loved this girl. That it was the sort of love he would one day give to his wife she did not believe. That did not seem possible to her.... On the other hand, there were many periods when she knew a fear that Kendall would marry Andree. She asked herself why he should not marry Andree. She had seen the girl, talked with her, found her beautiful and sweet—even good. Maude even felt a sympathy for Andree to the extent of warning Kendall against tampering with the girl's happiness. Her sympathies were with Andree rather than with Kendall. She had never experienced the slightest aversion for Andree, none of that aversion which a woman safe in the possession of what she terms her virtue is entitled by ruthless custom to feel for the girl who is no longer a maid. She was able to conceive of a union such as Andree's with Ken as possessing a sort of regularity, as being made more or less regular by the standards and conceptions of the society in which they were living.... But, nevertheless, when it came to marrying Ken her American prejudices and conceptions took on life and set themselves up as a barrier.

It was natural that she should be very curious about Andree and should wish the opportunity of meeting and studying the girl. She was rather frank and outspoken herself and could imagine herself discussing the situation with this girl and, perhaps, arriving at some determination. But the opportunity failed to present itself for days and weeks. Her brief chat with Andree on Bastille Day had proved nothing, and it was not until early August when a chance meeting in the Galeries Lafayette, where both girls happened to be shopping, gave her the opportunity she desired.

They met on one of the broad winding stairways of that enormous store, Andree descending, Maude ascending. Of the two Andree was the more self-possessed. She looked at Maude with that quaintly inquiring expression with which she seemed to greet all the world, but gave no other sign of recognition until Maude smiled and extended her hand.

"*Bon jour, mademoiselle,*" she said.

"*Bon jour,*" responded Andree.

"I've been hoping to see you for a long time. We hardly got acquainted in that little chat we had a month ago."

"You are sure you wish to be acquainted?"

"Oh, very."

"*Pourquoi?*"

"Why? That's difficult to put into words, isn't it? But I know about you—and you must know about me. We just ought to be acquainted better."

"Eet is possible. You will know me. Ver' well. I also would know you."

"Suppose we have *déjeuner* together, then. Have you finished your shopping?"

"Ever'thing—all is completed."

Maude turned and walked down the stairs with Andree. They did not speak until they had traversed the crowded aisles and reached the street. Each was thinking about the other, but with this difference: Maude was wondering what Andree thought about her, while Andree was not concerned in the least with Maude's opinion of herself. She thought of Maude only as some one in whom Ken was more interested than she liked, and wondered what this American girl would say to her.... Maude was impressed, not exactly in spite of herself, with Andree's appearance and manner. The girl was so slender, so dainty, so appealing, so childlike and fragile! One could not help wanting to defend her and befriend her.... But it was not befriending her to wish to take away the man she loved and who loved her, which was the thing that could not but rest in the back of Maude's mind. She had a feeling that Andree knew that desire was in her mind....

"Let us go to the Petrograd—it is only a few steps. I am living there now. A great many of us American girls live there."

"Ver' well," said Andree, who, it seemed, had placed herself on the knees of the gods and was prepared to let events wait upon her at their will.

They made their way to the rue Caumartin and turned to the right. Presently they entered the courtyard of the Hôtel Petrograd and made their way to a dining-room well filled with American girls in the uniforms of the various war-service organizations. Selecting a table in a sheltered corner, they ordered luncheon, nor did they speak except of casual matters until they had finished. Andree addressed herself to her plate with that quaint absorption which always delighted Kendall. It touched Maude now, as everything about this appealing little girl touched her. She found herself actually growing fond of Andree as one might grow fond of a lovable child.... And yet she had a certainty that she would not find Andree altogether childlike; that in all matters appertaining to her love she would be all woman and amply potent to defend herself and her rights.

"Now we shall speak," said Andree, looking into Maude's face with directness, almost with challenge. Her own face, if it showed any expression at all, spoke of hesitation, diffidence.

"What shall we talk of?" Maude asked, experimentally.

"It is for you to say, mademoiselle. It is you who make the suggestion that we speak together...." Then, with disconcerting directness, "You wish to speak about Monsieur Ware, is it not?"

"Yes," said Maude, "I should like to talk about him—and you."

"It is ver' well."

Now that it reached the point of discussing Kendall, Maude was nonplussed for a moment. How should she open the discussion, if discussion there were to be? What could she say that would not be an impertinence to this girl, whom, somehow, she did not want to offend? Maude even respected her, perceived that about Andree which demanded respect and consideration. She hesitated. Andree smiled and leaned a bit forward.

"Mademoiselle," she said, "perhaps it is that you are in love with thees yo'ng man also. Is it of that you wish to speak?"

"I am not in love with him, mademoiselle."

"Ah ... but that is not the ver' truth—no. I have seen. I do not know— maybe you theenk you do not love him, but you do love him. That is why I am willing to speak weeth you."

"I don't understand."

"I am willing to speak weeth you about Monsieur Ware bicause I love him ver' much and bicause you also love him. I theenk it mus' be bicause I know we both wish ver' much to have him always be happy. Is it not?"

"But I do not love him."

"Then, mademoiselle, it is not of a necessity for us to speak at all. If you are merely his frien', his acquaintance, you have no right to speak weeth me about him. It is so. *Mais*, if you love him"—she lifted her shoulders—"that is ver' different."

"He has not asked me to love him."

"That is well. I theenk he loves me very *fidèle*. Yes. But also he theenk of you ver' much. I have seen. You are of his country and are ver' pretty.

He theenk of you and compare you weeth me. I am French.... That is not American. He theenk about w'en he goes back to America, and then bicause I am ver' French and not American he is troubled. He theenk I do not onderstan', but I onderstan' ver' well. He say that he love Andree in Paris, and in Paris Andree is ver' nice, but in America, where all is so different, then he does not know what to theenk."

"And then?"

"And then he theenk of you, mademoiselle, of you who would not be foreign and strange and at whom his friends would not make to shrug their shoulder' and lift the eyebrow'—bicause I do not know the manner and the custom."

"Is that all that troubles you—not knowing the manners and the customs?"

"What else could there be, mademoiselle? I am not *très-jolie*—ver' beautiful—but also I am not so hideous. I do not know."

Maude shifted the subject because she was not ready to speak about the thing which would be troublesome more than manners and customs.

"Has he asked you to go to America with him?"

"No, mademoiselle. We have not speak of that."

"But you would go? You would leave your France and your people and go to a strange land?"

"I theenk, mademoiselle, that I would leave the worl' for Monsieur Ware."

"As his wife?"

"As to that, I do not care. If he wish, then ver' well. If he do not wish, then ver' well, also. The marriage—makes nothing to us. It is only the love.... But you, mademoiselle, you make of marriage the necessity."

"I would not marry him—I do not think I would marry him."

"You would love him—as I do?"

"No.... No.... You misunderstand. Even if I loved him I do not think I would marry him."

"And why? It is ver' strange. Perhaps it is some American custom."

"Of course I am American.... But the reason is yourself."

"Myself!... Oh, I do not onderstan'."

"I do not believe I could bring myself to marry him when he has loved you—as he has. When he has—been your lover."

Andree's eyes were wide with surprise. "It is ver' strange," she said. "What have I to make weeth it? Suppose one day he do not love me any more, but loves you ver' much. Then you will not marry him bicause of me? Oh, that ees ver'—how do you say?—ver' silly."

"It is hard to explain. Something inside me rebels against it. I would always think about it.... It would seem to me that he was tainted ... not clean as a husband should be."

"*Mademoiselle!*" Andree sat very erect, her lips compressed.

"Don't misunderstand me.... Please! I do not mean to offend. I expressed myself clumsily—and yet that was what I meant. It is nothing against you.... I have seen you, and I believe I can almost understand you. You are sweet and good—but you are different...."

"Much different, mademoiselle, for that if I love then nothing matters. I give, and I do not ask questions. I theenk not of myself, but of him. It is the truth. I say, can I make him ver' happy.... But I do not ask if I am so ver' good that he is not so good as I am?"

"I wish I could explain. I can never understand you wholly, and you— I'm afraid you will never be able to understand me at all. We have grown up in different worlds. You here, I in America.... Do you know that what you are doing is very bad in America? that a girl who does as you have done is an outcast? that no one will receive her in their homes nor have anything to do with her? ... People would say you were bad...."

"Oh, thees America! It is ver' *sérieux*. Is there not love in America, then?"

"Love is proper only when people marry."

"And in America I would be a bad girl?"

"Yes."

"Bicause I love ver' much and am *fidèle*?"

"Because you love without marriage."

"And that makes Monsieur Ware bad also—bicause he love' me?"

"It makes him—yes, people would say he was bad."

"It is a lie. He is not bad, but ver' good and kind. Do I make him bad? Oh, mademoiselle, that is a ver' silly thing. I would only make him good and happy. It is the ver' truth.... And bicause of me he is made bad and you must not marry him!... Regard me, mademoiselle, what harm do you theenk he has from me?"

"No harm from you. Oh, I mean it.... I—I don't blame him. If I were a man I think—yes, I'm sure—I should love you as he does.... But—"

"But he is bad, and I have made him bad?"

"It isn't you who make him bad...."

"Then he is not bad, for there is no other. I am ver' sure. He is *fidèle*."

"You don't understand. It is not *you* who make him bad, but the thing he is doing ... his relations with you. They are bad."

"It is mos' difficult—like some philosophy in a big book. I make him bad, but I do not make him bad, yet he is bad bicause of me...." Her eyes began to flash as she arose in Kendall's defense. "It is not true. What you say is ver' bad and wicked. For he is nevair bad.... As for me, I do not theenk I am bad. No. I do not theenk *le bon Dieu* believes I am bad. You yourself, mademoiselle, have seen me and speak weeth me. Do you theenk I am bad?"

"No, dear. I believe you are good.... I mean it. From the bottom of my heart, I believe you are good."

"It is well. Then, can one take something bad from one who is good? See! To be bad is to offend the good God. Have I offended the good God who smiles when there is a great love? I do not theenk. Have I made Monsieur Ken to offend the good God?... I should not be happy as I am if it were so.... Have I made him to do a wickedness? Am I a woman of that sort? It is not true. All I have desire is for him to be good and to be ver' happy.... That is not a sin, and it does not make a sin for him.... And you would not marry him even though you love him.... Mademoiselle, that is not a good love, not such a love as make the good God to smile.... It is a wickedness to love so...."

"My dear—"

"No.... Let me speak. Suppose thees Monsieur Ware have love me and marry me—and I am no more. I am dead. Then you would not marry him?"

"That is different altogether. There would be no reason why I shouldn't marry him then."

"But I tell you, it is the same. Behol'! he loves me so ver' much, and one day he does not love me bicause the war is done and he mus' go home, and it is not possible for him to carry me weeth him.... The theeng is ended. It is as if I were dead—as I should desire it to be. The love was the same as if I have marry him.... He would then nevair be weeth me any more. I would be as if

I were not.... And he would have taken no harm.... To say that he would be harmed is to say that to love a man more than any other theeng in the worl' is to harm him, and to say that, mademoiselle, is *impie—blasphématoire*—to say a theeng which is an insult to God.... No!... No!... You make a wrong.... Because he have love' then he is better—not more wicked.... I say to you, mademoiselle, that the love like I have for Monsieur Ware makes to keep him from a sin. I know."

Maude's eyes were not dry. She was listening to a thing that rang with truth and with goodness. She saw what she had never been able to perceive before, and it showed her that Kendall Ware could take no harm from Andree, let their relations be what they might, for Andree was good, with a simplicity and a faith and a purity greater and better than any she had ever known. American as she was, reared upon the traditions of Plymouth Rock, which are as unbending as the laws of the Medes and Persians, she perceived the truth, saw that to judge is a power withheld from mortals and jealously guarded by God....

"My dear!... My dear!..." she said, tremulously. "I—Can you forgive me?... You are right—*right*. Nobody could be harmed by you.... You are sweet and—and wonderfully good...."

Andree smiled wanly. "So we need speak no more. We have done. There remains but one little thing, mademoiselle. You love thees yo'ng man, and I love thees yo'ng man.... He loves me now, and until I am dead I shall keep him—keep him.... I shall make to fight for him as I can.... But I am sorry that it mus' make you sad—if I can keep him. I am ver', ver' sorry.... Good-by, mademoiselle, we shall not be friend'—no, that ees not possible—and one of us mus' be ver' sad.... I mus' pray that it shall not be myself...."

"Good-by," said Maude, extending her hand.

Andree turned and walked with quaintly stiff tread and daintily erect body out of the dining-room. Maude ascended to her room to think, to readjust herself.... Her state of confusion was almost as great as Kendall Ware's. She was conscious of her own inadequacy and of her inability to pierce to the true heart of events and see them as they would be seen by a mind at once perfect in logic and perfect in purity.... But, in spite of prejudices bred into her being from youth, she could not see Andree as otherwise than *right*, Andree as untainted by evil ... and it seemed a thing impossible that Kendall Ware could have been made one whit unworthier by any contact with her....

CHAPTER XXV

Kendall Ware went to his office on September 1st just as he went to it on any other day, anticipating a day like a hundred of its predecessors had been. He enjoyed the walk through the clear sunny air of Paris and felt not the slightest foreboding of heavy events to come. Fifteen minutes after his arrival the day had taken upon itself the importance of marking the close of an epoch in his life.... He was ordered to report himself in Brest on the morning of September 4th to board the first returning transport for America.

The order partook of the essentials of a calamity. It came so unexpectedly, with such sudden shock, that he did not sense immediately the full meaning of it nor what it involved. In the beginning he saw only the misfortune of being sent home, of being removed from proximity to the war. That alone was enough to give him keenest distress, but as he returned to his desk and sat staring gloomily at the wall before him this first effect was swallowed up and lost forever by the inrush of cold dread of the major consequences of his enforced departure.

"Andree!..."

He was face to face with the inexorability of the postponed decision. There was no time to work matters out gradually now, to hope for some miraculous solution. He must decide; he must answer yes or no.... What should he do about Andree?... Within twenty-four hours he must determine if she was to remain in his life, or if they had reached a point in the journey where one must turn to the right and one to the left to follow roads that never joined again on earth. He must determine whether or not he should marry Andree and take her home. It would be possible. There was time. He felt sure he could obtain the necessary permission to have her accompany him on the transport because he knew women were constantly returning on transports. Even failing that, she could demand her passport as his wife as a newly made citizen of the United States and go to America by way of Bordeaux and the French line.... But only as his wife could she cross the ocean; in no other way could she obtain the essential passport....

So that became the one question—to marry or not to marry!

If he did not take her with him, then what? How could he tell her?... What would she do if she discovered that she had lost him? There came to him a vision of the bridges crossing the Seine ... and it was harrowing!

The breaking of evil news is, perhaps, the most feared task that can fall to man. He fears it as he fears no other demand that can be made upon him.... It was inevitable that Ken should consider eluding such a black responsibility. Why not? It would be perfectly simple.... He was to see Andree to-morrow night. Well, there was no need to see her, and the night after that he would be on the train for Brest. He could step out of her life without a word, abandon her without farewell.... It would remove all complications—except the complication of conscience. It was a temptation which did not persist. Kendall Ware was no hero, but he was immeasurably above such an act of black cowardice. Besides, he could not bear to go without seeing her again ... if the decision were to leave her.

He must decide....

It was a sentence from which there could be no reprieve, implacable, inevitable. He had arrived at the most critical, the most momentous crisis in his life ... and nowhere could he turn for help. He stood alone, sole judge and executioner. There was no jury to pronounce verdict, no expert who could advise. He—Kendall Ware—must speak the word.... Never had he been so conscious of himself as an individual, of his existence as a distinct entity, of *himself*. It frightened him—that idea of himself as a responsible thing, of which life could require decisions. For the first time he realized the meaning of the words "free will" and he resented them. God had endowed him with the perilous gift of freedom to mold his own life, and he felt a cowardly resentment toward God.... But the stark fact was there. There was no avoiding it. There *must* be a choice, *some* choice ... and the combined populations of the earth could not take it out of his hands....

He was thankful for some minor matters of routine which would demand his attention until noon. After that he would be relieved from duty, with no occupation but to make ready for his departure.... It was a trifling postponement and he welcomed it eagerly. At eleven-thirty he left the office and walked down the Champs Élysées, almost for the last time. He pretended that he was walking aimlessly, but it was not true. He had a destination, and that destination was 12 rue d'Aguesseau and Maude Knox.

It was not that he felt the necessity of seeing Maude Knox, but that he wanted to talk to somebody, to talk to somebody who might have some understanding of his plight. It was not advice he sought so much as sympathy. Maude was the sort of person he could talk to, and talk was necessary.... He waited in the archway of the building until she came down.

"Well?" she said, in some surprise.

"I'm waiting for you. Can you lunch with me?"

"What has happened?" she countered. "I can tell by your face that something has happened."

"I've been ordered home."

She did not reply for a moment, for his announcement brought her also face to face with a climax in her life. *He was going home!* The *status quo* which had been endurable, if difficult, was to be altered. While he was there and she was there their relations might go on as they were, somewhat anomalous, but requiring no immediate decisions or arrangements. They could drift and allow events to take care of themselves.... But now he was going, and she realized that she did not want him to go. She realized what she had repressed and concealed was now insisting upon recognition—that Kendall Ware was very important to her, that his presence was very important to her, and that for a time to which she was unable to set an exact limit she had been hoping that their relations would be determined in a manner satisfactory to herself.... She was bolder in facing the fact than Kendall had been. She faced it promptly and adjusted herself to it ... and the fact was that she loved him....

"Where shall we lunch?" she asked, and it would have been impossible to tell from her tone that in the brief pause that came before her question she had withstood a shock and mastered a crisis.

"The Oasis is quiet and we can talk."

"But they're so slow!"

"That doesn't matter to-day. There's—there's so much to say."

"To me?"

He nodded. "I've got to talk it out with you ... because you are the only person who can do any good. The same things are behind both of us. We know the same sort of people back home.... Don't you see?"

"I think so. But, remember, I've been here as long as you have. I'm not the same. I've seen things, too.... I can't judge anything the way I would have judged it back home. I'll never be able to again."

They walked to the rue St.-Honoré and presently turned up the rue Boissy-d'Anglas to the quaint, quiet little English tea-room with its soft lights and absurdly carved fireplace and decorations. That fireplace, Bert had once said, looked like the life-work of a lazy man who loved to whittle. There they found a table—there were but three or four—and gave their orders to the thin, very serious Englishwoman who was the only member of the staff of the place who ever became visible. Nobody knew if she were the proprietress or merely a waitress—and nobody cared especially.

"It's rotten luck," said Ken.

"Yes."

"I'll be stuck at some desk job in Washington. It wouldn't have been so bad if they had given me a few months at the front—"

"Or if they never had sent you to France at all."

He looked at her a moment, then shook his head. "No. I wouldn't have missed these months over here. I've really lived; really appreciated being alive. No.... Whatever happens now, nobody can take this away from me...."

"It has been wonderful," she agreed.

"Just to see it—Paris, the people, the war going on—would be wonderful.... But I believe I've done more than merely *see*. I've *felt*."

"You've seen and felt, Ken, but how much has it changed you?"

"What do you mean?"

"I mean, what has seeing and feeling done to you? Has it made any permanent changes in you? Your experiences here have impressed you a great deal—but how long will the effect last when you get home?... When Paris is just a memory—and a subject for conversation? In ten years will you be any different as a result of all this than you would have been if you had never come?"

He hesitated. "I don't know," he said, slowly. "What do *you* think?"

"I think," she said, "that we will get back into the old environments and the old habits and will become just what we would have been. If we were to stay here, then we might change, broaden, really profit by our experiences. But we go home. We see the same faces, hear the same sort of talk, and are tied by the same sort of prejudices and theories and narrownesses that we used to accept without question. We will know better for a while, and then we will revert.... It takes something pretty big and startling to change a person forever."

"Big and startling.... You mean something in his own life and experience—something personal to him—that is big and startling?"

"Yes."

"Like—"

"Oh, like committing a crime, or making some supreme decision or sacrifice.... Anything that strains the very soul of a person so that it can never get back into its former shape."

"Love?"

"Not love itself, but something wonderful or terrible that comes as the result of a love."

"Then you don't think experiences change people, that it is—well, just making decisions that grow out of the experiences. It is reaching a crisis and then making a choice of which way you will go."

"I think that is it. I don't see how any event can change a person if he remains merely a spectator. I don't think any sort of happening will really alter a person for good and all unless it has compelled him to use every bit of his will and courage and intelligence to make up his mind what he will do about it. If he chooses the right way, then he becomes stronger; if he chooses the wrong way or dodges the decision, he becomes weaker."

"There's no dodging the choice," he said.

"And that is what's the matter with you, isn't it?"

"Yes."

"And the choice?" She knew very well what problem he was laboring over.

"Is Andree," he said.

"She was bound to be the problem. Couldn't you see that from the beginning?"

"That doesn't matter now—what I saw at the beginning. All that has happened has happened"—he paused and stared down at the table-cloth—"and I'm glad it did happen.... But now I've got to settle the bill."

"And you want my advice?" She looked at him queerly. "You have come to *me* for advice about this?"

"Not for advice. I just want to know what you think."

"About what—definitely?"

"Whether I should marry Andree?"

"Why shouldn't you?"

"So many reasons.... There's my mother. There's the vestibule of the Presbyterian church, if you know what I mean." She nodded her understanding. "There are all the things that have come down from Plymouth Rock.... There is something in me, something I can't get rid of, that is a result of all these things, which makes me hold back from marrying a girl who—with whom I have—who has been to me what Andree has been.... And there is *you*." He uttered the last sentence defiantly.

"That isn't fair—it isn't *fair*! You have no business to say such a thing to me.... You're the most tremendously selfish man I have ever met."

"Selfish!"

"In this whole thing you are thinking of nobody but yourself. You haven't thought of Andree—and then you—you say such things without—considering me."

"I do think of Andree," he said, quickly. "I'm afraid—for her. I can't bear to think of making her unhappy.... And you—It's a confused mess, Maude!..." He leaned across the table. "Maude, if there was no other woman in my life—if Andree were a thing of the past—would you marry me?"

She stared at him, biting her lips. "Ken Ware," she said, "that is the most impertinent—and selfish—question a man ever asked.... Don't ever do it again! Don't ever mention such a thing again! The idea! You want to have your cake and eat it, too. You're always at it—carrying on a sort of left-handed courtship with me.... Always hinting—and—and playing safe. If you decide you don't want this other girl, then you want to have me all prepared to fall into your arms.... I won't stand it. Never dare speak of it again—until you can come to me honestly and say that you *love* me—and that there is no other woman in your life—and that you want me to marry you. Then I'll tell you whether I will or not.... Do you understand?"

"I'm sorry. I've been clumsy ... and selfish."

"You have."

"But you'll tell me what you think—how this whole thing over here affects you? Don't think about my case in particular if that is offensive, but about the whole system, the whole idea of the relations between men and women as we see them here."

"I will, because I would like to find out just how I *have* been affected...." Suddenly she laughed. "I used to have an uncle who spent his life arguing abstractions. I remember he took the stand once that there was no reason why women should not smoke as well as men, that there was nothing inherently masculine about smoking and nothing immoral. He declared that women had as much right to smoke as men. My aunt listened to it until she got tired, so one evening she waited until uncle lighted a cigar and then took out a cigarette and put it between her lips.... Uncle stared at her and *roared*. He fairly snatched that cigarette, and it looked as if he was going to put my aunt out of the house.... Smoking for women was all right as an abstract question, but when it touched him personally it was quite another matter.... I think I am a little like him. I can sit down and say that these girls are within their rights. I can even see that they are good.... I believe your Andree is wonderfully good.... I can even say that if so many Americans were killed in this war that I would never be able to find a husband I might do the same thing—and I believe it would be *right* and moral for me to do it ... in the *abstract*. I can feel these things in Paris. But as soon as I come to a concrete instance and one which touches me personally—why, I'm Middle West and Plymouth Rock again.... One can never tell. Things can happen here— even to an American girl like me—that never could happen in America in normal conditions. With this war going on, with this horrible state of affairs, nothing else seems to matter much. Personal moral considerations seem to be so minute and unimportant as not to count at all.... There is something in the very air.... You see we don't know France—only a small section of it that we see about the streets. We don't know how the classes of France who stay in their homes and are never seen on the boulevards look at this matter. They may be as straitlaced as we are ... and we've been judging all of Paris by the Champs Élysées...."

"That doesn't decide the thing that's worrying me.... It doesn't even help.... I wonder if this war and everything connected with it won't change people back home."

"So that they would tolerate—Andree?"

He nodded.

"Never—if they found out that Andree had violated their laws."

"But you—what do you think about her?"

"Is that fair?"

"I don't see why it isn't. You've met her and talked with her. What do you think of her?"

"Ken, she is one individual, and I can tell you what I think about her ... but that doesn't make her stand for the whole code of ethics. The other thousands of girls may not be like Andree at all—they may be bad. Don't you see? It comes down to a matter of personal, concrete experience again.... But Andree...." She looked at him gravely. "I should hate to feel that I had broken faith with Andree or been unfair to her or caused her grief. She is very sweet and childlike—and *good*. She has no consciousness of having been other than virtuous because she has loved you.... I had lunch with her the other day. It was the first time I had ever lunched with a woman whom I knew to be violating our standard ... and it didn't hurt me in the least. I felt no repulsion or disgust ... but that was because I couldn't help feeling that she was good...."

"Then you think—"

"I think this: that all of us come to fit into our environment very readily. We come over here, and soon we are being absorbed by the things around us.... Presently we will go home, more or less in the frame of mind created by Paris ... and then the environment of home will begin to work. In no time at all we will have adjusted ourselves again and Paris will be almost as if it never had been.... I believe that is exactly what will happen. If we stayed here we should become as nearly Parisian as we could be made, but, going home, Paris will very rapidly be eradicated."

"And all that has happened here?"

"Will be part of a memory—something in a dream."

He shook his head. "I can't believe that. I know I shall never be just the same as I was before. I see your point of view, but it doesn't help me ... and I don't believe you are right."

"You don't want to believe it."

"I know—Andree makes all the difference. If you were a man and there had been an Andree you would have felt as I have. Somehow France means Andree to me. I never dreamed of any one like her. You don't know her—what a quaint, childlike, womanly, fairy kind of a girl she is. When I think of her she doesn't seem real, but like some mysterious being out of a magical country who has come to visit for a little while—to make me happy.... She does come from a mysterious country. Do you know that I don't know her name—just Andree? I have never asked. I don't know where she lives or how she lives. I don't know anything about her except that she appears and is with me a little while—and then disappears again.... That has made a difference—that quality."

"I would hardly have suspected you of being so romantic."

"It isn't sentimentality, at any rate.... And nobody can ever convince me that I've done wrong or that I've taken any harm from her.... Even if this should prove to be only an episode, it has been a beautiful episode with nothing but good in it.... But this mystery, this fairy element, has somehow kept the realities at a distance. I have simply gone along and *lived*.... Why, I have hardly thought of such a thing as marriage in connection with her. Possibly you won't understand that, but I understand it perfectly.... To marry Andree would be to make her real, material. The mystery would be gone."

"I think I understand."

"But to marry her and take her to Detroit!... Suppose I should take her home and then this story should come out—and it *would* come out somehow. What then?... When I think of that smug, gossiping crowd in the church vestibule, and of their looking at her and pointing at her and whispering about her—it seems like a profanation. I couldn't bear it.... And then—well, I've inherited some of it myself. I belong to that crowd. I've their ideas of marriage ... and the vestibule doesn't marry a girl who—has lived with a man...."

"You're afraid of them."

"I am," he said, and flushed.

"But if you loved her—really loved her—"

"I do," he said, quickly, "but can't one love without wanting to marry? That is a thing that puzzles me."

"I don't believe anybody can love and be willing under any circumstances to part with the person one loves."

"I don't know.... Isn't it, possibly, better to love and to be a part of a beautiful, rather mysterious, glowing episode and to have it end while it is beautiful and mysterious?... Then something always remains—something dreamlike and lovely. To come down to actualities, to marry, to take this mystery into the land of grocers' bills and house-cleaning and the every-day problems of marriage—why, it wouldn't be the same thing at all."

"I don't think you believe that. You're arguing with yourself and trying to salve your conscience.... You're afraid to marry Andree and take her home—"

"That is part of it. I admit it. But—and I am sincere when I say it—I don't know whether I want to marry her. I love her and she loves me.... She would be a wonderful wife—and yet, love and all, I don't know whether I want to marry her."

"You are just trying to deceive yourself. Either you don't love her at all...."

"Would you marry a woman who had done what Andree has done?"

"It would depend on the woman—and upon how much I loved her.... You can't generalize about that. It is a matter that nobody can decide except for himself in a particular instance. I do think, if I were a man, that I could marry your Andree without a thought...."

"But to take her out of her world—away from Paris where she is as natural and unconscious as the birds in the trees—and set her down for life in Detroit ... to be stared at and lied about and suspected ... it would make her miserable."

"Would it make her as miserable as to lose you altogether? If she had you and your love, no matter what unpleasant things were about, wouldn't that be better than to be left behind here alone?"

"Yes," he said, honestly. "Yes."

She looked at him a moment, studying his face, which was set and anxious and overcast, his eyes, which were dull and brooding, and a wave of compassion surged up within her.

"It has made you miserable," she said. "I'm so sorry."

"I deserve to be miserable."

"Possibly not. Nobody can judge, but—this affair has been almost inevitable. It wasn't your fault and it wasn't Andree's fault.... The circumstances were here, and you two got tangled up in them...." She glanced at her watch. "I must go now. I'm sorry I haven't helped you—for—I wish I might help you.... Shall I see you again before you go?"

"I'm afraid not."

"Then this is good-by." She held out her hand steadily. "I hope matters turn out for—for your happiness.... Good-by."

"I shall write you."

She looked at him and smiled queerly, but made no rejoinder. "No, don't come with me," she said, as he walked to the door. "I'd rather go alone.... Good-by and a safe voyage."

And so the first of the two women with whom his life had become involved stepped out of his life....

CHAPTER XXVI

When Kendall went to the apartment for dinner Arlette came bustling into the hall as she heard him open the door, and, poking again and again with a pudgy finger toward the rear of the place, she exclaimed, excitedly: "Monsieur Bert!... Monsieur Bert!..."

"Here?"

"*Oui, monsieur.*" She grinned with delight.

"Hey, Bert!" shouted Ken, delighted, for he had feared he would not see his friend again before he sailed. Bert came out of the door, half shaved, with a towel about his neck, and shook hands after the manner of healthy young men.

"Howdy, old-timer! Gosh! it seems good to get back to you and Arlette. How have things been going without me? Seen Madeleine?"

"Haven't seen her. Things have been going all right till to-day. This morning the blow fell."

"What blow?... You look as if somebody had stolen your pet goat."

"I'm ordered to America. Leave Wednesday."

"The devil!... Oh, say, that's rotten luck! What's the idea?"

"Don't know. Just my confounded luck, I expect."

"Wait a minute till I finish this shave and I'll help you weep.... How's Andree?"

They were walking back to Bert's room, and Ken did not answer until his friend stood before the glass, razor in hand.

"She's all right."

"How did she take the news?"

"She doesn't know."

"Doesn't know!"

"I just got my orders this morning. Won't see her until to-morrow night."

"Coming to dinner?"

"Yes."

"We'll pull a party—farewell party with all the trimmings, eh? I'll get Madeleine and we'll dig up a bottle of champagne and wring a *poulet* out of Arlette if we have to call in the police to help us. I'll bet they would, at that."

"It won't be a very merry party," said Ken, lugubriously.

Bert turned and looked at Ken. "Huh!... Something eating you again?"

"It's a rotten mess. I don't know what to do."

"About Andree? It isn't any mess at all. You've had a good time and she's had a good time. That's all there is to it. Now you've got to go home. She didn't expect anything else."

Ken was silent.

"Unless you've made her expect something else.... Now Madeleine and I had an understanding right at the start," said Bert.

"I wish I could get it off my mind for a couple of hours."

"Get it off, then. We'll go to the Folies or the Olympia or some place to-night. To-morrow I'll look up Madeleine."

Ken was willing to go anywhere, to do anything, so long as he was helped to keep Andree off his mind, and to think about something besides the inevitability of the decision. So, after, they went to the Folies, arriving after the performance had begun. They did not take seats, but made their way through the big table-filled room to the theater proper, and stood up with the crowd behind the railing. The house was full, but even when the house was not filled many of the spectators remained in the promenade to walk about and smoke and, possibly, to put themselves in the way of being accosted by some of the numerous and sometimes pretty *habituées* of the place.

The entertainment was directed to the American soldier, and much of it was in English. But it could not hold Kendall's attention. It was, in fact, a mediocre performance, with an act or so that was deserving of attention. After seeing the perfection of the performances at the Comédie Française Ken wondered at the halting stage management of this popular music-hall. It hitched along. Choruses seemed to improvise rather than to have been drilled. Nobody seemed to know just how to get on and off the stage, and when a scene or an act or a chorus number ended, it simply ended.... Every now and then animated conversations broke out in the back of the theater, and ushers walked about through the crowd, saying: "Hush!... Husss-sh!" The whole thing depressed Ken instead of lifting his spirits, and he actually experienced a feeling of disgust at the grand closing number in which the *première danseuse* appeared as an American cowboy, in white tights and waving an American flag.

"Let's get out of here," he said, impatiently.

"Suits me," said Bert, and they jostled their way to the street, ignoring more than one tentative *"Bon soir, monsieur,"* from young women whose cheeks were not guiltless of what the phrase of the streets termed camouflage.

"Want to walk home?" suggested Bert.

"Yes." Ken did want to walk. He wanted to tire himself so that he could sleep, for he was afraid of a sleepless night. So they started off briskly, cutting through dark and narrow streets to the Boulevard Haussmann and thence into the Avenue Friedland, which they followed to the rue Beaujon and into the Avenue Hoche. They climbed the stairs of the apartment, and Bert, as was his custom, searched the cupboards to see if Arlette had left anything unconcealed that might be eaten. But Arlette had been careful, as usual, and nothing was to be found except a box of dry cookies. It was not Arlette's intention that her young officers should waste their substance by eating up her supplies at unexpected hours.

Ken dreaded to go into his room alone and turn off the lights, so it was Bert who made the first movement to go to bed. Ken carried in with him a sleep-provoking book on militarism which an earnest friend had forced upon him, undressed, and stretched himself on the bed with the small light on his table to read by. He forced himself to read ... and presently fell asleep.

The next day was filled with errands and shopping. He wandered about the stores, selecting inexpensive souvenirs for his friends and presents for his mother and father. It was hot, and it irritated him to push and shove in the milling crowds that jammed the Printemps and the Galeries Lafayette, but it kept him busy and gave him an excuse for pushing his decision another hour and still another hour into the future.... His last errand was the selection of a present for Andree, a farewell gift, or a gift of some other sort. There had to be a gift, so he spent more money than he could afford in a little bracelet of gold set with tiny pearls.... Then he went home, for it was near the dinner hour.

Bert was there before him, wearing such an expression of sheepishness and chagrin as Kendall had never seen before on his friend's face.

"Where's Madeleine?" he asked.

Bert grinned mirthlessly. "Don't know," he said.

"Isn't she coming?"

"I left a note at her hotel inviting her."

"Didn't see her?"

"No. I went around to the hotel and there was a small boy in the *concierge's* room. He said Madeleine was out with an American officer.... Then I went up the street, and pretty soon I thought I saw her with a lieutenant. They were a block away and I hustled up to make sure, but they turned off and disappeared. Looked like she caught sight of me and ducked.... Anyhow, I went back and left a note. Maybe I was mistaken."

"Serves you right," said Ken. "You were so darn sure—you with your understandings.... Three weeks were too much for her, and she's passed you up for somebody who isn't always telling her she's just a temporary arrangement."

"Go chase yourself," said Bert. "It makes no difference in my young life."

But Ken noticed that every minute or so Bert strolled with elaborate nonchalance to the window and looked down the street. Ken smiled. Bert's manner was not that of a man whose heart suffers, but who has taken an injury to his pride....

"Here comes Andree," said Bert.

Ken did not go to look, as he usually did. It was not that he did not want to see Andree, but her arrival brought his affairs to the acute stage. He had put off and put off the struggle to reach a decision; had occupied his mind with other matters, crowding out as much as was possible any thoughts of Andree and of what he was going to do about her. True, the thing had been with him always, lurking in the background and ready to step out at the least encouragement. But he had not approached it directly. It had been a sort of dull ache that he was always conscious of, but which he had been able to stifle. Now she was coming, was almost at the door. It would be a matter of minutes only before he would have to tell her that he was going away.... Even now he did not admit to himself that he had reached a partial decision, indeed that he had not required to make a decision upon one point. That was taking her with him. He had told himself that it would be possible to marry her and to take her on the transport that carried him, but it was self-deception, and he knew it was self-deception. In his heart he knew now, as he had known, that to-night he would say good-by to Andree and go to America without her.... He might come back for her, might even marry her before he went away, to have her follow him on another vessel. But there would be a parting, temporary or permanent....

He had never asked himself if Andree would marry him. The idea that she would not do so had never entered his head, which was significant. It was that which made his decision doubly difficult, for she was wholly in his hands, had given herself to him to do with as he pleased, and her life was his to break if he wished to do so.... He persuaded himself that his hesitation was more on her account than his own, that it would be impossible for her to be happy in the conditions which would be found in America, or that perhaps it would be impossible. He believed that he was trying to decide what would be best for her—or almost believed it. It may be that he was not wholly selfish, not thinking solely of himself and of the effects of his marriage with Andree upon himself. At any rate, his anxiety for her was very real and very disturbing.

She was coming up the stairs utterly unconscious of what awaited her, confident in a future with him which would not be disturbed for so long a time that it need not now be considered. An event that is a year distant is very far away to a young girl. If Andree had known she would lose Kendall in a year she would not have thought about it now ... nor until the year was drawing to a close. It is the ability to hope that makes this possible. Something might turn up within the year.... But now she was stepping into the event! In a few minutes she would hear his voice telling her that he was going away to-morrow—not in a year, not in a month, but *to-morrow!*... When he told her that he must tell her more. A mere announcement of his departure would not suffice; he must supplement it by telling her if their good-bys were forever, or for a few days or months....

The bell rang and he went to the door and opened it. She stood there very demure and self-contained and grave—dressed in white as he had seen her first. She lifted her eyes to his and smiled and then became grave and wistful again, for she saw that he was not happy.... He held out his arms to her and drew her in, realizing that it was the last time he should ever draw her slender daintiness through that door, the last time she would ever enter that apartment. It was the beginning of the end of that phase in their lives, of the untrammeled romance, the quaint mystery, the adventurous sweetness.

"You are *triste*," she said, anxiously. "Is it that you have worked too hard?"

He shook his head.

"You are not *joyeux* to see me."

He took her face between his hands and looked down into her deep-shaded eyes. "You must not say that.... You must never say that. It is not true."

"Then I am ver' glad." She smiled. "Monsieur Bert and Mademoiselle Madeleine they are here?"

"Bert is here, but Madeleine hasn't come."

"I desire her to be here." She stepped into the *salon* and spoke to Bert. "You shall go to fetch her. Now.... Now. You shall run ver' fast."

"I asked her to come," said Bert.

"And she would not?" Andree's voice showed profound astonishment.

"I'm afraid she got tired of waiting for me to come back to Paris."

"But no, that ees not possible. She would not be tired to wait. She would be ver' glad when you return."

"We'll see. If she isn't here in five minutes she won't be coming."

"Why do you theenk?"

"Because I guess she has another American officer. I think I saw her with one to-day."

"Oh, *non, non, non!* That would be ver' bad. I do not believe. Mademoiselle Madeleine is *fidèle*. You shall see."

"Why are you so sure, mademoiselle?"

"*Pourquoi?*..." She shrugged her shoulders. "Bicause it would be so. If Monsieur Ken should go for three week, for three mont', for three year, I should wait and be *très-fidèle*. I should find no other *officier américain*. *Non, non*, it would not be well."

"There's Arlette's head," said Ken.

"No need to wait," Bert said, irritably. "She won't come."

"We should wait," said Andree.

"Until a quarter past seven, then."

But a quarter past seven arrived and Madeleine did not arrive.

"Let's eat," said Bert. "She's given me the sack."

"*Pauvre Monsieur Bert*. It ees ver' sad. Oh, she is *très-méchante*, ver' naughty. I do not onderstan'."

They went out to the table and sat down. Kendall sat in gloomy silence, Bert was suffering from wounded vanity, and Andree looked from one to the other uncomfortably.

"It is *nécessaire* to smile," she said, and touched Ken's hand with her finger-tips.

"I don't feel much like smiling, *mignonne*."

"*Pourquoi?*"

Arlette entered with the *potage* to save him from replying to her question, and, placing the huge bowl in the middle of the table, stood regarding Andree dolefully, with two big tears standing on her fat cheeks.

"Even Arlette makes to weep," said Andree. "It is ver' strange. What is happen?"

"*Pauvre mademoiselle! ... pauvre mademoiselle!...*" said Arlette, and, turning very abruptly, she scuttled out of the room.

"*Qu'est-ce que c'est?*... Why does she speak this theeng?" She turned startled eyes upon Ken.

He hesitated, bit his lip, then he reached out and took her hand and pressed it to his lips. "I have been ordered to America," he said, baldly.

She did not speak, did not stir. It seemed to him that her expression did not alter by so much as a shade. She was *still*. It was almost as if animation were suspended. Andree did not turn her eyes from his face, nor did she move or speak. She did not gaze at him questioningly nor accusingly nor imploringly—she merely gazed with that accompaniment of *stillness!*... He felt that he must speak and break that quietness which he could feel as with a physical pain.

"I got my orders yesterday.... I—it didn't seem possible. I couldn't believe it.... I only knew yesterday." He felt that he must clear himself of any guilt of concealment, of having known of this thing and kept it from her.

"*Quand?*" she said.

"I go to-morrow night—to Brest, and then to America."

She turned to her plate and began to eat. She had uttered no complaint, shed no tear, done none of the things he had dreaded she might do. There had been no painful scene, but he was not relieved. She was so *still*!

He fumbled in his pocket and took out the little jeweler's package and removed the bracelet. She watched him gravely, with no outward sign of emotion, and when he reached for her hand she gave it to him unprotestingly. He snapped the bracelet about her wrist. She looked down at it, and then up into his face.

"It is ver' pretty," she said, "and you are mos' good to me...." That was all, but every now and then he saw her staring at the bracelet and staring at it as if it were something strange and inexplicable. Once she reached across with her other hand and touched it, felt of it, as if to assure herself that it was really there, an actual thing and not imagined.

Ken tried to talk, Bert tried to talk, but the effort was futile. Dead, cold silences fell.... The sensations of that meal would remain with Kendall as long as he should live, a recurrent nightmare. Presently Bert arose. He did a thing which he had never done before—lifted Andree's hand and touched it with his lips.

"I must go, mademoiselle," he said. "Good-by."

"Good-by, Monsieur Bert," she said.

Then they were alone!

In the *salon* he drew her down beside him on the sofa and held her close.

"I am very sad, *mignonne*," he said. "I love you...."

She studied his face a moment and smiled at very trifle of a smile. "That is well," she answered.

"I am not going away because I want to. It is orders. I have to obey."

"*C'est la guerre*," she said, gravely.

"Yes, it is the war, but it's cruel—it's rotten. I want to stay here, to stay with you."

"I wish that also," she said.

Something was demanded of him. He must say something, must not keep this child in agony, not knowing what he intended to do with respect to her. It was her right to know.... He must decide, and he must tell her....

But again he put it off. There was time enough, and before he told her there was still the chance of one last happy evening.... He wanted that, wanted the memory of it, if nothing more.

"*Mignonne*, do you love me?" he asked.

"It is certain."

"Very much?"

"I cannot say how much."

"America is not far," he said, with some idiotic intention to comfort her. "The ocean can be crossed in a week."

"That is true," she said.

Her head was against his breast, her eyes staring into her lap. Ken looked straight before him, thinking, thinking. His mind was very clear, as if lighted by that painful white light which seemed to pour in upon his consciousness in moments of mental stress. It seemed to him as if his eyes could pierce the walls if he willed it, as if his memory could show him every minute incident in his whole life, as if he could see and understand everything—everything. He drew her to him fiercely, but even as he was sensing the softness of her slender body against his side he was seeing the vestibule of the Presbyterian church, he was watching it function. The individuals stood before him as if alive, every well-known feature distinct. It was photographic. He could see changes of expression, hear whispers, see cautious hands placed before gossiping lips ... and he could see himself passing through that little group with Andree on his arm!...

He could see his own home—his return to it. He could see his mother and feel the hostility that sprang to life the instant her eyes rested on Andree. He could read his mother's thoughts ... and his father's. There was the one bright spot. He could see his father kissing Andree diffidently and patting her hand and telling her how glad he was to see her and asking how his son had ever managed to capture such a pretty girl.... There would be no doubt of her welcome at his father's hands.... But his mother—that cold hostility, that hard-eyed suspicion!... And then, when she had him alone, the catechism he would undergo, and the resentment and jealousy she would exhibit....

He could see his friends and the neighbors of his childhood with their crass curiosity and their hints and whispers.... He knew their every thought

... could see their eyes fixed on Andree speculatively ... some of them hopefully!

It was that he would have to take her, too.... And then, if the story should come out!... But that would be little worse.... Perhaps he exaggerated, perhaps he saw his old friends and acquaintances in characters which were not truly theirs. There might have been more charity among them than he perceived, more kindness and less narrowness and insularity.... But he did not see them except as he feared they might be.

What of himself? How would he feel to find himself married to a girl who had violated the standards of Plymouth Rock, even though he had been the one to profit by that violation?... Even if none ever found it out but himself? He would know it.... It would constantly be recurring to him—or would it not? He did not know. The thing did not affect him now. It did not make Andree the less desirable and lovable and *good*. Perhaps that would persist—but his prejudices were deep-seated, had their roots in an older generation and were not lightly to be cast out....

But he loved her.... In spite of all that he saw and felt and feared, he knew that he loved her, and that to know she was removed forever from his life would be to lose a wonderful thing that he could not bear to lose.... The decision lay between love and expediency.... If only he could live in Paris and never return to America! How easy it would be then!

"Will you miss me?" he asked, clumsily.

She stirred in his arms and held her face up to his. "I shall be ver' sad," she said.

"Suppose—suppose something should happen to me and I could never come back?"

She held his hand very tightly. "I do not know," she said. "I cannot to theenk of that."

He must decide.... He must decide.... But he was afraid; he *could not* decide—not now, not yet.... There were hours ahead of them.

She asked nothing of him, made no demands, but waited, waited. He could feel her waiting, hoping for some word, some assurance that he was not going to desert her forever, that he would come back to her—and he could not give that assurance ... not yet.

"It might be six months; it might be a year before I could come back."

She smiled. "I would be here," she said.

"And *fidèle*?"

"You know," she answered. "There would be no thought only jus' for you...."

"But America is strange. It would not be Paris. You might be unhappy there."

"That ees ver' silly.... Where you are I shall always be happy."

He leaped to his feet and paced up and down the room, then stopped suddenly before her. "What shall I do?... What shall I do?" he said, hoarsely.

"I cannot say. I do not know."

"You know I love you."

"I believe."

"I can't decide. I can't tell what to do.... I don't know what I can do, what will be possible."

She made no answer.

"Can't we pretend just for a while, just for a few hours, that I am not going and that everything is going along just as it is? Can't we have just one more little moment of happiness?"

"It ees not *facile*—not easy—to pretend so."

"But we will try ... I want to see you smile. I want to see you happy once more. I've got to see you happy."

She sat erect and smiled, then the smile faded and she clenched her little fists in her lap. "Oh, I shall be so *solitaire*, so lonely—so lonely...." It was her only departure from that still calmness, her only approach to emotion, to giving away to grief, and it passed swiftly.

"See, I make to laugh now. For thees night I shall laugh, bicause you wish it, and I do not wish you to be sad and to make thees *grimace*.... You mus' sit here beside me now thees minute. You mus' to sit here and love me so ver' much, and we shall be mos' happy.... Oh, I shall theenk of thees Monsieur Bert and how ver' fonny his face made itself to look. He is ver' droll—thees high yo'ng man.... It ees ver' bad that you do not have a piano, for then I can dance for you.... You must to get a piano ver' quickly—now, now.... You shall send out to fetch one or I shall go away...."

"*Mignonne ... mignonne....*" he said, and buried his face in her lap....

She sat looking down at him very gravely, stroking his hair with her soft, slender fingers....

The taxicab hurried them down the Champs Élysées through the cool morning air—on their last ride together in Paris.... He was conscious of the city about them, of the essence of the marvelous city from which he was so soon to depart.... There is something in the air of Paris, something that one cannot escape, something intangible, enticing, exciting.... He would miss it, miss it very much.... Andree, too, was looking out of the window. She sat very still and did not speak. Her face was grave and expressionless with that look of abstraction which she wore as some wild bird of the forest wears its protective coloring.... He reached out and took her hand, holding it silently....

His decision had not been made. He had given her neither assurance of his return nor had he told her that they were about to part forever.... He did not know, and he could not decide ... there were now only minutes—seconds. He could see the Élysées Palace Hôtel ahead, his destination, where he would say good-by to her.... And again, with a weakness which made him despise himself, he evaded the issue.

"You will write to me—often?" he asked.

"Yes.... And you?" It was her first question since he had told her he was to go; the first time she had demanded anything of him.

"I shall write. I shall tell you everything.... Everything will come right somehow. It must come right."

"I have not your address." She spoke very calmly.

He wrote it on a slip of paper and handed it to her.

"But you have not my address—nor my name." She smiled with that quaint lightening of the face which always stirred him to tenderness.

He had not wanted to know her name nor her address. He had loved the mystery of it and of her. But the mystery must end. He gave her his memorandum—book and she wrote, but he did not look at the page, closing the book and placing it in his pocket.... She was still a mystery—he would look when it became necessary to look, and not before.

The taxicab was stopping. They looked at each other, but even now she gave no sign of distress, shed no tear.

"*Mignonne*...." he whispered, and drew her into his arms. "Good-by.... Good-by.... I love you...."

"Good-by," she said, gravely. "I also love you ... and I shall be always *fidèle*."

He opened the door and alighted; then he turned and lifted her hand to his lips. She did not smile; her face was immobile, her eyes were fixed on his face with a strange expression of detachment, of abstraction. He kissed her hand again and turned abruptly away. But he could not leave her so.... He turned; the taxi was starting. He called and ran toward the curb, but the chauffeur did not hear.... He was too late; the machine gained headway and swept around the corner—and she was gone....

CHAPTER XXVII

After a sleepless, uncomfortable night, spent sitting bolt upright in a compartment of the Paris-Brest train, Kendall arrived at the dirty, unkempt, unattractive seaport which was his destination. His baggage was taken from him by the branch of the army which looked after such matters, and he found his way to the provost's office, where he showed his orders and was told to report daily to see if his name was posted in the list of those to sail. No further information was given him as to the date of his departure nor the vessel upon which he should sail.

He secured a room at the Continental Hôtel, the best the city afforded, and found it unspeakable—and then for six interminable days he wandered about the town, waiting, waiting for the convoy which seemed destined never to arrive. He played innumerable games of bridge, walked a dozen times a day to a vantage-point on the old fortifications from which he could gain a panoramic view of the harbor and its jostling craft.... Far out at the entrance swayed and tossed an observation balloon, keeping ceaseless watch of the sea for lurking submarines....

No vessels came save one, the torpedoed *Mt. Vernon*, which had sailed early on the morning of his arrival. It staggered into port with a great hole in its side, and presently disappeared into dry dock farther into the bay.... Then the report spread that cholera had broken out in the town and was magnified to appalling proportions.... There was nothing to do but play bridge and walk to the harbor to look for an incoming convoy, and to eat and sleep. It was maddening....

The harbor ceased to be interesting. German prisoners compelled to labor on the docks became commonplace; scurrying destroyers failed to stir the imagination.... And then one morning Ken walked to his usual vantage-point and saw at anchor the gigantic *Leviathan*....

Presently orders were posted and his name appeared upon the list. He was to report himself with his hand-baggage at a certain point early next morning.... The morning was overcast and cold, with a chilling, slanting drizzle of rain, and everybody was out of spirits and uncomfortable as they waited for the lighter to carry them out to the transport. There was no shelter, and they stood about the deck of the little boat, backs to the slashing rain, for no sooner had they left the wharf than the rain descended in earnest.

Finally they were on board and were assigned to rooms, but this was not the end of the waiting. Forty-eight hours remained while the vessel was being coaled, but at last she started, a consort on either side and a flock of destroyers for convoy.

The voyage was not unpleasant, and it was interesting, at least, to watch the little destroyers plunging and rolling through the great waves until one night they disappeared and left the three transports alone.... There were six days and a half of plowing westward through the Atlantic, days when one wore constantly his life-jacket and rather expected to hear at any moment the detonation of the defensive guns or the explosion of a torpedo against the vessel's sides.... But at last land came into view—only to be obscured by fog that compelled the *Leviathan* to crawl along, feeling her way with the lead.... And then, as suddenly as it had come, the fog vanished and they were in the harbor, with the Goddess visible ahead and the sky-line of the metropolis over to the right.... Nobody left the deck. It was an experience and every man wanted to feel every second of it, witness every manifestation of it.... Vessels cheered them and they cheered in return.... It was America—home. They had been to the war and had returned, some of them battered, broken, but nevertheless returned. It was exhilarating, wonderful.

An early morning ferry-boat, crowded with civilians, ran under their bows, and some competent individual led the cheering. *Crash, crash, crash,* sounded the enthusiastic welcome of those who had remained behind, and every man on the transport knew that those cheers were for *him*....

The great vessel swung about and docked by the aid of snorting, grunting tugs, and after more delays and formalities they set foot on shore.... Kendall went directly to the Pennsylvania station to book a lower berth for Washington.

A week later he was in Detroit on furlough—in his old home, amid familiar surroundings ... under his own roof with his father and mother. It was very much the same. The war touched the life of the city but lightly. It was all as he remembered it, all as he had expected it to be ... and Paris and the distant war seemed to be matters that had occurred in a dream.... On Sunday he went to church with his mother and father and received the homage and congratulations of the vestibule....

That afternoon he went to his room to write—to write the promised letter to Andree. It was not easy ... for the decision had not yet been made. He wrote and destroyed and wrote again. He promised to return; he assured her of his love ... but when he read he was not satisfied.... He was in Detroit, in another world, and Andree did not belong to that world. He was surprised to find how well this world satisfied him and how unreal that other world he had known and loved had become.... This was *his* world, these were the things *he* was meant to do and the thoughts *he* was meant to think. This was America, and he was an American!...

He tried to think of Paris, to get back again into the spirit of Paris, but could not do so.... It had become unreal, distant, not appealing....

But Andree ... she was not unreal, not distant. She was very real, present in his heart—and yet she was of that other world, a stranger, an alien.... He loved her—but—There was always that *but*.

He wrote still another letter and read it. Yes, he had decided. He could not give her up. He would bring her here and let the consequences be what they might.... The letter was placed in its envelop and he drew out his note-book to look for her address.... It was there, those written words which should forever remove Andree from the land of lovely mystery.... But he did not open the book. It lay in his hand, but he dared not open it.... He went to the window and looked out upon the street, that typically American, typically Middle-Western street.... He stood so for many minutes, then walked toward the fireplace and tossed the note-book into the blaze.... The thing was done, the decision was made and was irrevocable ... and Andree would always remain a glowing mystery....

He went again to his desk and wrote another letter. It was brief:

Dear Maude—There is no woman in my life but you. When you come home I shall come to you for my answer.

He inclosed it, addressed it, stamped it, and went out to the post-box on the corner. Even now he hesitated a moment, but it was only a moment.... The letter dropped inside. It could not be recalled.

But he did not move from the spot. For a long time he stood staring before him with eyes that did not see the typically American street, with a consciousness that did not feel his typically Middle-Western surroundings.... What he felt was that something true and faithful and beautiful had found a place in his life never to be removed. What he saw was a vision of Andree, waiting ... waiting....